5357223
15.00
Jul95

Anderson
Rich as sin

DATE DUE			

ER

GREAT RIVER REGIONAL LIBRARY
St. Cloud, Minnesota 56301

GAYLORD MG

ALSO BY PATRICK ANDERSON

Novels
The Approach to Kings (1970)
Actions and Passions (1974)
The President's Mistress (1976)
First Family (1979)
Lords of the Earth (1984)
Sinister Forces (1986)
The Pleasure Business (1989)
Busybodies (1989)

Nonfiction
The President's Men (1968)
High in America (1981)

PATRICK ANDERSON

SIMON & SCHUSTER

New York ◆ London ◆ Toronto
Sydney ◆ Tokyo ◆ Singapore

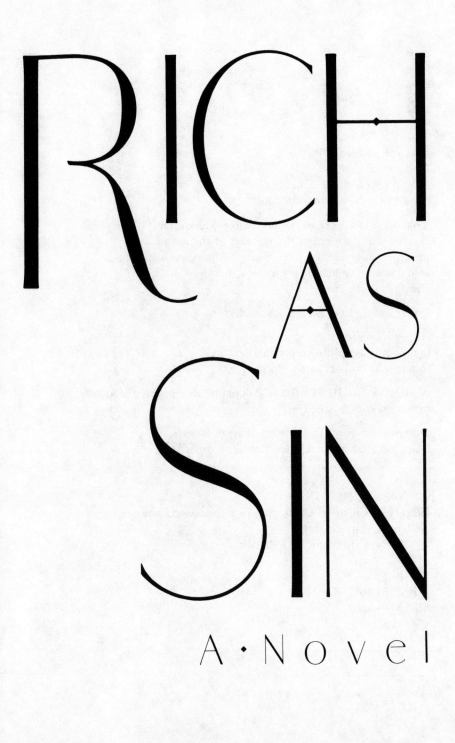

RICH AS SIN

A · Novel

Simon & Schuster
Simon & Schuster Building
Rockefeller Center
1230 Avenue of the Americas
New York, New York 10020

SIMON & SCHUSTER and colophon are registered trademarks
of Simon & Schuster Inc.

Designed by Nina D'Amario/Levavi & Levavi
Manufactured in the United States of America

Library of Congress Cataloging in Publication Data
Anderson, Patrick, date
    Rich as sin : a novel / Patrick Anderson.
        p.   cm.
    I. Title.
    PS3551.N377R5   1991
813'.54—dc20   91-11886
                                                          CIP

ISBN 0-671-69531-2

For M.

PROLOGUE

• • •

Houston / New Orleans / The Gulf Coast

•

The 1950s

1.

A LONESOME YELLOW MOON SAILED HIGH ABOVE THE COASTAL plains the night the lovers and their babies fled Texas. The twin girls whimpered in their mother's arms as their father steered the Oldsmobile through the desolate Gulf Coast, past skeletal oil derricks, toward the imagined safety of the Louisiana line. The babies were finally lulled to sleep by the melancholy strains of Hank Williams on the radio.

The very young mother, her body weak and bleeding, her mind benumbed by fear, distantly recognized the tortured voice, but she had never really *listened* to him before. Girls at her level of Houston society did not listen to hillbillies. They attended the symphony once a year, they listened to the Hit Parade ditties of Doris Day and Eddie Fisher, and they secretly shook their bottoms to the exotic new "race" music of Lloyd Price and the Clovers and Clyde McPhatter, but Texas petro-princesses did not listen to hillbillies. Too many of their parents were too recently removed from the indignities of hardscrabble farm life to welcome its plaintive music into the bright new world they inhabited.

But now, as the girl fled through the darkness with the man she loved, Hank Williams sang a song of infinite sadness, one that tore at her heart. One line would stay with her forever, about tears that came down like falling rain.

She had never known tears, not until she fell in love with the young man at her side. Now as they drove through the lonely autumn rain, fleeing the biblical wrath of her father, her tears overwhelmed her, tears not only for herself and her babies but for a world of frightened, helpless people she had never known existed.

"Christ!" her lover said, his dark eyes flashing to the rear-view mirror. It was the first time he'd spoken since Beaumont.

"What's wrong?"

"There's somebody after us."

"Oh no!" she cried. "It's him. You know it's him!"

Her fall from grace had begun innocently, nine months before, when she visited a friend in New Orleans, a banker's daughter who lived in a lime green Victorian mansion on Prytania Street. The first afternoon they wandered the French Quarter, two sixteen-year-old girls giggling at strip joints, dancing to Dixieland jazz played by street musicians, stopping finally for coffee at the Café du Monde, where a young man in a cream-colored suit bowed low and introduced himself.

Perhaps in Rome or Florence he would not have seemed so special, but she had known only sun-bronzed, raw-boned Texas boys, with their crew cuts and knobby faces and harsh twangs, and Mario was soft and white and angelic, a gentle cherub with liquid eyes, jet black curls, and a shy, musical voice.

He said he was twenty-three and had been a professional gambler since the age of twelve. He took them on a tour of the city in his Olds 88 and the next morning he returned for her alone. That evening, afloat in golden twilight, she gladly surrendered herself in his canopied bed in a cluttered apartment above an antique store on Royal Street. He played Puccini on his stereo and their bodies responded with magic; her sympathetic friend made excuses while the lovers pursued their newfound passion until minutes before her train left on Sunday.

They parted with tears and promises; but back in Houston, back with her Ford Victoria and the drama of the football season, she found her passion fading. When he called, begging to see her, she put him off. As if to punish her fickle heart, her body, always like clockwork before, rebelled. In time she understood she was carrying a baby.

Texas mythology of that era did not admit to sex among the daughters of the rich, much less unwed motherhood. The girl had no idea what to do. Her life seemed over; she imagined herself a suicide, with Puccini's music playing to mark her tragic passing. Instead, she called Mario; was not New Orleans the kind of city where there were doctors who could solve the problem?

Mario protested in two languages. They would not murder their precious child; they would marry and she would bear their baby. Again she hesitated, more calls went back and forth, pitting his passion against her confusion. Finally, inevitably, the man she feared most in the world overheard one of their furtive debates.

Her father was a famous man in his corner of Texas, famously rich and famously cruel. When she confessed she was pregnant, he first demanded the name of the father. When she would not reveal it, he hit her, told her his doctor would "fix" her the next morning, and locked her in her room.

She slipped out her window and drove to New Orleans and lived in hiding with Mario for the eight weeks it took her father's men to find her. By then, the doctor said it would be dangerous to abort. It was decided she would be sent to stay on her father's ranch in South Texas until her bastard child was born; then it would be given up for adoption and she would return to River Oaks High School.

It was, she would admit in later years, not an unreasonable plan, and certainly not an unusual one in Texas in those days.

But at the time her fury was beyond reason. Both her hate for her father and her love for Mario grew apace with the life inside her during her months as a pampered prisoner at the isolated Hill Country ranch.

In her last month she bribed a Mexican girl to mail a letter. In her last week Mario appeared like an avenging angel. She wept for him to see her so fat and awkward, but he proclaimed his love and they escaped in his Olds. Fleeing eastward, they circled Houston warily and were almost to Beaumont when her labor began.

They took refuge in a $5-a-night motel on Railroad Avenue, not far from the Spindletop Museum, and Mario found a doctor who for $200 cash would deliver the baby with no questions asked.

The doctor had brown teeth and nasty eyes. He leered at the girl's delicate beauty and expensive rings, gave her whiskey to dull the pain, and to everyone's amazement delivered twins, two girls.

Mario crossed himself, kissed his barely conscious lover, and marveled at God's blessings. Then he paid the doctor, who lit a Camel and counted the money twice.

"How long until she can travel?"

"How far?" the doctor parried.

"Dallas," Mario lied.

"Way she was bleeding, I'd wait."

"Wait how long?"

A shrug. "Two days?"

The doctor knocked ashes on the floor. "I figure you owe me another hundred."

"For what reason?" Mario demanded.

"Twins. You don't get two for the price of one."

"We had an agreement."

"I figure you owe me," the doctor repeated.

"I don't have another hundred dollars," Mario confessed.

"How 'bout them rings she's wearin'?"

Mario drew himself to his full five feet eight. "You'll not have her rings or another penny!"

"Ain't you some fancy wop?" the doctor drawled.

He left, but stood at the curb and gazed back menacingly, as Mario watched uneasily through the window. Mario did not trust anyone in Texas and especially he did not trust the doctor. Darkness fell, and he paced nervously as the girl and the babies slept and headlights swept their window. After a police car went by twice, Mario woke her.

"We must go."

"I don't think I can walk."

He carried her to the car, then the babies, and arranged blankets around them.

"I'm still bleeding," she told him.

"We'll be safe in Louisiana," he said, as if invoking a magical kingdom, where lovers dwelt in perfect peace.

They sped east on Highway 90, through Rose City, where a sign urged black people not to linger, and through Vidor, where a Dr. Pepper ten-two-and-four clock outside the Dairy Queen said midnight. The state line was near—Mario had the Olds up to eighty-five. One of the babies began crying. Then he saw the headlights coming up fast.

"It's only the police," he said with relief. "We'll say we're going to the doctor in Lake Charles."

He stopped. A red light flashed behind them in a night as black as death. A big-bellied Texas Ranger came to the window.

"Good evening, officer," Mario began.

"Get out."

"My wife is very ill, you see. We must . . . "

"Get out, wop," the Ranger said and jerked open the door and threw Mario to the ground.

Another Ranger came and the two men began kicking Mario. The girl screamed and the babies cried and then she saw the Cadillac behind the police car and watched her father climb out, a gaunt old man in a dark suit, alligator boots, and a white Stetson hat.

"No, no, no!" she cried as the Rangers dragged Mario into a ditch beside the road. One held the flashlight while the other used a hunting knife to perform an operation that was more typically performed on young bulls and stallions than on angelic young gamblers from the French Quarter.

Mario screamed and struggled, then whimpered, then was silent.

A moon-faced woman in white emerged from the Cadillac and lifted the babies from the girl's arms.

Her father's craggy face loomed near.

"Come on, darlin', we're going home."

The nurse climbed into the police car with the twins, and the car vanished into the night.

The old tycoon led his daughter to a vast Fleetwood, its tailfins sharp as swords.

The girl tried to pray, but in her heart she knew that the only God who mattered was beside her drinking whiskey from a bottle in a brown paper sack. "My babies," she whispered.

"Honey, your life's gonna be perfect now," he told her. "What say we git you your own little Coupe de Ville?"

He played the radio on the drive back to Houston, and once more Hank Williams sang of tears like falling rain. She had not known there were so many tears in the universe. Oceans of tears, continents of heartbreak. She huddled in her seat, summoning her daughters' tiny faces.

Part of her vowed to fight back, to find her babies, to defy her father. But as the music engulfed her, she realized that her courage was gone as surely as her lover was gone. This night had undone her girlish belief in love and justice and happy endings. Her father had taught her, more effectively than anyone would ever teach her anything again, that life could rip your heart from your breast with swift and terrible precision and leave you only the consolation of a Coupe de Ville.

PART I

• • •

Fort Worth

•

The 1960s

1.

ON THE JUNE AFTERNOON IN 1963 THAT WILDCAT BILLY RINGER turned up on her doorstep after so many years, Lillian Nash was content with her life.

Lily, who cared about words, would not have called herself happy; resigned was closer. But, overall, she was content. Howard was a good Christian man, a good provider, a strict but devoted father to their sons. There was, she accepted, no romance in their lives. Howard was preoccupied with his work at the bank, his duties as a deacon of their church, his civic clubs and social status, and he was not given to affection, or remotely interested in the things she thought made life worthwhile.

Lily loved the singing of Bing Crosby and Judy Garland, the movies of Clark Gable and Cary Grant, the novels of Herman Wouk and John O'Hara and Pearl Buck. Whenever a musical—*South Pacific*, say, or *Guys and Dolls*—made its way to Fort Worth, or more likely to nearby Dallas, more a center of culture, she ached to go, although she could rarely persuade Howard to take her.

Howard's passion was his status as chief accountant of the Farmers and Ranchers National Bank. He still dreamed of becoming a vice president, although in truth Lillian doubted it would ever happen. Howard, she had come to believe, was not rowdy enough to be a success in Fort Worth. He was a dour man, large and fleshy, with thinning hair and pursed lips, not a drinker or a backslapper or a hellraiser like the "real" Texans who daily made fortunes in oil and land development.

Still, the Nash family was doing well enough. Once Billy, their youngest, started school, Lillian had gone back to work, teaching English at W. C. Stripling Junior High, adding her $6,000 salary to Howard's $15,000. They owned their own home in Ridglea, out by the new country club, they drove an almost-new Dodge, and they were putting away money for the boys' college years.

Lily was content. Her girlhood dreams of romance and adventure had not come true, but whose ever did? She had her sons, her books and records, her secret dreams, and those things were enough, or so she persuaded herself.

He came early in June, just after school let out for the summer. Howard was at work, and the boys were out somewhere, playing ball, or prowling the open prairie to the west.

Lily was dusting when she heard the doorbell chime. Looking out, she saw a rusty, battered old Ford pickup in front of the house. Some handyman seeking work, she thought.

Still, she opened the door—and cried out in astonishment.

She would not have known the old man except that his eyes were ageless, shrewd, sparkling eyes that called back long-forgotten days when he had dandled her on his knee, brought her candy, shown her pictures of distant lands, called her his "Silly Lily," and in a hundred ways brought joy into her young life.

The rest of him was a stranger—a frail, stooped old man in khakis, scuffed boots, a work shirt, a denim jacket. A tentative smile brightened his unshaven face, then he doubled over coughing.

"Y'ain't forgot me, have you, Lily?"

She threw open the screen door and embraced him. Tears filled

20

her eyes, her first tears in so many years. "Oh, Billy, Billy, what's happened to you?"

"I got old, gal, that's all. How you been?"

She took his hand and led him into her spotless living room. "I'll put tea on," she said.

"You wouldn't have nothing more substantial, would you? For the cough?"

"I'll see." Howard usually kept a bottle of Four Roses at the back of the cupboard, in case his boss from the bank dropped by and wanted a drink.

Lily gave him the whiskey and he poured himself a generous portion. The last time she'd seen Billy was at her wedding reception. He'd consumed several bottles of champagne and told tales of the boomtown days until he passed out. Howard had never let her forget that one.

"Where've you been, Billy?" she asked, when they settled at the kitchen table.

"All over. Panama. Alaska—that's where I got this cough. Louisiana. Saudi Arabia for a while. Anywhere there might be oil."

She smiled. "Find any?"

"A little here, a little there. The competition has got a hell of a lot tougher in the past thirty years." He sipped the whiskey. "So how's Harry?"

"Howard? He's fine, he's the chief accountant of his bank." She smiled. "But of course you've always hated bankers, haven't you? We have three boys—I'm dying for you to meet them. Can you stay for dinner?"

"I've got no urgent plans. Matter of fact, there's some business I want to talk with you and Harry about."

"Howard," she corrected. "That'll be fine, Billy. Why don't you spend the night? The boys can double up."

He emptied his glass. "Let's see what Harry has to say. He might not take to a boarder." He yawned. "Lily, you suppose I could take a nap? I drove all night from Baton Rouge and I ain't as strong as I was."

She took him to a bedroom at the top of the stairs. The old man stood in the doorway, admiring the model airplanes that hung from the ceiling, the clutter of books and games and athletic gear. "Looks like this boy's a pistol," he declared.

Lily beamed. "This is Billy's room. He's our youngest. Oh, you don't know—he's your namesake, William Ringer Nash."

Billy Ringer grinned. "That's a real honor, Lily."

"How is Kent?" She had not thought of her cousin in years. He was a man her own age who had been raised by his mother in California.

"I lost him," the old man said. "A car wreck."

She held him close. "Oh, Billy, I'm so sorry."

"You're a good woman, Lily. Fine-looking, too, like your mama, God rest her."

The words, even from her aging uncle, warmed her. It seemed an eternity since any man had told her she was pretty.

"I'll take that nap now," he said.

Downstairs, Lily paced the kitchen. She had no illusions that her husband would embrace her black-sheep uncle. Somewhere in the attic was a scrapbook filled with clippings of the old man's glory days—pictures of gushers and mansions and limousines, headlines from the 1930s that proclaimed WILDCAT BILLY DOES IT AGAIN! But that was long ago. Now he was old and broke and sick and alone, with no one else to turn to. But what could they do? They had no room for him and they had to think of the boys' education.

With a sigh, she called Howard at the bank.

"What is it, Lillian?" he demanded. "I've got people waiting."

"Howard, you remember my uncle, Billy Ringer?"

"How could I forget the old reprobate? He's dead, isn't he?"

"No, he's here. He's having dinner with us."

"Dinner? In my home? What the devil does he want?"

"It's just a visit, Howard. He's never met the boys."

"Never gave a damn about meeting them, either. Lillian, he's come for money and don't you give him a dime. He threw away millions in his time, and he's got no cause to come to us for charity.

Don't invite him to stay, either. I don't want him filling my sons'
minds with crazy ideas."

"I don't think he'll corrupt them."

"Don't be impudent. If you won't get rid of him, I will."

Lily put down the phone. It had been even worse than she'd
expected. She picked up the bottle of Four Roses and ran water
into it, back to its previous level.

Her dilemma overwhelmed her. Billy could not stay, yet how
could she turn him away?

Lily sat at her kitchen table, gazing out at the sun-baked Texas
prairie, trying to think.

By the time Billy woke, the boys were home. Lily had found the
scrapbook and was showing them the yellowing proof of yesterday's
glory.

"Is he rich?" asked Sonny, who had a paper route, and was saving
to buy a car.

"No, dear, but he's had an exciting life. He's been all over the
world, and known famous people."

"What's the point if you don't save your money?" demanded
Mark, the son most like his father.

Billy, the youngest, was huddled over the scrapbook. "Boy, look
at that car—a Pierce-Arrow. And it says he found oil in the jungle!
What jungle, Mom?"

"Peru, son," Billy Ringer said from the doorway. The nap had
put color back in his face. "They had Indians with blowguns and
poison darts there who decided we were devils and we barely got
out with our skins. Lily, introduce me to these gentlemen."

The boys reacted to their newfound great-uncle more or less as
Lily had expected. Sonny was curious but skeptical, Mark was
disapproving, and Billy leaped into the old man's lap and was entranced by his tales of gushers and boomtowns.

At six, the front door banged, and Howard made his entrance.
He glared at Billy and did not offer to shake hands.

"How ya been, Harry?" the old man muttered.

23

"I'm well, thank you. To what do we owe this unexpected honor?"

"You owe it to Lily being my only blood kin, and me wanting to see her and her family 'fore it's too late. Fine bunch of boys you've got."

"I'm glad you approve of them," Howard said coldly.

Dinner was a disaster. When young Billy tried to quiz his uncle about his adventures, Howard cut him off with a sarcastic remark. Billy coughed a great deal, to Howard's vast annoyance. Finally the ordeal ended and the boys were sent upstairs. Lily was close to tears as she poured coffee.

"Lily, you reckon I could skip the java and try a little more of that cough medicine?"

"Of course, Billy." But when she brought the whiskey, Howard leaped to his feet.

"There's no cause for whiskey drinking in my home!"

Billy downed half the glass. "Oh shut up, you damn fool, and I'll tell you why I came, then I'll get out of your precious home."

"Please, Howard," Lily pleaded. "Let's go to the living room." She wished she had the courage to remind him of the Sunday School lessons he taught, about taking the stranger in, binding his wounds, washing his feet.

In the hallway, Lily clutched her uncle's arm. "I've got money he doesn't know about, in the Credit Union," she said. "I can give you a thousand dollars. Call me tomorrow."

"God bless you, child," the old man whispered.

They settled in the living room, Howard stirring his coffee, Billy sipping his whiskey, Lily nervously eyeing them both.

"Let's get this over with, Ringer," Howard said.

"Fine with me," Billy said. "Lily, you're gonna be my heir. Everything I've got goes to you and those boys of yours. And the way things look, you won't have long to wait."

"And just how extensive is this estate, Mr. Ringer?" Howard said with withering sarcasm. "Does she get that glorious vehicle you've parked in front of our house? Does she inherit your scrapbooks and dry wells and tall tales? Indians in Peru and castles in Spain?"

Billy coughed until his entire body seemed unhinged. Lily tried to steady his frail shoulders.

"Stop it, Howard," she pleaded.

When Billy Ringer spoke again, they could barely hear him. "It's hard to say how much it'll be," he whispered. "Nobody knows. Maybe a hundred. Maybe two hundred. Maybe more."

Howard slammed down his coffee cup. "You've come here, you've put us through all this, to tell Lillian you're leaving her *two hundred dollars?*"

The old wildcatter glared at the banker with a lifetime of contempt raging in his eyes. "No, you silly ass, not two hundred dollars, two hundred *million* dollars!"

Lily cried out. Howard's coffee cup crashed to the floor.

"I leased some swampland in Louisiana back in the forties. Hung on to it, all these years. I always knew there was oil there, but it was hid real good. But now we got it. A producing field. Nobody knows how much oil is down there. And it'll all be yours, Lily."

Howard slowly rose up, dazed, open-mouthed, trembling. With a supreme effort he said, "Billy, you old so-and-so, how about another drink?"

The old wildcatter ignored him. His head sank to his chest. Lily didn't know if he was drunk or exhausted or even dying. "Oh Billy Billy Billy," she sobbed.

Billy Ringer looked at her with eyes that had gazed upon much of the world's bounty, and now glowed with infinite sadness. "Don't cry, Lily," he whispered. "It's only money. It ain't like I was doing you a favor."

2.

BILLY RINGER VANISHED BACK INTO THE WILDS OF LOUISIANA. That fall, as the Nash family awaited word from him, two twelve-year-old sisters took up residence not far away, at the Gertrude Little Home, better known in Fort Worth in those days simply as the Home.

Gertrude Little donated her Victorian mansion on Camp Bowie Boulevard to start the Home in the 1930s, and it had never lacked for occupants. Babies of uncertain parentage arrived, and the orphaned survivors of floods and fires and highway disasters, and rawboned West Texas youngsters whose parents had gone mad or lost their farms or otherwise quit the parenting business. By the 1960s the mansion was squeezing in more than a hundred boys and girls.

Because of its location on the west side of Fort Worth, only minutes from the monied enclaves of Rivercrest and Ridglea and Westover Hills, the children from the Home attended Arlington Heights Elementary and W. C. Stripling Junior High and Arlington

26

Heights High with the sons and daughters of some of the state's richest oilmen and ranchers.

Lily Nash had taught many children from the Home at W. C. Stripling. She thought of them as a breed apart. Many of them, particularly the girls, moved in a kind of trance, like soldiers shell-shocked by battle. Some of the boys distinguished themselves at sports; life at the Home was good preparation for athletic combat, if not for much else.

But more often the children from the Home sat silently in class, rarely volunteering a comment, rarely connecting with the world around them. You could always tell them, Lily thought, by the wariness in their faces. By the shaved heads of the boys and the straight, unadorned hair of the girls. By the sack lunches they brought with an apple and a peanut butter sandwich made with two-day-old bread from Mrs. Baird's Bakery. And by the ill-fitting hand-me-down clothes that contrasted so starkly with the cashmere sweaters and suede loafers that monied girls in Arlington Heights wore and the expensive boots and pearl-buttoned cowboy shirts that the rich boys affected.

The sisters who arrived at the Home that fall had been living with a farm family in West Texas, but their foster mother suffered a stroke and her husband found himself unable to care both for the girls and his bedridden wife.

There was with these girls, even more than with most new arrivals, a scarcity of official information. They had no birth certificate, and the farmer was stubbornly vague about their origins. Their names, he said, were Mickey and Jessie, and they had adopted his surname, Ketchum.

When the time came to say goodbye, Ezra Ketchum hugged the girls stiffly. The one called Jessie was crying. Mickey's face was frozen in pain, but she shed no tears.

"Trust in the Lord, girls," was the farmer's parting admonition. "He brung you this far and I reckon He'll carry you the rest of the way."

Nadine Cottle, the Home's director, glared at the pious farmer. "This is most irregular," she told him. "We need documentation."

He squinted into the distance and drew five one-hundred-dollar bills from his pocket.

"This here's their nest egg."

Mrs. Cottle accepted the money uneasily. Dirt farmers like Ezra Ketchum rarely accumulated $500 in a lifetime, and even more rarely gave it away. Was this a bribe? Was he crazy?

"This is a lot of money, Mr. Ketchum," she said.

"There's this lawyer who'll call you," he said.

Nadine Cottle did not argue. When he was gone, she took a hundred dollars for herself and applied the rest of the bonanza to paying the Home's bills.

Mickey and Jessie were given bunk beds at the far end of a big dormitory room that housed forty girls aged six to seventeen.

"Where ya from?" a girl asked them.

"Matador," Mickey said.

"Where's that?"

"Motley County. Out by Lubbock."

"My name's Winnie. How come you're here?"

"Our mom had a stroke."

"How come you do all the talkin'? Don't she talk none?"

"When she feels like it," Mickey said.

"I talk," Jessie said. "I'm just tired is all."

"You two twins?"

"Sure we are," Mickey said. "Don't we look it?"

"I dunno. Sort of. But you look tougher than her."

"What's it like here?" Jessie asked.

Winnie leaned close. She was a bony girl with close-set eyes. "It's rough as a cob. Mrs. Cottle, she'll whip you with a belt. And the boys pick on the girls somethin' awful. How old're you two?"

"Twelve."

"No crap? You'll find out. You sure will find out."

Something in her voice made Jessie inch closer to her sister. "Whatta you mean?" Mickey demanded.

But Winnie only repeated, "You'll find out," and skipped away.

The next day a fight broke out on the playground between a big red-headed raw-boned boy named Luther and a smaller, newer boy.

28

The other boys formed a circle and cheered for Luther. Blood was spurting from both their noses. "Motherfucker," Luther muttered, as the smaller boy kept getting back up.

Mickey and Jessie and Winnie watched from the far corner of the playground. Finally Jessie turned away.

"Look," she said.

"Lookit what?"

"In the window. Mrs. Cottle. She's watching."

"She don't never stop fights," Winnie said.

The fight ended when the smaller boy went down and stayed down. Red-haired Luther spit blood and pumped his fists victoriously.

"He's from Mineola," Winnie said. "They're all mean in Mineola."

To the twins' horror, Luther came swaggering their way.

"You two, what's yore names?"

"Ketchum. Mickey an' Jessie Ketchum," Mickey said.

"Which one are you, babydoll?" the boy asked Jessie.

"I'm Jessie," the girl whispered.

"You like to fuck, Jessie?"

"You shut your dumb mouth!" Mickey yelled.

Luther's open hand shot out and hit her above the ear and she tumbled to the ground.

"You like to fuck, Jessie?" Luther said again.

Mickey rose to her knees but was stalled there. Jessie could not speak.

"Come on, you kids, it's time for cleanup!" Mrs. Cottle yelled from the doorway.

Luther spit blood on the ground. "I reckon I'll be seein' you gals," he said, and strutted away.

"The son of a bitch," Mickey muttered.

"He's mean as a snake," Winnie said. "They all are in Mineola."

The Ketchum twins were assigned to Lily Nash's seventh-grade English class and they fascinated her, so alike and yet so different. At first glance they seemed identical. They were the same size, barely five feet tall and perhaps ninety pounds, and their delicate features were identical, and both had thick golden hair. But then you began to see the differences. Jessie's hair was a shade lighter—it caught the sun while Mickey's was tangled with shadows—and Jessie clearly spent far more time washing and brushing hers. Jessie carried herself cautiously, delicately, while Mickey was all elbows and swagger. Jessie's fair skin seemed a stranger to the sun, while Mickey's was tanned and scarred from playground mishaps.

Somehow, Lily thought, the girls had started with the same raw material, and one had become a perfect little lady—a beauty, to anyone who had eyes to see—and the other a classic tomboy/ragamuffin, hard-edged, watchful, and tough.

They both were terribly bright, and that was rare among Home kids, but bright in different ways. Mickey had a literal mind. If you gave her a list of words to learn, she learned it, and she used her knowledge as a weapon. Lily would never forget little Mickey Ketchum wildly waving her hand when she knew the meaning of "ultimate" and the girl beside her, the pampered daughter of a Cadillac dealer, did not.

Jessie, for her part, rarely opened her mouth unless called upon, but her papers were gems. After the class read *Ivanhoe*, Jessie wrote the most remarkable essay. The child had entered the world of *Ivanhoe*; its knights and princesses and jousts were clearly more real to her than the Gertrude Little Home. In paper after paper, Jessie revealed a gift for self-expression and a potential for scholarship. And yet she remained painfully withdrawn; to talk to her was like pulling teeth.

Lily sent a note to Mrs. Cottle, the Home's director, praising both girls, but she received no reply. Cottle was a tough old bird and the Home was a hard place to grow up. Boys came to school bruised and battered from fights, and girls sobbing because of God-only-knew what abuse. The teachers wanted to protest, but it was pointless. The Home cared for a hundred children whom no one else wanted, and most people thought they were lucky to have a roof over their heads.

Lily, caught up in the unfolding drama of her own life, had little time for the Ketchum twins. Still, she opened her heart to them, gave them extra attention, a hint of love, and hoped that somehow it would help.

To the twins, school was a sanctuary from the harsh realities of the Home. Enforcement of the rules, when Mrs. Cottle was not on hand, was left to the senior boys, led by Luther, the sullen red-haired teenager. The boys, they soon discovered, were bullies, who beat up younger boys and humiliated girls.

Luther and two other boys caught Mickey behind the old barn on the far edge of the playground one day that winter.

"Let's see yore pants," he demanded.

"Do what?"

"Hike up that dress, gal. This is a pants check."

"You're crazy."

"Hike it up and no back talk. Let's see if yore pants is clean."

She tried to run, but the boys grabbed her and one of them started tugging at her dress. She kicked him and flailed at the others with her fists.

Luther was laughing. "Let the little bitch go," he said. "She ain't got nothing to see nohow."

"She kicked me in the nuts," one boy protested.

"Let her go," Luther said. "Her sister's the cute one."

Mickey skipped away from them, then turned back. "You leave us alone," she said. "We ain't doin' you no harm."

"We ain't doin' you none either," Luther said. "We gonna educate you, honey."

The boys' ugly laughter followed her all the way back to the safety of the mansion.

A delegation from the Home confronted art at the local museum one day. They were at first awed by the spectacle of a huge silent room, its walls covered with paintings. Most of them had never seen an oil painting except the one of Gertrude Little that hung above the mantle in Mrs. Cottle's office.

Many of the paintings were Remingtons, vivid scenes of cowboys and cattle and Indians, and that somewhat impressed the boys, although they didn't know Frederic Remington from Roy Rogers.

The intended highlight of the visit, however, was a glimpse of Thomas Eakins's *The Swimming Hole*. Although the men's naked bodies were shown only from the rear, and although their art teacher stressed the purity and innocence of the painting, the spectacle of bare buttocks on display in mixed company inspired many hoots and wisecracks from the Home's young men. *The Swimming Hole* would, a few decades later, be valued at $10 million, but Luther and his cohorts wouldn't have given ten cents for it.

"Turn round, let's see what ya got!"

"Shut yore eyes, gals, that's plumb filthy!"

"Looks like a buncha queers to me!"

As the flustered art teacher hurried the ungrateful orphans to the next exhibit, Jessie turned to her sister.

"It really *was* pretty," she said.

Mickey rolled her eyes. "I reckon they could have worn bathing suits," she said firmly.

But cultural outings were rare. Days and nights at the Home were slow as molasses. They had one black and white TV set, but it was generally tuned to westerns or wrestling matches. Many evenings the girls simply gossiped in the dorm or jumped rope or played hopscotch in the yard, or just sat watching the cars go by. On summer evenings the yard was thick with lightning bugs. Jessie had happy memories of the summer before, when they would catch lightning bugs on the Ketchum farm and put them in a mayonnaise jar with holes punched in the top. They'd watch the jar flash like a magic lantern, all evening long, and at bedtime they'd unscrew the top and set the fireflies free.

The Home was different, as they learned one sultry night. Jessie and Mickey were sitting on the back steps and the boys were racing around catching lightning bugs. Jessie was not paying much attention until Luther ran up and thrust his hand under her nose.

"How 'bout that!" he demanded.

A small, dull greenish-yellow ball, the size of a pea, glowed in his palm. Jessie did not at first understand. Then she screamed.

"Leave us alone!" Mickey yelled, as she too realized what the boys were doing: catching the fireflies, tearing off their wings, and molding their bodies into phosphorescent balls that would glow for hours.

"How can they be so mean?" Jessie sobbed, as the boys romped and howled in the deep shadows under the oak trees.

"They just *are*," Mickey said bitterly. "They're born that way."

One night after lights out the sisters heard the older girls whispering.

"Where's Emmy?"

"They got her."

"Took her to the barn."

"Where's Miz Cottle?"

"She ain't even here."

"It's Emmy's birthday. They're giving her a birthday party."

"Them dirty old bastards."

"It ain't fair."

"Aw, it ain't so bad."

Mickey lay in the darkness angry because she did not know what was happening. Jessie lay in the bunk beneath her, not wanting to know anything at all.

Late that night, the missing girl returned to the dorm. They awoke to her sobbing.

"What'd they do to you?" Mickey asked.

But Emmy just kept sobbing as if her heart would break.

3.

HOWARD AND LILY NASH DID NOT HEAR FROM BILLY RINGER again until December, when he checked into a cheap hotel on South Main Street and drove out in his pickup truck on Christmas morning to slip crisp new hundred-dollar bills into the boys' stockings. The old wildcatter looked more gaunt than ever. His oil field, he reported, was producing beyond his wildest dreams. He declined Howard's offer of a drink and was gone in less than an hour.

One Sunday a month later Lily took a call from a man who announced himself as Thomas T. Thomas, counsellor-at-law, of New Iberia, Louisiana. "Madam, I have the unfortunate duty to inform you that my client, and your uncle, Wildcat Billy Ringer, has embarked to a better world."

As Lily cried out in grief, the lawyer continued, "The last rites will be perpetrated at the New Iberia Memorial Garden at high noon tomorrow, that sad ceremony to be followed by a reading of the will in my office, conveniently located above the Red Rooster Café."

The Nash family left before dawn and barely arrived in time for the graveside ceremony. The handful of mourners were mostly old men in khakis. A young Baptist preacher read the Twenty-third Psalm and offered up a prayer. Lily thought it a shabby end for a man who in his prime had walked with senators, governors, even kings. She noticed a fat man in a green suit and a red tie, who kept eyeing her. Beside him, clutching his arm and sobbing, was a tiny woman with orange hair who like Lily was dressed in black.

As the mourners departed, and men in overalls began shoveling red clay onto Billy Ringer's pine coffin, the fat man approached them, hand outstretched. "Thomas T. Thomas offers his condolences, sir and madam, on the passing of your kinsman. Shall we repair to my office?"

The old woman in black poked his arm. "Oh, by the by," the lawyer added, "allow me to present the bereaved widow, Mrs. Ida Ringer."

"Widow?" Howard exclaimed.

The woman took Lily's hand. "Oh, my dear, he loved us both," she cried, and fell into Lily's arms.

They left the boys in the Red Rooster, to feast on RC Colas and Moon Pies, and they proceeded to the lawyer's office for a difficult afternoon. The lawyer told them some of the story with Ida present; then some more after she, pleading fatigue in the face of Howard's outrage, retired to the mobile home she and Billy had shared.

Billy and Ida had, the lawyer said, been "fast friends and close companions" for some years, but it was not until that fall that they had wed.

"But he'd already named my wife as his sole heir," Howard protested.

"True, and we drew up such an instrument in July," Thomas said, sipping from a Dixie cup of bourbon. "But after they were joined in matrimony, he suffered a change of heart, and we penned the new will, leaving everything to Ida."

"He was senile!" Howard roared. "Incompetent! We'll have the will overturned!"

The lawyer licked his thick lips, savoring the rotgut and the moment. "Sir, as the attorney for Mrs. Ringer, and as the brother-in-law of the county judge who placed his official seal of approval on it, I advise against such a course. Billy's lungs were gone, but there wasn't a man more *compos mentis* in the state of Louisiana."

Lily spoke for the first time. "Mr. Thomas, can you tell us precisely what the will provides?"

"Of course, dear lady. Right now the Ringer estate is worth upward of twenty million, and more royalties flow in every day. The will says that money is to be prudently invested, with yours truly as executor. Ida gets the interest, but can't touch the principal. When she's gone, the whole shebang, which by then could be worth fifty million or two hundred, goes to yourself, the beloved niece, minus of course certain legal expenses."

"There's no immediate bequest to Lillian?" Howard demanded. "To those boys of ours he loved so dearly?"

"It is as I have stated, sir."

"I think it's more than fair," Lily declared. "He loved her and he's provided for her and, God knows, we'll get more money than we could ever want, eventually."

"How old is that woman?" Howard demanded.

"Ida? Oh, seventy, give or take."

Lily stood up. The smell of rotgut was making her ill. "Howard, we'll call on Mrs. Ringer, then we have a long drive ahead."

Ida's mobile home was tiny but cozy—the boys played in the piney woods nearby—and she served Kool-Aid and told them of Billy's last years. "I never thought we'd tie the knot, but he insisted. He loved you and your boys dearly, Lily, but I guess he worried about me. I told him, 'Billy, don't fret about me, the Lord will provide,' but he said he'd give the Lord a little help."

"What can you tell us about your background, Mrs. Ringer?" Howard asked.

Lily wanted to say, "For God's sake, Howard, she's not applying for a loan," but the old woman smiled sweetly.

"Call me Ida," she said. "My background? Lord, there's so much of it. Mississippi is where I started out. I was a hairdresser for a time. I met Billy back in Gulfport in nineteen and thirty-one. I was working in a bar and he was what you'd call a steady customer. But I mustn't bore you with an old woman's memories. Anyhow, we'll all be getting to know each other better."

"How is that?" Howard asked. His eyes kept darting around the neat little trailer, as if he expected bandits to leap from nowhere and attack.

The woman's eyes sparkled. "Well, I thought it over, me having no family to speak of, except insomuch as you're my family now, and I just up and decided I'd move to Fort Worth."

And so she did, and proceeded to buy an imposing stone mansion on Rivercrest Drive, across from the golf course of the exclusive Rivercrest Country Club.

Howard was livid, but in time he calmed down. After a second trip to New Iberia, and a long talk with Tom T. Thomas, Howard learned that Ida had the power to determine which bank would manage the estate. It was then that Howard invited the widow to dinner, began calling her Aunt Ida, bought her drinks, and listened with unaccustomed patience to her views on everything from soap operas to the afterlife.

Lily soon realized what was afoot: Howard wanted Ida to transfer Billy's fast-growing estate to his bank for safekeeping.

Ida sweetly agreed.

The move meant little to her but everything to Howard. He could claim personal credit for bringing to the Farmers and Ranchers a huge account. Moreover, as he let it be known, that fortune would soon be his own. Before the year was out, Howard was a vice president of the F&R, and his salary soared to $22,500, whereupon he informed Lily that she should quit her job.

"I don't *want* to quit," she protested. "What would I do all day?"

"It doesn't look right, you working," he said. "Lily, we're prominent citizens. You need to think about charities, women's clubs, your place in the community."

"I don't give a hoot about those things," Lily declared. "All that money may just be a pipe dream, but those students of mine are real!"

Howard grumbled, but Lily kept on teaching.

4.

THE GIRLS OF GAMMA KAPPA SORORITY AT ARLINGTON HEIGHTS High School came to the Home every Christmas Eve. They came wearing cashmere sweaters and camel-hair coats and suede loafers and bright plaid scarves and they came bearing practical gifts like gloves and socks and caps. After everyone had exchanged cheerful hellos and opened their gifts and drunk some punch, the girls from Gamma Kap put on a skit about Santa Claus. Then everyone sang Christmas songs, although the Gamma Kaps sang with more enthusiasm about mistletoe and sleigh bells and the baby Jesus than the boys and girls from the Home did.

The sorority girls left at five for their own Christmas Eve parties and the Home girls went back to their dorm. Jessie whispered to her sister, "I hate them. They're just here for them, they're not here for us. They don't care anything at all about us."

Mickey was eating an apple she'd sneaked out of the dining hall. "They're just dumb," she said. "I got some neat gloves out of it."

"I hate them," Jessie repeated.

"You ain't got the spirit of Christmas," Mickey said, and offered her a bite of the apple.

Back in her office, Nadine Cottle did not have the Christmas spirit either. She did not appreciate the sorority girls who brought apples and Christmas carols but whose parents rarely donated the kind of money they spent on their Cadillacs and country clubs to support her orphans. Nor was she happy, late on Christmas Eve afternoon, to receive a call from George Peoples, the Home's lawyer and trustee. Peoples was the man who signed the checks, and when he called, it usually meant trouble.

"I understand you have two sisters called Ketchum," he began.

Mrs. Cottle remembered the farmer's $500 and the $100 she'd kept for herself. But how could he have known? "I . . . yes, sir, we do have them," she said.

"Are they well?"

"Couldn't be better. Jessie, she made straight A's last time, and little Mickey, she's a feisty one, always running and playing."

"Mrs. Cottle, I have an interest in those girls. I want them well treated."

"All my children are well treated."

"To repeat, I have an interest in the Ketchum girls. Do I make myself clear?"

"Yes, sir," she said meekly.

"I must personally approve any adoption. Do you understand?"

"Of course. But may I ask why . . . ?"

"No, you may not. Good day, Mrs. Cottle."

She put down the phone gingerly. He hadn't even known about the $100. All he'd cared about were those two Ketchum girls, the one with her nose always stuck in a book, the other a troublemaker, always fighting and complaining. She guessed she'd better keep a closer eye on those two, maybe do something special, make sure they knew how much she loved them. Mrs. Cottle tried to remember, didn't they have a birthday coming up in the spring? She would have to check their file. It was a restricted file, one she kept under lock and key, one that was lacking in certain basic data, but she was almost sure it gave their birthday.

The older girls who knew what the boys did on their birthdays didn't talk about it and the younger girls who talked about it didn't know. Mickey listened to whispers and hints and rumors and learned only enough to make her fear for herself and Jessie.

She had never forgotten the time Emmy was gone half the night and came back crying her heart out. After that she'd tried to make friends with Emmy, because that seemed the best way of finding out the truth. One lazy Sunday afternoon that spring, when they were out by the barn talking, Mickey said abruptly, "We're friends, aren't we?"

"Sure."

"Then tell me something."

"What's that?"

"What'd the boys do to you that night?"

Emmy looked away. "I don't wanna talk 'bout it."

"Come *on*."

"They make you swear not to tell."

"Swearin' don't count if they make you. I bet they made you, didn't they?"

"You think I'd of done that stuff if they hadn't made me?"

"What stuff?"

Emmy's face puckered like she would cry. "They call it the nitiation."

"The nitiation?"

"Yeah, like when you join some fancy club. That's what Luther said. He made a speech 'bout you been a girl but now you're gonna be a woman and we're gonna nitiate you. And then you gotta do the stuff."

"What stuff?"

"You know 'bout sex, dontcha?"

"Sure I do. We grew up on a farm. We seen the horses doing it. Is *that* what they make you do?"

Emmy made a face and looked away.

"Mrs. Cottle, she's an old bitch, but she wouldn't let 'em do *that*," Mickey said with alarm.

"You think! She told Luther she ain't no policeman, and she ain't gonna ask no questions, so long as the girls don't get pregnant."

Mickey was confused. "If they ain't gonna get pregnant, then what're they doing to 'em?"

"Don't keep asking questions!" Emmy cried. "This ain't horses, they got lots of things you can do!"

She started away, then came back.

"When's your birthday?"

"Next week."

"You gonna be thirteen? Both of you?"

"Yeah."

Tears filled Emmy's wistful brown eyes. "You better watch out," she warned. "I wouldn't treat a dog like they treat us girls. It's dirty and it hurts and I wish they were dead."

It was clear to Mickey that the sensible thing to do was run away. She'd been thinking about running away ever since she discovered Huck Finn.

Their English teacher, Mrs. Nash, was the sponsor of the Reading Club and she'd asked them both to join.

Not many kids joined the Reading Club, because they figured they already read enough, but to Mickey and Jessie staying after school one day a week looked pretty good. There were only six of them in the club and one of them was Mrs. Nash's son Billy, who was a ninth grader and kind of cute and funny.

The first few weeks they read *Huckleberry Finn* and talked about it. About how Huck could be so friendly with a black man. Mrs. Nash didn't think that was so bad—she said Jim was the best person in the book—but she was the only white person Mickey had ever met who felt that way. And they talked about the King and the Duke and the people in the towns along the river, and about Tom and Huck and how they were different. Mickey had never imagined there could be so many things to talk about in one book.

To Mickey, the point of the book—the greatness of the book, what gripped her imagination as nothing in any book ever would again—was that Huck had run away. Just up and *gone*. Lit out for the territory. She loved the part when Huck and Jim were on the raft, floating down the river. "It was kind of lazy and jolly, no books nor study," Huck had said, and that sounded like heaven to Mick.

She talked to Jessie one afternoon on the playground. There was a big fence around the Home, iron bars painted black with spikes on top, and through the fence they could see the cars on Camp Bowie Boulevard. Sometimes when the cars stopped you could hear the music from their radios, Elvis or Marty Robbins or those new guys from England with the funny haircuts. Mickey loved the music because it came from far away, proof of a big world out there, far beyond the Gertrude Little Home.

"It's like a prison here," she declared.

Jessie looked uneasy. "It's not so bad."

"I figure we ought to run away. Like old Huck Finn."

Jessie's eyes opened wide. "Run away? Where to?"

"I dunno. Back to Matador, maybe. Old Man Ketchum'd probably take us if we showed up. Or somebody else would."

"The schools are better here," Jessie said.

Mickey laughed. She figured schools were the same anywhere.

"Mickey, we don't *have* anybody," Jessie protested. "This is the only home we've got. We've got to stay here, till we're big enough to take care of ourselves."

Mickey saw the fear in her sister's eyes and she hated it; she tried never to show fear, no matter how much she felt.

"This isn't like Huck Finn," Jessie added. "There's no river to float down. Just big old highways that go on forever."

"We could hitchhike. That'd be our river. To Dallas or Houston or anywhere."

"The police would just pick us up and bring us back."

Mickey stared at her sister in frustration. She loved Jessie more than anything on earth, but she couldn't understand her. Jessie loved to read the books about "days of old when knights were bold," but she didn't want to *do* anything bold. She lived in her books, in her dreams, and pretended that the real world wasn't even there.

Mickey knew that Jessie was ten times more book-smart than

she'd ever be, but she prided herself on being the one with common sense. She'd vowed to protect her sweet, bookish, vulnerable sister, to shield her from the world's cruelties; sometimes she imagined that she would care for her sister forever.

But they saw things differently. They'd both of them wondered, ever since they were old enough to wonder, who their mother and father had been. Before the Ketchums, there'd been another foster family, named Bellson, who'd always said the girls' parents were killed in a car wreck, and that's what the Ketchums said too, except once Ketchum had gotten a long-distance call and grumbled about "that lawyer in Dallas," and after that he wouldn't say anything more and when Mickey kept asking he told her to hush.

Jessie said there wasn't any use in wondering, that it hurt too much, but Mickey couldn't stop wondering. She had a plan to sneak into the Home's office at night and look at their file and see if it told about their parents. She wanted Jessie to stand guard, but Jessie was afraid.

She had another accomplice in mind, the Home's janitor, a funny old man called Mr. Apple. He was bald and goggle-eyed and half-crazy, but he was good to the girls. Mickey knew he had keys to all the offices, and she was trying to figure if she should steal his keychain or try to talk him into helping her. She'd gone out to see him that morning in his little room behind the Home, in what used to be the stables, and she'd found him shaving, a scrawny little man with his face all lathered up, scraping at it with an old-fashioned straight razor eight inches long. She'd talked to him while he shaved—he claimed to have a daughter who was a dancer in Mexico City—and finally she told the truth, that she needed help getting into the office files to find her parents. Mr. Apple's goggle eyes grew bigger. "Oh, no, honey, Miz Cottle wouldn't like that, she'd tan our hides!" he said in his singsong voice.

That was that. If she wanted to break into the office, she was on her own. And breaking into the office wasn't her most urgent problem.

"Jessie, I hear talk the boys may try to mess with us, like they done Emmy."

Jessie looked away.

"Dirty stuff. They do it to all the girls, on their birthday when they're thirteen. Like we're about to be."

"Nobody knows."

"They have a list in the office, of everybody's birthday."

"Maybe if we're nice to everybody, you know, they'll leave us alone."

"Maybe pigs can fly."

"We could tell Mrs. Cottle."

"She don't *care*. She lets 'em do it. Honey, we're orphan girls and nobody gives a hoot what happens to us except us. I say let's get out of this dump!"

"It's our home," Jessie said in anguish. "It's all we've got."

Jessie didn't hate the Home so much. She guessed anything was better than a hardscrabble farm and a one-room school in Matador. She didn't even mind the rich girls anymore. The lesson Jessie had learned at W. C. Stripling was that she was as smart as any girl in her class, no matter how grand their homes or rich their fathers. It was a stunning discovery because it meant that someday, if she could survive the madness of her childhood, she could be a teacher or a doctor or anything. That was what kept Jessie going. Mickey wanted to meet the madness of the world head-on, but Jessie's was a more subtle strategy: to survive until things got better.

All this talk of their birthday, of an ordeal in store for them, confused and overwhelmed Jessie, and her tears were a knife in her sister's heart.

Mickey embraced the twin who was so unlike her. "Don't cry, darlin'," she pleaded. "Nobody can hurt us, long as we've got each other."

Mickey liked the brave sound of her words; she almost believed them.

5.

Lily Nash took a drunken call one day from Thomas T. Thomas, who declared that Howard had promised him money for approving the transfer of the funds to the Farmers and Ranchers, and that payment was overdue. Lily hung up the phone, and Howard indignantly denied the charge.

She did not know the truth of the charge, but she knew as the weeks and months went by that Howard was changing. He seemed determined to remake himself into the man's man, the true-blue Texan that he was not. He started playing poker with a group of bankers and oilmen who met once a week. He came home smelling of whiskey and she got the impression that he lost a good deal of money. He quit going to church regularly, but insisted that Aunt Ida come to dinner with them every Sunday. He started keeping whiskey in the house, and drinking heavily when Ida visited them.

His lust for the money was changing him, Lily knew, the tantalizing promise of vast wealth that dangled just beyond his grasp, torturing him. Lily, a Methodist minister's daughter, had never thought much about money. There were many fabulously wealthy people in Fort Worth, but she didn't worry about them. She saw them driving their Cadillacs, she read in the *Star-Telegram* about their divorces and debutante parties and oil deals, she taught their kids in school, but it never occurred to her to envy or resent them.

But Howard did. He brooded endlessly about the wealth that surrounded them. He followed the exploits of the Amon Carters and Clint Murchisons and Sid Richardsons as other men followed baseball. Sometimes in restaurants they encountered oilmen he knew, and she had seen how obsequious he became, bowing and scraping, and then when they were gone he would say bitterly that this one's wife ran around or that one would be belly-up in six months. It frightened her, how much he hated them.

Ida, for her part, took to wealth like a duck to water. She had hired a maid, a colored woman named Cora Lee, although it seemed to Lily that Cora Lee spent more time gossiping and drinking with her employer than she did cooking or cleaning. She also bought a cherry red Cadillac convertible, and used Cora Lee as her chauffeur, the two of them sitting up front and cruising Arlington Heights like a couple of schoolgirls.

Ida was a churchgoer, too, partial to Pentecostal preachers and tent evangelists. Howard tried without success to persuade her to attend Arlington Heights Methodist, not far from her home and more suitable socially, but she would cackle, "Methodists bore me, Howard—they've got no juice!"

Ida's house fronted on the Rivercrest golf course, and one Sunday she announced that she'd joined the country club so she could take up golf.

"Joined?" Howard cried. "Why it takes years, you have to be . . ."

"Well, not exactly joined," Ida explained. "The thing is, it's such good exercise, and there's that beautiful course just out my front door, and . . ."

"Wait a minute, Aunt Ida," Howard protested.

" . . . and so I went to see the manager and gave him a thousand dollars and said, 'All I want is to play that one hole in front of my house, and I'll get out of the way. when the real players come past, so how about it?' And he gave me the sweetest smile and he said, 'Miz Ringer, be my guest.' So I reckon you could say I'm a one-hole member of the Rivercrest Club."

"My God," Howard moaned.

Lily could hardly keep a straight face. Howard would have killed to be a member of Rivercrest. "So have you started playing golf?" she asked Ida.

"You bet! My hole, it's a par five, and I shot a seventeen yesterday, but I can beat that. Boy, do I feel great! My mama lived to be ninety, and the way I'm going I'll make a hundred!"

Lily smiled at Ida's little joke, then she saw the outrage in Howard's face, and it was chilling.

6.

THE GIRLS' BIRTHDAY CAME AND WENT ON WEDNESDAY WITHOUT incident, but Mickey kept a wary eye on Luther and the other boys, studying their bony faces for signs of menace. On the playground that Saturday she saw the boys smirking at her and Jessie in a way that made her shiver. She began to think how she could defend them, and she was more worried when she saw Mrs. Cottle drive away. Mrs. Cottle often went to see her invalid mother—at least that was what she said—and left the Home under the direction of Miss Tibbs, her assistant, who mostly took to her room to watch cowboy shows on TV.

By nine o'clock all the girls were in their dormitory. Jessie was on her bunk reading a paperback book.

"What's that?"

Jessie held the cover of the book up for her to see. It had a weird title.

"What is it, about baseball?"

"No, it's about this boy in a prep school up East, except he gets kicked out and he's real cynical. Mrs. Nash loaned it to me."

"What's a prep school?"

"Kind of a private school. You pay to go there."

"*Pay* to go to school? That's the dumbest thing I ever heard of. They oughta pay us!"

The lights went out at ten and Mickey was almost asleep when three senior boys slipped in.

"You Ketchum gals, Miss Tibbs wants to see ya."

Mickey shot to her feet. "What for?"

"You got a phone call."

"A phone call?" Jessie echoed. Was this every orphan's dreamed-of call, the miracle that would pluck her away to some more perfect world?

"You're lying," Mickey said stubbornly.

"Come on, she's waitin'."

Jessie took her sister's hand. "Let's see what it is."

Mickey wavered. "You better not be lyin'," she warned.

"Come on," the boy said.

The twins followed the boys out, torn between hope and terror.

"You'll be sor-ree," a girl called after them.

The boys marched them outside. The girls shivered in their thin cotton nightgowns.

"Where you takin' us?" Mickey demanded.

But she got no answer. The boys gripped their arms and led them across the schoolyard to the barn. One of them snickered.

The barn was used to store tools and sports equipment and it was supposed to be off limits. But tonight a rough table stood in the middle of its dirt floor; three candles adorned the table and three boys sat behind it like judges. Luther was in the center, and the light from the candles made his lopsided face gleam like a jack-o-lantern. Other boys, arms folded, stood around them in a circle. A bottle of Everclear gin stood on the table. And a bottle of baby oil.

"Welcome, sisters," Luther said.

Jessie felt her whole body start to shake.

"It's your birthday, and we're gonna have a party for you. This here's a solemn event, 'cause you're gonna stop being girls and gonna be women now. Let's drink us a toast to that."

One of the boys filled two Dixie cups with Everclear and handed one to each girl.

"Drink 'em down," Luther said. "Nothing like ole Everclear to put a gal in the mood for a party."

"I don't want any," Jessie whispered.

"We got us a party pooper here, fellows," Luther declared. Two boys grabbed Jessie and forced the gin down her. Two others held Mickey. Jessie gagged and spit out more of the gin than she swallowed.

"What about you, sister?" Luther asked. "You gonna drink your toast?"

Mickey seized the cup and threw the gin down in one swallow. It burned all the way down but she held her chin high, defiant.

"That's better," Luther said. "Now, kneel down, sisters, so the ceremony can begin."

"No, please," Jessie whispered, but the boys pushed her to her knees.

Mickey sank down beside Jessie, taking her hand.

"Sisters, we're here to nitiate you into womanhood," Luther said solemnly. "The thing is, women got to know how to please their men."

Mickey glared back at him; in the flickering candlelight Luther seemed a demon from hell.

"Please," Jessie pleaded. "Don't do anything to us."

"Sister, we're gonna make your young life beautiful. We never had us twins before. Which one's gonna be first?"

Luther unbuttoned his jeans. The weapon he revealed, risen to its full glory, was more huge and terrible than either of them had ever imagined.

They watched numbly as he moved toward them. The gin had left Mickey lightheaded, reckless.

"Let her go," she said.

Luther loomed above them. "Why's that, honey?"

"She's my sister. I look out for her."

"She's a little bookworm who needs to learn what's what!"

"No! I'll do the stuff you want."

"Honey, you'll both do what I want," Luther said. "You gals take them nightgowns off. Show us them little rosebuds."

"No, please," Jessie pleaded.

"Give her a hand, brothers," Luther said. "She's the cute one, ain't she? Plumb ripe."

Two boys yanked Jessie's nightgown over her head. She tried to cover her small breasts but two boys held her arms behind her.

"Leave her alone, I told you!" Mickey shouted.

"Shut up, you nasty little bitch," he warned.

Jessie sobbed helplessly as Luther swayed before her.

"This here's Prince Philip," he drawled. "Ain't he a big, handsome feller? And he wants to be your friend."

"No, please," Jessie pleaded.

"How'd you like to have Prince Philip up 'tween your legs, honey?"

"No, no," she whimpered.

"But then you'd get all knocked up, an' we got enough little bastards 'round here already. So you got to learn some other practices, don't you?"

Mickey struggled vainly against the boys who held her arms behind her back. When she tried to protest, one of them clapped a hand over her mouth.

"Answer me, gal!"

"Yes," Jessie whispered.

"Maybe you'd like to shake hands with Prince Philip," Luther drawled.

"No, please." It was, for Jessie, the most impossible of nightmares, that these terrible things could happen to her, for no reason.

"Listen up, honey. First we put some oil on your sweet little hand, so everything'll be real gentle."

One of the boys jerked Jessie's hand out and poured baby oil into her palm.

"Now, honey, shake hands with the prince."

"No, please," she said yet again, for she had no other words. One of the boys twisted her arm until she thought it would break.

"Come on, honey, the Prince is feelin' lonely. Give him a squeeze."

One of the boys seized her wrist and guided her hand forward. Luther towered before her, his huge, blue-veined, purple-knobbed erection inches from her face. When she hesitated, the boy behind her twisted her arm again. Luther's weapon, however awful, was less terrible than the pain she feared might break her arm. Her fingers encircled him.

"That's right, honey, now you shake his hand real soft and gentle."

She could barely fit her hand around it. Jessie was in a trance; she moved her hand up and down the shaft; it was hard as steel, yet soft too, with the gentlest of skin.

"Oh, you sweetheart," Luther moaned. "The Prince, he's gonna give you some sugar candy. Oh yes, yes."

Jessie felt him twitch, throb, grow beneath her fingers.

"Come on, gal, open that sweet little mouth!"

Suddenly Jessie understood what he was demanding. She screamed. The boy twisted her arm again, and she shut her eyes and pretended that she was not there, that she was not even alive, that she had never known this cruel, mad planet.

"Here comes the candy, sweetheart," Luther sang, and then she heard the howl of vengeance that was not her own.

As Mickey watched the outrage, she burned with fury. She thought her whole life had been leading to this moment. The question was always the same. Did you surrender to bastards like Luther, or did you fight back?

She had felt the grip on her loosen as the boys watched Jessie's ordeal with lewd fascination. As Luther was poised for his conquest, Mickey broke loose with a wild cry.

In one fierce motion she reached under her nightgown, yanked Mr. Apple's straight razor from the waistband of her panties, and slashed the disbelieving Luther where he was most vulnerable, in the place that all justice demanded.

His scream filled the darkest, most distant corners of the barn. He staggered back, spurting blood and howling.

"Holy shit, he's gonna bleed to death."

"She like to cut it off!"

"Go call an ambulance!"

Mickey brandished the razor until the boys drew back from her and Jessie. The fate of Luther was a more urgent issue. His comrades carried their fallen hero up to the house and in time an ambulance took him away.

Mickey hustled Jessie back to the dorm, where the other girls crowded around, begging for details.

"Luther cut himself shaving," Mickey told them.

She washed the razor off and put it under her pillow, in case anyone came seeking revenge. In truth, none of the boys who had witnessed Luther's undoing wanted any part of her.

Finally it was quiet in the dorm.

"You're so brave," Jessie whispered. She was still trembling. Mickey lay beside her, embracing her, whispering to her, trying to drive away the night's demons.

Mickey knew she wasn't brave. She was scared to death. But you did what you had to do to survive in a world of Luthers.

"What's going to happen to us?" Jessie asked.

They could hear the cars roaring past on Camp Bowie Boulevard, music blasting, the promise of faraway worlds.

"I don't know," Mickey admitted. "But there's one big ugly ape who won't bother us again."

7.

THE NASH BOYS WERE TEENAGERS, AND THEY CONTINUED TO live normal lives despite the promise of great wealth. Sonny, the oldest, was a junior at Arlington Heights, a good-looking, moody young man, a loner whose few friends were scruffy, unknown boys Lily could not bring herself to like. They spent their afternoons in pool halls or playing poker or cruising around in someone's souped-up car. Lily knew Sonny was smoking and she suspected that beer drinking had begun.

Lily's consolation was that Sonny's math teacher said her son possessed one of the most brilliant mathematical minds he had ever encountered. Whether he would ever use that mind for anything more ambitious than poker was what worried his mother. As much as she loved Sonny, she knew that part of him was unreachable. He could be charming, but he kept his distance, watching, calculating—to what end she hardly dared guess.

Mark, her middle boy, was the one most like their father, which Lily considered a not-unmixed blessing. Pudgy and solemn, he studied hard, made almost all A's, was a regular churchgoer, and showed little social skill and even less humor or creativity. Although Mark had little athletic ability he insisted on going out for football, because he craved the social acceptance the sport provided. Bruised and battered, he remained stubbornly determined to make the team—if it kills me, he seemed to be saying, and Lily feared it might.

Billy, her youngest, was Lily's joy. He was a happy, dreamy child who spent his Saturdays at the public library and had already read his way through the Hardy Boys, Mark Twain, Sherlock Holmes, Jules Verne, and most recently Ray Bradbury. He was popular and easygoing, an Eagle Scout and ham radio operator, and already girls were calling him on the phone most nights.

Often Billy would help Lily with the dishes and they would talk about books and poems and plays, and whether there was a God, and why men were put on earth, a million mysteries he was determined to solve. She thought he had inherited his namesake Billy Ringer's genes, that he would forever be pursuing some impossible dream.

Those were her boys: Sonny the brilliant loner, Mark the dogged athlete-scholar, and Billy the dreamer. Lily loved each of them, whatever his flaws, simply for what he was. She sometimes thought she was burdened with a singularly poor imagination, because the prospect of Billy Ringer's fortune never excited her. She could not imagine what she would do with his millions, because her three very different, far from perfect boys gave her a happiness that mere money, she truly believed, could never equal.

8.

LUTHER NEVER CAME BACK FROM THE HOSPITAL. THEY HEARD he'd been stitched up and sent to a foster home in Oklahoma. Even more astoundingly, unknown powers replaced Mrs. Cottle with Ben Dixon, who had been a junior high football coach in Haltom City, and who declared there would be "no more nonsense" in the Home. Some other senior boys were sent away and the ones who stayed left the girls alone.

The twins had little time to savor the new era. After breakfast one morning Ben Dixon told them to put on their Sunday dresses because someone wanted to meet them.

In his office, minutes later, they greeted a plump man who wore a three-piece suit with a gold watch chain, and a stately woman in a flowered hat.

"These are Mr. and Mrs. Gilbert, girls," Ben Dixon said. "They've come a long way to meet you."

At least, Gilbert is what Mickey thought he said. He had a way

of slurring his words. She would agonize for years over what name
he had spoken that morning.

"Aren't they adorable?" the woman said. "What's your name,
dear?"

"Jessie."

"I hear you like to read?"

"Yes, ma'am. I'm secretary of the Reading Club."

Mickey snickered; the Reading Club had so few members that
everyone was an officer. She studied the couple carefully. The
woman kept smiling even when she talked. The man had a few
strands of black hair combed up from the side over his shiny bald
head.

"I saw your report cards," the woman said. "You're quite the
scholar."

"I like school, ma'am."

"I believe I'll call you Jessica, my dear. That's a little more refined
than Jessie, isn't it?"

She turned to Mickey. "And you, dear, do you like school?"

Mickey resented the question. "I like sports better. I play softball
and run track."

The woman held her relentless smile. She could see, as anyone
could, that these twins were far from identical. They were the same
size, and both had good bones and intelligent eyes, but the differences leaped out at you. One was gentle, graceful, polite, feminine,
a perfect little lady. The other was awkward, tomboyish, sullen,
frizzy-haired, her elbows and knees scabbed and scarred from sand-
lot exploits. The contrast was in their school reports, too: almost
all A's on the one hand and quite average marks on the other.

Her husband, pink-faced and jovial, asked the girls a few questions and concluded by giving each of them a shiny new half-dollar.

"Mr. Dixon, if we could have a further word with you," the
woman said.

"Of course," Ben Dixon said, and asked the girls to wait outside.

When they had gone, the woman smiled sadly and said, "Well,
of course, it would be a pity to separate them, but . . . "

Outside the door, the sisters eyed each other nervously.

"You suppose they're going to take us?" Jessie asked.

"Nobody wants kids our age," Mickey said. "They want little pink babies who go goo-goo. We're stuck in this place. It ain't even so bad now."

Jessie smiled wistfully. "It'd be nice to live in a real house. And have our own room and an easy chair to read in and a bathtub."

The door opened and Mr. Dixon waved them back into his office. The visitors were beaming.

"Girls, I have wonderful news," Mr. Dixon said.

"Oh, my dear," the woman said, and rushed across the room to embrace Jessie.

"The gentleman and his wife are going to adopt Jessie," Mr. Dixon explained.

Jessie twisted free of the woman. "What about Mickey?"

Ben Dixon stepped forward. "The trouble is, they just don't have room for two children."

"Then I'll stay here," Jessie cried. She ran to Mickey's fierce embrace.

"See, we belong together," Mickey said earnestly, as if sweet reason might prevail. "We've always been together. Since we were born. Through all the foster homes and all kinds of crazy stuff. She's the sweet one and the smart one and all that, and I'm kinda raggedy-looking, but, see, I take care of her."

"We'll take care of her now, dear," the woman said in a sugary voice.

"No you won't, you old bitch!" Mickey yelled. "You can't take her. You . . . "

"Mr. Dixon, we'll wait in the car," the woman said sternly. "Come along, Fenton."

The couple marched out to their waiting Buick. Ben Dixon knelt and put his arms around the girls. He was a balding, sad-eyed man who had no children of his own.

"Girls, I know this is hard, but it's a wonderful opportunity for you, Jessie. They can do a lot for you. The grades you make, they'll send you to college."

"College?" Jessie whispered.

58

"You'll have it made," Ben Dixon told her.

"But what about Mickey? What about us?"

"Jessie, go pack now," he said firmly.

"No," Mickey cried. "No, you can't!"

She struggled against his grip.

"Go pack," he commanded and Jessie left in a daze.

Mickey was crying and kicking, but he held her tight. "Honey, you've got to think of her. They can give her so much. It's better for one of you to have a good home than for both of you to stay here."

"Then make 'em take me."

"After you called her an old bitch? Mick, you've got to be brave."

He held her until Jessie returned. It wasn't long; she hadn't much to pack.

The sisters embraced, both sobbing helplessly, Jessie saying, "No, no, I won't go without you," and Mickey telling her, "You have to, Jess, it's what's best for you."

"It's time now," Ben Dixon said.

The girls embraced one last terrible time, hugged as if they could make themselves indivisible, then Ben pulled Jessie free and his secretary led her out.

He and Mickey watched through the window as Jessie's new parents greeted her with big smiles.

"Where are they taking her?" Mickey asked.

"I can't tell you, honey."

"Can I write to her?"

"They want a clean break."

They saw Jessie look back, her eyes searching for them, imploring them, as the couple hustled her into the Buick.

"Goodbye, baby," Mickey whispered. "Goodbye, Jess."

She could stand no more. She broke loose and ran out the door, across the yard, after the black sedan that was blending in with the other cars on Camp Bowie Boulevard.

"Come back, you bastards," she screamed. "She's my sister, bring her back!"

Mickey dashed into the street, ignoring cars that honked and swerved to miss her. She was a good runner; she had run the last leg on the girls' 440-relay team at school. She could see Jessie's face at the back window. The Buick stopped for a light and she drew closer, screaming, "Stop, stop, stop!"

She'd catch them, she thought, and throw open the door and pull Jessie out and they'd run away, hitch a ride, escape this place forever.

She came close enough to the Buick to read the numbers on its license plate, but then it broke free of the traffic. She ran harder, her lungs bursting, but the car was pulling away. Jessie's face was a forlorn dot in its distant window.

The half-dollar was still clutched in her fist. She sailed it after the Buick with all her strength.

"I don't want your stupid money—I want my sister," she cried, and collapsed by the side of the road. She did not know or care when Ben Dixon lifted her into his arms. As she had been torn from her mother, now she was torn from her sister. The better part of her was gone, the part she loved most dearly, and she feared that for the rest of her days she would be angry, empty, and alone.

9.

Months passed, a year. howard's drinking grew worse. Every time he saw Ida cruising Camp Bowie Boulevard in her red Cadillac convertible, he came home in a fury. He hated everything about her now. He hated her Mississippi drawl that made "girl" come out "gull." He hated her giving money to a glib young tent evangelist who lusted for his own TV show.

"She's wasting tens of thousands of dollars," Howard raged. "She has no right. That money is ours."

"She's an old woman," Lily said, trying to calm him. "Be patient, Howard. Our turn will come."

"No. The old witch will live forever."

"Don't talk like that. I hope she does live forever. She's had a hard life and these are her golden years."

"I think Ringer gave her that money just to torment me," he raged. "I can see the old bastard, down in hell laughing at me!"

Lily worried about Howard, about his drinking, his gambling, his temper, his debts. She could hardly talk to him anymore. Howard was angry, overweight, florid, half-crazed, living only for the day when he could claim the Ringer fortune.

Sometimes she thought of divorcing him; she'd thought of it for years. But there were so many terrible uncertainties. She couldn't raise three sons on her schoolteacher's salary. Nor did she trust Howard, or the Texas courts, to provide for her decently. Indeed, she wasn't even sure the courts would give a divorce, much less child custody, to a woman who for no clear reason wanted to leave a churchgoing bank executive; they might think she was crazy. And even if she had enough money—no doubt Ida would help her—there remained the stigma that attached to divorce among respectable, middle-class Texans. She could bear it, but she wasn't sure she could inflict that shame on her sons.

Aunt Ida, meanwhile, had never been more chipper. "Look what I can do," she cried one Sunday. To their amazement, she leaped into the air, clicked her heels together, and landed as gracefully as a ballerina. "Let's see any of you youngsters match that!"

One day, Ida announced that she intended to move to Waco and transfer her money from the F&R to a bank there.

"You can't!" Howard roared.

"Oh yes I can," Ida said serenely.

"But why?" Lily asked. "Are you unhappy with the F&R?"

"No, honey, they've treated me good. But my horoscope said I needed a change. Me and Jerry Max prayed on it, and the Lord said He wanted my money in Waco. Jerry Max thinks he can get his TV show started there."

"That man's a fraud!" Howard cried.

"No, he's a servant of the Lord," Ida insisted.

Howard got on the phone and shouted at Thomas T. Thomas, but to no avail. Howard thought he had bought Tom T.'s collusion, but the tent evangelist had bid higher.

"I'll have her committed," Howard raged. "She's crazy as a loon!"

"No you won't," Lily warned. "If it came to it, I'd testify that she's as sane as you or I."

Howard stormed around the kitchen, knocking chairs over, and finally settled at the kitchen table, his face beet red. "For heaven's sake, what does it matter where the money is?" Lily asked.

"You don't understand," he stammered. "I owe the bank money."

"We can repay them."

"You don't understand," he repeated miserably.

One evening that week Lily overheard Howard talking to Sonny. The boy was about to graduate and his brilliance at math had given him the choice of many colleges. But Howard was telling Sonny he might have to stay home and attend TCU, that they lacked the money to send him away.

"It's that old woman's fault," Howard said. "With your brains, son, you should go to Rice, or even MIT, but we can't afford that. You'll suffer so she can drive her Cadillac and give her money to a fraud like Jerry Max Crump."

Lily was shocked—it was a lie, they had money saved—but she so feared Howard's temper that she said nothing.

As Ida's move to Waco drew near, Howard made another abrupt about-face. He stopped drinking, started going to church again, and doted on the old woman. He helped her lease her house and arrange her moving plans. He insisted she attend Easter services with the family and bought her an orchid corsage. His sudden affection for Ida filled Lily with unease. Sometimes she wished Billy Ringer had never returned, when she thought of all the torment his money had brought into their lives.

On the Saturday before Ida was to move, Lily was weeding in her garden. She enjoyed the solitude and the hot Texas sun, but she was thinking about something she didn't enjoy at all, something that had happened that week to Mickey Ketchum.

After Mickey's sister Jessie was adopted and taken away, Lily had increasingly become the girl's friend and confidante. She had seen, everyone had seen, how inconsolable Mickey was when Mr. Dixon insisted he couldn't tell her where Jessie was. Lily found out later how Mickey had tried to outsmart the powers-that-be.

All she had to go on was the name of the family—Gilbert, she thought—and the license number of the car they had driven away from the Home.

Mickey first called all the Gilberts in the Fort Worth phone book. When that didn't uncover Jessie, she went to the public library and made a list of all the Gilberts in the Dallas and Houston phone books. Then she helped herself to an empty library office and placed two hundred dollars worth of long-distance calls before someone caught her.

The police were summoned, and it took all of Ben Dixon's guile to keep Mickey out of reform school.

That was when Mickey came to Lily for help. She knew from TV that the police could trace a license number to the car's owner. She'd already called police headquarters with a story about finding her best friend's uncle, but the cop who'd answered had laughed at her.

As it happened, Lily knew a policeman, and he checked and told her the license in question had belonged to a rental car and he couldn't demand that Hertz tell him who had rented it without official approval. So that was another dead end.

"I know she's tried to write me," Mickey told Lily. "I figure either the Gilberts stop her letters or they steal 'em when they get to the Home."

"The Gilberts are the people who adopted her?"

"Kidnapped, I call it," Mickey said with a bitterness far beyond her years.

A few days later Mickey ran away. The police picked her up in Houston a week afterward. Armed with a city map and a page ripped from the phone book, she was going door to door in search of families named Gilbert. She'd hitchhiked there, and stolen food from grocery stores, and when the police stopped her it took two of them to subdue her.

This time, it took Lily's best efforts, along with Ben Dixon's, to keep her out of reform school.

"Mickey, I think it's an outrage that they won't tell you where Jessie is," Lily told her. "But the best advice I can give you is to do your best in school. Prepare yourself for life. Then, when you're older, you can find your sister."

Mickey seemed to accept the advice. At least she stayed at the

Home, and advanced to Arlington Heights High, where in time she became the school's first hippie. She grew her hair long and frizzly, and gloried in beads and feathers and bizarre costumes from junk shops. In the early days of the war in Vietnam, she became one of the city's first and most visible anti-war activists.

Her classmates thought her crazy and probably a Communist, and that week they struck back. Lily had just heard the news from a friend who taught at AHHS.

Each spring the students voted to elect their most popular classmate, the most studious, most likely to succeed, and so forth.

There was also a joke category, Ugliest Man On Campus. A football player was always elected UMOC, as a tribute to his popularity.

This year, however, was different.

The class leaders cooked up their little joke, a write-in vote. During an assembly, when the winners were announced, the student body president grinned merrily as he declared:

"And now, for Ugliest Man On Campus, we've got a real monster. Someone who's set new standards of grungy clothing, ugly hair, and subhuman hygiene. I give to you, our Ugliest Man On Campus, maybe in the entire world, Comrade Mickey Ketchum!"

The auditorium rocked with laughter. The principal, Mr. Moreland, a stalwart of the American Legion, flashed a cold smile of approval.

Students stood and jeered at Mickey who, until her name was called, had been reading a book. When she realized what had happened, and the student body president summoned her to the stage, she tried to bring it off. She marched up the aisle in her hippie outfit, mugging and waving, but at the last moment she screamed, "Fuck all you bastards!" and ran from the auditorium in tears.

Lily Nash, kneeling in her garden that hot May afternoon, imagined Mickey's pain and grieved for her. She was glad when Howard called her from the back door, breaking her reverie. She looked up, slapping dirt from her hands.

"Ida called," he told her. "Sonny and I are going to help her move."

"The movers are supposed to do it all," Lily said.

"Well, she called, so she must want our help," Howard said with maddening logic.

He and Sonny left, and Lily returned to her gardening.

An hour passed quickly. Then the phone rang and she hurried inside to answer it.

"Lillian?"

His tone was oddly grim, even for Howard.

"Yes?"

"I have terrible news. Aunt Ida is dead."

Lily gasped. "What happened?"

"When we arrived, she said she'd be right down. We went to the kitchen, then we heard a scream. We found her at the bottom of the stairs. She must have tripped."

"Oh my God," Lily whispered. "I'll come over."

"There's no need," he said.

She went anyway. She arrived to see them carrying Ida's body out. The sheet covering her had slipped down. Ida's head lay at an unnatural angle and her face was frozen in rage. Billy Ringer's widow had not gone gladly into that good night.

Lily could not imagine Ida falling down her stairs, that spry old trouper who could leap up and click her heels.

The police asked few questions. Howard was, after all, a banker, a pillar of the community, and soon to be very rich—rich as sin, as Lily's clergyman father used to say.

Sonny, tense and withdrawn, would not speak to her. Once home he locked himself in his room.

Howard lumbered to the bar he had installed in their "family room." He poured a drink and settled heavily in his big leather chair. After a moment's hesitation, Lily poured herself a drink, too, her first in years.

She sat in her smaller chair. The Mama Chair and the Papa Chair. She burned with a million resentments; anger she had never let herself admit boiled to the surface.

"It was a blessing," Howard said.

Lily did not bother to reply.

"It would have been a tragedy for her to waste away with cancer or something," he added, in case she did not understand why Ida's broken neck was a blessing.

She fought against her anger. "Howard, I don't know what happened today. I'm not sure I want to know."

"A tragic accident. Those stairs—I'd warned her."

"You don't fool me," she cried, and trembled with frustration and anger. He put down his drink and reached for her hand. She yanked it back as if from a serpent.

"All that money is ours now," he told her. "We're rich, Lillian."

"No."

"Oh yes. We're very, very rich. Everything is going to change. Our dreams will come true."

"No."

He scowled at her. This sullen woman was spoiling the most beautiful moment of his life.

"What do you mean, no?"

"How can you be so stupid, Howard?"

"What the hell do you mean?"

"*We're* not rich."

"Don't you understand? She's dead. You've seen the will. We're *rich*!"

She turned a new face to him, the proud, ravaged, tear-bright face of a woman he had never seen before.

"*We're* not rich," she said again.

He gasped, as he began to grasp the enormity, the finality of her words.

"*We're* not rich, you son of a bitch," Lily said triumphantly. "*I'm* rich!"

PART 2

. . .

Fort Worth / New York /
Washington

◆

The 1980s

1.

THE FIRST TIME JESSICA ALBERT SAW BILLY NASH THAT DAY HE was leaning against a dinosaur licking mustard off his fingers.

Something endearing about him, even at a glance, made her eyes linger as he chewed his hot dog. He was not exactly handsome, but he was a pleasant-looking young man—slender, with sandy hair and blue eyes, and a sweet, bemused expression.

Suddenly, his eyes met hers. His mouth full of hot dog, he winked.

Jessica blushed and hurried away.

She was supposed to be attending a lecture, but an afternoon on the Mall had been infinitely more inviting. Now she found herself drawn toward the one monument she'd not had the courage to visit.

An hour later Jessica turned away in tears from the black wall of the Vietnam Veterans Memorial, shattered by its fifty thousand silent names.

She did not know or care who pressed a handkerchief into her hands, or whose shoulder she rested her head against. But when she regained control, she looked up into the solemn face of the young man she had glimpsed with the hot dog, beside the playground dinosaur outside the Museum of Natural History.

"Don't talk," he said. "I understand."

They walked along the winding sidewalk, back toward the Capitol.

"I didn't follow you," he said. "At least not consciously."

They passed an empty bench. "Could we sit a moment?" she asked.

"Of course."

"I found his name on the wall, and everything came back, all at once. He was just a boy who lived down the street. I was fourteen when he went off to the Army. I sent him cookies, and he sent me a postcard. He would have been married now, with children and . . . "

"It's what the memorial is for," he said. "To make us remember, to make us feel the pain of being human, perhaps to make us better people."

He was in his thirties, and he seemed at once gentle, funny, and wise.

Jessica stood up. "I'd guess we'd better . . . go somewhere." Already, somehow, it was "we."

"Any place you say."

"The National Gallery?"

They walked along, framed against a bright panorama of monuments, tourists, and spring blossoms.

Jessica was blessed with classic features and golden hair that swayed languidly about her shoulders. She wore a simple green cotton dress, and her walk was at once graceful and jaunty.

"I'm Billy Nash," he told her.

"That's a nice name. Are you from here?"

"I'm a Texan," he declared.

That fact stunned her. "Really? You don't look like a Texan."

"How do Texans look?" he demanded, his state pride aroused. "Have you ever been there?"

Had she been there? Even the thought of Texas stirred up fear and pain that Billy Nash could never imagine. "I was there once, when I was a child," she managed to say. "But I grew up in Little Rock, Arkansas."

It was a vague answer, but he did not press her.

"I'm Jessica Albert," she said, as if that, at least, was a fact she could share.

"Where do you live now, Jessica Albert?"

"Outside Baltimore. I teach at a small college there. I'm in Washington for a poetry workshop."

"What kind of poetry?"

"Mostly Emily Dickinson."

They crossed 14th Street and she wondered if he had any idea who Emily Dickinson was, or if he thought her strange.

Finally he said, "I guess the one about death is my favorite. How does it go? 'Because I could not stop for death . . .'"

She finished the stanza for him:

> "He kindly stopped for me—
> The Carriage held but just Ourselves—
> And Immortality."

She was moved that she and this stranger should love the same century-old poem, yet she was uneasy too. Who *was* this Billy Nash?

She had an unsettling sense that she had seen him before. He might have been an actor in some half-forgotten film, a shadow from another life.

The vast, domed National Gallery loomed ahead. "They say one man built it," she said.

"He used his money wisely," Billy said. "We have good museums in Texas now. Texas has changed a lot."

Not enough, she thought.

Curiosity overcame her good manners: "What do you do?"

A slight frown hinted his displeasure. "I'm a traveling salesman. We have a family business."

"What kind of business? Do you make things?"

"Buy things, sell things, make things."

73

"A mysterious business."

He laughed. "It's a mystery to me."

His evasions, his stubborn privacy, intrigued her. In his khakis and sneakers and polo shirt, he might have been any of a thousand tourists on the Mall, yet with every moment he seemed more unique.

Inside the National Gallery, they wandered alone through a gallery of Rembrandts.

Abruptly, he said, "Come on, I'll show you my favorite," and led her through a maze of galleries. Suddenly, he took her arm and swung her round.

"There!" he said.

Jessica gasped. The life-size portrait of a young woman hung before her.

She was leaning against a rock, beneath a tree on a hillside, with her dark hair tossed by the wind. A sunset lingered on the horizon as storm clouds blew in. The young woman wore a salmon-colored dress, with a blue sash at the waist and a gossamer scarf loose around her neck. Her pale, sad, lovely face was somehow hopeful, as she awaited the ominous storm, the gathering darkness.

She was Mrs. Richard Brinsley Sheridan, painted two centuries earlier by Thomas Gainsborough, in the last year of his life.

"The playwright's wife," she murmured.

"She was an actress," Billy said. "So incredibly beautiful—she looks like you."

"No, don't say that," Jessica pleaded, for she saw not Mrs. Sheridan's beauty but her fragility in the face of the oncoming storm.

"Let's go now," she said, and Billy took her hand and led her out of the museum and across the Mall to the Hirshhorn Museum's outdoor café. It was festive there, with huge sculptures scattered about the courtyard. He ordered two glasses of wine, then fumbled in his pockets. Jessica paid with her last twenty-dollar bill.

"I have money here somewhere," he grumbled. She wondered if Prince Charming was penniless.

They sipped the wine and did not talk for a time. Jessica thought about Mrs. Sheridan for a moment, then she forgot Mrs. Sheridan as she and Billy exchanged a smile.

Finally he said, "Let's think about dinner."

Jessica made a face. "There's a conference dinner I'm supposed to go to."

"I have something, too," he told her. "But I'd rather be with you."

"I don't have much money left. But there are cheap ethnic restaurants."

He dug in his pockets again and came up with a wad of bills. "Trust me," he said.

He hailed a cab, and ordered the driver to Adams-Morgan, where they settled on Hazel's, which boasted of its Southern cooking. They ordered beer and two plates of ribs, with cornbread and blackeyed peas.

"Hazel's ribs aren't as good as Angelo's in Fort Worth," he said. "But they're good."

"You're from Fort Worth?"

"Yep, good old Cowtown. Ever been there?"

"Tell me about it."

He sipped his beer. "It's a crazy place. It was a stockyards town, a cowboy town, so it has a Wild West, six-gun tradition. But it was never pretentious like Dallas. It's grown a lot in the past ten years, but not really changed much. Except for some fancy restaurants, and a few stabs at culture."

"What kind of culture?"

"Some great museums. A ballet company. A semi-professional theater. I've done some work with them."

"Work?"

"Some directing, some producing. We did a *House of Blue Leaves* that was a hoot. Do you like the theater?"

"Love it. I directed *Romeo and Juliet* at our school. In college, I was the world's worst Cordelia."

"Have you ever been married?" he asked abruptly.

"No."

"I'd think men would be beating down your door."

"Being in graduate school studying literature is like being a nun, and I was in graduate school forever. I mostly dated other graduate students, who tended not to be very exciting. Then I started teaching and . . . well, I was almost married last year."

"What happened?"

"He was the chairman of my department. A widower. Seventeen years older. Attractive in his way."

Jessica sighed.

"What happened was he met a rich widow and they eloped to Italy."

"He was a fool."

"Oh, I know," she said. "But I felt the fool. Left at the altar and all that."

"At least you didn't marry him. I married the perfect woman. All my friends said so. She was so perfect she drove me crazy."

A trio was playing jazz in the back room. She felt at ease with Billy, relaxed, and she didn't want the evening to end. But it was crazy. He might be attractive, but he was a salesman from Texas, the last place on earth she was interested in seeing again. It was maddening, to meet someone you liked, just before your trains pulled out of the station, bound relentlessly in opposite directions.

After coffee, he looked at his watch. "I should go by my hotel and check my calls."

She wondered if he was trying to maneuver her to his hotel room. The idea did not shock her, but she would have appreciated a more romantic approach. He hailed another cab and took her to the elegant Hay-Adams Hotel, across Lafayette Park from the White House. As they entered the lobby, a little man with a foreign accent dashed up to them.

"Mr. Nash, the White House called and called. We looked everywhere for you. Where have you been?"

"Out eatin' barbecue, Oscar," he said, exaggerating his drawl.

Oscar staggered away in despair, and they took an elevator to a corner suite overlooking the park and the distant White House lawn.

76

Billy glanced at some messages. She could stand it no longer. "*What* calls from the White House?"

He blushed, like a boy with his hand in the cookie jar. "There was a state dinner tonight."

"*A state dinner!*"

"It's not important."

"Billy Nash, how do you think that makes me feel?"

"Flattered?"

"I don't want to keep you from a White House dinner. Why didn't you *tell* me?"

He looked annoyed. "Number one, we gave them enough money that we can go to their dinners or not go—the choice is ours. Number two, I wanted to be with you."

He smiled hesitantly. "So don't be cross with me."

She sat down, dazed.

"Are you rich?" she asked abruptly. "It doesn't matter, but I want to know."

"I told you, I'm a traveling salesman."

"It's disorienting," she said. "The White House. This suite. Do you have any idea what it costs?"

"None at all. The company pays. But if it offends you, let's leave. I'll stay at the Y, it doesn't matter."

She laughed helplessly. "No, please don't stay at the Y. The view wouldn't be nearly so grand."

He took two business calls, barking out numbers and instructions, then put down the phone. "Sorry," he said.

"Come sit," she said.

He sat beside her on the long white sofa, studying her face as he had studied the Rembrandts in the National Gallery.

"I feel very close to you," he said.

"I know. I feel the same way."

"I've tried to analyze it."

"Don't."

He laughed. "I can't help it. I don't feel any of the usual defenses, from either of us. No games, no pretending. I look at you and I feel only contentment. A kind of peace. God, I saw you on the Mall, so beautiful that . . . "

"No, don't say that . . . "

"I *did* follow you, you know. On the Mall. I told myself, I have to talk to that woman or I'll kick myself the rest of my life."

"I saw you too. Eating a hot dog."

"Jessica, do you feel anything at all of what I'm feeling?"

"Of course. Something is happening to me and I don't know what it is. All I know is that it's wonderful."

"Have you considered the possibility that we're falling in love?"

She smiled wistfully. "It doesn't happen like that. Love takes time."

"Don't be so sensible. Maybe, once in a lifetime, it hits you like a freight train. Maybe that's how you know it's real. Maybe, when that happens, you have to gamble everything."

"What's real is that tomorrow I go back to my little world and you go back to Texas."

He seized her hands and spoke with sudden passion. "It doesn't have to be like that. Stay with me tonight. I don't mean for sex; I don't care about that, not tonight. But we belong together. I couldn't bear it if you left now."

"I don't think I could either," she admitted.

In a moment, he led her into the bedroom. They could see the White House in the distance. "I have some extra pajamas," he said. "They may be a little large."

Jessica laughed. "Better baggy pants than none."

Soon they were in bed, snuggling close, enjoying the easy fit of their bodies. She would not have minded making love, but she knew he was right, that they dare not risk breaking the spell. There would be other nights for sex, perhaps, but never another night of this yearning, this mystery.

They whispered for a time, then Billy fell asleep. She lay close to him, listening to his steady breathing, glad for his warmth. She had known many men in her life, liked a lot of them, loved a few, but intimacy had never been so easy, so inevitable. To be here wasn't "like" her—she was cautious, sensible—but she had rarely felt more right about anything. If it wasn't love, if it was only illusion—no matter. The memory would be real, even if her traveling salesman vanished with the dawn.

In the morning they had breakfast in bed and Billy told someone in the White House a harrowing tale of intestinal flu. She was dressed by then.

"So you think it's goodbye, do you?"

"I know it is. My bus leaves in two hours."

"Come to Texas with me."

His words stung. She had steeled herself for goodbye. "I'd like to see you again, but that's insane. I have work to do. Papers to grade."

"That's what's insane. Do you want to spend the rest of your life grading papers?"

"I love my work," she said stubbornly.

"Okay, you love your work, but you could do so much more. You love the theater? We'll start a theater."

"Sometimes I think you're crazy."

"Sometimes I am. Come meet my family."

"Billy, I'm sure your family is wonderful, but . . . "

He laughed aloud. "Wonderful, hell! They're a disaster. But you have to meet them. Just come for the weekend. You can fly back Monday."

"How do you know I can get reservations this late?"

He gestured impatiently. "I have a company plane."

He took her hand. "It's up to you. My driver will take you to your hotel. If you want, he'll bring you to the airport."

She gazed at him in wonder, this mysterious boy, this traveling salesman who could conjure up magic carpets, who in a day had turned her life upside down.

Jessica fled; she had absolutely no idea what she was going to do.

She returned to her hotel, tormented by doubt. Her dusty little room was hardly as big as the closet in Billy's suite. She thought of all her years in cheap hotels and shabby off-campus apartments.

Worse, she thought that all her life she'd been hiding from reality in the dank, airless womb of literature. She let herself think the unthinkable: that sometimes she hated her narrow little life.

Abruptly, she made up her mind.

Billy's driver pulled onto the runway and stopped beside a graceful Sabreliner jet. The pilot tipped his hat and helped her aboard. Inside, the plane was all leather and brass and burnished wood.

"Somethin' to drink, miss?"

"No. Thank you."

"I'm Buster Watt, miss. Anything I can do, you let me know. Billy, he'll be along any minute."

She settled in one of the cool leather chairs.

"Tell me something, Mr. Watt. Does the company treat all its salesmen as well as it does Billy? I mean, private planes and suites at the Hay-Adams . . . "

"Salesmen? What's that scamp been telling you?"

"He . . . he said it was a family business. That, I don't know, they make things."

Buster laughed good-naturedly, showing big white teeth.

"Make things? Money, mostly. What's your line of work, miss?"

"I . . . I'm a teacher."

"Not in the business world, so to speak?"

"No."

"Never heard of Nash International?"

"No."

"Never heard of the Nash brothers of Fort Worth? Or Sonny Nash?"

"No."

"You done led a sheltered life, miss. You've seen that Hay-Adams Hotel?"

"Yes, we went there."

"Billy's trying to buy it. Sonny bought another hotel, across from Central Park, because he couldn't find one in New York that could cook up a decent chicken-fried steak. What kind of credit card you carry?"

She told him.

"They bought the bank that owns it. You might have one of their computers, and most likely you've flown on the airline Sonny just picked up. The bottom line, miss, is that them three boys is worth upwards of three billion dollars."

She looked out the window and saw Billy walking toward the plane, still in khakis and sneakers and a polo shirt, boyish and beguiling.

She thought of Emily Dickinson and the carriage, of Mrs. Sheridan and the gathering storm, of the mustard on Billy's fingers, of his soft kisses.

More than anything she wanted to flee.

Instead they went soaring toward Texas.

When Jessica stepped from the plane, the hot Texas wind hit her like a fist. She had forgotten the violence of the elements, the blistering summers, spring's blinding sandstorms, winter's relentless icestorms, the northers and tornadoes that came racing across the prairie any time. First she was stunned by the heat, then they were encased in a cool Mercedes, with tinted windows, soft music, and Billy's telephone. Yesterday's "traveling salesman" became a Texas tycoon, barking commands to unseen minions.

She huddled against the door, staring out as the city she had forgotten rushed toward her again.

At its outskirts, Fort Worth seemed the ugliest place in the universe, a raw, desolate shantytown stretched out beneath the pale, pitiless sky. She was shaken by the wrenching memories the landscape brought back, even after nearly twenty years.

Billy pointed his finger toward the jagged skyline ahead. "That's ours."

"What's yours?"

"That building—the tallest one," he said. "We thought the Bass boys were getting too big for their britches, so we built us one taller than theirs."

His skyscraper rose sleek and silvery for more than fifty stories.

"I thought there was a depression in Texas, because of oil prices?"

"There is. A lot of people have gone under. People you thought were bulletproof. It's a tragedy."

"But you . . . "

"We've been lucky. My brother Sonny stays a step ahead of the game. Sonny's ruthless, but a genius in his way. You'll meet him."

"I'm not sure I want to."

"Oh, he can be charming. And he does admire beautiful women. You'll meet my mother, too. You two will get along fine—she loves books and art."

"You didn't tell me the truth about your money."

"The truth might have scared you away."

"It still may."

He turned to her. "I see dollar signs in women's eyes. One Chicago debutante spent an evening introducing me as 'Mr. Cash.' Yesterday was wonderful, to be anonymous, to have a sensational girl like me just for myself."

They left the freeway, drove through Forest Park, then turned onto Camp Bowie Boulevard. A sign proclaimed a "Cultural District" and, sure enough, three museums had sprouted across from the Will Rogers Memorial Center.

"Look at them," he said proudly. "The Kimbell, the Carter, and the Modern Art Museum. You won't find another city this size in America with three museums of that caliber. As soon as I'm caught up, we'll spend a morning in the Kimbell."

They turned onto Crestline Road and passed Rivercrest Country Club. The city's shabby outskirts were far behind them now, and a cool, green oasis greeted them. The houses grew ever grander— she marveled at one amazing pink marbled mansion with a fountain before it—and then he turned off Crestline and drove through an imposing gate. Majestic brick and stucco houses lined the street.

"This is Westover Hills," he said. "It's sort of an enclave. Sort of a cliché, you could say. But it's pleasant and the security is good."

He turned in a driveway, passed a wall of hedges and towering oaks, and abruptly stopped before one of the most beautiful homes Jessica had ever seen, all glass and stone and polished wood, perched like a gull on the edge of a wooded hillside. Inside, one room flowed into another, decorated with bright Indian rugs, graceful modern furniture, neon sculpture and a breathtaking collection of art. She discovered a Dufy, a Matisse, an O'Keeffe, a Cassatt, and a Hockney arrayed in his living room.

"This is incredible," she said, lingering before them.

"I was lucky," he said. "I bought them before prices went through the roof."

"What is it like, to have paintings like this on your walls? I'd feel guilty."

He laughed. "You get over that. If I hadn't bought these paintings, someone else would have. And probably taken them out of the country. I'll enjoy them for a time, then give them to the Kimbell. No guilt there."

He led her down a skylit hallway. "Here's my guest room. You can stay here, or you can use my mother's guest house. She's on Rivercrest Drive, not far from here."

"Will people talk if I stay here?"

"They'll talk whatever you do. With the possible exception of Washington, D.C., Fort Worth is the gossip capital of the world."

She looked around. Fresh wildflowers filled an Oriental vase. Lovely etchings adorned one wall. The windows overlooked a green river valley.

"I'll stay here," she said.

"Good. Now why don't you rest? We meet my mother at seven at the club."

Billy kissed her and left. Jessica threw herself on the bed, her thoughts in turmoil. The ugly outskirts of the city had been replaced by this incredible luxury. She had kissed a traveling salesman and he turned into a prince. The magic of their meeting had been followed by the shock of returning to this city.

She had known Fort Worth in another life, and had escaped it. And now a sweet, radiant man had brought her back, to confront the ghosts of her past. Gratefully, she fled into a troubled sleep.

. . .

Jessica woke up wondering what to wear to a Texas country club. Billy, who had changed to slacks and a short-sleeved shirt, reassured her. "Nobody dresses in Texas in the summer—it's too damn hot. You look great."

Rivercrest Country Club, newly rebuilt after a fire, was as green as old money. As Billy led her to a dining room overlooking the pool, people called his name and hurried to shake his hand. He introduced her as "my friend Miss Albert" and she felt the eyes of Texas very much upon her. They chatted with a woman called Birdie who said she was eating at the club because her cook was just back from Paris and had taken to her bed.

When they finally reached their table, Billy ordered Margaritas and raised his glass. "Welcome to Texas, home of the world's only jet-lagged domestics."

As Jessica laughed, his eyes cut anxiously toward the door.

"There's Mother now." Jessica spotted a slender, tanned woman with close-cropped reddish hair, a stylish rust-colored dress draped with a Hermès scarf, and wrists hung with gold bracelets. She, too, was soon ringed by friends and well-wishers.

"The thing about Mother is, no matter what she has now, she's had a hard life," Billy said quietly. "It wasn't easy being married to my father, then she went overnight to having millions. She had to be tough to keep from being robbed blind. But she has a soft center—if she likes you she'll kill for you."

He leaped up to peck his mother on the cheek.

"Mother, this is Jessica Albert from Baltimore. My mother, Lillian Nash."

The two women studied one another from behind their decorous smiles. Lily Nash spent a great deal of time and money perfecting and enhancing her face, body, and hair, and she was as youthful as any woman her age had a right to be.

Jessica, confronting the older woman's cool, penetrating gaze, was dazzled and confused. *Where have I known you before?*

"What do you do in Baltimore, Miss Albert?"

"Please, call me Jessica. I teach English at Goucher College." She told a little about the school.

Rich as Sin

A waiter, unbidden, brought Lily a gin and tonic. "*I* taught English once," she said. "The state of Texas in its wisdom paid me six thousand dollars a year. But the kids made it worthwhile. I look back on those years at W. C. Stripling with pleasure."

"I'm sure you do," Jessica said quickly.

Like a landslide, her memories came. Billy's mother—younger, plumper, plainer—had been her English teacher that awful year at the Gertrude Little Home. The Reading Club. *Huck Finn. Ivanhoe.* But the dowdy schoolteacher had become this svelte, cool-eyed millionaire. And the urchin Jessie Ketchum was now Dr. Jessica Albert.

Lily Nash did not recognize the child she'd taught so briefly many years before, and Jessica knew, at once and irrevocably, that she must not reveal her secret. Jessie Ketchum was dead and buried, and it would benefit no one to resuscitate her.

"And what brings you to Texas?" Lillian asked.

"I brought her to Texas, Mother," her son injected.

"Let her answer for herself."

Jessica opted for honesty. "Mrs. Nash, I met your son yesterday in Washington. He asked me to come and he's very persuasive. It doesn't make much sense."

"She's here because I intend to marry her," Billy declared.

Both women were stunned by his pronouncement. Lily downed her drink and sent a waiter scurrying for another.

"Well, she's pretty enough to marry," Lily said finally. "But is she tough enough?"

"Pardon *me*," Jessica said. "But I haven't agreed to marry anyone. Frankly, Mrs. Nash, I have the same doubts that you do. This isn't a life I'm prepared for. Or interested in, for that matter."

The older woman sighed. "Call me Lily," she said. "I like your spirit. If a woman won't stand up for herself in this world, no one else will. But you see, it isn't a life that anyone is prepared for. Billy is my baby, the one I worry about. Sonny's hard as a rock, and Mark has icewater in his veins, but this is my romantic. The one who'd fall head over heels for a girl like you—and I don't fault his taste—and not think about the consequences."

Billy protested: "Mother, when I married Sandy, everybody—yourself included—agreed she was perfect for me, and you were all dead wrong. Next time out, I follow my own instincts."

"I may leave," Jessica declared, the color rising in her cheeks.

"Don't, I'm starting to like you," Lily said. "You see, if Billy had an income of a hundred thousand a year, he'd be an ideal husband. The problem is, his income is more like a hundred million. Whoever marries him will have to deal with greed and jealousy and temptation on a scale you can't begin to imagine."

"I may be tougher than you think," Jessica declared.

"That's true," Lily Nash admitted.

"Dammit, Mother, I wish you'd quit talking about the horrors of wealth. Unlike my brothers, I have a lot of fun."

Lily laughed. "Billy is my philanthropist, my bleeding heart. Has he told you about his project for the homeless? That's admirable, of course, but he also has that hippie guru he supports, and his project for space travel."

"It's not space travel, Mother, it's . . . "

He abruptly fell silent. The entire room fell silent. One moment there was a hubbub of chatter and laughter, then an eerie hush.

"*Damn!*" Lily Nash muttered.

Two people were moving across the room, a man and a woman who, Jessica saw at a glance, were unlike anyone else she had ever known. The man was tall and broad-shouldered, with slick black hair, a hard body, and arrogant, chiseled good looks.

The woman was nearly six feet tall, with fiery red hair, flashing green eyes, and the kind of body that is rarely seen outside of centerfolds and chorus lines. Her body was all too visible in her costume: a gold fishnet dress, with what appeared to be the skimpiest of bikini panties under it.

"She might as well be naked!" Lily Nash muttered.

The woman also sported golden slippers and an array of diamonds, rubies, and emeralds. She dragged an ermine wrap behind her on the rug. The man wore faded Levis, crocodile boots, and a skin-tight Carta Blanca T-shirt. He grinned at people as he passed between the tables, but the woman kept her head high, as if the other guests were beneath her notice.

"Hi there, Mama Lily," the woman said. "Hey, Billy—how's your hammer hangin'? Who's she? You gotcha a new honey?"

Billy looked pained. "Jessica Albert, meet my brother Sonny, and his wife Emily."

"Call me Puss," the woman said. "Everybody does."

"Why don't you put some clothes on?" Lily demanded.

"You know, Mama Lily, I was about to do that very thing," Puss said. "I said, Sonny-pie, we gotta go home and get decent 'cause we got a houseful of people."

Sonny gave Puss's ample bottom a leisurely pat.

"I bought this publishing house in London the other day. I didn't mean to, but I was squeezin' this holding company and they threw in the publishing house to sweeten the deal. They said they used to publish T. S. Poppycock or whatever he's called."

"T. S. Eliot?" Billy asked.

"I guess. Anyway, their editor flew in. He thinks I'm gonna burn his books and rape his babies. Why don't you come meet him?"

"Okay, maybe we'll be out."

Jessica watched Sonny intently: the dark, sardonic eyes, the blade of a nose, the wide, cruel mouth. His animal magnetism was undeniable—she could understand what drew him and Puss together, and it wasn't T. S. Eliot.

From the first she was both fascinated by Sonny and a little afraid of him.

As Sonny and Puss departed, Lillian Nash said bitterly, "He had to bring her here. He had to rub everyone's nose in her."

"I say thank God she had the bikini on," Billy countered.

"Not that people in this town are saints," Lily said. "But in public at least they make a show of decency."

"The thing is, Sonny loathes Fort Worth society," Billy told Jessica.

"That's putting it nicely," Lily said. "He tortures people every way he can—that creature he married is the final straw."

"There was a Roman emperor," Jessica said. "Maybe it was Caligula. Besides violating the wives and sons and daughters of the aristocracy, he made a horse his proconsul, and all the senators had to march in and kiss the horse's ass."

"Don't tell Sonny that story," Billy laughed.

They went through the buffet's ample array of Mexican dishes.

"I'll say this for Sonny, he saved my life when he bought that penthouse on Fifth Avenue," Lily said as they ate. "When Fort Worth gets me down, I fly up and spend a week seeing shows. The trouble is, New York spoils you. Our hometown productions look pretty puny after Broadway."

"I keep telling you, Fort Worth needs a professional theater," Billy declared.

"You say that, but you don't do anything about it," his mother shot back.

"I may yet," Billy declared.

"What would you do?" Jane asked.

"Well, look at the Alabama Shakespeare Festival. A man named Blount gave them twenty million to build a new theater and hire a full-time company. They have an annual budget of four million now, three dozen professional actors, and play to half a million people a year. If they can do it, why can't we?"

"Do you propose to put up the twenty million?" his mother asked.

"Maybe half, and then shame others into giving the rest. But I won't spend that kind of money unless it's run the way I think it should be run."

"Hire the right director," his mother suggested.

Billy grinned. "Maybe Jessica and I could run it together."

"*What?*" Jessica exclaimed.

"Sure. You love the theater, don't you? Somebody has to make the decisions."

"You can't dictate to artists," she protested.

"For twenty million dollars you can make polite suggestions," Billy said. He finished his coffee. "Enough talk of art. It's time to face reality. Let's go visit Sonny and Puss."

. . .

A quarter moon guided them out the Jacksboro Highway and Boat Club Road to the hillside where Sonny Nash had built his dream house high above Eagle Mountain Lake.

They rounded a curve and confronted a vast stone fortress, part castle and part bunker, with soaring walls and improbable turrets. It was unlike any home Jessica had ever seen before. A fog drifting up from the lake nestled against the castle's walls, adding to its dreamlike aura.

"Sonny designed it himself," Billy said. "He'd been to England and by God he wanted a castle. The damn thing cost nine million, a ridiculous amount of money, but Sonny was making a statement."

Jessica laughed. "What was his statement?"

"I think it freely translates as 'Fuck you, world.' "

They passed through a gate and stopped in a stone courtyard packed with powerful cars and motorcycles. Billy led her into a kind of medieval banquet room with a beamed ceiling and huge stone fireplaces roaring with fires. Air conditioning kept the center of the room chilly. Thirty or forty people were scattered about: bikers in black leather, men in business suits as well as men in jeans and boots, women in jeans and shorts, one glum, red-faced gentleman in tweeds, and one "outlaw" country singer whose music Jessica had loved for years.

"Hey, baby brother," Sonny called, bounding up to them. He poked his face close to Jessica's and winked. "Smile if you're gettin' any."

She made the only possible response: she laughed aloud.

Sonny beamed. "So you like it here, huh?"

"Love it." For the moment, she half-believed it.

"Hey, Puss, come say howdy."

Puss had changed into a flowing white gown.

"Hi, honey," Puss drawled. "How ya doin'?"

"Fine," Jessica said. "Fine."

"You gonna marry Billy and join the Nash family circus?" Puss demanded.

"We just met yesterday."

"Listen, baby brother, if you don't marry this gal, you're nuttier'n

I thought," Sonny roared. "Here, Miss Jessie, welcome to Texas."

He reached into his jeans and pressed a ring into her hand, a gold ring with a ruby the size of a pea.

"Sonny, I can't keep this," she protested.

"Sure you can, it's a present."

"It's too valuable. You should . . . give it to Puss."

"Honey, I got a hunnerd like that," Puss said disdainfully.

"Sonny, please."

"Little lady, are you gonna hurt my tender feelings?" Sonny said, his eyes narrowing. "Why don't you try it on?"

Jessica slipped the ring on her finger. "It's beautiful," she said, truthfully.

"So're you, little sister," Sonny said. "So're you."

"Down, boy," Puss muttered.

A Mexican boy in a tuxedo brought champagne. Whole pigs were thrust into the fireplaces at either end of the room and roasted. A Western band played Bob Wills songs but few of the guests were listening.

People drifted by. A cowboy in a white Stetson carrying a coffee can. A U.S. senator who talked with Sonny about the new savings and loan regulations.

When the senator wandered off, Billy said angrily to his brother: "This S&L thing stinks—I don't want any part of it!"

Sonny looked amused. "It's Christmas on the Potomac, buddy-boy. It's a honeypot, and we'd be damn fools not to dip our peckers in it—beggin' your pardon, Miss Jessie."

He strolled off, in his rolling, cowboy gait, leaving a plump, pink-faced man in tweeds standing before Billy.

"I'm Derek Hopsworth, editorial director of Sterling & Sissons," the man announced, "and I'm given to understand that you, sir, are the younger Nash, and my new master."

"The youngest, actually—there are three of us," Billy said. "But, yes, my brother said he'd bought your firm, and he asked me to talk to you. This is Miss Albert."

The editor nodded vaguely in Jessica's direction. "Do you realize what a disaster this is? We've published some of the greatest writers of the past century."

"What's the disaster, Mr. Hopsworth?" Billy asked. "Has anyone asked you to lower your standards?"

"Not *yet*," the editor said pointedly.

"Maybe we'll raise your standards," Billy said. "Maybe we can pump more money into your operation. Why assume we're Yahoos?"

The Englishman was sweating heavily, and his eyes were dull with whiskey. The poor man had crossed the Atlantic, to deepest, darkest Texas, to confront the barbarians.

"Didn't you publish Somerset Maugham?" Billy asked.

"Why, yes, some of his books."

"I'll never forget reading *The Razor's Edge* and *The Summing Up*. Heady stuff for a teenager in Texas."

"And Sylvia Plath," Jessica added.

"Why, yes. Do you know her work?"

"I gave a paper once for PMLA; I compared her imagery to Emily Dickinson's."

"You see, Mr. Hopsworth, we're not total illiterates," Billy said. "Let's talk tomorrow."

"Why . . . thank you, sir, thank you," the editor said, and collapsed in a chair by the fire.

"Well done," Jessica declared.

"We Texans often benefit from low expectations," Billy said drily.

Soon the barbecue was served and people settled in chairs and on the floor. Two girls near Jessica were giggling about a "ceiling camera." When she asked Billy what they meant, he said, "Sonny and Puss inspire a lot of rumors. One is that they have a camera over their bed, to record their greatest hits, so to speak."

"Do they?"

"How would I know?"

He went for more barbecue and she was joined by a very attractive dark-haired man in his forties. He introduced himself as Philip Kingslea, a writer.

"And do you like writing?" Jessica asked, trying to make conversation.

The writer laughed. "Do I like writing? No, but it beats living your life, doesn't it?"

"I enjoy my life," she said.

He glared at her, his eyes a dark blue, ringed by the thickest, blackest lashes and eyebrows she'd ever seen. His gaze was hypnotic, angry, and sad, all at once. "You enjoy it, do you? Then get the hell out of this city." He moved away just as Billy rejoined her.

"Who is he?" she asked angrily.

"It's a long story," Billy said. "He wrote a novel twenty years ago, about what a terrible place Fort Worth is. He's mostly in California now, writing screenplays."

Jessica turned her attention to Sonny as he moved about his party, always the star. She noticed Puss following him with her eyes and seething when he lingered with a woman.

Sonny called to the cowboy who was carrying a beer in one hand and a coffee can in the other.

"Why does that man carry a coffee can?" Jessica asked Billy.

"That's Cal Hurd. He owns the biggest ranch in the Panhandle. He's a pal of Sonny's."

"Yes, but why the can?"

Billy looked uncomfortable. "Well, Cal chews."

"Chews?"

"Tobacco."

"Oh my God," Jessica said.

Soon Sonny began sending people outside, where there was to be a cockfight. Jessica told Billy she wanted to leave.

"No problem," Billy told her. "I have to say good night to a couple of people."

She hurried to the courtyard, but the men had formed a circle there, so she ran down to a knoll overlooking Eagle Mountain Lake, where the air was fresh and cool. The men were soon shouting behind her, and she could hear the cries of the gamecocks. She could not have felt more alien among head-hunters in Borneo.

"Scared?"

Sonny had joined her. He looked amused.

"A little."

"Billy's the sweetest kid in the world."

"It's not Billy that scares me."

Sonny's smile widened. "We're a pretty wild bunch, huh?"

"It's not the world as I've known it."

"It's not the world as anybody's known it," Sonny said. "If you have enough money, you can make your own world."

"That's the scariest part, I suppose," she said.

"Did you know my castle has a ghost?"

"No."

"Or maybe you don't believe in ghosts."

"I believe strange things happen on this earth."

"There's no reason anybody has to die," Sonny said. "I mean, somebody strong, they're gonna live on. Lyndon Johnson—you think he's dead? He's too mean to die. Or Hitler or old Joe Stalin? They're still around. They don't talk to us much, but they cut the cards now and then."

He was deadly serious.

"What about good people?" she asked, fascinated now. "Do they live on, too? Is goodness as strong as evil?"

"I don't know many good people," Sonny said. "Name me a few."

"Emily Dickinson. Louis Armstrong. Abe Lincoln. Do they live on?"

Sonny grinned. "Maybe, if they're mean enough. Come to one of my séances and we'll see."

Billy joined them. "She's mine, brother."

Sonny lifted his hands in innocence. "I've been a perfect gentleman—right, Miss Jessie?"

"Perfect," she agreed. "Forgive us for leaving, but I believe it's been the longest day of my life."

He opened the car door for her. "Good night, little sister," he said. "Don't be a stranger."

For that moonlit instant Sonny Nash seemed neither arrogant

nor ruthless. She kissed his cheek impulsively and then she and Billy sped wordlessly beside the silent, fog-bound lake, heading home.

When Jessica awoke the next morning, she might have thought it all a dream, but Sonny's ring glittered on the table beside her bed.

She stretched lazily as she thought of Billy, how patient and kind he was. Glorious sunlight filled the guest bedroom. After a while she went to the blue-tiled bathroom, brushed her teeth, pulled on a robe, and walked barefoot down the hallway. She found him in bed, still in his pajamas, reading a *National Geographic*.

"Good morning," he said.

"It could get better," she said, and slipped in beside him.

He was a wonderful lover, generous, tender, and unhurried. When they rested, she laughed aloud.

"What?" he asked.

"I hit the jackpot."

"We both did."

They lay close, their bodies one, until she heard someone banging pots in the kitchen.

"Who's that?" she asked in alarm, pulling away.

"That's Olivia, my housekeeper."

"How long has she been down there?"

"Don't worry about it."

"You mean she's heard dozens of women moaning in your bed?"

"I mean it's great to be appreciated."

She held him close again. "Any woman would appreciate you."

Billy laughed. "Well, nothing remains to make my morning perfect except one of Olivia's breakfasts."

They put on robes and he led her to the kitchen and introduced her to the stately black woman who was assembling a Texas-sized breakfast. They settled on the deck with coffee. "Is there an agenda?" she asked. "Or can we go back to bed?"

"No such luck. I have to meet that Englishman, but I've arranged for you to have lunch with Kay, my brother Mark's wife. You'll like her; she can tell you a lot about the town. If you're game, she'll meet you at Shady at one."

"At what?"

"Shady Oaks. A country club. It's nearby. Buster will drive you."

"Why weren't Mark and Kay at Sonny's last night?"

"Mark *never* sees Sonny outside the office," he said. "He and Kay went to Indonesia last Christmas, to avoid Sonny and Puss."

Shady Oaks stretched out on a hillside just west of Westover Hills. The manager greeted Jessica at the door and led her into a dining room that overlooked the golf course. "Miss Albert, Mrs. Mark Nash," he said grandly.

Kay Nash smiled and extended her hand. "Also known as Kay," she said. "Welcome to Texas."

She was a small, trim woman in her thirties with short auburn hair, a deep tan, plump cheeks, and shrewd eyes. She wore an apple green Adolfo suit and the most striking earrings Jessica had ever seen: black jet and diamond pavé chevrons atop thumbnail-size emeralds.

"Thanks, I guess," Jessica said. "I love your earrings."

"Do you? A little gift I bought myself. Drink?"

Jessica hesitated. "I hardly ever drink at lunch."

"Welcome to Texas," Kay said again, and called for two Bloody Marys.

"Rumor has it that you're a schoolmarm from the East who Billy has vowed to make his prairie princess," Kay said. "And I'd bet you're tempted. Dazzled. And scared. Am I right?"

Jessica nodded. "He's wonderful, and I'm so confused."

"There's much to be confused about. How can I help you?"

"Tell me about the family. The city. Everything."

"Well, it's bound to be different for you than it was for me. In the first place, I'm a Texan, so I knew the territory. And of course Mark is very different from Billy. Mark and I met at UT—the University of Texas, in Austin. We were pinned senior year—he

95

was a Kappa Sig, I was a Theta. Back then, they were rich, but not crazy fuck-all rich, the way it is now. Back then it was millions, not billions."

"What about Billy's first marriage?" Jessica asked.

"A big mistake. Billy tried to do the conventional thing with a conventional girl, but he's not a conventional person. A lot of people underestimate Billy. He's very un-Texan. Non-macho, but very strong in his way. Determined to be his own man. He needs someone he respects, and who respects what he is."

"That's the only kind of marriage I'd want."

"Sure, but it's hard to be the equal of a man who has a billion dollars. This is a man's town. They'll peek down your dress and ask about the children, but very few of them assume you have a brain. If you marry Billy, you'll be Mrs. William Ringer Nash, and it won't always be fun. When push comes to shove, it's *his* money."

The waiter took their orders. Kay ordered a fruit salad and Jessica a club sandwich.

"Tell me about Mrs. Nash."

"Lily? Have you met her?"

"Last night. She was tough, but friendly in her way."

"Good. You don't want to cross her."

When their food arrived, Kay asked for wine and Jessica settled for iced tea. "You asked about the city. Well, it's unique. I could take you, within ten minutes of here, to twenty homes that have Matisse on the walls and Mozart on the stereo and sons at Yale. I could also take you to some of the most dangerous dives in America—and you'd be surprised how much traffic there is between those elegant homes and those sleazy dives. Puss and Sonny are prime examples—Sonny has raised slumming to an art form."

"We were at Sonny's last night. There were some pretty strange characters there."

"It's a city of extremes. Beneath the veneer of culture, it's a rough place. You'd be surprised how many men go armed. Even the more enlightened men don't talk about much except money and football. It's easy to get into an argument, but hard to find a serious discussion.

"Do I sound negative? Is that horror in your face? Actually, most of the people are quite nice, and it's a good place to raise children. People drink a lot, of course. Mark says Fort Worth is made up of the drunks and the ex-drunks—he's a pillar of AA now, as he'll be the first to tell you."

Kay sipped her wine. "The social system here is Byzantine, with hundreds of layers and alliances, but it comes down to how much money you have. That, and high school. People gossip endlessly about what happened twenty or thirty years ago. She was a cheer-leader and he was a football star and she had an abortion, *et cetera, ad infinitum*. Sometimes I think that life in Fort Worth is just their senior year at Arlington Heights—replayed over and over for fifty years, until everyone dies of boredom.

"None of that would matter to you, of course. If you're a Nash, you're in the stratosphere, miles above the people who are plotting to have their daughters properly brought out at the Steeplechase Ball and properly wed at St. Andrews Episcopal. If you marry Billy, my advice is join the League, be sweet to everyone, give a smashing Christmas party every year, have your babies, get an apartment in New York and a place in France, and latch onto a worthy cause."

Jessica brightened. "Billy wants to start a professional theater."

Kay greeted the idea calmly. "If you get the chance, run with it. Don't think about the money. The family has more money than you can imagine."

"May I join you? Or is this a private party?"

A tall, platinum-haired woman in a pink Chanel suit stood by their table, a drink in her hand and an ironic smile on her face. She might have been forty or fifty; a former beauty with classic bone structure but a face lined with inner pain.

"Pull up a chair," Kay told her. "Jessica Albert, meet Myra Fontaine."

The woman scoured Jessica with her eyes. "Goodness," she said, in a raspy, smoker's voice. "I thought your name was Dorothy."

"Dorothy?"

"Yes," the woman said, enjoying a long sip of her vodka and

tonic. "I thought you came from Kansas in a tornado, looking for the Emerald City."

The three of them laughed. "Does that make you the Wicked Witch?" Kay demanded.

"Some would cast me in that role," the woman drawled.

"I do feel a little like Dorothy," Jessica admitted. "I've just come here for a visit, and . . . "

"Oh, I know all about you," Myra Fontaine said. "You're the talk of Westover Hills. I expect to be the first to know when you set a date."

Jessica threw back her head and laughed. Her predicament seemed outlandishly funny. "Ms. Fontaine . . . " she began.

"Call me Myra, honey," the older woman said. "I may be obscenely rich, but I'm common as dirt."

"Myra, I'm terribly fond of Billy, but I may leave here tomorrow and never see him again."

"I'll bet a thousand dollars that you don't," the woman shot back. "You want some of that, Kay?"

Kay shook her head. "I'm praying that she never leaves," she said. "I need her."

The words startled Jessica. Somehow, in this carnival, she had made a friend.

"Well, if he lets her go, he's crazier than everybody thinks," Myra said. "You missed the excitement at Sonny's last night, my dear."

Jessica looked at her incredulously. "Were you there?"

"I blew in just in time for the cockfight. Except the real cockfight was later. That cretinous senator called Phil Kingslea a degenerate, and Phil called the senator a whore, and blows were exchanged, but they were both too drunk to do serious damage.

"And Miss Puss was seen making eyes at some hoodlum and Sonny slapped her and she called him a few exceptionally vile names, but that's par for the course, isn't it? Oh, and Maggie Plum turned up with her husband, of all people, as if to dispel those fascinating rumors about her and the ballerina."

Kay rolled her eyes. "I don't think we should expose Jessica to all the local dirt at once," she warned.

"Forgive us, honey," Myra said. "But a lunch without gossip is like a day without sunshine. And now I must run. A date with my shrink. *Adios*, Miss Dorothy."

She paused, enjoying the moment.

"In case you're wondering who this Wicked Witch is," she added, "I'm the lady who shot her father. Kay can fill in the details—it's Texas History 101."

She exited the dining room grandly, head high, with many eyes upon her.

"I think I'll fade out with a stinger," Kay said. "Join me?"

Jessica wasn't sure what a stinger was, but it sounded like a good idea. "Please."

"It's true," Kay said. "She did kill her father. The court called it self-defense. She inherited fifty million dollars, back when that was big money."

"Is she married?"

"She has been. She and Sonny are friends, oddly enough. Probably lovers, years ago."

Jessica's stinger arrived, and stung sweetly.

"You haven't told me much about Sonny," she said.

Kay shrugged. "You met him last night?"

"Yes."

"How was he?"

"Charming, in his way. He insisted on giving me a ring." She took the ring from her purse and showed it to Kay, who only laughed. "Wear it, it's not stolen."

Then she added, "Sonny gave *me* a ring once. Then he made a pass at me."

"Wonderful," Jessica sighed.

In truth, more than a pass had been involved. Sonny's advances came to a head on Kay and Mark's first anniversary. Mark had gotten plastered and she wasn't far behind. Sonny drove them home, dropped the unconscious Mark on a sofa, and carried Kay up to bed.

But that was not a tale to tell this sweet child. Instead, Kay said: "Be warned. Innocence only provokes Sonny. He's utterly amoral.

He's also ruthless, shameless, a genius, dangerous, cruel, a little crazy, and, as you saw last night, quite charming when he chooses to be. Personally, I avoid the son of a bitch."

"I don't know what to do," Jessica confessed. "I may go home and forget I ever heard of the Nash family."

"I don't envy your decision," Kay said. "But I don't mean to discourage you. You could have a fabulous life. Fort Worth really is the best city in Texas. It still has a human scale. Dallas and Houston are utterly bizarre."

Jessica finished her stinger. Out on the golf course, men in bright shirts and pants rode white carts in the blazing Texas sun. "I can't deal with this," she whispered. "I'm a very normal person. I teach English."

"Texas can be tough," Kay said. "Men have their pleasures on a silver platter, and we women have to fight for ours. Still, life is interesting. My advice is go for it."

Back at the house, she napped in Billy's bed, then awoke in late afternoon and found him reading in his study.

"How was lunch?"

"Fun. You were right, I like Kay a lot."

"Mark's lucky to have her," he said. "Hell, the town's lucky to have her. She single-handedly raised the money for new wings on two hospitals."

"When do I meet Mark?"

Billy made a face. "Don't be in any hurry. Look, let's go spend the night at the ranch."

"What ranch?"

"My ranch. We can be there in time for dinner. We'll ride and swim tomorrow. I won't have to share you with anyone."

Within a half hour they were aloft in his little twin-engine Piper, sailing west into the sunset. Jessica was torn between the glorious view and a gnawing fear of the plane's fragility.

"Don't worry," he told her. "A rowboat doesn't fall off a lake, and planes don't fall out of the sky."

She thought the analogy imperfect, but surrendered to the sunset.

"So what did Kay tell you at lunch?" he asked.

"She said a lot of good things about you, and your mother, and Fort Worth in general."

"And maybe a few bad things."

"Tell me something. Everybody says what a genius Sonny is. Exactly what does he *do*?"

Billy pushed his sunglasses higher on his nose and adjusted the levers before him.

"Do you know what a hostile takeover is?"

"When you buy somebody who doesn't want to be bought?"

"Right. It's a kind of corporate rape."

"Is that all? He buys companies, like a big fish swallowing smaller fish?"

"It's a combination of things. A grasp of the economic system. A gambler's instinct. And an utter lack of sentiment, particularly about the oil business. For a long time, oil was a religion in Texas. It's what people had instead of God.

"But Sonny saw that the bottom could fall out of the oil business, and he decided we should diversify. He began buying up defense-related companies, and when Reagan came in, our profits went through the roof. Now Sonny gobbles up anything that looks good— manufacturing, textiles, TV stations, chemicals, airlines, S&Ls, you name it."

Billy sighed. "Let's make a deal—no more talk of Sonny."

"Deal," she said. "The mind boggles—I mean, I can barely balance my checkbook."

"Look, there's the ranch."

The plains, barren for so many miles, suddenly flowered beside a winding river. Thick trees shaded a stone ranch house and its pool and tennis court and bright flowerbeds and stables.

"It's beautiful," she said.

"It's my favorite place in the world. When my family gets to be too much, I come here, unplug the phone, and tune out."

He landed in a field and taxied up to the stables. A sorrel mare pranced out to greet them.

"There's a couple who look after things," he explained.

He led her into a cool stone house perched on a bluff near the river, with a view of cottonwoods and the last purple afterglow of sunset. Someone had already built a fire in the living-room fireplace, and the room was bright with Navajo rugs and baskets of wildflowers and Western art.

Billy opened two beers and set to work barbecuing ribs. They listened to nightbirds sing, until Billy pushed a button and Beethoven filled the night. While the meat cooked, he surprised her by lighting a joint and offering it to her. She smiled and shook her head.

"Don't like it?" he asked.

"I haven't smoked in years," she told him.

They ate beside the pool, under the stars.

"What're you thinking?" he asked her, after one silence.

"About you," she said. "And teaching."

"How much you love it?"

"Not really. We have a group of teachers who meet for drinks every Friday afternoon. Sort of TGIF, except we call it SOTS. Sick Of This Shit. You wouldn't believe how many so-called students are openly hostile to the English language these days."

He laughed. "You should hear my mother on that subject."

"I guess I was wondering if I could make the transition from that world to your bigger, more challenging world."

"Sure you can."

After dinner, they moved into the big, high-beamed living room and settled before the fire. "Question," she said.

"Shoot."

"Last night, your mother said something about your science-fiction projects. What did she mean?"

Billy grimaced. "I take a lot of heat for some of my projects. The thing is, I'm interested in science, in the future, in peace, in how people can live together on this planet, in a lot of questions that we don't have answers to yet."

"So what's the sci-fi?"

"I've supported a project to transport material from place to place.

Like in the movies—you enter a booth in Texas and get out of another booth in New York."

"Far out!"

He smiled good-naturedly. "Maybe nothing will come of it, but if it did, my God, I'd make more money than Sonny."

She laughed and put her arms around him hungrily.

Making love that night was different from the first time. Their bodies were acquainted, their lovemaking more relaxed, more intimate, with a hint of pleasures yet to be. She fell asleep thinking that she didn't know where this strange romance was leading, only that it was sweet and seductive and that she didn't want the journey to end.

They awoke at dawn, ate a quick breakfast, and went out to the corral. Billy saddled two horses. Jessica's was a gelding called Sam. "Gentlest horse in Texas," he promised.

The prairie shone pink and gold in the morning sun. The trail curled among sunflowers down to the river, where an old stone dam made a shady, inviting pond.

"Swim?" he asked.

"Forgot my suit," she said.

"Me too."

They paddled about in the green, slow-moving water, while the horses swished their tails patiently on the bank. When they emerged from the water, Billy unrolled his saddleblanket and they came together eagerly in the morning sun.

"You're a fabulous lover," she said lazily, as they rested in the shade.

"I love to please you," he said. "I want to please you for the rest of my life."

"That's a long time."

He seemed not to hear. "I want children. I want to do some good in the world. I want to be happy, and to make you happy. Is that so terrible?"

"No, it's beautiful."

"Then why do you hesitate?"

"Maybe it's too good to be true. Your mother was right, it'd be simpler if you didn't have so much money."

"Do you want me to give it all away? Don't think I haven't thought about it. When I was twenty-five, I tried to. But I've learned I can do good with my money, that's the challenge."

He grinned. "Hey, it's too early for this. Let's head back. It's been a nice ride."

"Both of them," she said, as she reached for her jeans.

He held Sam while she mounted, then they started back the dirt path along the river. She was excited. This was the real Texas, she thought, not the country clubs or Sonny's circus, but the peace and privacy and joy she could have here at the ranch with Billy. What was she so afraid of? She knew the answer. She was afraid of the past, of her memories of the Home, of the helplessness and hopelessness she had felt that year. Could she ever be happy in a city where she had once been so unhappy? The memories of the horrors and the humiliation were coming now in waves. Would these people who had so much ever understand the loneliness she had known? Would she not always feel a stranger here, a fraud, an impostor? She had built a new life; was she now to surrender it?

And yet . . . and yet . . . The past was far behind. She was a different person, successful and self-confident. As Billy Nash's wife, she would have to fear no one.

She was falling in love with him for the right reasons. Not because of his money, but because of him, because of his quirks and surprises, because he was kind and funny and endlessly fascinating.

The money was part of it. Only a liar or a fool would deny that. The money gave life a new dimension, new possibilities.

They crossed a field of red and yellow wildflowers; she was daydreaming to the easy clip-clop of Sam's gait when a sudden hissing made her blood run cold.

Sam reared, and she was flying through space.

. . .

She woke slowly, confused, in the bed at the ranch house, with Billy and two other men peering down at her.

"What happened?" Her head hurt terribly.

"You took a spill," Billy said. "A rattler spooked Sam."

"Your head could use a couple of stitches, miss," said a white-haired man. "But it'll hold till we get back to town."

"This is Dr. Ames," Billy explained.

"I'm Mark Nash," the other man announced. "I flew the doctor out, as soon as my brother called."

Kay's husband was not what Jessica had expected, but what Nash had been? He was stocky and round-faced, with thick lips, a flat nose, and piggish eyes.

"Are you sure you're all right?" Mark asked.

"I . . . my head hurts," she said.

"But besides that . . . " Mark pressed.

"She just woke up, leave her alone," Billy said.

"I don't know why you put her on a horse," Mark said. "The family could be liable for . . . "

"Will you shut up?" Billy snapped.

"Why don't you two settle this outside?" the doctor suggested.

The brothers grumbled but left, and Dr. Ames established that she could focus her eyes and count to five.

"You're a lucky girl," he told her. "The next time you go riding, wear a crash helmet. Okay?"

"I promise."

He gave her two aspirin and went to call his office.

She was alone for a moment, then Mark Nash reappeared. "I regret that we've not met before," he said formally.

"It's all been rather sudden," she said.

"My wife gathers that you and Billy are quite serious."

"Your wife is a lovely person," she said. "And it was good of you to come today."

Mark was not disarmed. "I'm always concerned when there's a question of company liability," he said.

"Liability?"

"We'll handle your medical expenses, of course. But I'd like to be assured that there's no . . . "

"Did you think I was going to *sue* you?"

"Someone in the family has to consider such realities," Mark said.

She couldn't believe what this man was saying. Where was Billy?

"If you and Billy are contemplating marriage, be advised that I will urge a binding pre-nuptial agreement, so far as company assets are concerned, lest there be any misunderstanding about. . . ."

She tried to block out the drone of his voice. She thought of sweet, bright Kay, married to this lout. She remembered Kay's Bloody Mary and wine and stingers and she thought, *You fool, if I was married to you, I'd drink like a fish too . . .*

"Billy, for God's sake, where are you?" she shouted.

He rushed into the room. "What's wrong?" he demanded.

"Get me out of here, please get me out of here," she cried.

That night, back in Fort Worth, they lay in his bed, a million miles apart.

"My brother is a fool, but don't let him come between us," he said. He had said it a dozen times.

"I can't do it," she told him. "I can't marry you. It's impossible."

"Forget Mark," he pleaded. "Forget Sonny."

"It's not them," she said. "I don't like them but it's not them."

"Then what is it?" he pleaded.

"It's . . . it's something in my past that I can't talk about, can't explain. But it comes between us. I thought I'd put it away, but all this has dredged it up."

"Tell me what you mean," he pleaded.

"I can't. I truly can't talk about it."

"You're not being reasonable. You're acting like someone afraid of ghosts."

"I am," she said. "I am afraid of ghosts."

She thought of what William Faulkner had said, that the past is not dead, it's not even past. How could you explain that to someone who didn't feel it in the pit of his being? Perhaps she was irrational, but her pain and her fear were no less real for that. How could he understand, as she did, that the past could be the present, could be a cold hand that dragged you back relentlessly from the fragile glories of today to the black pit of yesterday?

Jessica flew back to Baltimore the next morning.

2.

ONCE MICKEY WANTED TO BE AN ACTRESS. SHE FELL IN WITH A little theater troupe in Denver and made her stage debut as Lucy Brown in *The Threepenny Opera*. The director loved Mickey and Mickey loved being someone else. You learned your lines, you put on a costume, and for three hours every night your troubles flew away. The director raved about her "vulnerability" and wanted her to play "a punk Joan of Arc" in his next production. But then Mickey's guitarist boyfriend was offered a recording contract and they roared off to Nashville. Two months later he ditched her for a Cajun cutie, but by then Mickey had lucked into a job as a photographer for a local paper.

The paper assigned her to the police beat, covering fires and car wrecks and other disasters. That's life, Mickey thought: One day you're St. Joan, and the next day you're chasing fire engines.

She got along fine with the cops, who were pretty much no-crap guys. One day a detective she knew introduced her to a DEA honcho named Whittaker, whose problem was that he had a big bust planned and he wanted pictures, but his photographer was sick. The next day Mickey was shivering on a rooftop in East Nashville while down on the street a dealer handed over four kilos of cocaine to two undercover narcs.

Then all hell broke loose. The dealer started shooting and one of the agents was wounded. Mickey kept cool, snapping pictures of the whole mess, and she wound up as a key witness in the dealer's trial. By the time the bad guy went down for twenty years, she and the DEA guys were pals for life.

Then Whittaker called again. "The agency needs women who can handle themselves, McGee," he declared. "The work is challenging, the benefits are good, and you're part of a cause that matters. Think it over."

She thought it over. At first she thought it was nuts. Her, a narc? It wasn't that Mickey was a druggie. She'd smoked a little dope, but mostly she figured life was weird enough without chemicals. She'd known too many people who'd scrambled their brains on coke or acid or speed. That was why she'd blown her chance to be St. Joan, because the guitar player had been so wired he couldn't have made it back to Nashville without her. If you wanted to be philosophical about it, Mickey had no problem with the war on drugs.

But it was more than that. Mick loved her freedom. She'd run loose for a long time, job to job, town to town, guy to guy. The trouble was, she was tired of bouncing around. Maybe it was time to settle down and maybe the DEA was the place. The agents told her it was like a family, that you'd never be closer to anyone than to the people you worked with, and that part grabbed her. She'd had boyfriends (and briefly a husband, which was why she was Mickey McGee now, a name she reckoned marginally better than Mickey Ketchum), but she hadn't had a family since the day years before when they'd taken Jessie away. She'd looked for her sister all those years, looked for her until various irate boyfriends had called her crazy and obsessive and a lot of other names. Mickey didn't care.

Jessie's memory was more real to her than the boyfriends' complaints.

She'd been back to the Home a dozen times, but nobody there knew where Jessie was, and the Home's lawyer wouldn't even talk to her. She'd gone to cities all over Texas, calling people named Gilbert. She'd searched through high school and college albums, put ads in newspapers and magazines, followed up all kinds of leads, hired private detectives when she could afford it. But it had all led nowhere. It was like the earth had opened and swallowed Jessie up.

But she'd never given up. In Nashville, covering the police beat, she'd made calls and checked local records. And now the DEA opened up a new world of possibilities. The agents bragged about their state-of-the-art technology. The supercomputers that could tap into IRS and Pentagon computers, into bank and insurance and credit card records and police files, and a thousand other sources.

Mickey was obsessed, she admitted it. But when she was thirteen, they'd taken away the only person she'd ever loved and it was like they'd ripped out her heart. Now she was sure she would find Jessie. With all the DEA hardware behind her, how could she miss?

Thus, one June afternoon in the early 1980s, Mickey McGee found herself on a bus rolling into the big Marine base at Quantico, Virginia. The bus stopped before a complex of buildings that held classrooms and labs and housing for DEA and FBI trainees.

Mickey climbed out and stretched. She was a wiry, wary young woman in jeans and a T-shirt, with a mop of sandy hair, no make-up, and a hands-off glint in her eyes.

"Hey you there!" someone yelled.

Mickey saw a huge black man in a DEA shirt glaring at her.

"You talking to me?" Mickey replied.

"Yeah, I'm talking to you. You some fucking tourist? Get your ass inside and register!"

Mickey bristled. Bozos like this had been yelling at her all her life and most often she told them where to go and what to do.

Not this time.

Instead, she picked up her bag, smiled sweetly, and said, "Be right there, sir."

That was the actress smiling; the real Mickey McGee was thinking: *I'm coming, Jessie baby, I'm coming as fast as I can.*

110

3.

JESSICA LEFT TEXAS CONVINCED SHE WOULD NEVER RETURN. Billy Nash, she told herself, had simply been a sweet, bizarre interlude in her otherwise sensible life. Back amid the ivy-walled sanity of her campus, she thought of their weekend together as a lovely dream from which she had now awakened.

She had, however, underestimated his determination.

His first ploy was no less effective for being a cliché: he sent roses. But Billy sent them Texas-style, three dozen a day. If at first she was annoyed, soon she was overwhelmed.

Abruptly, after a week, the deluge stopped. It was like feeling her heart stop. Since he surely had not run out of money, she had to ask herself if he had run out of interest. Or—this thought, with unexpected panic—had he fallen for some other woman glimpsed in a museum or across a crowded room?

The next day, a new surprise arrived, hand-delivered by the owner of Baltimore's finest rare-book store: a letter that Emily Dickinson, aged twenty-eight, had written to her mother setting out the qualities she sought in a man and the extreme unlikelihood, as she saw it, of finding one who possessed them. It was, to Jessica, a quite priceless gift.

At noon the next day, as she left Hunter Hall, he was leaning against a tree. She cried aloud and ran into his arms.

"That wonderful letter—how can I ever thank you . . . ?"

He grinned. "Marry me."

She had no answer to that.

He had stopped off on his way to New York, and she agreed to join him for a weekend at the Pierre.

A chauffeured limo whisked them about New York—to Broadway, to the Village, to Chinatown—and she was reminded of something Scott Fitzgerald wrote, that to have money was like having fins, letting you glide about the city, from one cool sanctuary to another.

The best of it was to have him away from his family. Billy Nash made a lot more sense with Puss and Sonny and Mark half a continent away.

He did not mention marriage that weekend. He drove her back to her campus and went on his way, leaving her to ponder the sudden emptiness of life without him.

He called two weeks later. He was returning to Washington for yet another state dinner, and wanted her to be his date. She spent half her life's savings on a shimmering green gown, piled her blond hair atop her head, and set off to meet the President.

The East Room of the White House was brilliant, the food and wine were magnificent, and the entertainment, featuring Sarah Vaughan and Joe Williams, was all anyone could ask. Yet the evening seemed artificial and choreographed. It was less a social event than a political ritual, in which everyone played a part: the politicians, the diplomats, the media stars, the corporate czars, the black opera singer, the Polish football coach, even she herself, though her role was purely decorative. She was quickly aware that almost no one she met had the slightest interest in her, except insofar as she might marry into the Nash billions.

At one point she whispered to Billy, "Who's paying for all this?"

"A grateful nation," he whispered back. "Lighten up."

Billy, less analytical than she, and far more at ease with conspicuous consumption, was having a grand time. Raffish in his tuxedo, clutching an unlit Cuban cigar, he more than held his own at their table with the opera star, the Secretary of State, a senator's giddy wife, and a pompous newspaper columnist. Billy was properly deferential, but his wealth created an aura that only he could ignore.

After dinner, the President and First Lady began the dancing, and soon Jessica was spinning in Billy's arms, trying to lose herself in the music, to enjoy to the fullest this once-in-a-lifetime evening.

Then, abruptly, Billy surrendered her to the President. He was beaming, his cheeks a bright pink, his grin contagious, and he danced divinely. Jessica disagreed with just about everything the man had ever said or done, but she couldn't resist his charm.

"When are you youngsters going to tie the knot?" he asked.

She looked at him, her eyes wide with surprise.

He winked back. "Marriage is a wonderful state," he said. "Everyone should try it—at least once."

The dinner broke up just before midnight. Jessica and Billy, exhilarated, hurried back to their hotel, the Four Seasons in Georgetown, and stopped in the terrace bar for a nightcap.

"He's amazing," Jessica said. "His magnetism. It really is hard to take your eyes off him."

"He had his eyes on you, too," Billy said.

"Just be glad he's not thirty years younger, mister."

The next morning, over coffee, he said again that she should marry him.

What had seemed so impossible two months earlier in Texas seemed quite inevitable that morning in Georgetown.

They were married that afternoon by a tipsy JP in Hagerstown, Maryland. Billy rounded up the necessary witnesses in a nearby bar, and the JP hugged everyone tearfully after the groom paid him with a crisp five-hundred-dollar bill.

They drove to Wintergreen, a ski resort south of Charlottesville, for the most secluded of honeymoons. Billy called Nash International's head of public relations and told him to announce the marriage; after that, he wanted to lie low until things died down.

Billy owned a condo atop the highest mountain in Wintergreen. They swam and played tennis a few times, but mostly they stayed inside, making love more or less non-stop.

"I wish we could stay here forever," she told him, the morning of their departure. "I think sex might supplant literature in my scheme of things."

"Alas, reality awaits," he said.

"Texas is reality?" she asked.

"Not really," he admitted. "But after a while you don't know the difference."

As the NI jet carried them back to Fort Worth, Billy was moody and withdrawn, and when they sailed above the pine forests of East Texas, he said to her:

"One thing you have to understand is that a lot of people in my hometown consider me eccentric at best, and a nut case at worst. I bug them because I have money and don't worship it. They understand Sonny, because he wallows in money like a pig. He may be a ruthless amoral son of a bitch, but people admire him. He's a *hero*. But to some people I'm a freak and you're going to be a freak's wife. That doesn't mean they won't kiss our behinds—they will— but a lot of them will be waiting for us to fall on our faces."

His words pained her. "Billy, all I want is for us to be happy. We can shut out all the rest of it."

"We'll try," he promised.

NI's chief PR man met the plane and drove them back to town. He was a fast-talking, olive-eyed man named Nick Rugatti who wore a Texas A&M ring and came bearing magazines and a pile of news clips.

"So what about our marriage?" Billy asked. "How did it play?"

"Not bad," Nick said. He started handing over clips. "Here's my favorite."

Billy glanced at the headline on a supermarket tabloid, laughed aloud, and passed it to Jessica.

BOOK-LOVING BALTIMORE BEAUTY BAGS BASHFUL BILLIONAIRE!

"Bashful Billionaire," Billy mused. "I've been called worse."

"I'm glad they didn't add an 'n,' " Jessica said.

"Say what?" Nick said.

"Bangs, instead of Bags. Beauty Bangs Bashful Billionaire. It would have sold more papers and how could I deny it?"

Nick glanced at Billy. "You brought home a live one."

"She'll sneak up on you," Billy agreed.

"Well, anyway," Nick continued, "you need to see at least the *Star-Telegram* and the Dallas *Morning News*. And *Time*'s regional guy is pushing us."

"What about TV?"

"I say stall them, until we get the print media off our backs. Jessica, honey, we need to sit down and brainstorm, like what you want to say."

"What if I didn't want to say anything?" she asked. "What if I was a private person who didn't want to tell all?"

Nick looked uneasy. "The thing is, Nash International is sort of Big Daddy in the community, and if it looked like you were snubbing the local papers, it'd be lousy PR. She's met Puss, hasn't she?"

Billy nodded.

"Well, Lillian and Kay are tops, with all those charities, but with Puss you have certain regrettable tales circulating that create problems, image-wise. So that's all the more reason that you be . . . positive."

"You're saying I should not say shit or fuck, or embrace feminism or pro-choice or nationalizing the oil fields?"

"Not unless you wanna give me a heart attack," Nick said. "Look, the reporters aren't gonna push you. But people will want to know about your background, how you met, and your courtship and all that crap."

"My background?" Jessica said. "What about my background?"

"Basic stuff. Where you grew up. Where you went to school. Your teaching career."

"My father was a doctor in Little Rock. He's dead now, and my mother is in poor health. I don't want anyone bothering her."

"Okay, no problem," Nick assured her. "Listen, don't worry, the media is gonna eat you up. This is the romance of the century!"

Indeed, when the time came, the reporters treated Billy and Jessica like royalty, which in a sense they were.

Lily Nash gave a luncheon at Rivercrest to introduce Jessica to her friends. They were women who had raised their children, kept or buried their husbands, and had little left to prove to anyone. They were, Billy told her, women who had Renoirs on their walls and Blackglama minks in their closets, but would offer you a home-cooked meal and more likely serve milk than Montrachet. One rather shy woman Jessica met that day had, Billy told her later, recently underwritten an entire Metropolitan Opera production of *Aïda*, complete with elephants.

A few of the women, like Lily Nash, showed signs of serious dieting and cosmetic surgery, but more had clearly decided to eat and drink as they pleased. They gossiped about their grandchildren, teased Jessica about being a "Yankee," and solemnly advised her to start having her babies.

When Kay followed with a luncheon at Shady Oaks, for her friends, the air was more rarefied, the exchanges more subtle. There was less drinking, and more scrutiny, for these were Jessica's peers and potential rivals. The older women had worn Dior or Chanel; the younger wives were more trendily clad by Blass, de la Renta, Valentino, Ungaro, and Givenchy.

Jessica felt as if she were back in sorority rush, being told she was wonderful by people she barely knew. She was indeed vigorously recruited for the Junior League and the opera guild, for bridge, tennis, golf, prayer breakfasts and square-dancing, for a wine-tasting society, sky-diving lessons, and a tour of China. She met one fascinating woman who had written her thesis on Colette, another who endlessly used the phrase "the whole nine yards," and another who kept calling her husband "a real kicker," whatever *that* meant. For the most part, Jessica was impressed by these beautiful, self-assured young women, with their easy gossip of hairdressers and shopping sprees and debutante balls; she smiled a lot, listened carefully, and watched her words.

Everyone asked how she liked Texas, and she sang the praises of her new home, careful not to reveal her deepest, darkest secret: that she had a terrible time spending money.

Jessica had tagged along once when Kay went on a shopping spree at Neiman Marcus. It was like following a whirlwind. With three saleswomen and an assistant manager in tow, Kay had for two hours relentlessly bought, bought, bought, and never once looked at a price tag. Jessica peeked at them, though, and when the orgy ended she was sure that Kay had spent more money in one afternoon than Jessica had earned in three years of teaching. When they left the store Kay was exhilarated—flushed and breathless. Her pleasure seemed almost sexual, and Jessica was limp with disbelief. She had scrimped and saved for too many years; money was real to her, in ways it was not to the other Nashes.

Lily had driven up one day in a gorgeous new Mercedes sedan. She'd bought it for Jessica, she said, "because it matches your eyes." Jessica drove the car a few days but didn't enjoy it. She'd owned only one car in her life, a battered old Toyota, and she felt pretentious in the Mercedes, and terrified of putting a dent in it. Finally she told Billy how she felt—that she was happier driving his three-year-old BMW—and he shrugged and said to take the Mercedes back, that his mother wouldn't care.

Midway through Kay's party, Jessica had an odd exchange with a petite blonde named Daisy Bragg. Jessica had mentioned that she was paying her new maid six dollars an hour.

"Six dollars an hour?" Daisy said sharply.

"Why yes . . . " Jessica said, taken aback. "Isn't that about right?"

"Well, it's none of my business, but if word gets around, we may have a revolution on our hands."

"What do you pay?"

"I start them at the minimum wage, then raise them to four dollars."

"Four dollars an hour?" Jessica protested. "That's—what?—seven thousand dollars a year? Nobody can live on that."

"You might be surprised what they can live on," Daisy said. "Anyway, I give my girls a bonus at Christmas if they behave. Four or five thousand."

Jessica was puzzled. "I guess it comes out about the same. But why not just pay six dollars to begin with?"

Daisy Bragg's eyes glittered like stars. Her pearls had cost enough to pay her maid for at least three years.

"Frankly," she drawled, "there's a principle involved, and if you don't understand, I don't think I can explain it to you."

The edge in Daisy's voice made Jessica hope that she did not learn about her giving back Lily's Mercedes. She was dead sure that Daisy would use it to paint her as weird, an outsider. She began to sense that, as Billy had warned, there were people who would love to see them fall on their faces.

By the end of the luncheon, she had divided Kay's friends into three groups. Many of them, she thought, had nothing beneath their bright surfaces—they were cheerful, content, empty-headed, and in their way quite nice.

In others, like Daisy Bragg, she glimpsed malice; perhaps they would have resented any "outsider" who married Billy.

Finally, amid the chit-chat and gossip, she saw in some women signs of empathy. The Texas culture, Jessica had come to think, viewed intelligent women as subversive to social order. But these women's eyes seemed to say, "Later, when we can, we will talk." It was as if they belonged to a secret sorority; these women, she hoped, would be the friends and allies who would help her survive in her new home.

That evening Jessica told Billy about her exchange with Daisy Bragg.

"I should have warned you," he said. "I dated Daisy for a while. I won't say she regrets losing me, but she might lust for my cash flow now and then. Her husband, a lawyer named Carson Bragg, is a rival of mine."

"A rival? In what?"

"On local issues. Preservation, that sort of thing. Some of us want to convert the Will Rogers Auditorium into an arts center, for example, but Carson champions the good people who want to keep on having hillbilly concerts there. You've heard of limousine liberals? Carson's a Porsche populist."

Jessica's thoughts shot back in time. She remembered Daisy Bragg now. The year she lived at the Home, Daisy had sat next to her in home room all year and only spoke to her once. Jessie Ketchum had been, in Daisy's thirteen-year-old eyes, an untouchable.

She had finally broken her silence when elections were held; she seized Jessie's arm and declared, "I'm running for cheerleader and you'd better vote for me."

Jessica had not, but Daisy won nonetheless.

Soon Jessica remembered two other women at Kay's party from that year in junior high. But she was sure that none of them would ever associate the shy orphan of yesteryear with the glamorous young wife of today.

She wanted to tell Billy everything. Part of her was proud of the metamorphosis she had made, from grub to butterfly, from the Gertrude Little Home to Westover Hills. But she could not open that door to the past for fear of what monsters might emerge. She could no more explain her blind, visceral fear than a child can explain its fear of the dark. It was as if by admitting the past she would reenter it, would be helpless and vulnerable again, would feel those boys' hands upon her again, tearing at her body. The pain was too great, so she kept her secret to herself.

Of all the Texas-style hospitality that awaited her, it was an evening with Sonny that Jessica would remember longest.

She met that morning with a landscape architect who was going to replace the formal garden that Billy's first wife had installed with a "natural" look, using wildflowers, grasses, ferns, rocks, ponds, and waterfalls to remake their backyard as a dreamscape from Rousseau.

Next she saw her doctor, then hurried to lunch and tennis with

Kay at Rivercrest. By the time she arrived home, she wanted nothing more than a quiet evening with Billy. But he announced that Sonny was taking them to dinner.

"Do we have to?" she groaned.

"We have to," Billy admitted.

They were to meet Puss and Sonny for drinks at the Carriage House, a restaurant off Camp Bowie Boulevard where Sonny often held court. It was a shadowy no-frills steakhouse that served excellent food and stocked Sonny's favorite champagne, Louis Roederer Cristal.

Puss and Sonny arrived just as they did, roaring up in his fire engine red 1957 Cadillac with its Texas longhorn hood ornament. Sonny, Billy said, had once driven a Duesenberg, until he decided it was un-American.

He came striding toward them, a cocky grin on his face, both arms outstretched. He was wearing sharkskin boots, tight yellow slacks, a black silk shirt, gold chains, and wraparound Ray-Bans. Puss's backless, mostly frontless dress echoed the fiery orange of her hair.

Inside, a bottle of Cristal waited in ice beside Sonny's table in the back room.

"You're looking good, little sister," Sonny told Jessica. It was their ritual greeting.

"You too, Sonny," she said.

"I oughta look good—I took some clowns for sixty million dollars this afternoon!"

"Did you buy somebody?" she asked.

Sonny rocked with laughter. "The gutless so-and-so's gave me the sixty million to go away."

"There's times I'd give that," Puss drawled.

"How're your Brownies?" Jessica asked her. It was not widely known—it would spoil her image, she said—but Puss sponsored a Brownie troop in the black neighborhood of Lake Como. It was, Jessica assumed, Puss's rebuke to the society belles who toiled over charity balls but never laid eyes on a person in need.

As Puss rattled on about the trip to Six Flags she and her Brownies had taken, Sonny scowled and went off to talk to some men at the bar. When he returned, he said it was time to go, and soon they were in his Cadillac, speeding toward the North Side, home of the restored stockyards and the famous Texas-sized honkytonk called Billy Bob's.

Their destination was the celebrated Mexican restaurant Joe T. Garcia's. Various of Sonny's friends were gathered outside, around big tables in the moonlight. Sonny ordered pitchers of Margaritas and no one was in a hurry about eating. Some of the men had dates, and other young women came and went, chewing gum and saying little.

Sonny's entourage told jokes, downed Margaritas and Mexican beer, laughed loudly, and largely ignored Jessica and Billy, who talked about their plans for the garden. Once Sonny loudly declared, "The only thing she was good for was fuckin' and she wasn't much good for that. Only woman I ever met who could screw up a blowjob!"

His cronies broke up.

"Who's he talking about?" Jessica whispered.

"His first wife," Billy told her.

Jessica could not help laughing. "Your brother is so crude, so unspeakably tasteless that he achieves a certain grandeur."

Billy nodded. "That's an important point to understand."

Sonny's friends were mostly shadowy men in their thirties with no clear means of support. They talked vaguely of "plans" and "deals," of restaurants they would open and nightclubs they'd owned and lost. All the while, their eyes rarely left Sonny.

In time, huge Mexican dinners arrived; Joe Garcia's had no menu, everyone was served the same incomparable platter. The evening had become surreal, and it seemed quite logical when Sonny announced that their next stop was the Caravan of Dreams.

This proved to be a bar/restaurant/theater downtown, a few blocks from the courthouse, in the restored area called Sundance Square, in honor of the Sundance Kid. They climbed the stairs to the crowded rooftop bar, which featured a fifty-foot glass and steel geodesic dome that encased cacti from Tehuacán and the Sea of Cortes.

Sonny commandeered tables and ordered pitchers of beer. They were surrounded by the new skyscrapers that dominated the downtown skyline, the Nash Tower prominent among them. Many had whole floors of lights left on, creating stripes and crosses that could be seen for miles. Jessica asked Billy why they did this.

"Call it tradition," he said. "Like a beacon, to reassure travelers on the prairie. Back in the thirties, Dallas had a famous landmark, the Flying Red Horse, which an oil company put on top of its building. You could see it for fifty miles. And in Fort Worth, in the fifties, we had a huge neon flag on top of the courthouse."

"Hey-ho, look who's here!" Sonny bellowed. Jessica looked and saw familiar faces: her sister-in-law Kay, the writer Philip Kingslea, and Kay's friend Myra Fontaine.

"Whatsa matter, sister Kay," Sonny demanded. "Hubbie gone off to pray?"

Kay made a face. "Every time the price of oil goes down, attendance at the Bible study classes goes up. We heard this is where the action is."

"You heard right," Sonny said. "We're taking the newlyweds for a night on the town."

The newcomers pulled up chairs near Jessica. "You didn't follow my advice," Philip Kingslea said. "About getting out of this town."

"I know. But I was in love."

"It's been the ruin of many a poor girl," the writer said. "Now look at you, part of Sonny's entourage."

"Are you and Sonny friends?"

"I wouldn't put it that strongly. He interests me. I just don't think of him as a human being."

Myra Fontaine puffed on a Marlboro. "Sonny's human," she said in her raspy voice. "He just isn't civilized. He's *Homo sapiens* in his natural state, circa fifty thousand years ago."

"You're saying he'd be as happy using a sharp rock as a leveraged buyout?" Philip asked.

"Happier," the heiress said.

"You people talking 'bout me?" Sonny demanded.

"Singing your praises," Philip assured him.

"I was just talking about women," Sonny said. "How they're always telling men"—and here he mimicked nastily—'Oh, you're not in touch with your feelings, honey, tell me what you *really* feel.' "

Sonny shook with laughter. "The trouble is, what a man is feeling, nine times out of ten, is 'Baby, I just want to fuck you and get out of here!' "

"Listen to the great lover," Puss injected. "He can't take care of me, much less all the other women in Texas."

"The whole damn Cowboys squad couldn't take care of you," Sonny growled. He stood up and stretched. "This party ain't very lively."

Sonny led his friends toward the wall that surrounded the rooftop bar. Jessica leaned back and looked around her—at the full moon, at the skyscrapers rising out of the prairie, at the geodesic dome looming above them, at the bizarre mixture of students, bikers, cowboys, Yuppies, millionaires, debutantes, drug dealers, and tourists, all gathered on the roof of a bar called Caravan of Dreams, in a block named for a bank robber, near a courthouse that once was topped by the world's largest neon American flag.

The moment was unreal, yet wonderful. She felt high, in a good way, and wished they were home, so she could tell Billy the news she'd hoarded all evening.

Sonny and his entourage lined the wall now, and as his friends cheered he began showering Houston Street with scraps of paper.

"Come on, you may as well see the show," Billy said.

At first she was confused. Teenagers below were racing about the street, leaping into the air, fighting for pieces of paper as they fluttered down from the roof. Sonny's friends howled with delight.

Suddenly she understood. Sonny was throwing crumpled bills—money—to the children.

Traffic ground to a halt, as teenagers fought over bills and a few motorists joined in.

Jessica stepped back. "This is awful," she said.

Billy nodded, but he seemed as fascinated as everyone else.

A police car arrived and a beer-bellied patrolman gazed up.

"Sonny, how about knockin' it off, you got traffic all screwed up."

"No problem, Homer," Sonny called back.

The policeman chased away the youths. A black teenager went racing down the street, pumping the air with a fistful of bills, triumphant.

Jessica and Billy returned to the table.

"How'd you like our little show?" Philip Kingslea asked.

"It's sick," Jessica said, hoping her brother-in-law would hear.

"Don't feel involved," Kay said. "Sonny does many things we aren't responsible for."

Philip Kingslea grinned. "Bread and circuses," he said. "Hail, Sonny, we who are about to die salute you."

"Hey, Sonny," one of his cronies yelled. "What was them bills? Ones or tens or what?"

"Twenties," Sonny said. "I tried hundreds once, and we like to had World War Three."

A tall, distinguished man in his sixties approached their table. He wore a white linen suit and regimental tie, unusual garb for the Caravan of Dreams.

"Why do you persist in making a spectacle of yourself, Sonny?" he said in a voice that carried across the rooftop.

"I guess I enjoy it, Walter," Sonny drawled.

"You're scum, nothing but scum."

Sonny rose and faced the man. "I'm sick of your shit."

"And this city is sick of yours," the man continued. "I suggest you take that baggage . . . "

He glared at Puss, who yelled, "Fuck you, you old fart!"

" . . . take her back to Houston or wherever she came from, and stop polluting our fair city."

"It's you who's gonna leave, Walter," Sonny raged. " 'Cause I'm gonna run your skinny ass right outta Texas!"

"Scum," the man said again, and marched away.

"I'll ruin you!" Sonny rose menacingly, but Myra Fontaine took his arm and spoke soothingly. Muttering to himself, Sonny sat down.

"You can't let him talk to me like that," Puss said bitterly. "Who the fuck's he think he is, calling me *baggage*?"

She turned to Jessica. "I'm not trash," she said defiantly. "I'm as good as anybody in this stupid town."

Jessica and Billy caught a cab home. Olivia was reading when they arrived. She offered to make coffee. But Jessica sent her to bed and spooned up ice cream for them.

"Who is that man and why does Sonny hate him so?" Jessica asked when they were settled.

"His name is Walter Lamont," Billy explained. "His daughter, Felice, was Sonny's first wife. The Lamonts go back about as far as you can go in Fort Worth—Hiram Lamont was a rancher, in the 1880s, and built one of the city's first great mansions, up on Summit. They found oil on their land in the twenties, and Walter has built up a conglomerate with oil supplies, tankers, electronics—the works."

"Are they rivals of yours?" she asked.

"Not really. They're perhaps a quarter our size. The problem is that Sonny hates Walter."

"Why?"

"Mainly because of the divorce. Felice is a wonderful woman. Of her generation in Fort Worth—in Texas—she was the prize, and Sonny set out to win her. This was fifteen years ago, when Sonny wasn't . . . well, he wasn't *Sonny* yet. Just this rather dynamic guy who was starting to make a lot of money. So he swept Felice off her feet and married her and they had a son and then, naturally, he was bored with her. I think Sonny resented Felice because she was so much better a human being than he is. He abused her—verbally *and* physically—until she took Willie and left."

He took their bowls and put them in the sink.

"When Felice told Walter what had been going on, he wanted to take Sonny to court. He wanted criminal charges." Billy sighed. "It was sticky. There were legal questions. If he beat her, and she

125

didn't complain at the time, could she go to court months later? And you get into whether a man can rape his wife—you wouldn't consider Texas enlightened on that one. What Walter really wanted was to keep Sonny from ever seeing Willie again.

"The trouble was, Sonny had his cronies ready to swear to some pretty unpleasant things about Felice."

"Like what?"

"Sex. Drugs. Whatever. None of it true, but Sonny's pals would have made it sound good. Thank God, they settled out of court. Sonny set up a trust fund for Willie, and he got visitation rights."

"And then came Puss?"

"Puss has a certain style. And Sonny enjoys inflicting her on the city. Let's face it, Sonny could marry Lena the Hyena and people in this town would kowtow to her."

"Walter Lamont wasn't kowtowing. What was that remark about taking Puss back to Houston?"

Billy shrugged. "There's a story that she was a call girl in Houston for a time."

"Is that *true*?"

"I don't know. I know that several private detectives haven't been able to produce any—no pun intended—hard evidence."

Jessica had to laugh. "I'm sorry," she said finally. "It's all too much. I can't believe I have a brother-in-law who throws money off rooftops and a sister-in-law who's an ex-hooker."

"He's redistributing the wealth. Maybe she was, too."

"This isn't a normal life you live."

"I never said it was. Look, let's go to the ranch for a few days."

She took his hand, savoring the news she'd been saving until this whirlwind of an evening wound down.

"I have something to tell you," she said. "I hope it makes you as happy as it makes me."

"Everything you do makes me happy."

"Billy, we're going to have a baby. I saw the doctor today."

He embraced her, tears in his eyes. They settled on a sofa in their living room, holding hands.

"I want to give this child a sane childhood, Billy."

She did not have to spell out what she meant.

"I agree," he said. "When I was a kid, I mowed lawns and threw the *Star-Telegram*. Thank God for that. How was it for you in Little Rock? It sounds like a sensible sort of place."

Jessica hesitated. She was so tired of deceiving him.

"There's something I never told you." She squeezed his hand. "The Alberts adopted me. I never knew who my real parents were."

Billy frowned, bemused. "How old were you?"

"Very young," she said. She couldn't talk about the Home yet. Perhaps she never would. "The Alberts meant well, but they were older and not really suited for raising a child. When I went off to college, I began to think for myself. I demanded that they tell me what they knew about my birth parents and they said they couldn't. We were never close after that."

She laughed. "So I guess I can't make you any promises about the genes I'm contributing to this offspring of ours."

"My God, who could have more perfect genes than you? Just hope that our kid doesn't inherit whatever rogue gene produced Sonny. Talk about the bad seed!"

"I had a sister," she said. "I don't know what happened to her. I tried for years to find her but she'd vanished."

Billy was curious but didn't want to vex her with unwanted questions. "We have lawyers and investigators," he said. "If you want to use them . . . "

She hesitated. The conversation had gone afield. "Maybe later," she said. "For now . . . for now my life is just about perfect."

He kissed her fingers and held her hand against his cheek.

"Sometimes I can't believe it's true," she told him gently. "Sometimes I think I'm Cinderella and at midnight it'll all be gone."

"It won't be gone," he told her. "It's only going to get better. You wait and see."

4.

"HEY, LOOK AT THE MICK! WOULD YOU FUCKING LOOK AT HER?"

"Hell, that ain't Mick. That's Farrah fucking Fawcett!"

"Screw you guys," Mickey grumbled.

They were in the lobby of the DEA's office in Southwest Washington, and Rafe Klayman and Lon Tate were giving her a hard time, which was nothing new.

Rafe touched her silk dress. "No crap, Mick, you look great. Look at her, Lon! Get her out of jeans and sweatshirts, get her hair done, put a decent dress on her and some makeup—and she's Miss America!"

"She ain't bad," Lon Tate admitted. He was a huge black man, a one-time pro football player. Rafe Klayman was white, a wiry West Virginian, a gung-ho ex-Marine. They had been the stars of their training class—the best athletes, the leaders.

"I feel like a jerk," Mickey grumbled.

In truth she was a new woman, in the clinging yellow dress and ash-blond wig, with her face artfully painted.

"So where's the party, Mick?" Rafe asked.

"I'm checking out a place called El Mundo in Georgetown," she told them. "Flash, cash, and Eurotrash."

"Mick, you look real foxy," Lon Tate said. "But you got to stand up straight, smile a little, show some flash yourself. You don't wanna look like an impostor."

"I feel like one," she admitted.

"Be careful, Mick," Rafe said, as she started out the door, a little unsteadily on her high heels.

The two men exchanged a glance.

"The Mick emerges as a looker," Lon said.

"It's only a disguise," Rafe said, and they laughed in the easy way that men dismiss the foibles of the weaker sex.

Mickey took a table against the wall in El Mundo and ordered a glass of wine. The girl she was looking for wasn't here yet, so she watched the place fill up with the Happy Hour crowd. Mickey was in no hurry. She was starting to like being a bimbo.

She'd known, after just a few weeks at Quantico, that this was what she'd be doing if she made it through training. She'd just squeezed through the academic part of the program, all the chemistry and report writing and legal stuff, and she'd been only so-so on the range and at physical training.

But what she'd really aced was the practicals, the make-believe when you sat down with a dealer and told him you were a coed or a Mafia guy's girlfriend or a call girl and talked him into selling you drugs.

Conning people came easily. You had to be loose and funky and cynical as all get-out. It was what she'd done as a photographer, flattering people until they smiled for the birdie. It was what she'd done as an actress, too. People were funny; they saw what they wanted to see.

In training she'd acted out roles with other agents, but now it was for real. Mickey met dealers in bars and restaurants and gained their confidence and eventually she'd make the buy. There wasn't much danger. Usually there were other agents nearby, as witnesses and for protection. Most of the time she enjoyed it, because most dealers were scumbags who didn't give a damn what their dope did to people.

And yet she was immensely frustrated, because her little buys were trivial alongside the real drama that consumed the DEA field office in Washington that fall.

Just as she and Lon and Rafe had arrived, two agents had been gunned down on a playground in northwest Washington. They'd gone there to meet an informant, with other agents watching from nearby, but the killer had shot from across the street with a high-powered rifle and escaped by car.

It was, for the entire DEA, an electrifying moment. Drug dealers had traditionally avoided violence with the DEA, on the assumption that they could only lose. But if two agents could be shot down in cold blood in Washington, D.C., it meant the rules of battle were changing. It meant America's drug wars might soon be as bloody as those in Latin America.

A forty-man task force was working day and night to find the killer. Lon and Rafe had been assigned to the task force, the only first-year agents thus honored. And Mickey was jealous, sitting in El Mundo waiting for some two-bit dealer to appear.

Something else frustrated her. She'd thought that once she was an agent, she'd be able to use the NADDIS computer to look for her sister. She'd built it up in her mind as this new-age *deus ex machina* that would go click-click-click and cough up the twin she'd been searching for all these years. The trouble was, the task force was using NADDIS around the clock, and she couldn't just waltz in and borrow it for her personal use.

But Mickey was patient. She'd waited a long time; her day would come.

After a while she spotted the young blonde at the end of the bar. People came and chatted with her. Sometimes she and another girl would go to the women's room together. Sometimes she'd slip something into a guy's pocket. She was a busy little bee, and when the moment came Mickey sat down beside her.

The girl was pretty and nervous. She chain-smoked Virginia Slims as her eyes darted about the bar.

"Hi, I'm Mickey."

"Mickey? That's cute. Boy, what bones you've got. I'm Julia. Want a drink?"

"Sure," Mickey said, and Julia waved to the Iranian bartender.

"What do you do?" Mickey asked.

"Me? I'm an ex-student at Georgetown. I mean, I was doing too much coke and I flunked out. So now I'm sort of, you know, hanging out."

Mickey said she was a legal secretary, new in town. She talked about how she missed her boyfriend and listened to the girl complain about her parents and finally she asked if Julia knew where she could score any coke.

Julia looked coy. "Why would I know that?"

"The thing is, these guys at my law firm are always asking me if I have any. I'll bet I could move eight or ten grams a week, if I had a good source."

"I could call you if I hear of anything."

"That'd be great," Mickey said. "Here, take this." She produced a card from her purse; on it was the address and number of a Washington law firm. "Call me any time."

Julia walked off and Mickey finished her wine. She felt like hell. Here she was in Washington, the capital of big-time bribery and corruption, where lobbyists, politicians, and contractors worked out sweet deals that cost the taxpayers billions—it seemed crazy to be busting your ass to nail a kid like Julia.

Mickey shrugged and left El Mundo and found Rafe Klayman leaning against a light pole on M Street.

"Surprise!" she cried.

"How about dinner?" he said.

She didn't argue. She wished he was here because he found her irresistible, but probably he just figured she was such a klutz he'd better check up on her. "Sure, but I gotta go home first and change back to the real me."

An hour later, they settled over beers at the Tune Inn, not far from the apartment Mickey shared with another woman agent on Capitol Hill. She was back in jeans and a sweatshirt, with her short, sandy hair liberated from the wig.

"So how did it go?" Rafe asked.

"I met this girl. She's dealing and she'll probably call me in a couple of days. I'm bummed about it. She's a messed-up kid, pushing a little dope."

"She's a messed-up kid who'll mess up other people if we don't stop her," Rafe declared. He dropped some quarters in the jukebox.

"What'd you play?" she asked.

"Hank Williams."

"Senior or Junior?"

"There's only one Hank Williams," Rafe said.

He was like that. Dogmatic, you might say. She remembered the first time she saw him, the first night at Quantico. All the new trainees gathered in a room with the staff, and each of them had to tell why he'd joined the DEA.

Some of them mumbled about career opportunities and improved salaries and the like. Then Rafe got up, this wiry little guy with a hillbilly twang and tattoos on his arms and fire in his eyes, and said he just finished ten years in the Marines, and he fought in Vietnam, and he loved the Corps, but there was only one war being fought now, the war against drugs, and if the politicians wouldn't let the Marines fight that war he was going to join the outfit that could.

By the time he finished, everyone was cheering, even the staff, and Rafe was their star. He and Lon Tate, who'd been a pro line-backer before he hurt his knee, were the two best athletes in the class and they'd become best friends, too.

Lon was going with Ruby Blake, the agent Mickey shared an apartment with, and sometimes Mickey wondered if Rafe had a girlfriend or had time for one. He was, she knew, divorced.

"These Mickey Mouse buys I'm making, they seem so unimportant compared to what you guys are doing," Mickey said.

"Wrong, McGee," he said. He had small brown eyes that shone

when he talked, and rough skin and a broken nose and a beautiful mouth. "What you're doing is important. That girl tonight, she might buy from a guy who buys from the guy we're looking for."

"Do you have any leads at all?"

The waitress brought their burgers and fries, and Rafe ordered more beer. When she was gone, he said, "We know he's young and white and smart and probably flies his own plane and maybe lives in northern Virginia."

"How smart?"

"Think about it, Mick. Suppose you could fly and wanted to make big bucks selling coke. What would you do?"

"Are you saying the same guy is both the pilot and the distributor?"

"It looks that way."

"Then I'd get me a SOS in Colombia and fly the stuff in myself. That doubles your profit and cuts down on the number of people who can screw you."

"Right," Rafe said. "So, say you're moving a hundred keys a month, to four or five distributors, what do you do if you think one of your guys is about to flip?"

"And I'm facing life in the slammer? That's easy. I zap the sucker."

"We busted a Porsche salesman who said he bought from a guy named Brad. But before he can take us to Brad, he goes jogging one day and gets his neck broke."

"That's rough jogging."

"Then we bust Broussard, who works in this spiffy Eye-talian clothing store. And he gives us the same vague description of his source—thirty or so, white, well built—except he calls him Seth. And our guys say they've got to meet Seth, and Broussard says he's set it up, that Seth's going to meet them at the Stoddert School playground. Except when they show up, somebody shoots them with a high-powered rifle from an apartment across the street."

"So are Seth and Brad the same guy?"

"We think so. The other question is why he shoots our agents.

133

We know why he kills *his* guys—because they can identify him. But why shoot our guys?"

"Because he's doing too much coke and he's paranoid?"

"Maybe. But maybe he's making a statement, changing the rules, declaring war."

Mickey thought about it. "Once, could be he freaked out," she said. "If he does it again, it's war."

"That's how we figure it. This man is dangerous. But we'll find him. Believe me, we'll nail his ass."

Mickey pounded the table with her fist. "*Dammit*, I wish I was working with you!"

Rafe Klayman unfurled his lopsided smile. "You're doing fine, Mick," he told her. "It's all the same war. Just keep it up."

A few days later Mickey had a call from Maxie, who ran the music room. The music room was pure magic. You could have dealers call you there, and Maxie supplied the sound effects. If somebody thought they were calling you in a bar, Maxie could serve up music—rock, jazz, hillbilly, you name it. Or banging and clanking if you were supposed to work in a factory, or a baby crying or a jet going over or traffic noise or whatever you needed.

The thing was, agents didn't go live in slums or try to maintain twenty-four-hour identities. That was too dangerous, too depressing, too everything. Instead, they zipped in, made their buys, and zipped out. But they had the documents, the disguises, the cover stories, the cars, the money, even the sound effects, to convince the crooks they were whoever they were pretending to be.

Maxie played her a tape of the call. It began with Maxie reciting the name of a law firm.

"Hello? I'm calling Mickey."

"I'm sorry. She's in a meeting."

"Would you ask her to call Julia? Or come by the club this evening?"

"I'll give her the message."

It took Mickey a minute to remember the nervous blonde sipping rum at El Mundo. She'd hoped Julia wouldn't call. But she had.

That evening Mickey went to the bar and bought six grams of coke from her, with another agent nearby as a witness.

"Hey, Mick, we need you!"

Mickey looked up from her computer. The DEA wasn't all kicking down doors. A lot of the time you did paperwork until your eyes were on fire.

"You need me, you got me. What's up?"

"We busted this kid Julia and it's a disaster."

"How so?"

"She won't stop crying. She's been crying for two hours. She's fucking driving us crazy. You're her pal—you talk to her!"

Mickey groaned and went downstairs and found Julia perched on a bench in a holding room. When she saw Mickey, she began to howl.

Mickey threw up her hands. "Hey, come on!"

"Awwwahhh! You were my friend!"

"I'm not your friend, I'm a DEA agent."

"You asked about my dog. You bought me a drink. You *lied* to me!"

"I'm a cop, I lie to everybody."

Julia sobbed as if her heart might break. Mickey thought she would start bawling too if the kid didn't stop.

"Dammit, stop that! We gotta talk!"

Julia kept sobbing.

"Hey, *please*, talk to me!"

"There's . . . nothing . . . to . . . talk . . . about. Just lock me up . . . I'll hang myself in my cell!"

"Will you listen? We don't want to put you in jail. We just want to talk to you. So shut up bawling!"

Julia fished a Virginia Slim from her purse. "I was just trying to make money to go back to college with. Is that so awful?"

"Look, face the facts. We caught you in a felony. You *could* go to jail."

"For how long?"

"A couple of years."

"Awwwahh!"

"We can make a deal. Just tell us who sold you the coke."

"You mean rat on my friend?"

"Some friend! Look, tell us who this creep is, and we'll go to bat for you with the judge. Probably you'll get a suspended sentence and can go back to school."

The girl snubbed out the cigarette and blew her nose. "Suppose I told you I did coke last weekend with a senator?"

"You did what?"

"I mean, he's older than my father, but he's a real wild man. Could that get me out of this mess?"

Mickey stood up. "Hold it right there," she said. "I'm going to get my supervisor."

5.

Jessica and billy's daughter, whom they named melissa for Lily's mother, arrived one May afternoon with a minimum of fuss, a good baby from the start.

Billy was in the delivery room, holding her hands, as the doctor dangled their pink and perfect daughter before them.

That night they celebrated with a bottle of Pouilly-Fumé de Ladoucette, which Billy smuggled into the hospital, and when she went home a cornucopia of flowers and gifts awaited her. She was also met by Bridget, a pink-cheeked young Scot who was to be Melissa's nanny. After a week Bridget set off for California, but Jessica didn't mind. She'd decided that she and Olivia could care for the baby. Olivia had worked for Lily for a dozen years, and she wasn't going to skip for California.

Jessica had loved her pregnancy. Her breasts were huge, her husband adoring, and their love life increasingly inventive. She'd had a perfect excuse to give up coffee and alcohol, and to arrange her social life exactly how she wanted it.

That meant a minimum of baby showers, and it also meant that except for a drink on Christmas Day, she was able to banish Puss and Sonny from her life, although reports of their doings arrived daily.

It was said that she had attacked him with a hot poker, that he'd left her tied naked atop a pool table for two days, that they'd taken a mulatto transvestite to bed: Puss and Sonny stories rivaled football and the price of oil as the city's favorite topic.

Jessica enjoyed the stories; she just didn't enjoy Puss and Sonny. The two people she did enjoy most, during and after her pregnancy, were her sister-in-law Kay and her neighbor Myra Fontaine.

Kay surprised her by calling one afternoon and saying urgently, "If anyone asks—I was at your house for lunch!"

"Okay," Jessica said, "but what . . . "

"Can't talk now—later!"

The next morning, a more relaxed Kay arrived for coffee. She wore a new tennis outfit that showed off her trim figure to good advantage. If Kay had ever worn the same outfit twice no one had noticed.

"Didn't mean to panic yesterday," Kay said, stirring her black coffee. "But I thought I'd been found out."

"What had been found out?" Jessica asked.

"My fling with Phil Kingslea," Kay said. "Hadn't you guessed?"

"I'd never thought about it. I . . . do you want to talk about it?"

Kay shrugged. "Why not? It's how I keep my sanity."

"But doesn't Mark know? Or care?"

"Oh God, who knows what Mark knows or cares about? He cares about Jesus and AA and money. And he doesn't give a damn about sex. He never did, although in the bad old days he'd at least give it a shot when he was smashed."

Kay pushed her coffee aside. "Do you mind if I have a drink?"

Jessica laughed. "I'm not your mama. You know where it is."

Kay returned in a minute with a Bloody Mary.

"Mark looked pretty good in college," she said after a while. "He was pompous, sure, but he was rich, and not at all stupid, and he hadn't put on so much weight then. By the standards of the Kappa

Sig House, he was a prize. Jesus, what did I know, what does any girl of twenty know? Other boys were worrying about finding jobs, and here was this millionaire who wanted babies.

"So I married him. And he grew progressively richer, fatter, and duller. Somewhere along the line I realized that it was boys like Phil, who started out with nothing, who were angry and hungry and passionate, who were interesting."

"Billy's interesting."

"Yes, you're right, he is. Dammit, I married the wrong Nash brother. Wouldn't trade, would you?"

"Maybe Puss would."

"Ha! Talk about the frying pan to the fire."

"Kay, I sympathize, I really do, but where does it lead? Do you want to marry Phil Kingslea?"

"He's not the marrying kind. And, let's be honest, the Nash money is addictive. Anything I want, I can have."

She bit her lip. "No, that's not true. *Anything money can buy, I can have.*"

"How . . . how do you meet Philip, without being found out?"

"In charming, out-of-the-way motels," Kay said drily. "Yesterday we thought we saw someone watching from across the street. Post-coital paranoia. So I slipped out the back and called you. I'm sorry, it's not fair to you. But, who knows, maybe someday you'll want me to return the favor."

Jessica laughed. "That's the dumbest thing you ever said."

"No offense," Kay said. "But you never know."

6.

DWIGHT WINGO, THE DRUG ENTREPRENEUR WHO WOULD BRING such turmoil into Mickey McGee's life, was the son of a minor player in the Watergate scandal.

His father, John Wingo, a lawyer and Republican fund-raiser in Arlington, Virginia, had at a crucial moment been asked by a senior Nixon aide to fly a padlocked Louis Vuitton suitcase from Washington to Key Biscayne in his private plane. John Wingo suspected that the suitcase contained illegal campaign contributions, yet he eagerly performed the task requested of him. Like many others, he assumed that only good could come from serving the President's men.

In due course the Special Prosecutor beckoned, and John Wingo's testimony helped send the senior Nixon aide to Allenwood. Wingo himself was given a suspended sentence and disbarred, whereupon he devoted himself to selling real estate, drinking heavily, and cursing Richard Nixon. He remained, however, a loyal Republican;

this was a man who had, in 1952, named his only son for his party's candidate for President.

While John Wingo was surviving Watergate as best he could, his son Dwight (who loathed his given name and was known to friends as Dee) was an MP, assigned to the U.S. Embassy in Saigon, surviving the final days of the Vietnam adventure. Like his father, Dee Wingo often cursed Richard Nixon, but unlike his father, who was partial to Johnnie Walker Black, the son used hashish as his buffer against a hostile world.

Dee Wingo had for several months been sleeping with the sixteen-year-old daughter of a Saigon merchant, and as the fall of Saigon grew near the merchant was desperate to get himself and his daughter out of the country. He came to Wingo for help, and revealed that his most liquid asset was two pounds of the purest heroin.

Wingo consulted an MP sergeant who said that for $5,000 he would guarantee that he would not be searched on the flight back to California. For another $5,000 the merchant and his daughter could be put aboard a military transport bound for Manila.

It was for Wingo a most agonizing decision. He was fond of the girl, but her father was a pig, and not to be trusted. Wingo eventually concocted a plan that reflected the hard-won pragmatism of a year in Vietnam. He put the girl on a plane to Manila, with $100 and his assurance that her father would follow soon, then he returned to Saigon and blew the merchant's head off.

Two weeks later, in San Francisco, Wingo sold the heroin for enough money to support him while he pondered his career plans.

It was first necessary to visit home. His unrepentant father was prospering in real estate. "I gambled and lost, simple as that," he said of his downfall. "With any luck, Nixon would have burned those damn tapes and I'd have been a federal judge." He urged his son to enter law school.

Wingo instead drove to Florida to investigate opportunities in the drug trade. He had no thought of dealing in heroin, which he considered a dangerous drug that attracted dangerous people. Rather, he went from Miami to Mexico to study the growth and distribution of marijuana, and in particular the merits of smuggling it over the border in small planes. He was an expert pilot and that seemed a likely way to gain a foothold in the business. But his study convinced him that smuggling marijuana from Mexico did not, in the long run, make any sense at all. Marijuana was too bulky and the border was too well guarded.

In the spring of 1976 Wingo returned to Miami to continue his research. One afternoon he happened upon an airport rally for a squeaky-voiced Georgia politician named Jimmy Carter who said that if elected President, he would never tell a lie. The man was either insane, Wingo thought, or the biggest liar in America.

Wingo might have quickly forgotten Jimmy Carter, but that evening, in a bar in Coconut Grove, he chanced to meet a young Georgian named Richmond Morris, who was an aide to Carter, and a lawyer named Lita Howe who had done local fund-raising for him. Curious, Wingo bought drinks and in time was invited back to the woman's apartment, where Lita introduced him to cocaine.

It was his first experience with the drug, and he was impressed by its brilliant and energizing high. He was impressed, too, that savvy young professionals like Rich Morris and Lita Howe had made cocaine their drug of choice.

Wingo abruptly reached a conclusion that would make him one of the richest men his age in America: cocaine, then still seen as a rich man's drug, a kind of illicit champagne, was destined to become the marijuana of the 1980s. *It simply had to be.* From the consumer's point of view, it was a superior drug. To the supplier, it was far easier to transport, and thus promised greater profits at less risk.

He began to study the cocaine trade, and it was soon obvious that all roads led to Colombia. Unlike marijuana, a humble weed that would sprout almost anywhere, cocaine grew only on a few isolated slopes in the Andes Mountains, and from those slopes it made its way, by a process he did not then understand, to Bogotá and Medellín.

Wingo flew to Medellín, a city of one million souls, a great many of whom wore expensive gold chains and drove even more expensive German cars. He checked into the best hotel, made himself conspicuous in the best bars, and presented himself as an American pilot named Wilson who wished to purchase several kilos of cocaine.

The first thing that happened was that two young toughs lured him into an alley and tried to rob him. They reckoned without the survival skills he'd learned as an MP, and he left one with a concussion and another with a broken arm. He would have killed them but did not want to offend their superiors.

The next morning he received a call from a man who identified himself in passable English as Hector Ugarte, a businessman who would be honored if Mr. Wilson would join him for lunch in the city's finest restaurant.

Ugarte proved to be a small, dark, pockmarked man who wore a white suit and a handpainted tie with pink elephants on it; he arrived in a chauffeured limousine, was fawned over by the maître d', and insisted on ordering champagne.

"My apologies for the unfortunate incident last night," he said.

"Were they your people?"

"On behalf of the Orchid City, my apologies."

"I was in Vietnam. I can take care of myself."

"One must, in this world. And what has brought you to our city?"

Wingo had come too far to bullshit.

"There is a growing demand for cocaine in my country. I'm a pilot, looking for a reliable source of supply."

Ugarte stared at Wingo for a long time. Despite his gaudy clothes, Wingo recognized him as a dangerous man, a killer.

"Let me speak frankly, Mr. Wilson. If what you say is true, we can make a great deal of money together. If it is not true, your life is very much at risk."

"What I say is true."

"I hope so, because you are right about cocaine. The world is changing. When Allende came to power in Chile, he imprisoned or exiled the leading producers of cocaine. The business shifted to my country, where the government is more sensible. We are in transition from a fragmented industry to a centralized one. We have the supply, your country has the demand, and the possibilities are unlimited."

"But there is the problem of transportation."

"Yes. I am still sending my product to your country in suitcases with false bottoms, a few kilos at a time. We are near a new stage of development. The time has come to transport hundreds of kilos by air. For that we need reliable pilots, planes, and landing strips. Do you have a plane?"

"I'm prepared to buy one."

"If you will deliver hundred-kilo shipments to agreed-upon destinations in the United States, I will pay you a thousand dollars per kilo."

Wingo stood up. "You must think I'm crazy."

Ugarte seized his arm. "A businessman cannot afford hurt feelings. Tell me your concern."

Wingo sat back down. "A thousand a kilo is absurd, when I'm taking most of the risk and you're making at least twenty thousand per kilo."

"I have expenses. And I supply the product."

"My goal is not to be only a pilot," Wingo continued. "I grew up in Arlington, Virginia, across the river from Washington, D.C. I know that area like the back of my hand. It's filled with young lawyers and politicians and students, people who have money and work under pressure. Right now, there's only a trickle of coke, coming from Miami or California by car. I want to develop that market. I'll start by making one flight a month. I'll pay you twenty thousand per kilo. With any luck I'll be moving a hundred kilos a month soon. After a year we'll renegotiate. Agreed?"

Hector Ugarte broke into a greedy grin. "Agreed!" he murmured.

The partners flew to Miami and paid $300,000 for a Merlin III that Wingo believed would suit his needs. He then returned home for a crucial period of planning. His most pressing decision was where to land his shipments. With the entire Eastern United States to choose from, he chose his native Virginia. He visited Charlottesville, where fine old antebellum mansions were being bought up by wealthy Easterners. One more rich newcomer flying in and out would cause little talk. Wingo therefore leased Davenport, a thousand-acre estate that featured both a historic mansion where

144

Thomas Jefferson had often dined, and a landing strip added by the previous occupant, a recently indicted New York financier.

Wingo flew two dry runs before he carried his first shipment, and he concluded that the actual flying was the easiest part of the business. The sky was vast and the chances of a prudent pilot being caught were slim. The dangers were on the ground.

Wingo spent months building his distribution network. He sought out bartenders, lawyers, and men who sold expensive cars or clothing. He wanted people who were clean-cut and intelligent and had no criminal records or associations. He dealt with these men anonymously, at times and places of his selection, and when he met with them he wore wigs and dark glasses and drove cars rented under false names.

By the end of the first year Wingo had five associates buying twenty kilos a month and the question was what to do with the millions in cash that were pouring in. He turned for assistance to his father, who was prospering in the Tyson's Corner real estate boom.

His father knew bankers who asked no questions about large cash deposits, so long as certain commissions changed hands. Wingo & Wingo Realty, via various dummy corporations, soon owned several of the biggest hotels and apartment complexes in Fairfax County.

As his wealth multiplied, Wingo was increasingly anxious to quit the drug business, although that was a delicate matter, since one did not simply walk away from Hector Ugarte and his associates. In truth, Wingo wanted out of real estate, too, because it bored him.

His new dream, the new frontier for his relentless ambitions, was politics. He had kept in touch with his friends from the Carter campaign. Richmond Morris was now a presidential adviser, and Lita Howe graced the White House policy planning staff. Wingo invited them to lunch at Sans Souci, a fashionable restaurant near the White House, treated them to a lavish meal, and in parting he gave each of them an ounce of the finest cocaine.

The festive lunches at Sans Souci became a monthly event. Rich and Lita were the only people Wingo gave cocaine who knew his real name, but, like his father fifteen years before, he assumed that only good could flow from having friends at the White House.

Rich Morris, to show his gratitude, had Wingo appointed to something called the President's Council on Economic Progress, which won him a free lunch at the White House and a chance to be photographed with the President.

That sort of publicity, plus Wingo's generous campaign contributions, marked him as a comer in Virginia politics. He had learned from Richmond Morris that old-style politics, where you worked your way up the ladder from local to state to national office, was dead. In modern politics, if you had enough money for television, you started at the top. Wingo had the money, and his dream was to await the proper moment, then run for office as a dynamic young northern Virginia businessman.

In the meantime, he had work to do.

Wingo realized that in his business he might have to kill. The issue was not moral but logistical: what was the safest way to dispose of a problem? You could hire people to kill for you, but they were by definition not people you could trust.

In time a problem arose with one of his distributors, a Porsche salesman named Robbins. A disgruntled girlfriend turned him in, and Robbins faced a long term in prison.

Robbins didn't know Wingo's name, and had only seen him at night, when Wingo was disguised. Still, it remained possible that Robbins could somehow identify him.

Wingo's first move was to send Robbins $100,000 cash with a note saying: "For your defense fund—Brad." Brad was the name the car salesman knew him by. Wingo then went to France for a month.

When he returned, several bartenders told him that undercover agents had been asking around about a dealer named Brad. At that point Wingo changed his plan.

Robbins was free on bond, living in a condo in McLean. Wingo rented an apartment nearby and observed the car salesman's habits, which included daily jogs along the C&O Canal. When Wingo was sure that Robbins was not being protected, he followed him one evening.

Wingo kept in shape through Nautilus and karate classes. He also belonged to a gun club and went to the range weekly, but gunplay was not appropriate here. Rather, he jogged toward Robbins in the dusk, raised a hand in greeting, then with one expert burst of energy broke the salesman's neck.

By the time Ronald Reagan became President, Wingo had settled into a routine. He made a run to Colombia every other month, and his distributors moved more than a hundred kilos a month. His real estate empire was worth tens of millions, and he wanted out of the drug business; the problem continued to be his friends in Colombia. He knew their minds. Active, he was useful to them; retired, he was a potential problem, better off dead.

Wingo was menaced by the DEA on the one hand and the cartel on the other; for the first time he began using his product to excess. He advanced from snorting to the more violent pleasures of free-basing. In the short run, at least, he felt invulnerable.

Wingo soon made friends in the Reagan administration. The younger ones were as partial to his gifts as their Carter counterparts. He also kept in touch with Lita, who had gone to work for a prominent senator. Soon Wingo was supplying her with two grams a week, which she and the senator consumed during all-night parties in her Watergate apartment. It seemed to Wingo that the legalization of cocaine was inevitable, since everyone he knew in government was using it.

One evening Wingo met one of his distributors, Broussard, the manager of a posh Italian clothing shop, for their monthly exchange of money and drugs.

"There's this guy been buying from me," Broussard said. "Hip-looking guy, nice hair, dresses good. He wants to meet my source."

"Forget it." Wingo did not deal with strangers.

"Look, Seth . . . "—Seth was the name Broussard knew him by—"the thing is, this guy makes me nervous. Keeps asking questions. Like, did I know a dealer named Brad? You suppose he could be a cop?" Broussard asked.

"He wants to meet me?"

"Yeah, exactly, to deal with you directly."

"Then we'll meet," Wingo said.

He told Broussard to bring the guy to the Stoddert School playground in Glover Park the next afternoon at four.

But the next day at four Wingo was in an apartment across from the school, one of several apartments he kept in the area. He had with him a high-powered rifle.

When Broussard arrived, there was an immediate hitch. Not one guy but two were with him. One early twenties, one mid-thirties, both bejeaned and bearded; they looked like your basic Mutt and Jeff cop team. A set-up. The question about Brad had been the tip-off; they were still looking for the Porsche salesman's supplier. Either the DEA was about to bust Broussard or they already had. Wingo was angry at Broussard, angry at these DEA bastards, angry at all these idiots who were trying to screw up his life.

Wingo might have acted differently if he had not been free-basing for three months. He might simply have walked away and dealt with Broussard later. But the drugs had taken their toll. He was impatient, angry, paranoid. He wanted to lash out, to punish his enemies, to crush them.

Wingo shot the older cop first, then the younger, then Broussard. They crumpled, one, two, three, and then all hell broke loose. Men with guns were running in all directions. Wingo slipped down the stairs and drove away without incident.

The slaughter of two DEA agents in broad daylight caused a great outcry. Wingo flew to the Bahamas for a few days to think things over. But all he could think was *Fuck these cowboys. Fuck the government.* They'd better understand that the game was serious, that cowboys could still die with their boots on.

Such was Dwight Wingo's fury when Mickey McGee arrived in Washington to put people like him in jail.

7.

Billy nash returned from a week in London fired up about his long-discussed theater project.

"I went to the theater every night," he told Jessica. "I saw a sensational *Man and Superman*. A *Guys and Dolls* that knocked me out. The new Tom Stoppard. And I kept thinking, Why do I have to go to London or New York for this? Why can't Fort Worth have a first-class professional theater? The money's there, if we just shake the tree!"

Jessica encouraged him, and not only because she loved the theater. Billy had been traveling more than she liked, both on business and to his various philanthropic projects. There was Homes for the Homeless in South Texas; CUP, the Center for Universal Peace, in Geneva; and WISH, the World Institute for Spiritual Healing, near Taos. There had been chaos in Taos since a police raid revealed that the WISH staff had made mescaline central to their spiritual journey.

Jessica saw the theater as a project that would keep him closer to home. As they talked, a glorious vision sprang up before their eyes: the gem of a theater, the brilliant opening night, the respectful notices in the *New York Times*.

Billy invited two dozen of their friends over for drinks and a sumptuous buffet, then he outlined his hopes for a world-class professional theater in Fort Worth. It was, for Jessica, a fascinating and sometimes disturbing evening. Big money was being discussed, and prestige and culture and community image too; for the first time she saw some of the egos and animosities that lurked beneath the smooth surface of their little world.

Billy began by saying that to launch the theater he envisioned would cost around $25 million, and that he and Jessica (he was kind enough to add) were donating an initial $10 million.

Then the free-for-all began.

Birdie Phelps, the woman with the jet-lagged maid whom Jessica had met her first night in town, wanted to know if this theater would lean, as she put it, toward "*Hamlet* or the Three Stooges." She also questioned the need for another theater in town, and Billy patiently explained that he was talking about first-rate professional actors, of the level you'd see on Broadway. "Professionals, like the Cowboys or the Rangers," he added, to make the point perfectly clear.

There were more conflicts. A gay interior designer took umbrage when Birdie spoke scornfully of Tennessee Williams's plays. A liberal lawyer wondered aloud why there weren't any blacks at the meeting.

But Billy's biggest critic was a lawyer named Carson Bragg, the husband of Daisy Bragg, the ex-girlfriend of Billy's who'd questioned the wages Jessica paid her maid. Billy and Carson had clashed before, over preservation and other local issues. The Braggs saw Billy as a rival to Carson's political ambitions, and liked to paint him as a radical who was using the Nash fortune to bankroll effete causes.

Carson questioned whether the time was ripe for a new theater, with the Texas economy in shambles. Billy argued passionately that there was no better time to build the theater, that they would be showing the world that cultural growth went on in Texas despite the economic cycles.

Then Carson questioned Billy until he admitted that he hoped to see the theater named for his mother's uncle, Billy Ringer.

Carson seized on the admission. "With all due respect, I wonder if that's the sort of image we'd want to project. As I recall, Wildcat Billy drank like a fish, spent some time in jail, and was broke for twenty years before he brought in that Louisiana field."

Billy's face reddened. Jessica feared he would explode. But Myra Fontaine spoke up before he could.

"I might comment on that," she drawled. The sad-eyed heiress was sitting on a cushion in the corner, under a Matisse, nursing a Scotch. "My father was an oilman, and as most of you know, our relationship left much to be desired. But I'll say this—if it wasn't for men like my father and Billy Ringer, who fought and bled to find oil, some of us who are driving Porsches and dripping pearls wouldn't have a pot to pee in."

Kay broke the tension by drily announcing, "Billy, put us down for a million."

People cheered, and Myra Fontaine quickly added, "Me, too. That's providing I get to play Lady Macbeth."

"Fantastic," Billy said, genuinely moved. Jessica thought Carson had blundered, that his attack on Billy Ringer had tipped the balance Billy's way.

Birdie Phelps, for all her doubts, pledged a half million, and an elderly oilman named Mosley did the same. Billy called the meeting to a halt soon after, glad to quit when he was ahead.

After the guests had left, Jessica and Billy unwound with a drink in the study. Jessica was furious at Carson Bragg, but Billy would hear none of it. "It was a great meeting," he insisted. "You have fights, you spill some blood, but you move ahead."

Jessica was still mad at his critics, but she had to admit that, any way you looked at it, $3 million was a good night's work.

While Billy Nash battled to bring the city a professional theater, his brother Sonny quite effortlessly became a movie mogul.

He had not intended to. Sonny bought Ultima, the faltering Anglo-German conglomerate, primarily for its Alaskan oil reserves and Colombian emerald mines, only to discover that he had also bought Excelsior, America's second-oldest and third-largest film company. Curious, he scheduled a trip to Los Angeles, where he was greeted as a conquering hero.

Sonny had no great interest in movies. He had no great interest in anything that required him to remain silent for two hours. His favorite films were *The Texas Chainsaw Massacre*, *A Fistful of Dollars*, and John Wayne's *The Alamo*.

Still, it was Sonny's new Hollywood toy that brought him to Billy's office one bleak March day. Out the window, far below them, the frozen Texas landscape seemed to stretch on forever.

"How's it going, baby brother?" Sonny wore jeans, boots, a cowboy shirt, and a tweed jacket.

Billy looked up from a report on toxic wastes; visits from Sonny were infrequent enough to unnerve him.

"Okay, I guess. Melissa's starting to walk."

"That's when your troubles begin. Once a woman's mobile, there's no stoppin' her. How's your money-grubbin' comin'?"

"Slow," Billy admitted. "We're four million short. People I'd hoped would give a hundred are giving fifty or twenty-five. And the corporations have really wimped out."

He picked his words carefully. Sonny had not yet contributed to the theater, although he expressed a certain sardonic interest in its progress.

"You could kick in another four and quit all this fiddle-fartin' around."

"I won't do it," Billy said stubbornly. "If the community wants this theater, the community has to support it."

"Since you've already kicked in ten, your position ain't one of perfect logic," Sonny said. "Look, I know how you can raise some money."

"Great. How?"

"You know about this movie studio I bought?"

"A little."

"A fuckin' madhouse. Some of the babes are prime, but the so-called executives, what a bunch of fruitcakes. And they're saying, 'Oh, Mr. Nash, for just forty million dollars I can make this perfectly *divine* epic about Liberace and his cocker spaniel.' You wouldn't *believe* the shit. The only reason I go out there is to party. You ever meet Beatty? I never seen a man who looked so pussy-whipped. I shoulda been a fuckin' actor, I'm better-lookin' than those clowns."

"You couldn't take the cut in pay, Sonny."

"True. Anyway, I told Phil Kingslea I'd give him ten thousand a month to go out and read scripts. I trust him more than the fruitcakes and anyway it'll get him unstuck from Kay."

"What do you mean?"

"What do you think I mean? Everybody in town knows he's banging Kay except that brain-dead brother of ours. Not that I blame her. Can you imagine fuckin' Mark? Jesus, it'd be like fuckin' a seal."

"Sonny, I have lost the thread."

"The thread is, I own this studio, and all these movie types are always saying how they just *adore* Texas, so why don't we use 'em to raise money? Have us a big wing-ding where the locals rub elbows with the stars. People eat that shit up. Whatta you think?"

Billy gazed at his brother in wonder. "Sonny, I love it."

Billy's goal was a hundred couples at ten thousand each—a million dollars, minus expenses. But for that kind of money, it had to be the party of the year—"The Weekend of the Stars," they called it.

Sonny volunteered his castle, arranged for the world premiere of a new Charles Bronson movie, and summoned a veritable Milky Way of stars for a June weekend in Cowtown.

And the brightest of the stars, in Billy's eyes, was April Flynn.

She was a precocious sixteen, featured in her first movie, a star in her second, one of those child-women like Elizabeth Taylor or Jodie Foster who comes along once in a generation. April was thin and radiant, with a wistful innocence few men could resist.

And here was April Flynn, walking along the battlements of Sonny's castle, listening politely to Sonny's monologue, as her mother and Billy followed behind.

"See, honey, you can see my skyscraper from here—it's that big bugger, the biggest one, sticking up there."

"Fabulous," April said breathlessly.

"That's my boat down at the dock," he continued. "You stick around, we'll do some waterskiin'."

"I'd love it."

"Darling, have you told Mr. Nash about *The Second Smile?*" asked April's mother, Doris Flynn.

"Oh, yes, Mummy," April said.

The Second Smile was a script about a teenage girl dying of cancer, and her love for the young doctor treating her. Philip Kingslea believed it could win April an Oscar.

"I'm thinkin' hard about that 'un, Miss Doris," Sonny told her. He wore a shimmering silver-gray suit and a mogul's canny, narrow-eyed expression. "I reckon the question is if April oughta do something more upbeat."

"Oh, look at the gulls!" April said, and pointed to the birds circling the lake.

The graceful motion of her arm left Billy breathless.

She turned to him. "All I want, as an actress, is to be as natural as those gulls. To float, to be perfectly myself, and never intellectualize."

"Honey, you're prettier'n any old bird," Sonny said.

"Your daughter is very special," Billy told Doris Flynn.

"She possesses a rare innocence," she replied. "I've tried to nurture it. No boys, no television, or violent movies, none of that. Just acting lessons, voice lessons, dance lessons—I've deliberately sheltered her. Later, when she's a woman, she'll rely on art, but for now she has magic. I hope your brother understands that."

Billy did not reply; Sonny understood what he wanted to understand.

April turned back to them. "Mummy, Mr. Nash has the most wonderful idea."

"Call me Sonny, sugar."

She smiled shyly. "You tell them, Sonny."

"April was tellin' me she studied Shakespeare, and I had this flash—she ought to do Juliet."

April's mother peered at him suspiciously. "Do you mean a film version, Mr. Nash?"

Sonny winked slyly. "Nope. See, my baby brother here is trying to start a highbrow theater, but he's having trouble with his money-raising, this being a lowbrow neck of the woods. But suppose your grand opening was gonna be this little lady doin' Juliet. Wouldn't that sell some tickets, Billy?"

Billy was stunned. "It would be sensational, if it's possible," he said.

"That's what I do—I make things possible," Sonny said. "When's your theater gonna be ready?"

"A year from now, I hope."

"Okay, so she does this cancer thing, then something upbeat, and then she does Juliet. How's that sound, honey?"

"Like a dream come true," April said, and hugged him impulsively.

Gulls soared above the lake. Sonny marched on, puffed up with pleasure.

How he loves playing God, Billy thought. But this time he couldn't argue.

8.

THE SENATOR WAS OUT OF CONTROL.

Everyone knew that, including the good people of his home state, who kept returning him to office nonetheless.

The senator was a genial man and a champion of noble causes. The problem was that in middle age he had developed a fondness for illegal drugs and teenage girls that worried even his most stalwart aides. First marijuana, then cocaine, used at parties with an endless succession of young women he would bed once and never see again.

The senator behaved as if he were above the law, and indeed his life's experience supported that belief. Then one day the Attorney General of the United States came to call.

The senator thought the Attorney General was a moron, and had said as much in an effort to block his nomination. The Attorney General, for his part, considered the senator a degenerate and a security risk. More immediately, the senator, by virtue of his chairmanship of the Legal Affairs Committee, had blocked many of the new administration's judicial nominations.

Indeed, the senator assumed the Attorney General was coming in supplication, to plead for confirmation of the latest batch of nominees.

But supplication was not on the Attorney General's agenda.

"Well, Mr. Attorney General, to what do I owe this unexpected honor?" the senator asked grandly.

The Attorney General settled into the chair across from the senator's desk. He noted Bernie Fiegleman, the senator's top aide, lurking in the shadows across the room.

"Senator," the Attorney General replied. "One of us is going to have a news conference this afternoon."

He smiled nastily, the senator frowned, and Bernie Fiegleman sucked at a bloody hangnail. He was the latest in a line of clever young men who thought he could calm the senator and make him President.

"How is that, Mr. Attorney General?"

"If I have a news conference, it will be to announce your pending indictment on a variety of drug-related charges."

The senator's pink face flared tomato red. Bernie Fiegleman drifted into view.

"Those charges," the Attorney General continued, "would be based on a four-month investigation by the DEA. I have highlights here."

He began piling papers on the senator's desk.

"These are affidavits from young women. And here are pictures you may find interesting."

The senator was in boxer shorts. One of the girls was snorting through a straw.

"The girl with the tattoo is only fifteen, which adds an additional charge," the Attorney General noted.

"You incompetent oaf," the senator bellowed.

"Be quiet," said Bernie Fiegleman. "What are the options, Mr. Attorney General?"

"The other news conference I mentioned. The one where the senator announces his resignation as chairman of Legal Affairs."

It made perfect sense. If the senator resigned, his successor would be far more friendly to the administration's judicial nominations. If he didn't resign, the combination of cocaine and teen sex might finally be too much for his home state voters to swallow.

"The Education Committee is available," Bernie said. "We could work a switch."

"The nation would clearly benefit from the senator's leadership in education," the Attorney General said.

"If he resigns, there will be no charges and no leaks?" Bernie demanded.

"Now just a damn minute," the senator thundered.

"You have no choice," Bernie said.

"That's correct," the Attorney General said. "Except that the DEA has one requirement."

"Which is?"

"The director is outside. He can speak for himself."

The DEA director glared at the senator as he might have at Al Capone.

"As I told the Attorney General," he said, "whatever political arrangements you people work out is not my affair. But we have one requirement in a case like this."

"Which is?" Bernie said again.

"We want to know where the defendant secured the drugs."

"Mother of God," the senator sighed. "Send them to Lita. I got all my coke from her."

Lita Howe was the daughter of a Miami cop, a cheerleader in her day, but at some point she realized she was smarter than the people around her. She went to law school when women were first going to law school, and it was there that she developed a taste for cocaine.

She went into practice for herself and became a player in local politics. When Jimmy Carter began campaigning in Florida, early in 1975, she picked him for a winner and rode his bandwagon all the way to the White House.

Ah, the White House, *there* was a blast. If the Georgians trusted

158

you, you had such incredible power. And yet, almost from the start, they saw it going down the tube. They blamed the President, blamed the media, blamed each other—it didn't matter, their glorious power was slipping away. At Lita's level, they sought consolation in sex, drugs, and rock-'n'-roll. One of the bright spots of the four years was good old Dee Wingo with his endless supply of coke. And he never asked for anything. Jesus, they'd have given him Amy's tree house and the Pentagon, but he just kept buying lunch at Sans Souci and bearing gifts of sanity powder.

In the end, the Gipper routed the Peanut Man and they were all out on the street. At Lita's level, ex-Carter hotshots were just about unemployable. Big business didn't want them, the party regulars didn't want them, nobody wanted them. A dozen of them quickly advanced from the White House to the unemployment lines. They met twice a month when they went to pick up their checks, then they'd go have a hot dog for lunch. One day the girl selling the hot dogs looked familiar, and it turned out she'd been in Rosalynn's press office.

Then Lita got lucky. She met the senator at a party. He liked her looks and he liked her even more when she confessed she had a little coke in her purse. They partied for a few nights, then he insisted she come to work for him.

He expected her to supply him with coke, so she called her old friend Dee Wingo. He took her to lunch the next day, told her of his soaring political ambitions, and gave her four grams of coke. He loved thinking that she gave him a line to a powerful senator.

Lita handled women's issues for the senator. It was a good job, and there was always the fantasy that he'd make it to the White House, before they were all too old to care, but the way he kept screwing around that didn't look likely. She slept with him once or twice a month, but he preferred women who were a lot younger and dumber than Lita.

When the two DEA agents came, she thought they wanted to discuss policy. But when they started reading her her Miranda rights, she knew the party was over.

"Ms. Howe, we have information that you've been providing the senator with cocaine," one of them said. "It'll be easier for everybody if you'll tell us your source of supply."

Lita was cool; she was, after all, a lawyer. "What's your source of information?" she asked.

"The senator's own statement."

Suddenly his resignation from Legal Affairs made sense. A great battle was in progress, and she was being raped in a distant corner of the battlefield; it was pointless to resist.

"I've had one source for several years," she said. "A real estate man named Dwight Wingo."

"We'll want you to help us locate him," the other one said.

"He won't be hard to find," Lita said bitterly. "He thinks he's running for governor."

"Mick, what're you coverin'?"

"My ass, mainly."

"I got one for you."

"Shoot."

Lon Tate looked bigger and angrier than ever, but weary, too, after months on the Stoddert School investigation. She thought it was strange how people changed. Back in training, he'd been an ebony god; now he was another burned-out cop, driven half mad by the ubiquity of evil.

"You know about the senator?" Tate asked her.

"Hey, I gave 'em the girl who gave 'em the senator, then the bastards boxed me out."

"It's hush-hush. Heavy political shit. He'd been doing a lot of coke. Got it from a gal in his office. And she said she got it from this real estate dude in Tyson's Corner. But when we wanted to wire her, the bitch dug in her heels."

"Tell me more."

"The cat's name is Wingo, Dwight Wingo."

"Like Wingo Starr?"

"Calls himself Dee. Was in 'Nam. Now he's in real estate with his father. Dabbles in politics."

160

"And coke too?"

"Probably he's just some jerkoff who likes to impress the girls. But what's his source? The thing is, Wingo hangs out in Tyson's Corner, and we think the guy we're looking for is out there. So maybe they plug in."

"So what's the drill?"

"He's single. Likes to hustle the ladies. We figure he'd be a fool for a hot little number like you."

"Oh crap, Lon! I don't want to be your bait for this turkey."

"Duty calls, sweetpants. Put on your red dress and your high-heel sneakers and we'll nail this sucker!"

"Wingo Starr," Mickey grumbled.

9.

SONNY NASH HAD MET EVERY AMERICAN PRESIDENT SINCE LYN-
don Johnson and he thought them all fools. Not fools of equal
magnitude, of course. Ford and Carter had been hopeless, but he'd
had a certain respect for LBJ's toughness and rough charm.

Nixon had been Sonny's favorite President. At least until he
wimped out on Watergate—why didn't he *burn* the fucking tapes?—
he'd been one mean mother. He remembered something Nixon said,
when he was threatening to bomb Hanoi back to the Stone Age:
"Always make the other guy think you're crazy enough to do any
damn thing."

Such was Sonny's state of mind as he planned the destruction of
his former father-in-law, Walter Lamont, a revenge he had intended
since the night Lamont insulted him on the rooftop at Caravan of
Dreams. Sonny planned carefully; then one day he struck.

The next morning his brother Billy rushed into his office waving
the *Star-Telegram*.

"Dammit, Sonny, what is this?" Billy demanded.

162

"Read what it says," Sonny said. " 'Nash International Makes Hostile Bid for Lamont & Co.' It's God's own truth. Pretty soon we'll have us a new business and Walter Lamont will be out on his skinny old ass."

"Why wasn't I told about this?"

"I don't recollect you asking."

"Don't give me that. I'm the vice president of this company."

"Yeah, vice president in charge of high-mindedness and lost puppies. This is business, kiddo."

"It's a personal vendetta against one of the finest men in Fort Worth. A friend of our family. The grandfather of your son, for Christ's sake!"

"It's business," Sonny repeated. "Which happens to be directed at a sanctimonious old fart who once tried to take me to court for raping my own damn wife. What goes around comes around, baby brother. This time Walter Lamont gets his."

Billy paced the office in frustration. There were pictures of Sonny and politicians, Sonny and movie stars, Sonny on horseback.

"He'll fight back, you know."

Sonny flashed a killer smile. "I sure hope so."

"I have a say in what this company does. I don't approve of this."

"Read the by-laws. I can do any damn thing I want as long as one other principal approves. And guess what? Mark approves."

"You may not even make money in this market."

"Listen, as long as I don't tell you how to save the whales, don't you tell me how to make money. Lamont's undervalued. I can sell the oil reserves alone and get back what I'm paying."

"The by-laws say all three of us have to agree to any change of company policy."

"So?"

"So a vindictive personal assault on an old friend, that will irreparably harm NI's reputation, is a change in policy."

"Bullshit. Making money is our policy. If I was giving money away, that'd be a change in policy. That's why I'm running this company and not you."

"I can challenge this, Sonny."

Sonny bit off the end of a cigar and spit it toward his wastebasket. "Don't make me laugh," he said.

Lily Nash was not surprised to receive an angry visit from her son Billy that afternoon. In theory, she had the power to veto any company decision her sons made. But it was a power she had never exercised. Fifteen years earlier Lily had made a stunning discovery: her son Sonny loved to make money as much as she loved to spend it. She loved a week or two of unbridled luxury at Claridge's or the Gritti Palace or the Hôtel du Cap. She loved the beaches at Little Dix and Windermere Island and Cancun. She loved shopping at Baccarat and Cartier and Israel Sack and Neiman's and Louis Vuitton and Gump's and Jordan Marsh and I. Magnin. She loved, as the song said, an occasional man. After half a lifetime of unhappiness and drudgery, it had been a revelation to discover the pleasures the world offered to the very rich.

And Sonny made it possible.

When Lily first inherited Billy Ringer's fortune, she faced a terrifying question: Who could she trust? Texas was filled with lawyers and bankers and high-grade hustlers who promised to make her vast fortune even vaster. She tried one, then another, very respectable men, but it always seemed (insofar as she could decipher the figures they put before her) that whatever profits they made were eaten up by their fees, commissions, and endless expenses.

One year her banker-adviser confessed to a loss of $4 million—he blamed it on the market, oil prices, the government, everything but his own insufferable arrogance. It was a terrifying moment. If the fool could lose $4 million, why not $40 million, why not all of it? Lily, desperate, fired him and assumed day-to-day control over her empire. Within two months she was close to a breakdown.

That was when Sonny came to her. "I'm gonna bail you out, little lady," he said, to her vast relief.

Sonny had majored in math at Rice, then spent a year at the Stanford Business School. On his way back from California he'd stopped in Las Vegas and won $40,000 at roulette. He spent half of it for a Ferrari 250 GTO, and upon arriving in Fort Worth invested the other half in oil leases that soon made him a millionaire. It was then, rich in his own right, that he came to the rescue of his mother.

In the next dozen years, Lily watched in awe as Sonny parlayed her hundred million into billions. He had an astonishing ability to see over the horizon. Gold, natural gas, computers, oil tankers, cable TV, shopping malls, pharmaceuticals, electronics—he bought each at the perfect moment, reaped a golden harvest, then moved on.

Sonny's enemies called him ruthless. Lily called him single-minded. She knew well enough that he'd always had a mean streak. When he was twelve, neighbors charged that he'd doused their cat in gasoline and set the poor creature aflame. A few years later, when he started to drive, black leaders in Lake Como protested that Sonny and his friends had been speeding through their community throwing cherry bombs at innocent pedestrians.

Lily did not doubt that Sonny had been guilty on both counts. Perhaps it was a rationalization, but Lily liked to think that Sonny's cruel side was in part a reflection of the city he had grown up in. Fort Worth was a violent place; it always had been and, as far as anyone could see, always would be. It had been a military outpost first, put there to defend against marauding Indians, and after that a cattle town with more than its share of legendary brawls, bars, outlaws, and shootouts. From Butch Cassidy and the Sundance Kid to Bonnie and Clyde and Machine Gun Kelly, Fort Worth had tolerated, even welcomed, desperados. Lily could remember, about the time her sons were born, an outbreak of gang warfare when local gamblers kept putting bombs in each other's cars.

It was a town where schoolboys settled disputes with their fists and their elders often settled them with guns. Lily thought that somehow the social Darwinism that Sonny had learned in the playground, combined with stray genes from his father and her uncle Wildcat Billy, had led to the economic Darwinism that he practiced so brilliantly as an adult.

Not long after Lily withdrew from the day-to-day management of her fortune, her two younger sons stepped forward to claim their roles in Nash International.

Mark came first, and was content to follow in Sonny's wake, bringing order to his brother's disorderly deals, basking in reflected glory. It helped that Mark was terrified of Sonny, who throughout their childhood had given him a good thrashing at least once a month.

Billy was a harder case. At first he'd wanted no part of the family fortune. He had a trust fund and he was content to spend his twenties living the counterculture life, drawing his income and giving most of it away.

In time, however, Billy could not ignore the fortune Sonny was compiling, so he cut his hair, bought a suit, and reported for duty at Nash International.

Lily and her sons negotiated a simple agreement whereby profits were split four ways and power three ways. A majority of two brothers could make decisions. Lily in theory could overturn anything her sons chose to do, but Lily had read *King Lear* and did not intend to reclaim surrendered powers. At least not while profits continued to soar.

Billy was at first assigned to community relations and advertising. As time went on, he became president of the Nash Foundation and was content giving twenty-odd million dollars a year to worthy causes.

But it began to gnaw at him that while he was playing with millions, Sonny was playing with billions. He was trying to do good with the foundation, but Sonny wielded the bulk of the family fortune with the social conscience of a rattlesnake.

There had been, for one example, alarming reports about the pollution that one of their chemical plants was causing in a West Texas town, but Sonny bluntly rejected what the health officials were saying.

The more Billy regarded Sonny's power, the more he resented it. His personal projects, his marriage, and the Ringer Theater had all distracted him, but now his brother's assault on Walter Lamont rekindled his passion for change.

"Mother, it's an outrage," he told Lily that afternoon.

"I agree."

"Walter is our friend."

"I realize that."

Walter Lamont was, in fact, a good deal more than a friend. He had been Lily's lover and very nearly Billy's stepfather, in the first years of her freedom, until she concluded that she didn't want to break up his marriage and, in any event, he was too old for her.

"All it would take would be one phone call from you, and Sonny would pull back."

"Sonny would be humiliated."

"Which would be good for him."

"Or it might destroy him. For all his strength, Sonny is delicately balanced. If his ego was severely bruised, he might never recover."

Delicately balanced. It was, Billy thought, a generous way to describe the volcanic rage that seethed beneath Sonny's cool facade. Jack the Ripper had no doubt been delicately balanced.

"He needs restraints, Mother."

"He's made us very rich. I have to give him his head."

"If he destroys Walter Lamont we'll all look like thugs. Predators."

"No, that's not how most people will see it. They'll say that when Walter took his company public, he knew this could happen. They'll say he was a fool to take Sonny into court six years ago. And they'll note how much money Walter will make from the buyout."

"But we're not most people, Mother. We're moral, decent people, leaders in this community, and this is not how the company that bears our name should operate."

"I agree. But I'm not going to overrule Sonny. The Lamont buyout is something I must give Sonny in return for all he's given me—and you, too."

"I'm disgusted."

"Very well, be disgusted. But if I overruled Sonny he might very well go off on his own. And I'd be back where I started, with no one to manage my money."

"You'd have me and Mark."

"Both of whom I love dearly, but neither of whom I'd care to entrust with a billion dollars. I might not sleep quite so well."

"You could invest it prudently and live happily ever after."

"Perhaps that's the point, my dear. It's not only that Sonny keeps doubling my money. It's that he makes life so interesting. The older I become, the more his moneymaking is the central drama in my life. Seeing money grow, seeing millions turn into billions, is the ultimate thrill."

"Mother, please, don't be cynical."

"I'm not cynical, Billy. I'm addicted. Perhaps you will be too, someday, when you're older. I'm addicted and Sonny feeds my addiction. How could I let him go? More tea?"

Billy took his frustrations to Jessica that night.

"It's disgraceful," he declared.

"What will happen?"

"What will happen? Walter will try to raise money to outbid Sonny. He'll appeal to the SEC. Standard anti-takeover tactics. But Sonny will grind him down. If Walter was smart he'd take the money and run, but he's too proud."

"You make it sound so brutal."

"It is. That's the point. Walter will never know what hit him. All the rules have changed, with these damned junk bonds and leveraged buyouts. Someone like Sonny, with unlimited capital, is king of the jungle."

"What are you going to do?"

"I want to challenge Sonny. More and more what he does repels me."

"He makes money. Is that so bad?"

"The way he *does it* is bad! Dammit, can't you see that?"

Jessica took his hand. "Billy, please." She hated to see him upset, and she didn't think confronting Sonny was the answer to anything.

He stared moodily into the treetops. They were having drinks on their deck, high above the river valley. It was a sweet, dogwood-scented May evening, and she wanted them to enjoy it.

"You haven't asked about my day," she said.

He laughed, made himself relax. "Okay, how was your day?"

"Maddening. First the architecture committee met. Total chaos. People bringing sketches they'd done on cocktail napkins, literally. When I said our theater should be as excellent as the Kimbell, Boots Ferguson said the Kimbell looks like a Quonset hut. I almost screamed."

"It's just his Aggie sense of humor."

"Then, this afternoon, the search committee met. If anything, it was even worse. We're down to two candidates for artistic director. A middle-aged man who's solid but unexciting and a young man who's clearly brilliant but possibly controversial."

"How controversial?"

"Well, some of his concepts have been pretty avant-garde. And I think he's gay."

"You think?"

"Pending further evidence, that's my best guess."

"The older man, he's competent?"

"Solid as a rock."

"He's your man."

"He'd be predictable. The younger man would be exciting."

"Jessica, believe me, the first artistic director of this theater should not be gay."

"Not even if he's brilliant?"

"I know this city. Above all, you have to be respectable. You could stage the most brilliant plays in America and what people would talk about was that your director was living with another guy."

"It's not fair."

"We need money, respect, and goodwill. We don't need gossip. Later, when the theater is established, we can take chances."

"It's so crazy," she said. "You're the rebel, but you're so conservative on this."

169

He bristled, for the second time that evening. "It's easy to be far out if you're putting on a show in somebody's basement. I'm trying to start one of the finest regional theaters in America."

Jessica should have bit her tongue, but she was tired and annoyed.

"First-rate theaters aren't built on compromise," she declared. She immediately regretted her words—so prim, so holier-than-thou, so inadequate to the complexities that he understood far better than she.

It was Billy's turn to flare. "Well, thanks a million, Miss Perfection! Do you have any other words of wisdom for us? Anything else you'd like to get off your chest?"

She glared back at him. It was their first real argument, it was stupid, and it should be ended at once. But part of her was enjoying it.

"As a matter of fact there is something, if you can stand some constructive criticism."

"By all means," he said grimly.

"The other night, when we had the Coxes over, did you and R. T. really have to smoke a joint?"

"Oh God, is this my latest sin? I smoked a joint?"

"You don't have to shout."

"It is not heroin, Jessica. It is not LSD. It is not cocaine. It was one harmless little joint. I'm a grown man, and if I want . . . "

"That's the point. You're a grown man. This isn't the sixties anymore. I just don't see why you have to do something illegal in our home."

"The Westover Hills police are not going to drag me off to jail."

"Maybe not. But you're the one who talks about gossip and being respectable. Is this really something you need to do?"

"I'll take it under advisement," he grumbled, and they lapsed into an uneasy silence.

"Never go to sleep angry," the JP who married them had advised, and most often they followed his advice. Making love struck them both as the best possible end to the day. But this night their king-sized bed seemed as vast as a battlefield, and they stayed apart, each to his or her own troubled thoughts.

Jessica was sorry she'd snapped at him about the theater, but glad she'd confronted him on the marijuana. She was no fanatic—she'd smoked in college—but she didn't see why her daughter should be raised in a house where people sneaked off to smoke illegal weeds. Why couldn't he understand that?

Billy, for his part, was furious at Sonny, angry with his mother, and now mad at Jessica, too. Why? Because she hadn't seemed to understand the political realities about the theater? Because her barb about his "conservatism" had stung? Because she'd seemed to defend Sonny? Because he was taking out his frustrations with his family on her? He could not help thinking—although he knew it an unworthy thought—that he had given this woman everything, and she should show some appreciation instead of sniping at him about smoking a joint.

It was not that he did not love her. She was to him the most wondrous of women, radiant and gentle, beautiful inside and out. Then why did he feel this discontent? Billy guessed that in the tedium of day-to-day life—even their most blessed lives—it was impossible to maintain the intensity of first love. You had your frustrations and you snapped at whomever was most close at hand, however perfect she might be.

He wondered sometimes if any one woman could entirely satisfy him. He even questioned whether the concept of romantic love—upon which, for better or worse, he had based two marriages—was valid. "Modern marriage is for seven years," said a woman he knew. Was that rank cynicism? Or realism? People came together, took their pleasures, and drifted apart, an endless cycle of affection and farewell.

Sometimes, in his darkest moments, he questioned his capacity for love. During Billy's teens, his father had been half-mad, lusting for the Ringer fortune, drunken and brooding, and he had hated and feared him. As the youngest son, overshadowed by Sonny and fearful of him, he had learned to live by his wits.

The lesson of his childhood had been that you were on your own in this world. Love was a nice idea, but self-preservation was the reality. Billy could be charming, and he loved to please women, but he knew he had never given all of himself to any woman, not even to Jessica. Part of him held back, watchful and aloof, secure in his isolation.

He met many extraordinary women in his travels, and they made invitations, spoken and unspoken. He'd pursued no affairs since marrying Jessica, but he loved new women, the kaleidoscope of their minds and bodies, and he hated to think all that wonder and warmth was lost to him forever.

Billy thought himself an essentially moral man, and he was frustrated by his uncertainty. What harm would an occasional night of pleasure do, if it remained his secret? He loved Jessica, but he wasn't sure what that meant, and his ignorance maddened him. Billy, like many men, was torn between the joys of family and the joys a world of women offers. He dreamed of a life of perfection, and it galled him to think that somehow, in his marriage, he had achieved only happiness.

10.

MICKEY MCGEE AND RAFE KLAYMAN MOVED ABRUPTLY FROM friends to lovers. One night after dinner at the Tune Inn he'd walked her to her door, and the next thing she knew he spent the night. It was the best night of her life, and a few days later she moved in with him.

She'd never known anyone like Rafe. He was, to begin with, the toughest man she'd ever met. He'd been born and raised in a rough, raw mining town in West Virginia and grown up a fighter. He'd been a decorated Marine in Vietnam, then quit the Marines for the DEA when peacetime duty became too dull for him. He hated drugs and the people who dealt them, and was never happier than when he was busting some dealer.

For all his toughness he could be more tender, more loving than any other man she'd known. He'd had one marriage fail, he'd known war and violence, and he wanted their lives together to be an oasis of peace and love and sanity. He was small and squinty-eyed and balding, and not much of a talker, but no man had ever made her happier. No man she'd known before, Mickey believed, had been so truly a man.

She'd known some stinkers in her time, starting with that bastard Luther back at the Home. She'd fixed him, and there'd been a lot more she'd had to stand up to, one way or another. She'd found out in high school that guys wanted you to fit a mold, to be Barbie, smearing your face with lipstick and batting your false eyelashes and telling them how wonderful they were. Mickey had never played that game. Jeans and sweatshirts were more her style, and speaking her mind, and if some wiseguy called her names, she called him names right back. Most of them were bullies, picking on smaller people, and if you stood up to them they backed off.

She'd had boyfriends, but most men only wanted one thing and when they got that, they rolled over and snored. Even out of bed, they were mostly interested in drugs and booze and football and other women. She hadn't expected that she'd ever be serious about a guy again, then Rafe had come along.

He told her she was beautiful so often that she almost believed it. And he meant beautiful her way, in her jeans and sweatshirts, her hair shaggy, her face innocent of makeup. The funny thing was, she began to change, not because he asked it but because she wanted to please him. She bought some nice dresses to wear when they went out. She began to use makeup. She even went to a fancy "salon" on Connecticut Avenue and paid sixty bucks to have her hair styled and tinted, and when Rafe saw her his face lit up like Times Square.

Her happiness with Rafe made her less and less gung-ho about her work. Sometimes she wished she could bag the DEA and stay home and make babies. But that wasn't how it was. Rafe admired her because she did her job well, and, with half his salary going to his ex-wife for child support, he needed a woman who pulled her weight. Nor did she think that, with two teen-aged sons he rarely saw, and an all-consuming job, he wanted another child.

So she kept on with her job, and this new assignment, the real estate guy Dee Wingo who maybe was dealing on the side.

It wasn't that Wingo was so important, Lon Tate said. All their information so far was that he was a legitimate businessman who maybe liked to impress his friends. But he'd supplied the Howe woman, who'd supplied the senator, and because of that connection they had to nail down every corner, because their handling of the case might someday come under top-level scrutiny.

Wingo fancied himself a devil with the ladies, so the plan was for Mickey to come on to him as a rich, sexy young thing, to dazzle him until he came across with coke.

They worked out her new persona carefully. She was to be Michelle deCoursey, scion of an old Richmond family. Her parents, now deceased, had left her several million dollars. She was an interior designer, who wanted to resettle in Tyson's Corner and invest in real estate there. She'd go to Wingo for advice, and let nature take its course.

There was, in fact, a real-life Michelle deCoursey; if Wingo bothered to check, he would find that her story was true, except that the real Michelle had been living in France for three years.

Mickey liked her new role. She bought a new wardrobe, had her hair elegantly done, and fixed her face more artfully than ever before. "I wouldn't have recognized you," Rafe said when she left home that first morning. "You look like a movie star."

She kissed him primly. "Don't worry, it's just the same old me," she told him.

In truth, she loved having an excuse to be glamorous, to be the kind of woman she'd always resisted being. She thought a lot about her sister Jessie, who'd always been so ladylike, and she liked to think that this was how Jessie was today, wherever she was, a great lady.

Her first session with Wingo went like magic. His eyes lit up when she walked into his office, and within minutes he was offering her sherry and inviting her to lunch.

Wingo had bushy hair and a Savile Row tailor and he wasn't bad-looking if you liked Neanderthals. He wasn't stupid, Mickey thought, but he was certainly strange. He loved it when she babbled about her First Families of Virginia pedigree, and at lunch that first day he let drop that he "hoped to run for statewide office sometime very soon." He talked endlessly about how Jack Kennedy was his hero, and he was convinced he could be the new Kennedy.

They drove around and looked at some apartment buildings that afternoon—she'd said she had $2 million to invest—but he talked more about politics than real estate. He had no clear party affiliation, nor any particular interest in the issues of the day, only a vision of being adored by the cheering masses. Mickey began to wonder if drugs had inspired these visions of grandeur.

But that wasn't her problem. All she wanted him to do was to offer her a little coke, then their relationship would come to a screeching halt. He didn't mention drugs that first day, and she didn't press him. It might take two or three meetings before the moment arrived. Mickey didn't care. She was enjoying being glamorous. When she got home to Rafe that night, she'd show him just how much fun a movie star could be.

Even before Michelle deCoursey entered his life, Dee Wingo was near a turning point. Drugs were the dead hand of the past, threatening his future, and he'd persuaded Hector Ugarte to let him out. He had agreed to make one more flight, with all the profits going to the cartel. He was in effect paying several million dollars for his freedom, but it was better than a bullet in the head.

The shootings at the Stoddert School had brought him to his senses. That had been a crazed act, by a man doing too many drugs under too much pressure. It had brought down far more heat on him than he wanted to deal with. And yet his defenses had held. The DEA had turned northern Virginia inside out and found no link between the killer they sought and respectable Dwight Wingo.

Wingo felt reborn. Drug-free now, he saw the world clearly again, saw his future ahead, a smooth transition to the next phase of his plan. Elections were coming and he would run for lieutenant governor. It was a nothing job, but he could make it a stepping stone to the governor's mansion.

He was rich and respected, wooed by both parties as a candidate for office. As Wingo saw it, the only element missing was the right wife, his Jackie Kennedy, to dazzle the voters and ease his march to power.

From their first meeting, he'd thought Michelle might be the one. He could see her at his side at political rallies, could see her as the perfect hostess, could see her presiding over the governor's mansion.

He needed to know more about her, of course. Her money was for real; he'd checked that. But sometimes he sensed something mysterious behind that dazzling smile. Wingo didn't want surprises. He wanted a beautiful woman who would win votes, raise his kids, and not pry into how he lived his life. He wanted, in short, the perfect political wife, and Michelle deCoursey quickly became the leading contender for that honor.

"Is that one of your buildings?"

"You can see five of my buildings from here," Wingo boasted.

They were high above Tyson's Corner in Wingo's little Apache. The Beltway curved below them; all you could see were roads and parking lots crammed with cars, and ostentatious new hotels and office buildings. Wingo Country.

It was the third time she had seen him and he had not yet mentioned drugs. But the fact that he flew his own plane—she had not known that until this morning—had grabbed her attention fast. Being a pilot didn't make you a dealer, but it helped.

"When I was a boy, this was just a crossroads," he was telling her. The noontime sun sparkled on his gold Patek Philippe watch; the plane seemed to fly itself. "Some people named Tyson really did own the land where two roads crossed. Just a filling station and a corner store. But Washington kept growing. The Beltway came through. All those cornfields became gold mines."

"Where's the building you want me to buy?" she asked.

"There, across from the exit ramp, the one with the pool on top. Two million down, it pays for itself, dynamite tax benefits, and you live free in the penthouse."

"Super! Can I see it today?"

"Not today."

"Why not today?" she pouted.

"Because I have a surprise. How's your afternoon?"

She looked coy. "Flexible."

"I want to take you someplace special. I'll have us back before dark."

"Oh, I love surprises," Mickey cried.

Soon they were sailing south above the Blue Ridge, with the Shenandoah River twisting lazily off to the west. Mickey wasn't crazy about this detour, but Wingo was acting harmless enough. Soon he was telling her his life story.

"You see, Michelle, my background is very different from yours. You're an aristocrat, but my father grew up on a farm in Oklahoma. He went to law school after the war, on the GI Bill, and came to Washington. He did well in law for twenty years, but then he trusted some people he shouldn't have trusted and lost everything."

Mickey tried to look entranced.

"But my dad fought back, made a new career in real estate. All in all, this country has been good to us. That's why I want to go into politics, to give something back."

"Are you really going to run?"

"It's all but certain that I'll run for lieutenant governor next year. And that's just the beginning."

"It's so exciting," she enthused.

Soon they were over Charlottesville, circling the university and the great white dome of the Rotunda. "Mr. Jefferson is my inspiration," Wingo confessed. Then they flew south over thick green woods. Suddenly they were going down. Mickey gasped as he aimed them between two lines of trees, with only inches to spare, and brought them down in a long pasture.

She had learned something: Wingo might be a bullshit artist, but he had nerve, timing, and control; he could be more dangerous than he looked.

"Where are we?" she asked.

Wingo beamed. "In the eighteenth century."

He helped her down from the plane, then held her hand as he

led her through the woods. She hated his touch, and disliked being alone with him here.

They emerged suddenly from the woods, to gaze upon one of the grandest homes Mickey had ever seen: a graceful mansion, atop a gentle hill, adorned by a dome and four massive columns. As they admired it, two huge white dogs raced toward them, barking wildly.

Wingo silenced them with a word or two.

"Are we supposed to be here?" Mickey asked.

He laughed. "This is mine, Michelle. It's called Davenport. Mr. Jefferson's own architect designed it. I bought the place for a song. It was a crime how run down it had become. I'm restoring its original glory. And I want you to help me. Davenport needs a woman's touch."

"It's like a dream," Mickey said.

"Someday I'll live here," Wingo told her. "I'm looking for the right woman to share this with me, to be the mistress of Davenport."

He flashed his slickest smile. "Perhaps I've found her," he declared.

Mickey felt ill.

11.

W<small>ALTER LAMONT LIKED TO JOKE THAT HE</small>'<small>D LIVED LONG ENOUGH</small>
to see Fort Worth progress from the speakeasies of the 1920s to the
fern bars of the 1980s. "If you call that progress!" he would roar,
laughing heartily.

In truth, Walter loved Fort Worth in all its manifestations, from
the cowtown of yesteryear to the cosmopolitan city of today. For
more than a hundred years, the Lamonts had grown and prospered
with the city, and he was proud of their part in making it great.

He knew all about the drunken cowboys and Hell's Half Acre
and the gangsters and how the stockyards once stank—that was
yesterday's news. Today's news was that Fort Worth was the most
livable, progressive, arts-minded, prosperous city in Texas—maybe
in the nation.

People who had once laughed at Texas, and never heard of Fort
Worth, now came to marvel at the Kimbell and Carter museums,
the Water Gardens, the Fort Worth Ballet, the Japanese Gardens,
the Van Cliburn Piano Competition, the Texas Boys Choir, the

Colonial golf tournament, Casa Mañana, the annual rodeo and fat stock show—not to mention the economic wonders wrought by Carter, Richardson, Tandy, the Bass brothers, the Lamonts, and—yes—even the Nashes.

Friends had for years urged Walter to run for mayor, but he could never see the point. He could serve just as well behind the scenes, as the leader of a small band of businessmen who made key civic decisions. The two achievements Walter was most proud of were helping ease the way for peaceful school integration and masterminding the preservation of the stockyards and the Victorian mansions built by the cattle barons.

The Lamont family had built one of the first of those mansions, on Summit Street, high above the Trinity River. Then Walter's father had moved them to Rivercrest Drive in the 1930s, and there Walter lived today.

Walter had attended Choate and Princeton, but his only child, his daughter Felice, had gone to Arlington Heights High School and SMU. Walter had been making a statement: Texas could provide his daughter with as good an education as she could get "back East." And he had been right: Felice was as fine and cultivated a woman as any father could hope for.

He had only this regret: If he'd sent her away to school, perhaps, somehow, she'd have escaped the tragic mistake of eloping with Sonny Nash the night of her debut at the Assembly Ball.

He understood her decision. Sonny had been rich, handsome, dashing, and infinitely persuasive. How was a girl of twenty to know he was rotten to the core?

She had a fine son from the marriage, of course. Walter had studied Willie closely, and found blessedly little of his father in him. Now Felice was married a second time, to an eye surgeon named Mendelson, a decent, cultivated man—everything Sonny Nash was not.

Walter's one remaining regret was that Felice and her husband had no interest in managing his empire, and he had no son to inherit it. He sometimes dreamed of hanging on long enough to pass the reins to Willie, but the numbers weren't right.

For several years he'd been brushing away feelers from conglomerates that wanted to buy him out.

Now, out of nowhere, came the infuriating news that the man he despised most in the world proposed to buy his company against his will—to steal it, as far as Walter was concerned.

Walter Lamont had never imagined that such a thing could happen. As soon as he heard the news, he called for his lawyers. He didn't know the details yet, but he knew this: as long as breath was in him, he'd never surrender his life's work to Sonny Nash.

His lawyer and lifelong friend, George Duvall, arrived looking grim. He brought with him a young man called Sidney Timberlake, who had glossy blond hair and wore a pin-striped suit.

"Sid just joined us, fresh out of Yale Law. He's been making a study of LBOs."

"Of what?" Walter asked.

"Leveraged buyouts," George said. "Let's get started, Walter, it may be a long morning."

What young Timberlake began to explain, in a Boston Yankee accent, was that American business was in the midst of a revolution. A man named Milken, at a second-rate brokerage house called Drexel Burnham, had begun issuing high-risk, high-interest bonds—"junk bonds"—to finance the takeover of huge companies, often by much smaller companies headed by reckless entrepreneurs who were willing to assume huge debts.

"I'd read about this," Walter told the lawyers, "but I never imagined it could happen in Texas. We do business differently here."

"It *is* different," George Duvall agreed. "These people aren't interested in building businesses. Often the first thing they do is bust up the company—sell off its most profitable parts, to bring down their debt."

"I suspect, Mr. Lamont," Sid Timberlake interjected, "that what's been happening in the East has given Sonny Nash some ideas. He's done smaller deals—usually they started out hostile but wound up friendly."

"You mean the other side surrendered!"

"Yes. Sonny is different from the raiders up there in one important regard. They're highly leveraged. He has vast amounts of cash at his disposal. It puts him in a much stronger position."

Sid's haughty style rubbed Walter Lamont the wrong way. For fifty years he'd seen Yankees come to town, thinking they were smarter than everyone else, and finding out differently.

"Young man, you aren't a native of this city, so I wouldn't expect you to understand this, but Sonny is a paper tiger. This company has been in my family for a hundred years. It's part of the bone and sinew of this city. The community will not tolerate an act of . . . of cannibalism of this sort."

The young man's eyes narrowed in disbelief.

"Mr. Lamont, with all due respect, Lamont & Company is a public company. You are chairman of the board and CEO, but the stockholders own the company. And many of them, offered a substantial profit, from as progressive and profitable an outfit as Nash International, may see no reason to turn it down."

"No reason to turn it down?" Walter raged. "This is my company. The shareholders are my people. The employees are my people. This is my city. They'll rally behind me. Sonny Nash is the scum of the earth."

"Business is business, Mr. Lamont. And profit is profit."

"Dammit, can't you understand? This *isn't* business. It's a personal vendetta."

George Duvall looked uncomfortable. "Sid, let's get to the specifics," he said.

"Right. We know now that Sonny has bought at least five percent of Lamont's stock—at that point he had to file a 13D with the SEC. If past history is any guide, he'll soon have ten to twenty percent."

"Impossible!" Walter Lamont cried.

"You've been trading at sixteen. I hear Nash is offering twenty-four."

"If so, it proves he's irresponsible!"

"Not necessarily. Companies like yours tend to be undervalued. He may plan to buy the company, bust it up, and sell parts off for a quick profit."

Walter Lamont gasped, unable to speak.

"Sid, what are our defensive tactics?" George Duvall asked.

"Well, there are various objections we can raise in the courts or with the SEC, but in the end, barring a miracle, to keep the company you have to outbid him."

Walter stood up. "Young man, you may know the law, but you don't know this city. Now, if you gentlemen will excuse me, I have a phone call to make. I think I can settle this matter rather simply."

The two lawyers left as requested. Sid Timberlake cast one glance back at the big, shambling, white-haired man, who looked more like a rancher than a corporate CEO. Sid liked the old man, whether or not the feeling was mutual.

Walter's secretary had four or five messages of support from friends—he had expected more—but he left them unanswered. Instead, he called and made a lunch date with the editor of the *Star-Telegram*, Hall Wilkin.

They met at the Petroleum Club at one and took a table by the window. Walter finished his first Gibson before he got down to business.

"Hall, I don't question your putting that story on the front page—it's big news. But I think I should give you some perspective on Sonny and what he stands for. This isn't just another business story. This is a threat to the social and economic climate of this city."

"Tell me more," the editor said.

"I've known the Nash family for thirty years. Lily's husband Howard was no good. Worked for the F&R Bank, drank too much, finally stole some money and skipped town—part of the problem is Sonny's got the genes of a crooked little bank teller. Lily's a different breed of cat. When I first met her, she taught my daughter Felice at W. C. Stripling. She was a plump, shy little thing then, nothing like the woman you see today. Lily had an uncle, Wildcat Billy Ringer, an old reprobate, but late in his life he brought in a big field in Louisiana. Hell of a thing, him having this fancy new theater named for him. Anyway, he died and left it all to Lily. Actually to his widow, and to Lily after that. The widow was quite a character. Bought a house on Rivercrest Drive, just down from me, and used to play the hole across from her house. She finally fell down her stairs and died. Lily inherited the money, her worthless husband skipped town, and here's this schoolteacher left with a hundred million dollars."

"Fascinating," the editor ventured.

"I helped her in those days, gave her some advice. The poor girl didn't know who to trust. She was going through personal changes too—slimmed down, went blonde, and discovered the opposite sex, so to speak. I'll say this for Lily, once she got her hands on money, she figured out there's more to life than teaching *Silas Marner*."

Walter chuckled at his own joke. "Anyway, other people managed her money for a few years, then Sonny took over."

"And performed miracles," the editor said.

"He's made money, yes. But the point is how he made the money, and what kind of man he is. Unfortunately, I know Sonny rather well."

Walter Lamont stared moodily into his Gibson.

"He married your daughter," the editor prompted.

Walter nodded. "I came to know what a cruel, ruthless man he is. Subhuman, really. A criminal type. Look at that creature he's married to now."

"He's awfully successful."

"Blast it, that's not the point. He's a Jekyll and Hyde. Mark my word, he'll crack someday, and disgrace this city."

"Walter, I spoke to our business people. They tell me this is a more or less standard tender offer. Part of a trend in a changing business environment. You could make a large profit or you can resist. Obviously we will report whatever happens. Is there something else you wanted of us?"

Walter scowled at the editor. "My phone has been ringing all morning. Friends. Stockholders. Employees. Total strangers. All telling me to fight this. All pledging their support. It would be easy for me to take my profit and retire. But I owe something to this city. I don't think we want this kind of gutter, dog-eat-dog business tactics to infect Texas. I think honor and tradition and civic pride mean something. That's why I'm going to fight Sonny, all the way, with no quarter asked and none granted."

"Sounds like a whale of a story," Wilkin said.

"It presents you with a rare opportunity for leadership."

"How do you mean?"

"You should run an editorial tomorrow morning, denouncing this scheme. Saying it's bad for the city. That Sonny should be ashamed of himself. That all true Texans oppose this kind of gutter behavior. That way, after I've beaten this back, you can share the credit."

"Let me see what I can do," the editor said cautiously.

That night, Walter regaled Tilly, his wife of forty years, with visions of how he would rout Sonny Nash. He broke out a bottle of 1948 Nuits Saint-Georges, and recalled the time when, as a boy, he'd caddied for J. Edgar Hoover, and Bob Hope had given him a cigar. He told of seeing Ben Hogan win at Colonial, and of the gridiron glories of Sammy Baugh and Davey O'Brien at TCU. He loved to tell the story of the time the coach told Sammy Baugh to hit the receiver in the eye, and Slinging Sammy replied, "Which eye?" He repeated his grandfather's tales of shootouts in Hell's Half Acre, and recalled meeting Billy Rose during his great Casa Mañana Exposition of 1936, and talking with John Kennedy, in Suite 850 of the Hotel Texas, only minutes before he left for his rendezvous in Dallas.

"Not bad for a cowtown!" he would declare, after each tale of the city's past glory.

In truth, this raw, proud frontier city was his life, his universe, and it was inconceivable that it could let him down. After the candles burned down, Tilly came to his bed and they cuddled like newlyweds.

He woke early the next morning. Across Rivercrest Drive the golf course sprinklers made rainbows in the sun. He picked the *Star-Telegram* off the porch and carried it back to the kitchen. He started coffee, poured orange juice, and then casually opened the paper and thumbed to the editorial page.

To his dismay, the morning's lead editorial called for increased defense spending. The next one questioned the need for higher teachers' salaries, and the last praised the Girl Scouts.

After a moment of outrage, Walter laughed. The editorial page was printed up early. After their late lunch, there hadn't been time to rush an editorial into print. He would have to wait a day or two.

His self-confidence lasted a moment or two, then he seized the phone and called Hall Wilkin's unlisted home number.

"Hall, Walter here. Hope I didn't wake you, but I'd hoped for an editorial this morning."

The editor did not hesitate. "I took it all the way to the top. They saw it as a personal matter."

"I explained that. It's a civic matter of the greatest magnitude."

"Walter, I have great respect for you. But some of our people think the takeover trend is good for business. They say management gets complacent."

"Complacent?" Walter sputtered.

"Not you, necessarily. But I'm afraid the best I can do is be neutral on this one. Good luck."

Walter Lamont put down the phone. He felt the fight oozing out of him like blood. For the first time in his life, he was afraid.

12.

MICKEY FELT SICK, RIPPED APART, BROKEN. HOW COULD SHE have been so stupid? She'd gotten lazy, guessed wrong, and now there was this spark inside her fighting to live. And what could she want more than Rafe's child? A child to give the love she'd never had from the parents she'd never known. A child to be as perfect as she was imperfect. A boy, maybe, as strong and brave as his father. She wanted Rafe's child, wanted a dozen of them, how much more sense that made than to spend the rest of her life putting idiots in jail. Already, her body was moving serenely toward the miracle of a new life.

And yet it was impossible. Cruelly, maddeningly impossible. Rafe already had two sons he barely knew. He was working day and night, up for promotion, and the last thing he needed was a pregnant girlfriend. Sure, maybe he'd say, Go ahead, have the baby, we'll get married—then what? He was a cop. She'd have to quit her job and he'd be out working his tail off and either they'd stay together and be miserable or they'd split and she'd be miserable and make her child miserable. And if there was one vow Mickey had sworn it was never to bring a human being into the world if you were only going to make it miserable—millions of people were already doing that.

She dreamed that she could go to him, could say, Rafe, make it right, tell me you'll quit the DEA and get a sensible job and we'll have a barbecue pit and a swing set and be as happy as Ozzie and Harriet.

That was a sweet dream, but it wasn't how it was going to be. It wasn't even close.

The clinic was in Foggy Bottom and took credit cards and all the other women in the waiting room were black or brown. A few had men with them but most were alone, except for that spark inside them. They smiled shyly and watched the Saturday-morning cartoons while they waited.

The people in white were very efficient. Mickey spread her legs and shut her eyes and soon enough they said she should rest for an hour and take it easy for a week. When she walked out of the clinic, her strong young body felt fine. The problem was in her heart, in her soul, where she raged with sorrow and anger until she almost wished she was dead.

A week after her visit to the clinic, Mickey woke feeling rotten. Rafe had left for work and it was time for her to go back, but she wasn't sure she could face it. She drank coffee until she was wired, frenetic, hating herself and the world, then for the hell of it she called Wingo's office.

"I'm afraid he's out of town, Ms. deCoursey," said his snooty Brit secretary.

Mickey slammed down the phone. She guessed this was the trip he said was about shopping malls in Florida and she thought was about cocaine.

Mickey was edgy, half-mad, ravaged by the thing she had done. She saw Wingo's smug face before her, she thought how she despised him, for his arrogance, for his smooth talk, for his undeserved wealth. If she could wipe that smirk off his face it might in some small way lessen her pain.

She began to dress, to paint her face, to become Michelle. Transformed, she climbed into her blue T-Bird (whose previous owner was now a long-term guest of the federal prison system) and began the two-hour drive to Charlottesville.

It was mid-May, high spring, a glorious day to sail through the Shenandoah Valley, but Mickey had no eye for the scenery. She took the bypass around the city and began the search for Wingo's estate. She'd only been there by air before, and she had to search the back roads for a time. But when she saw that white dome floating above the trees, like a beacon from another century, there was no mistaking it for any place else on earth.

The gate was locked, but Mickey knew where he kept the key, under a rock, just inside the woods. She drove the half-mile up to the house and parked on the oval drive before the columns. His dogs came roaring at her, Hungarian sheepdogs, programmed to kill, but they remembered her, and she remembered the words that calmed them. They followed, docile as kittens, while she walked round the house. When she was sure she was alone, she used a pass key to let herself in.

This was the no-no part, the stuff the lawyers said you must never do. She'd heard all the lectures on probable cause and illegal search and seizure, but the way the law protected the bad guys sometimes you couldn't do your job unless you cut corners. She wouldn't plant drugs on Wingo, but if this illegal search turned up drugs she'd fuzz the facts and return with a search warrant.

She looked downstairs first. His desk was locked and none of her keys would open it. She tried closets, bathrooms, the basement, but found no drugs, no weapons, only expensive wine and trendy clothes and state-of-the-art electronic gear, as if his only crime was Yuppiedom.

She located his safe, behind a portrait of Lord Fairfax, but safe-cracking was beyond her talents.

In Wingo's bedroom, with its fine view of the lawn and boxwood gardens, she found mirrors arranged in ways she suspected Mr. Jefferson had not imagined, but no drug stronger than Advil.

She went out to the barn, banging through the stalls and storage rooms and those sad old shacks he called the slave quarters; they held history, ghosts, someone's terrible memories, and a family of field mice, but no contraband.

The more she looked, the angrier she became. Had she been wrong about Wingo? Had she been crazy to come here? She leaned against the side of the barn, conscious of the beauty and history around her, angry that it was wasted on such a fool as Wingo. She had failed, and it was time to get out of here.

Then she heard the roar of his plane.

At that moment, back in Washington, Rafe Klayman was face to face with the witness he'd sought for months.

Their investigation of the Stoddert School killings had stretched on and on. All they knew was that a white male, thirty or so, description vague, had rented an apartment across from the school, paying cash to the owner, an old woman with poor eyes and no curiosity. When he'd wanted to execute two DEA agents, he'd lured them to the park across the street, gunned them down with a high-powered rifle, and calmly driven away.

He'd left behind no fingerprints, no clothes, no papers, and neighbors who were extremely vague about him. He'd had no telephone in the apartment; they suspected he'd used a pay phone across the street.

There had been nothing to do except scour the area. When Rafe had knocked on every door within six blocks of the apartment, he turned around and started over.

Then the boy walked in. He was twenty, red-haired, agreeable, a Georgetown student.

"I lived downstairs," the boy said. "But I left town just before the shootings. Actually I flunked out. You mind if I smoke?"

Rafe didn't care if the boy mainlined if he'd keep talking.

"The story I heard was that he was a traveling salesman. The perfect guy to have upstairs, right? I saw him a couple of times.

Once, on the stairs, he was carrying some boxes, and I asked if he wanted me to help, and he brushed by me. The next time, I almost didn't recognize him, because he looked different, like he'd dyed his hair or something.

"But, the thing is, I knew what he looked like. Kind of fleshy, not bad-looking, but cold as ice."

Lon Tate joined them.

"Lon, this fellow lived downstairs from the apartment on 40th Street. Go on, Joey."

Lon coiled on the edge of Rafe's desk.

"Well, I came back to school, and my roommates told me about the shootings and you guys asking questions, and I didn't figure I knew anything worth telling, then last week I was in Georgetown and there was this guy, in a blue Bentley, not ten feet from me, stopped at a light. There wasn't any doubt in my mind, it was the guy upstairs. And it was so weird. I mean, a salesman, driving a *Bentley?*"

"Did you see his license plate?" Lon asked quietly.

"Yeah, sure. He had a Virginia vanity plate. REALEST. I mean, either that's some cool existentialist slogan or he's in real estate. Anyway, I figured I'd better call you guys."

As soon as the boy was gone, Lon said, "I'll check the plate."

"You don't have to," Rafe said.

"How come?"

"Wingo, Mickey's guy, he drives a Bentley. And lives in northern Virginia. We thought he was just some clown."

"Jesus Christ," Lon said. "Come on."

They ran to the computer room and grabbed Rizzo, the chief computer cowboy. Lon gave him the numbers of the pay phone across from the apartment and Wingo's office in Virginia. "See if there were calls between these, Gene," he said.

Rizzo punched his keyboard with stubby, nimble figures, a wizard at work. He accessed directly into the Virginia Bell terminal. He was an Alice Cooper freak; as he worked Alice wailed about death and dismemberment.

"We ran hundreds of dealers through this," Lon said. "The only

192

two who ever called that pay phone, or were called from it, were the one who got his neck broke and the one who got shot in the park."

"But we never ran Wingo?"

"He wasn't a known dealer," Lon said bitterly.

"Shit," Rafe said.

Rizzo kept punching keys until a printout popped into view; he ripped it off and studied the rows of figures.

"Goddammit, what does it say?" Lon roared.

Rizzo shrugged. "There were twenty calls between the two numbers in the last eighteen months."

Rafe pulled Lon out into the hallway. "Wingo's the killer. What the fuck was wrong with us?"

"Where's Mick?" Lon asked.

"I don't know. I called home. She's not there."

"We better find her."

When Mickey heard the plane coming in, she knew she should get out of Dodge. She had no backup, no weapon, and no good reason for being there.

The trouble was, she wasn't feeling sensible. She felt angry, stubborn, reckless; she felt like smashing someone, and Wingo was her best candidate.

So she leaned against one of the white columns, supple and Michelle-like in white linen pants and a flowered blouse, smiling her most indolent smile as Wingo emerged from the woods.

She felt strangely at peace. She loved being Michelle; she was a beautiful mask to hide behind. She'd always been stubbornly herself, even when it had cost her dearly. Being Michelle had taught her a profound truth: most people wore masks all the time, and they made life infinitely easier.

Wingo carried a blue duffel bag in each hand. He wore jeans and was unshaven. The dogs leaped beside him, rejoicing at his return. When he saw her, he stopped open-mouthed.

"What are you doing here?"

"Don't be a bear, Dee Wingo—I'm surprising you."

She skipped down the steps and kissed his cheek. "I decided to buy the condo, so we should celebrate. How was your trip?"

"It was good. How long have you been here?"

"Just drove up."

He touched the hood of her car, wondering why it was cool if she'd just arrived.

He led her to the mansion. As they stepped into the foyer, with its ornate chandelier and winding staircase, he tossed the duffel bags into a closet and locked it.

"Dirty laundry?"

"I have to call my office," he said. "Open some champagne. We'll sit out back and watch the sunset."

"Wonderful," she said.

As soon as he vanished into his library she rattled the closet door, sure those duffel bags were filled with coke. "Bastard," she muttered, and went to the kitchen. She opened a bottle of champagne, found a paring knife and stuck it inside her pants.

Wingo called a man who was just back from France, and he was not altogether surprised by what he learned. He slipped through the French doors to the T-Bird and jerked wires loose under the dash.

Then he joined her on the veranda, while the sun floated toward the trees. The dogs settled nearby, growling to themselves. He raised his glass.

"Cheers."

"So your trip was a success?"

He wore an odd smile. She had an unsettling sense that he, too, was playing a role.

"I'd been in a partnership I wasn't happy with, and now I'm out of it. I'm not interested in business now. I don't need more money. I care about this house, this land, serving my country."

"What a fine way to feel."

"I can be governor of this state in five years," he said. "And after that—who knows? A progressive Southern businessman—a veteran with a beautiful wife—might be just what this country wants."

Mickey looked coy. "But you don't have a wife."

"Not yet," he said, still with the odd smile.

The dogs leaped up barking, and raced across the lawn after a squirrel. They watched as the squirrel barely escaped up a tree.

Mickey sighed. "This reminds me of nights at college, when we'd smoke a few joints and watch the sunset."

He smiled indulgently. "At Sweet Briar? Imagine!"

"We were naughty. Did you ever smoke dope?"

"A little hashish, in 'Nam."

"I tried cocaine once. What a high."

"Would you like to try some more?"

"Do you have some?"

"I might. Stay here tonight. There are a lot of things we could try."

"I have to get back. My aunt is in town."

"Your aunt? There's so much I don't know about you, Michelle."

"There's not much to know."

"Oh, I'll bet there are many mysteries. After college, you went to France. Correct?"

She heard the warning bells. She didn't care about the coke now, just about getting out. "That's right. I love France. It's green like Virginia. Look, Dee, I . . . "

"But you came back home."

"Well, home is home, isn't it? Maybe I'm like you, and I want to contribute something."

"Yes, maybe you're like me," he said.

The sun was behind the trees; dusk engulfed them. Crickets sang and bats darted about the eaves of the mansion.

"Here's a mystery. A man I know was in France last week. He went to the museum where you worked. And guess who he met?"

"Who?" she said weakly.

"He met you, Michelle deCoursey, from Virginia, still working in Dijon. Isn't that strange?"

"It's a mistake." She stood up. "Look, Dee, let's talk tomorrow, okay? We'll close the deal."

She started away. He watched her.

"I don't think your car will start," he said. "Let's talk some more."

He leaped up and seized her wrist.

"You little bitch, who are you?"

She kneed him in the balls. When he doubled over, she kicked the side of his head. He fell to one knee, bleeding above his ear, then lunged, threw her to the ground, groping for her throat. Mickey jerked out the knife and slashed at him. He screamed as the blade sliced his palm. The dogs were barking wildly. He twisted the knife from her grasp.

She broke free and ran toward the house. "Get her!" Wingo cried to the dogs. "Kill!"

She reached the back door just ahead of the yelping dogs, slammed it shut, and locked it.

She saw him out the window, tying his handkerchief around his hand, and she thought of fleeing into the woods. But she'd be crazy to run with those two dogs after her. Her chances were better in the house.

She grabbed the phone—it was dead.

She went to the pantry and threw the breaker switches; darkness would be her ally. She seized the heavy iron tongs from the fireplace.

The dogs howled at the back door. But where was Wingo? She wanted to surprise him at the door. A gun, she'd give her arm for a gun.

The back door crashed open and he was there, bloody, cradling a MAC-11.

"Bitch!"

She swung the tongs, staggered him, and retreated down the dark hallway.

She heard him cursing. She crouched in the dining room, clutching the tongs, wondering where to make her stand.

He was silhouetted in the doorway. The MAC-11 was as potent an automatic weapon as was made, a cop-killer.

"Look, whoever you are, this is crazy."

His flashlight beam moved up the hallway.

"Tell me who you are, then you can go."

"Okay," she said, "I'm a reporter, that's all."

"Come here and we'll talk."

She slid a chair toward him.

One burst of the MAC-11 blew the chair into a hundred pieces.

"Get her, you dumb fucks!" Wingo yelled.

One of the dogs charged, hot-breathed and slobbering, knocking her backwards. Mickey, screaming, jerked her knife upward and found the animal's throat.

The dog died at her feet. The other one inched toward her.

"You want yours, Bozo?" she muttered.

The flashlight beam shot down the hallway. The MAC-11 roared again as she crouched behind a sideboard.

"You're messing up your pretty mansion, Wingo."

"Get her, Fritz, kill!"

Mickey retreated into the foyer, then up the staircase as the dog advanced. Halfway up she stumbled and he lunged, his teeth tearing into her leg. She swung the tongs and felt his skull crack.

She pulled herself to the top of the stairs. The pain helped her focus: kill or be killed. Wingo was below her now, in the foyer where Mr. Jefferson had danced, shining his light around.

She still might have fled into the woods. Or played hide-and-seek with him upstairs.

But that was what women had always done: run, cowered, hesitated, pleaded, let themselves be picked off one by one. Her training had reinforced her own deepest instincts: take the initiative, take it to the bastard.

Wingo was stalking a wounded woman, thinking her helpless.

But, whether or not he knew it, Wingo had a problem. He had to climb those stairs.

She watched him come, cradling the MAC-11, sweeping the flashlight beam before him, cursing as he stepped over the carcass of his dog. She waited until he was ten steps from the top, then she raced forward and flung herself through the air.

She held the tongs before her, hit him like a cannonball, and the two of them tumbled down the stairs. The tongs and his gun and flashlight flew away, and they landed in a heap on the marble floor of the foyer. Rising to her knees, she pounded at his face, sliced at his eyes.

"Bitch!" He rolled atop her, gripped her throat. She kicked, kneed, bit, scratched, but he pounded her head against the floor.

Abruptly he loosened his grip. His bloody face was inches from hers. "Who are you?"

"DEA," she whispered, as if those magic letters might save her.

"Who knows you're here?"

"They're out there."

"You're a liar, sister. You're dead." He choked her again. She began slipping into the void.

He raised up, poised to finish her, and her free hand found his balls. She squeezed with all her fading strength, squeezed until his balls popped like eggs, squished like jelly. He screamed and flopped away from her. She saw the tongs, swept them up, crashed them against his head. He whimpered and lay still.

Mickey sank to the floor, bleeding, battered, broken. Neither of them moved. She escaped from her pain into a hazy dream. She saw Rafe, her sister Jessie, the Home, the Tune Inn.

The sounds of car doors, crackling radios, men's voices, awoke her. She wondered idly about the commotion. It seemed unrelated to her pain, to the darkness she craved.

The door burst open. Beams of light, weapons glistening. Rafe knelt over her.

"Are you okay?"

"I hurt bad."

"Is that Wingo?"

"Yeah. We had a falling out."

Rafe laughed. The medics were hurrying in. "What the hell did you do to him?"

"I violated his rights," she confessed, and returned to her dream.

13.

SONNY'S CAMPAIGN AGAINST LAMONT & COMPANY ROLLED ALONG with military precision. His lawyers beat down Lamont's legal objections, his labor specialists won over Lamont's unions, and his PR men painted him as a dynamic young tycoon trying to revive a corporate dinosaur.

Walter Lamont was like the commander of a besieged city, who sees his food running low, his soldiers deserting, and the townspeople increasingly hostile. He tried to organize a buyout group of his own, appealing to bankers who were his lifelong friends, but they told him bluntly that his chances of prevailing against Sonny's all-cash tender offer were all but invisible.

Walter was eating little, drinking heavily, sleeping poorly, but he would not surrender. In this battle his staunchest ally was young Sid Timberlake. Somewhat to his amazement, Walter had come to feel affection for this young Yankee, whose advice always made more sense than anyone else's.

"The problem," Sid often warned, "is that if he's irrational, if

199

he's determined to have this company no matter what, then there's no telling how high he'll go."

Walter feared that. Sonny *was* irrational—and how could anyone bid against a madman with a billion dollars?

In retrospect, Walter saw that it all went back to that night at Caravan of Dreams when he'd told Sonny what he thought of him and his sluttish wife. This, finally, was Sonny's revenge.

The best strategy Walter could devise was for Sid to file every legal objection he could concoct. "If we can stall him long enough," Walter quipped, "either he'll lose interest or I'll die."

"Not funny, Mr. L," Sid said.

"I'm serious," Walter said. "Not about me dying, I wouldn't give Sonny that satisfaction. But, I keep telling you, the man is mad. Someday he'll self-destruct. I only hope it's sooner rather than later."

Sid dropped by Walter's office at five one September afternoon, as he often did. The older man poured them both a Scotch. Sid loathed whiskey, but Walter disliked to drink alone, so the young lawyer accepted the unwanted spirits as part of his job.

"Well, my boy, what's new?" Walter asked. His first drink of the day, if nothing else, cheered him.

"We're running out of appeals," Sid said. "And out of time."

"You, Sid, out of appeals? I don't believe it."

Sid jiggled the ice in his drink. "There is one possibility."

"Yes?"

"Sonny has a bad record. He's tried strong-arm stuff before, smaller scale, and sometimes been beat back. He entered into a consent agreement with the SEC a few years ago, and was censured by the New York Stock Exchange. He's had problems with the IRS."

"Insofar as the man has a guiding philosophy, it is that he should not pay taxes," Walter said. "But where does this lead us?"

"Well, maybe it's stretching it, but I'm thinking of filing a RICO complaint against him."

"A what?"

"The Racketeer Influenced and Corrupt Organizations Act.

Mostly used against the mob. It requires showing of a 'pattern' of racketeering. As I say, it's stretching it. But it opens up his past record, his morality, so to speak."

Walter Lamont was delighted. "Sid, you are a genius."

"Just a slick lawyer."

"It's perfect—it gets to the heart of the matter. Because Sonny *is* a criminal. A mobster. A thug with a billion dollars. By God, let's let the world know it!"

"It'll make him mad as hell, and . . . "

"Wonderful!"

" . . . and in the end probably be thrown out of court . . . "

"We're talking about the court of public opinion. Dammit, why are you sitting there drinking my whiskey? Get cracking! Go with it, boy, go with it!"

Sonny was enjoying his morning romp with Puss when word came that Walter Lamont was calling him a gangster.

Sonny's love of sex was, if anything, even greater than his love of money. The way he saw it, when he was eighty he'd regret the women he hadn't slept with far more than the money he hadn't made.

He and Puss dedicated their mornings to sex. They had coffee, juice, and uppers in their bedroom suite, enough to get them going, and they'd frolic at leisure, with the Today Show on the tube, or maybe a porn movie, depending on his mood. When he was sated—he was not convinced that Puss was ever entirely sated—they would relax in the Jacuzzi, and ease down for a Texas-sized breakfast. Sex was the best way Sonny had found to start the day. It cleared your hangover, put a smile on your face, and left you in a good frame of mind for business.

Sonny had seen a *Reader's Digest* article that said the average American male his age had sex 2.7 times a week. All he could think was, Jesus, what pigs they must be married to—he was doing better than that every day.

Sonny had learned at an early age that women liked to fuck as much as men and that, all things being equal, most would rather fuck a rich man than a poor man. That was the good news; the bad news was that a lot of women were pretty damn sorry in bed. They were crippled by hang-ups, thinking this or that was wrong or dirty. Even those who were eager to please often lacked the basic skills. Some of the smartest women he knew were hopeless in bed. They'd spent years getting educated and never learned to fuck half as good as the Mexican gals who cleaned their homes. Sexual illiterates, he called them.

As Sonny saw it, sex was a sport, like tennis, and at any given moment there were twenty or thirty women who were truly world-class. He figured that to be world-class a woman needed a great body (although up to a point enthusiasm could compensate), energy, humor, creativity, and the competitive edge that makes a champion. He'd met maybe a dozen world-class players in his life, and Puss was the best of the bunch. She could be a sassy bitch on her feet, but on her back he'd never met a woman more blessed with enthusiasm and God-given talent.

Sonny had done his share of tomcatting, but it grew tiresome. You met too many women who were angry, who were crazy, who wanted to talk your arm off, who dreamed of romance when all you wanted was a romp. He still had women stashed around the world, pit stops for the weary traveler. Some were pros, but more were the wives of men who worked for him. By and large, ambitious wives performed better than pros, for they were motivated by the dream of millions of dollars, not the simple payment of a few hundred.

Still, when he was home, Puss satisfied his needs. She could fuck his socks off, she could make him laugh, she didn't ask questions, and as far as he could see she didn't run around. All that, plus she drove the country club crowd bananas, the way she talked dirty and let her tits hang out and dragged her mink coats on the rug. He loved that.

On this morning, Puss had slowly brought him to a point of sheer bliss, of whimpering, weak-kneed, childlike ecstasy, when the bedside phone shattered his perfect moment. "Fuck!" Sonny roared. Only the most urgent calls were put through to the bedroom. His

executives knew that if they interrupted him without good cause
there would be hell to pay.

"What the hell?" he growled.

"Sonny, it's Nick."

Puss stretched languidly as he talked. She enjoyed their morning
playtime; she thought it was how she and Sonny communicated
best. The rest of the time was mostly one-liners and arguments,
but in bed they were Fred and Ginger, two hearts beating as one.

Puss had given a great deal of thought to sex, and the main
conclusion she had reached was that men and women really were
different. It was important to Sonny to think that millions of women
wanted to fuck him—he had to prove it every so often, lest he think
he was slipping. Puss, for her part, had figured out by age twelve
that millions of men wanted to fuck her. The fact had long since
ceased to thrill her. She was happy with Sonny. It wasn't even his
money so much. At his best, he was the funniest son of a bitch
she'd ever met.

"Nick, you cunt, this better be good."

Nick Rugatti, NI's top public relations man, took a deep breath
and told Sonny about the RICO suit that Walter Lamont's lawyers
had filed.

"Our lawyers are ape-shit," Nick concluded.

Sonny was on his feet, stalking the bedroom, the phone to his
ear. "Wait a minute," he said, "you're saying that old fart is calling
me a gangster?"

"That's right. It's a law against racketeering. They mostly use it
against the Mafia. It's . . . "

"I'm the richest fucker in Texas and he's calling me *gangster*?"

"Hell, Sonny, it's funny in a way."

"Funny, my ass! Get the lawyers to my office!"

Sonny slammed down the phone.

"A gangster. He called me a fucking *gangster!*"

"You braggin' or complainin'?" Puss drawled.

He turned on her. "Shut up, you stupid bitch!"

He slapped her and she tumbled back against the headboard.
Puss huddled in the middle of the big round bed and pretended

she wasn't there. She knew his temper and she wanted it directed at Walter Lamont, not at her.

Puss knew, as no one else alive did, that Sonny had once killed a man. They'd stopped in a hillbilly bar outside Baytown and a truckdriver made three mistakes: being drunk, asking her to dance, and calling Sonny a motherfucker. He'd asked the guy outside, and when the guy bloodied his nose, Sonny grabbed a rock and bashed his head in. They drove away unseen, nothing happened, and Puss had sense enough never to mention it again.

Puss made herself invisible now, as Sonny's fury slowly passed from fire to ice, from private rage to the cold malevolence of the public man. He dressed without speaking and soon was speeding downtown. Puss didn't know what was happening, but she knew his temper, and she feared now as she had often feared that someday he would kill again.

At a certain intellectual level Jessica was offended by Sonny's assault on Walter Lamont, yet at a more personal level almost nothing that Sonny did was real to her. It was as if his wars were fought with toy soldiers, his deals done with Monopoly money.

Her life increasingly centered on Melissa. The child was an endless joy to her. She had not known she would feel that way. Until she married Billy, Jessica had not expected to have children. She'd thought that if she married he would probably be an academic, and most of the male academics she knew were so cranky and otherworldly that she thought them exceedingly ill-suited for fatherhood.

Marriage to Billy had changed everything. He wanted a child, and she had been happy to oblige. Thanks to his money, motherhood was no burden. She could have played the Great Lady—a role she knew well, from certain Victorian and Southern novels—visiting the nursery occasionally and receiving her children before dinner, as a general reviews his troops.

But Jessica felt the pull of motherhood with an intensity that startled her. She could happily spend all day with Melissa. It was important to her to be there for her child's first step and first words.

She wished Billy shared her passion, but he was at the office when the first step came, and in London when his daughter one day announced, " 'Lissa want din-din."

Instead, it was Olivia who shared those moments with her, and Jessica had come to love her wholeheartedly. Olivia was simply a good person to have in your life, a woman of dignity, intelligence, and compassion, whose love of her and Melissa was total. A widow with grown children, she had begun living with them when Melissa was born, and she was friend, surrogate mother, cook, and house-keeper as well. Jessica had offered to bring in another woman to clean, but Olivia wanted no other woman in the house.

More and more Jessica found excuses to skip tennis games and luncheons with Kay and Myra and her other friends. Even the Billy Ringer Theater no longer seemed so urgent. The planning meetings had become agony for her. It was incredible how much ego, ar-rogance, and sheer pig-headedness a group of educated people could bring to a worthy cause.

"Why weren't you at the finance committee meeting yesterday?" Billy asked one evening.

She was not surprised by the question. She had skipped three committee meetings that month. "I couldn't bear to spend another evening listening to their endless bickering."

"We need to be represented."

"Billy, you've been using me as your stand-in, and those meetings are driving me nuts. Do you know the difference between starting a theater and having a baby? Starting a theater takes longer and hurts more."

"We're making progress."

"Fine, but you should go to one for every one I go to."

He sighed. "Okay, just tell my secretary when it's my turn."

"Thank you, Billy." She didn't want to argue. Their last argu-ment, about marijuana, had cleared the air, and everything had been good since then.

"But it's not just the theater," he persisted. "I get the impression that you're tuning out."

"You *get the impression*? From whom?"

"It doesn't matter. The point is, people are saying you're stand-offish. I know it's stupid, but we live in a goldfish bowl."

"Should I dedicate myself to tennis and bridge and long liquid lunches at the club?"

"Is it so awful?"

"I enjoy Melissa more."

"I'm not saying you should ignore Melissa. But there is such a thing as balance. You don't want to smother her . . . "

"*Smother* her?"

"She doesn't need you around the clock. People want to be your friend. Don't use Melissa as an excuse to be antisocial."

She felt both anger and a certain reluctant guilt. *Was* she anti-social? Was she, in fact, ill-suited for the social role that Billy's wife should play, and using her daughter as an excuse?

Billy took her hand. "I understand how you feel. I'm not exactly Mr. Gregarious. But the Nash money carries with it a role in this community. You married that. And it's not so bad. Just give it a chance."

She kissed him. "You're so incredibly patient."

"Not really. But thanks."

"I will try to do better."

She might have stopped there. But there was something on her mind, and this seemed the moment to raise it.

"I've been thinking, Billy."

He laughed. "About what?"

"About after Melissa starts school. It's not that far away. Then I will have time on my hands."

"Sounds great."

"The thing is, before you met me, I spent ten years being trained to do something, and then doing it. I liked teaching. I was good at it. Now, when I'm having lunch with Kay and her friends, I'm not happy the way they are, because I think there's somewhere else I should be. I feel adrift, a little useless."

It was not easy to say, and she prayed that he would understand.

"Useless? You're a great mother, you've . . . "

"I love being a mother. But after Melissa starts school, I might start teaching again."

"Teaching? Where?"

"There's TCU. And North Texas and SMU aren't that far away. Surely somebody would hire me."

"Oh, they'd hire you all right. But what about Melissa?"

"Melissa? A minute ago you said I was smothering her. It wouldn't be so hard. I could teach a light load at first."

"Jessica, one of the great things about our lives is we're free to run off to Paris for a weekend, or whatever. We couldn't do that if you were working."

"You work."

"I make my own hours. I don't have students waiting for me at nine on Monday morning."

"It would require give and take. But it really is important to me."

"I try to be open-minded," he said.

"I know you do."

"But I really don't see it. Just think about it. We don't have to decide this instant."

"That's true," she agreed.

He reached for a magazine. Calm returned. Jessica would indeed think about it. But she didn't think she would change her mind.

14.

THE CASE AGAINST DWIGHT WINGO CAME DOWN TO HIS WORD against Mickey's. Wingo had left a few tracks and no smoking guns. No witness placed him near the Stoddert School the day of the shooting, nor had any murder weapon been found. Phone records showed that he had spoken with two drug dealers, but he insisted he was buying a car from one and clothes from the other. Lita Howe testified that he had given cocaine to her and Richmond Morris, but the former White House aide, now a prominent Washington lawyer, indignantly denied her story, and Wingo's lawyers pictured her as a vengeful ex-girlfriend out to save her own skin. A government accountant tried to show that Wingo's real estate empire was built on drug money, but his convoluted testimony put half the jury to sleep.

The prosecutor called Wingo a psychopath and a cold-blooded killer, but the defense produced a parade of Virginia civic leaders who hailed him as a model citizen. Wingo's lawyers hinted at a shadowy plot, begun by two spurned women, and carried out by a corrupt DEA, motivated by greed and politics.

In the end, the trial turned on Mickey's testimony. She was the eyewitness, the one who had seen him unload two duffel bags of cocaine, the one he had tried to kill. As much as she despised Wingo, Mickey dreaded her courtroom appearance. She'd rather have Wingo coming at her with his dogs and a MAC-11 than face some lawyer trying to twist her words around.

The cross-examination, when it finally came, was even worse than she'd feared. Wingo's lawyer charged that she'd become caught up in the Michelle fantasy, that she'd fallen in love with Wingo, that she'd slept with him and wanted to marry him, that he'd rejected her, that she'd gone to his estate to threaten him, and that when he told her to leave, she tried to kill him, then her fellow DEA agents had planted cocaine in his house and plane.

A hundred questions began "Isn't it true that . . . ?" and none of it was true, but the defense lawyer's lies took on a cruel, tempting reality of their own; they opened the door to another world where she was the crook and Wingo a victim.

It was an outrageous story, perhaps just outrageous enough to be embraced by one anti-government nut on the jury. As Mickey denied the allegations, fighting to keep her temper, she would glower at Wingo, the picture of respectability in a blue suit and regimental tie, then gaze yet again at the jurors and wonder, Could they possibly believe this garbage?

She tried to be crisp and professional, but she did slip once, near the end.

"Isn't it true, Miss McGee, that after Mr. Wingo rejected your demands, you became incensed and attacked him with the fire tongs?"

"He attacked me with an automatic weapon and two dogs."

"But he was the one who wound up unconscious?"

"I wound up with a broken wrist, a dislocated shoulder, and fifteen stitches in my leg."

"But Mr. Wingo was the one unconscious on the floor with a concussion, wasn't he?"

Mickey glared at Wingo's smug face and broke into a smile. "You bet your buns he was," she said proudly.

While the jury was out, she and Rafe and their friends waited nervously in a tavern across from the courthouse. As the hours slipped past, the place was swept by rumors, one being that Wingo had bought a juror.

"They can't believe that bastard," Mickey moaned. "He can't walk."

"He wouldn't walk far," Lon Tate muttered.

"I screwed up," Mickey cried. "I should have come back at that lawyer harder."

"You were great, Mick," Rafe told her.

Abruptly, in the late afternoon, the jury had a verdict. The DEA agents rushed to the courtroom and took their seats in the front row as the jurors filed in.

"Ladies and gentlemen of the jury, have you reached a verdict?"

"We have, your honor."

Mickey gripped Rafe's hand.

"And what is that verdict?"

The jury foreman, a chubby accountant, licked his lips nervously.

"On the two counts of murder, we find the defendant, Dwight Wingo, not guilty."

Mickey groaned and huddled against Rafe. The murder case had been weak, circumstantial, but the DEA had wanted badly to win it. If Wingo walked now, Mickey would be to blame, for playing cowboy when she should have built the case carefully. She'd quit, she'd have to quit before they fired her.

"On the charges of conspiracy and possession of cocaine with intent to distribute, and of assault upon a federal officer with intent to kill, we find the defendant"—the foreman paused, and Mickey's heart stood still; that was her case, the duffel bags, the attack on her—"guilty as charged," the foreman concluded.

The courtroom exploded with cheers. Conspiracy and attempted murder would put Dwight Wingo away for thirty years or more. Mickey was crying and hugging Rafe. The judge pounded his gavel. The jury foreman was still trying to speak.

"Your honor, could we say one thing—two things—more?"

"Of course."

"We want to recommend a maximum penalty for the defendant."

Wingo's lawyer shouted his protests. The judge silenced him.

"And we would also like to commend agent McGee for the fortitude with which she conducted herself."

Mickey's eyes burned with proud hot tears.

Then Wingo was on his feet. He spun around, facing Mickey, not ten feet away.

"Listen to me, bitch," he said amid a sudden hush. "I'm going to get you. One night you'll wake up . . . "

"Fuck you, scumbag!" she whispered.

" . . . you'll wake up and I'll be there. I'll make you pay if it takes the rest of my life!"

The guards pulled him away. Mickey was trembling, her victory shattered. They would celebrate soon, but for that instant, even with Rafe and their friends surrounding her, she felt alone and vulnerable, as if she were the one sentenced.

A dozen of them celebrated at the Tune Inn that night. They carried on like crazy people but no one complained. Indeed, grateful citizens who'd followed the Wingo trial on TV kept sending over rounds of beer faster than they could drink them.

"Three weeks off," Rafe declared. "Damn fine outfit we work for."

"Let's get out of town," Mickey said. "The damn reporters are driving me crazy."

"They want to make you a star," Lon Tate said. "Tiny Tiger Zaps Drug Lord."

"Screw that," Mickey muttered. "I hate talking to reporters. They get everything wrong."

"Hell, Mick, let's go to Florida," Rafe said, killing a beer.

"Gas up the car," Mickey said.

Rafe sighed. "Hell, Mick, why don't we just get married and be done with it?"

Mickey choked on her beer. A hush fell over the table.

"What did the man say?" Ruby Blake asked.

"Don't get any ideas," Lon Tate told her.

"I never take advantage of a drunk man," Mickey said glumly.

Rafe did not recant when sober, and two days later they were married, with Lon as best man and Ruby as maid of honor. The newlyweds drove straight through to Panama City, where Rafe had rented a cabin on the beach. There wasn't much to do there except fish and make love and drink beer and lie in the sun and listen to Jimmy Buffett on the radio.

"I'd forgotten how normal people live," Mickey admitted, one clear, hot morning on the beach.

"I don't think normal people fuck this much, Mick."

"That's their problem."

Mickey rubbed some lotion on her legs while Rafe dozed. Her scar wasn't pretty but the tan helped. She hated to think of this trip ending; maybe it wasn't reality but it sure was heaven.

Except for Wingo. That bastard Wingo.

She watched some kids playing in the surf. It was crazy, in this bright, clean, timeless world of sky and water, to fear a man who was locked in a maximum-security prison hundreds of miles away.

But she did. Two nights before, on the coastal highway, some idiot had almost run them off the road. Just a drunk, Rafe said. She wondered. She thought a lot about Wingo, about his vow of revenge. You could bet he was living to escape, and that he had money stashed away and people on the outside to help him. Could he have sent someone to kill them? Or was that pure paranoia? She tried not to think about it.

One night they built a fire on the beach and watched the stars over the Gulf and for the first time she told him about Jessie.

"I've got to find her," Mickey concluded. "It's like I have this other half that was stolen from me, and I'll never be whole until we're back together."

"We'll find her, Mick," he promised, with that quiet, fist-in-the-fire determination he had, and she thought she'd been crazy for waiting so long to tell him.

Mickey gazed out at the timeless, flawless dazzle of the Gulf, a light so bright and pure that every noontime was like the first blinding instant of creation. She knew what she wanted now. To love this man and to keep their love as perfect as it was that day. To have his child. And to find her sister. Surely, if she tried hard and was as good as she could be, those modest dreams could come true.

15.

JESSICA WAS DRESSING FOR YET ANOTHER MEETING WHEN AN unexpected visitor arrived from West Texas.

All those boring meetings had paid off; the Billy Ringer Theater was starting to happen. An architect had been chosen, a brilliant design approved, and construction had begun at the Lake Worth site. Plans were under way for the theater's opening, and Sonny had invited the world's most famous actor, the President himself, to the festivities.

She was brushing her hair when Olivia knocked. "Miss Jessica, a lady to see you."

"Who is it?"

"I don't know. There's a policeman too."

Jessica went to the door.

The policeman tipped his hat. "Miz Nash, this lady says she wants to see you. But she don't *know* you."

Westover Drive was not precisely private property, but if you

214

drove along it looking out of place you might be asked a few polite questions.

The woman was in her twenties, with a handsome face and a determined look. Then Jessica saw the child. A boy with a large head, slanted eyes, and a dreamy smile. Jessica tried not to react, but there was something horribly wrong.

"I . . . I'm Jessica Nash."

"I'm Tammy Barber, Mrs. Nash. This is my son Josh. I'd like to talk to you about the Carvex plant."

"The what?"

"The chemical plant in Pearl? Out in West Texas? The Nash family owns it. It gave my son Down's syndrome."

"My God," Jessica said. "Come in."

"It's all right, ma'am?" the policeman asked.

"Yes, Jimmy. Thank you. Come in, Mrs. . . . "

"Tammy Barber. Just Tammy."

"Call me Jessica. Would you like coffee or a Coke or tea?"

"A Coke would be nice. We drove straight through from Pearl."

Olivia brought Cokes and they settled in the living room. The boy nestled on his mother's lap. Melissa appeared, gazing intently at the visitors.

"Melissa, this is Mrs. Barber and her son Josh."

"Josh. You want to play, Josh?"

After a bit of coaxing, Josh agreed. Melissa took his hand and led him out to her playground, casually assuming command, although she was at least two years younger.

"She's so sweet," Tammy said. "So perfect. Josh'll never be like that. He never had a chance. Down's happens at conception, if the chromosomes in the sperm or the egg are damaged."

"I don't know anything about this plant," Jessica admitted.

"Carvex is the biggest thing in Pearl, particularly with oil off so bad. Almost a thousand people work there. They make about a billion pounds of acetic acid a year, and all these chemicals they use in paints and dyes and things. Nash bought it five years ago, from a German company.

"For a long time nobody thought much about pollution and toxic wastes. There's just always been that yellow smoke coming out of the smokestacks. But so many people started getting sick."

"Sick with what?"

"A lot of things. Diabetes. All kinds of cancer. Then the Down's cases. There've been four cases in the last six years. Statistically, that's off the charts for a place the size of Pearl. A doctor from Baylor University came to see us. He says there's no doubt that methyl ketone in the air and benzene in the water caused it."

Tammy Barber looked embarrassed. "You get to where you talk like a scientist. The thing is, I'm the healthiest person you ever met. I ran track in high school. I never smoked or even drank beer, much less did drugs. My husband played football and he's a state trooper now. I was only twenty when Josh was conceived. It's not right—not me and three others."

Jessica couldn't speak.

"Oh, Carvex has scientists who swear on a stack of Bibles that it's just coincidence about our kids. But common sense tells you that's not true."

"There's a lawsuit, isn't there?" Jessica asked. "I read about it." In truth, she'd been so busy that she rarely read the paper.

"That's right. A lawyer named Conway has brought a class action suit. But no court can change Josh. The important thing is to close that plant down."

Tammy Barber blinked back tears. "We're afraid to have another child. Half the women in town are. What are we supposed to do, leave our homes? Is a chemical plant more important than human beings?"

"What do you want me to do?" Jessica asked.

"This lawsuit could go on forever. And all the while, more people will suffer. I think NI should shut down the plant, not hide behind its lawyers. I read in the paper that you were a mother, and I hoped you'd care."

Jessica felt a profound sense of shame, and of responsibility, too. "Tammy, I'll talk to my husband. I'm sure he doesn't know about this. We're going to New York tomorrow for the weekend—I'll talk to him then."

. . .

The Nash Foundation had contributed $7 million to the American Council on Theatrical Arts for a program wherein young actors would perform in schools all over America. ACTA's board, which included luminaries of New York society and culture, had decided to show its gratitude by inviting Billy and all other interested Nashes for a weekend in Manhattan.

The interested Nashes proved to be Billy, Jessica, Kay, and Lily. The company Sabreliner flew them up on a Friday morning, and limousines whisked them to the Plaza, where suites overlooking Central Park awaited them.

Jessica had looked forward to the trip, her first to New York since her and Billy's courtship. But the visit from Tammy Barber had shaken her. She wanted to talk to Billy, but she wanted to catch him in the right mood, and there was no opportunity amid the excitement of the flight up.

Two surprises awaited them at the hotel. One was Philip Kingslea, who said he was in New York to see his publisher but was clearly Kay's escort for the weekend.

An even greater surprise, when they gathered in Lily's suite for drinks, was a young man Lily introduced as "my friend Alex Molina." Spanish, thirtyish, liquid-eyed, and dashing in his tuxedo, Alex said he was in the import-export business, but just what he was doing with Lily remained a mystery.

ACTA's officers joined them in Lily's suite, among them a striking woman called China Siddons.

"Oh, God, you're all so attractive!" she cried, moments after entering. "We knew you were wise and good, but who would have thought you'd be so attractive?"

"We're so glad you're here," said Jack Billings, a stockbroker who was ACTA's chairman. "Your grant will make this program soar."

"It's exactly the sort of thing I had in mind when I started the foundation," Lily said.

Jessica felt very alone in this crowd. She wondered if she should tell Lily about the chemical plant. Was Down's syndrome the "sort

217

of thing" she cared about? She wondered how much one chemical plant meant to her, or one little West Texas town.

"We're glad to be here," Lily said. "Ten years ago, we Texans hardly ever came to New York. We were intimidated. But now . . ."

"Now you've decided to buy it," Philip Kingslea quipped.

"Well, a few blocks on Fifth Avenue," Lily conceded.

"Don't mean to rush you, but there are some fabulous people waiting for us," China said. She was a very thin woman of uncertain age, wearing a burnt orange dress. She was not conventionally beautiful, but blessed with lovely dark eyes, dramatic cheekbones, and absolute assurance.

They piled into limousines for the short ride to Lincoln Center. Billy, Jessica, and Philip Kingslea shared one limo.

"You lost Kay," Jessica said.

"She'll turn up," the writer said.

"I'll say this for the Nash women," Billy grumbled, "they're never lonely."

"No reason they should be," the novelist said.

"Kay's not worried about Mark?"

"You have a dirty mind. I'm just a friend of the family."

Billy sighed. His feelings for his brother Mark were not so affectionate that he could feign outrage at Kay's affair with Philip. "God, we look like the Snopeses, with all our bizarre entanglements."

"You and I aren't bizarre," Jessica reminded him.

Philip laughed. "Billy, you Nashes are very rich, and these people are very sophisticated. They wouldn't care if Kay and your mother arrived with the Hells Angels, as long as you keep writing checks."

"Thanks," Billy said. Then, "Who's China Siddons?"

"A rich widow," Philip said. "Who dabbles."

"How rich?"

"New York rich. Not Texas rich."

"Dabbles in the arts?" Jessica asked.

"Whatever. Speaking of dabbling, how do you like Señor Alex?"

Billy groaned. "Jesus, why can't my mother take up knitting?"

"She can knit when she's old," Jessica said. "And he's adorable."

"Are you going to have a thirty-year-old Spanish lover when you're sixty?" her husband demanded.

"If you're not around, I certainly hope so."

In a glittering hall at Lincoln Center they were met by dozens of glowing faces, movers and shakers of the social, financial, and theatrical worlds. Jessica trailed after Billy, who was relentlessly lionized. She met a number of women who were involved with the theater as writers, actors, directors, and producers.

She met other women who were younger and thinner and blonder. These were dressed in bright, gossamer creations and sported a long-necked hauteur. They focused their attentions on Billy, spoke rapidly, and listened hardly at all. When Jessica ventured a word about the Billy Ringer Theater, they were bemused by the idea of a theater in the distant wilds of Texas.

Eventually, Jessica sought refuge with Philip Kingslea, who was positioned in a corner enjoying champagne, Beluga caviar, and the spectacle around them.

"Having fun?" she asked him.

"Working," the novelist said.

She thought self-consciously of her simple black dress. "I feel like a mouse. Those women are so gorgeous."

"Don't be stupid. You're the most beautiful woman here."

"I don't feel that way."

"Let me tell you about these women. They've starved themselves until they have no asses under those two-thousand-dollar dresses. They're built like boys and think like men."

Jessica laughed. "Who are they?"

"Culture vultures. Idle women who leech onto whatever's fashionable. Women who marry rich men all dull as they are. One assumes they must fuck these men from time to time because neurotic children arrive sporadically. Mostly the men dedicate themselves to making money and the women to spending it."

Across the room, China Siddons had Billy alone, her face close to his, hands fluttering, eyes flashing, her dress billowing in a phantom breeze, her profile as sharp and chilling as a blade.

219

"Ah, tell me about Texas, you fascinating man," Philip murmured.

"What?"

"That's what China just said to your husband."

"She's so chic. She looks French."

Philip was amused. "China? She'd love that. She's Bronx-born and bred. But with a genius for marrying well."

"How old is she?"

"Ageless. A courtesan. Her most recent husband was a kindly old stockbroker she killed with an overdose of oral sex. They found him with a smile on his face. The perfect crime."

The party moved on: more limousines, snaking through the rain-bright streets. Their destination was a corner table in the Grill Room at the Four Seasons. An '83 Perrier-Jouet Fleur de Champagne greeted them. Jessica sat between Philip and Alex. The Spaniard chatted easily of art and the theater. Billy was at the other end of the table, between his mother and China Siddons. There were many toasts before the consommé arrived, essence of pheasant, followed by a majestic Mouton-Rothschild, filet of sea bass, risotto with morels and roasted porcini, and tournedos of beef with foie gras.

Jessica looked from face to face. Kay was chatting vibrantly with Jack Billings: how happy she was away from Mark. China talked intently to Billy. The widow was drinking Perrier and hadn't touched the food.

A woman called Scooter who produced plays Off-Broadway asked Philip about his novel-in-progress.

"Can you tell us what it's about?"

"It's about three hundred pages."

"Don't be coy."

"It's about a serial killer," Philip said.

"Goodness. Who does he kill? Innocent virgins?"

"Book reviewers. They're dropping like flies. Unspeakable deaths. Before the *coup de grâce* they're chained to a tree, made to listen to their own writings, and given a chance to repent. The evidence points to a penniless novelist."

Brandy appeared. Jessica fought to stay awake. When finally they started to leave, China Siddons blocked her path.

"I'd like to take you shopping in the morning. Buccellati, Bendel's, Saks, Hermès, Dinoffer—whatever your favorites are."

Jessica drew back at the sound of the woman's staccato voice. "I'm sorry. I promised myself I'd go to the Frick in the morning."

"The Frick? Don't you have museums in Texas?"

"Why, yes, we have wonderful . . . "

"Then we absolutely *must* go shopping."

"The thing is, I don't really need anything," Jessica said. "Well, if you know a good used book store."

China was aghast; Jessica was amused. She knew, as China apparently did not, that rich Texas women could satisfy their fashion needs without jetting to Manhattan. They had Neiman Marcus, Foley's, Sanger Harris, and a score of other excellent stores competing to serve them. Buyers and designers called Jessica almost daily, dreaming that she would emerge as a superconsumer like Kay. What did not exist in all of Texas, as far as Jessica could see, was one really good used-book store. No citadel of fashion in New York—nor any cathedral or theater or museum—could give her more happiness than a solitary hour browsing among dusty old volumes. She would meet her dearest friends there, summon up her happiest memories, and be thrilled beyond measure if she discovered a gem or two to take home and treasure. But she did not think China Siddons would understand this quite unfashionable passion.

"Then you must join us for lunch at Wilbur's," China persisted. "It's our little neighborhood bistro. I've already asked Billy and the others."

Jessica surrendered to the inevitable. "That sounds wonderful," she sighed.

"Did you meet the Spaniard?" Scooter asked China as their car headed uptown. "Positively delicious."

"The Spaniard is spoken for. There's really nothing like a billion dollars to take twenty years off a woman." China sighed. "And that adorable Billy Nash, he's worth a billion himself."

"They say he has two brothers."

"One a monster and one a pig, I'm told."

"Nobody's perfect."

"How can such an attractive, incredibly rich man live down there in Fort Apache with that dull woman who buys her clothes at the Goodwill Industries?"

"Ah, you noticed."

"You would not believe what that creature said to me," China confided. "I offered to take her shopping. And she said, 'Gee golly, I really don't *need* anything.'"

"An amazing failure of the imagination," Scooter said.

"In my experience, if a man is exceptionally endowed—in mind, body, or pocketbook—he wants to feel appreciated. So here is this ninny married to a billionaire and she asks if I know any used-book stores."

"Can this marriage be saved?"

"An interesting question." China sank back in the soft leather seat of her limousine, crossing and recrossing her thin legs. She looked up Park Avenue and saw only green lights, as far as she could see. She took that for an omen and laughed aloud.

Jessica dressed without waking Billy, and took the elevator down. The Palm Court hummed with excitement, but she hurried past, out into the muggy morning air. In her teaching days she'd learned never to eat in hotel dining rooms. She bought a carton of juice from a vendor outside Central Park and walked up Fifth Avenue, enjoying the city's Saturday-morning calm.

The Frick was deserted and she was soon lost in its grandeur; after the last hectic days, this was heaven. She was standing before Rembrandt's *Polish Rider* when someone spoke.

"They claim that one of his students did it."

The young man wore khakis, loafers, a green plaid shirt, and a tweed coat with suede elbow patches. His face was framed with a curly reddish beard.

"They must be mad."

"The thing is, everyone has bad days," the young man said. "It's as if, three hundred years from now, someone said Hemingway didn't write *Across the River and into the Trees* because . . . "

"Because it wasn't *The Sun Also Rises*."

"Exactly." He looked at her with piercing blue eyes.

"Would you like coffee?" he asked.

"I . . . I think I'm late for lunch."

"A pity."

Jessica blushed. "Yes."

"Goodbye," he said. "Enjoy."

She drifted down to a Goya. The young man had shaken her and she wasn't sure why. Not, she thought, because she was tempted by a handsome stranger in a museum. She was beyond that, wasn't she? Was it because their brief exchange had triggered memories of her university life, had carried her back to a world she had loved and left so far behind?

Or was she flattered by his attentions? Since her marriage she had been hugely admired, but mostly because of Billy's money. This young man had been drawn to her just for herself, a thirtyish woman, casually dressed, in a museum on a Saturday morning in New York.

That was how Billy felt, when they had met on the Mall: flattered to be admired—to be loved—for himself and not for his money. Sometimes she wondered if the day-to-day reality of marriage could ever live up to his romantic dreams of perfect love. They often saw things so differently. This trip was an example: he loved the flattery and the glitter that she found agonizing.

She looked at her watch and felt a touch of panic. No matter how much she dreaded lunch, she hated to keep people waiting.

The restaurant was not far away, over on Lexington. But as she set out, a light rain began to fall. She waved in vain for cabs and finally walked the last three blocks holding a newspaper over her head. As she neared the restaurant, a cab almost ran her down.

She entered the restaurant as she might have entered a church, seeking refuge: later she would think how bedraggled she must have looked.

An imperious man she took to be the maître d' did not notice her. The restaurant was cool and dim; a long, elegant room flanked by a crowded bar. The people gathered there were beautifully coiffed, confident, stylish. She felt underdressed; was this China's cozy little bistro?

The maître d' greeted other arrivals with hugs and first names, but Jessica remained invisible.

Finally she called to him.

"One moment, one moment," he snapped, and scurried away.

She tried again. "I'm Mrs. Nash and I'm meeting friends."

"Where are your friends?"

She was taken aback. "I don't see . . . "

"Then you must wait," the man decreed, and was gone again.

Jessica was cold and tired and wet. She wanted to sit down very badly.

When the man dashed by again she said rather loudly, "My friends must be late and I'd like a table, please."

The maître d's arched eyebrows were question marks, pointing at her. He evaluated her wet clothes, her stringy hair, as other men would evaluate her body. Should she drop China Siddons's name? She couldn't bring herself to speak it.

"Very well," he said. "Follow me."

He led her into a side room she hadn't noticed before. Its mood was funereal; she'd been banished to the twilight zone. He deposited her at a gloomy corner table. Jessica groaned—where was China, Billy, anyone?

She saw others like herself, sitting silently, like prisoners awaiting execution. They were different from the people in the front: Some of the women had gray hair; some of the men were fat and wore double-knit suits. They were tourists, drawn to the fashionable East Side bistro they'd read about in guidebooks, unaware they'd be received as untouchables.

A waiter passed. She'd not been given water, a menu, anything. "Waiter!" she said loudly.

He loomed, dark and surly. "Yes?"

"I'd like some hot tea."

"If Madame will wait."

"I won't wait! Please bring it immediately."

He brought the tea. People nearby applauded. The waiter dropped a menu on the table, which revealed that her tea had already cost her $3. My God, she thought, I left one of the great museums in the world—I left that nice young man—for this rude, gloomy, overpriced charnelhouse.

"Jessica, darling! What are you doing back here?"

It was China, a vision in pink, her hair concealed in a turban.

"Didn't I tell you two? Nobody *stirs* before then. Come on, you shouldn't be caught dead here."

She led her back into the warmth and gaiety of the front room, where Kay, Philip, Scooter, the Billingses, and a few others were enjoying their first drinks of the day.

The maître d' bustled up. "Henri, you scamp!" China cried. "How could you put our friend in Siberia?"

Henri was a mix of disdain and surprise.

"Please . . . " Jessica protested.

"This is Mrs. William Nash," China said. "As in the Nash brothers of Texas, who are buying up New York."

Henri's facade crumbled. "If Madame had only identified herself."

She did not deign to reply. She only wanted to be rid of this man, out of this city, far from this awful woman, this humiliation.

Billy arrived, amid much fanfare, and kissed her cheek. "Sorry I'm late. A water main exploded and screwed up traffic."

"It's all right. I had the most wonderful morning in . . . "

"Billy, we've suffered an outrage." China had a voice like a dentist's drill. "Jessica came early and was *banished* to *Siberia* with the *tourists!*"

Jessica had overlapping fantasies. In one she broke a chair over China Siddons's turbanned head. In the other Billy bought this hellhole and turned it into a McDonald's.

The maître d' apologized anew. The hubbub went on for an

eternity. China maneuvered Billy into the seat next to her own, where she continued to dominate the conversation. Jessica watched with grudging admiration as China orchestrated their little party. She was bright, witty, energetic, and well informed. She brought others into the conversation long enough to flatter them, then eased them out. She had done her homework on the Nash family: she knew about Sonny's takeovers and Billy's good works. She insisted that Billy describe several of his projects, which he did gladly.

Over coffee, China said: "Jessica, dear, tell us all about your wonderful new theater in Fort Worth."

Jessica hated being called upon like a schoolgirl, but the champagne had made the day brighter.

"It's the Billy Ringer Theater," she said. "Named for Lily's uncle, who was an oilman. It's really my Billy who made this happen. We expect to have our premiere in the fall. We're opening with *Romeo and Juliet*. An exquisite young movie actress, April Flynn, will be our Juliet."

"Then I'll take twenty tickets for opening night," China declared. "I'll charter a plane, organize an expedition, and descend on deepest, darkest Texas."

"Fantastic!" Billy declared. "That's just what we need."

Jessica had never been so happy to leave a place in her life. She hurried to F. A. O. Schwarz and bought a four-foot Teddy bear for Melissa, so the day was not a total loss.

As they dressed that evening, she tied Billy's black tie for him— he had not mastered the art—enjoying the easy intimacy of the moment. She wore a strapless black velvet gown, with a gold sash, and the diamond necklace Billy had given her for their second anniversary.

"You look great," he told her. "That velvet against your skin— fantastic! You ought to splurge more on clothes."

"It seems like such a waste. These women who never wear the same dress twice. I love Kay but, my God!"

"Indulge yourself. When we come to New York I want to show you off."

Their limousine inched down Broadway: walking would have been faster. Their hosts were treating them to *Cats*. As Jessica stared out the window at the bustle of Broadway, her thoughts were of Tammy Barber and the people in Pearl. She had not yet spoken to Billy—they'd hardly had a free moment—but she could not forget the Carvex plant. Was it the misery of people like Tammy that paid for her velvet gown, her diamonds, this limousine?

They shared a box with Kay and Philip. In time the curtain went up, the cats began to prance around the stage, and it was all Jessica could do not to groan aloud.

Philip Kingslea, too, was bored by *Cats*, but not by his weekend with Kay. The woman fascinated him: her money, her energy, her anger, the amazing distance between her inner and outer lives. As Mrs. Mark Nash she had everything, wealth beyond belief and a famous passion for spending it.

But the inner woman had nothing. She saw herself the victim of a Faustian bargain: to marry a rich man she did not love, she had surrendered her soul, her self-respect. When she drank, and they drank too much together, she was filled with self-loathing. The first time they went to bed, she begged him to hurt her, to punish her, but he would not, and it was with tenderness that he had won her love.

Sometimes she hinted that she would leave Mark if he would marry her, but Philip was not interested. He believed that in time rich women always reminded you who paid the piper. He liked to sleep with rich women, because they pursued pleasure more reck-lessly than other women, and had more interesting problems, but he thought only a fool would marry one.

Philip believed that vast wealth was unnatural, that to possess a billion dollars was like weighing four hundred pounds; it was not the way people were meant to live, and in time it made them crazy and dangerous. Sonny, for example. Philip had known Sonny since childhood and he thought him a freak, an accident of nature, a creature who possessed a certain dark fascination but was not re-motely human.

Mark was the least interesting of the Nashes, an oafish accountant who happened to deal in millions of dollars instead of thousands.

Billy was interesting because he had the humanity that Sonny lacked and the imagination that Mark lacked. Billy's problem was that he would have made an excellent English teacher at Hockaday or Madeira, but fate had cast him as history's first hippie-humanist billionaire, and there was no certainty that such an exotic creature could survive on this unforgiving planet.

Then there was Puss; Philip fancied her the happiest of the Nashes, a carhop in paradise.

And finally, Sweet Jessica. A lamb gamboling among the wolves. If Billy's survival was in doubt, what hope was there for his starry-eyed bride?

He watched her applaud politely as the curtain fell on the first act of *Cats*.

"I may throw up," he whispered, and was rewarded with her most fetching smile.

They sipped champagne between acts, feeling quite regal. But Billy was moody, and as the theater lights dimmed, he whispered to Jessica, "I feel like hell. I'm going back to the hotel."

"I'll go with you," she said.

"No, enjoy the show." Before she could argue, he was gone.

It was only as they left the theater that she realized China Siddons had not been with their party, in either of the boxes. Nor was she at their next stop, Le Cirque.

Without China, the second night's dinner was more subdued. Lily strove to keep up the conversation, but everyone had said all they knew to say about Texas and Broadway and the new theater project.

Jessica couldn't eat; she felt sick as she wondered if everyone assumed Billy and China were together.

"He had a terrible headache," she told people, feeling a fool.

When she arrived back at the Plaza, Billy wasn't in their suite.

She thought of calling Kay, but she was ashamed. When finally Billy returned it was as if she'd never seen him before.

"I couldn't sleep," he said. "I took a walk. I feel better now."

Jessica tried to think, to be logical, but her brain did not engage.

She could say, "Were you with China Siddons?" and he would say no and be offended. Or he would say yes, and then what would she do? The choice was too confusing, too hideous. She might have raged, wept, accused, stormed out of the suite, but instead she hugged her pillow and went to sleep.

There was no champagne and no laughter on the next day's flight back to Texas.

"Sick, sober, and sorry," Kay mused. "Does anybody remember that old hillbilly favorite?"

Lily and Kay nursed Bloody Marys, Billy gazed glumly out the window, and Jessica's mind still echoed with the unanswerable question from the night before: What had he done, and what should she do?

"We missed you at dinner last night, William," Lily said finally. She called him William when she was angry.

"And we missed you at lunch, Mother."

"I'd seen—and heard—enough of that China creature for one weekend."

"You could have brought Alex. He was overflowing with wit and wisdom."

Kay groaned. "Are we over New Jersey? Is there something toxic in the air?"

Billy wouldn't let go. "Mother, I'm damned if I know why you have to run around Manhattan with a man younger than I am."

His mother eyed him coldly. "Because, my dear son, when I was your age I was an overweight schoolteacher with an obnoxious husband and three sons to raise. Happily, life has given me a second chance."

"There is such a thing as discretion," he persisted. "At least Kay can pass Philip off as a friend of the family."

"Don't talk to me about discretion," Lily snapped. "Unlike my three sons, I am a single person."

Kay opened her eyes. "Billy, you mind your own fucking business. And I use the word advisedly."

"I think some of us have seen enough of New York for a time," Lily said.

"I may open an office of the foundation there," he announced.

"Not with my money, you won't," his mother said, and Billy did not argue with that.

Two days after their return to Fort Worth, as Jessica was driving downtown to see Billy, she felt a headache coming on.

Perhaps it was the heat, she thought. Or more likely her frustration about Billy. With her active imagination, she had sometimes worried about plane crashes and kidnappings, but infidelity was a calamity she had not considered. Should she confront him? Or turn her eyes away? She kept coming back to square one: she didn't know the facts. Had he been with China? Or only out for a walk? Was she a wronged wife or a paranoid fool? Did she want the truth or a soothing lie?

She resolved, like many another suspicious woman, to watch her man closely. If he announced a business trip to New York, there would be trouble. To her relief, he was busy with plans for a major Nash Foundation grant to SMU, in nearby Dallas.

Her thoughts were also on Tammy Barber and the Carvex plant. She decided to be businesslike; to that end she called Billy's office and asked for an appointment.

He was puzzled. "Sure, come on by. But what for?"

"Let me explain when I get there."

Did he think she was coming to confront him about China Siddons? If so, let him stew. Perhaps, when he found she'd "only" come about the Carvex plant, he'd be so relieved he'd give her everything she wanted. She laughed at that Machiavellian logic, and it was then that the headache struck.

She stopped in a drugstore on West 7th Street. As she waited at the check-out counter, she sensed something familiar about the sullen young clerk, but preoccupied with her meeting with Billy she gave the woman little thought.

She paid for the aspirin and was turning away when the woman declared, "I swear I know you from somewhere."

Jessica shook her head. "I haven't lived here long," she said. She had these encounters, with people who'd seen her picture in the papers; they embarrassed her.

"You lived at the Home. I'm Emmy Rollins and I knew you."

Jessica froze. "No."

"Sure, your name was . . . Jessie, that was it. You had a twin sister. My God, I remember the time your sister, she like to killed that damn Luther."

"No, you're mistaken."

"The heck I am." Emmy's round face hardened; her hand seized Jessica's wrist. "Look there," she cried triumphantly.

"No, please."

"Lookit that mole. You know why I remember that? 'Cause you were so perfect. I used to say that mole was the only thing that kept Miss Jessie from being perfect."

She grinned and released her arm. "So what're you doin' now, honey? Looks like you done okay for yourself."

"I have to go." Jessica hurried out the door, into her car. Emmy trailed behind, bellowing from the doorway, "You stuck-up bitch, who do you think you are?"

Jessica ran a red light at University Drive and almost hit a Mrs. Baird's Bread truck. She could see the Nash Tower ahead, but her hands shook too badly to keep driving, so she turned into Forest Park and pulled over.

She remembered Emmy well enough. Seeing her now had shaken Jessica, shaken her far more deeply than the possibility that her husband might have slept with a woman in New York. It was as if a door to her personal hell had been jerked open and she was face to face with the demons of her past. She was thrust back into the night that she and Mickey had been tormented in the barn behind the Home.

Hardly a day, hardly an hour passed that she did not relive that cruel "birthday party." The nightmare endured: the candlelight, the boys' leering faces, the Everclear gin and baby oil, the shame of her nakedness, the boy twisting her arm, the horror of Luther's erection, her overwhelming sense of helplessness in a hostile universe—all that, climaxed by Mickey's bloody vengeance.

231

Only weeks later she had been carried away to her new home in Little Rock. As much as the loss of Mickey had hurt, it had been heaven to be in her new home, with her own room, nice clothes, and all the books she wanted. She had nightmares at first, to the dismay of the Alberts, but they attributed them to the generalities of her past, not to that one never-confessed night of horror. There was no one she could tell about that—not the Alberts, not her friends, not the doctors, no one.

The Alberts, middle-aged and conservative, wanted most of all a proper daughter who would make them proud. Jessica played the role gladly; they gave her security, she gave them perfection, or at least good grades and modest behavior. Mrs. Albert feared sex most of all: it was not only not to be done, it was not even acknowledged. That was fine with Jessica. Of sex she only knew the humiliation of that night in Texas. Ever since, she had asked boys to leave her alone.

The problem was her beauty. At the Home she had been a skinny thirteen-year-old in hand-me-downs. But in Little Rock her looks began to blossom, enhanced by the fine clothes and cosmetics her adoptive mother lavished upon her. She never quite rejected her beauty; for years it all too often brought her unwanted attentions, when she only wanted to be left alone, but it was part of her and she was proud of it. Still, at its worst, she thought of beauty as a curse, one that brought her far more heartache than joy.

Looking back, Jessica thought it a miracle that she was ever able to have normal dealings with men. That she did she attributed to a combination of biology and good fortune. She had been lucky in her lovers. The first, her senior year in college, had been a would-be poet, who guided her gently into physical love. If he could not purge her memories of sex as violence, he could at least give her another image of sex as tenderness and sharing. She had taken only four lovers before Billy Nash.

She had worked hard to build a new life for herself, and she had succeeded beyond her wildest dreams. The past was buried, if never forgotten. Then, in an instant, Emmy's hand on her arm had been like a devil's claw, dragging her back. The past was her Pandora's box, seething with monsters; the child in her, confronting them, could only flee.

The top floor of the Nash Tower was given over to the executive suites, a conference room, a dining room and kitchen, and a small gym. All three brothers had offices there, as did their mother, although hers was rarely used.

The brothers' offices were the same size, but Sonny's was considered the most choice because of its spectacular view to the west—the Will Rogers Memorial Center, Arlington Heights High School, planes taking off at Carswell Air Force Base, and the distant, dusty prairie that stretched on endlessly, into the past.

Billy's view to the north was less grand, but he was content. He could identify the rooftop of Joe Garcia's, the stockyards, and the spot where LaGrave Field had once stood, in the golden days of the Fort Worth Cats baseball team.

When Jessica entered, he was hunched over the antique table he used for his desk, surrounded by papers, dressed in khakis and a plaid shirt. His office was brightly decorated with mobiles and modern art.

"You look busy," she said.

"It's this SMU grant, for an environmental center. Giving money away is not as easy as it sounds. At a big university you have all these bureaucracies that touch on the environment—biology, chemistry, policy planning, whatever. And they all say, 'Oh sure, give us your money and we'll do great things.' What they don't say is that they'll raise their vision beyond their own narrow fields and think seriously about how the university can help save the environment. So I have to get to know the professors and deans, all the players, and figure out what they should be doing, and then bribe them into doing it. That's why I've been in Dallas so much."

"So how's it going?"

"On paper, great. The prospect of twenty million dollars inspires eloquent promises. But I have to nail things down."

233

He grinned. "The glamorous life of a Nash brother."

She smiled back. He looked so boyish, so incredibly sweet; how could there ever be anything but love between them?

"So what's on *your* mind?"

"Billy, a woman came to see me last week. Tammy Barber. She lives in Pearl, near the Carvex plant. She brought her son who was born with Down's syndrome. Three other children have been born with it there. Doctors say there's no doubt that pollution from the plant caused it—there's just no other reason for four cases in a place the size of Pearl. And high rates of cancer and other things, too. There's a lawsuit."

"I'm very familiar with it," he said. "You say this woman came and brought her child?"

"Yes."

"What did she want?"

"She's afraid the lawsuit will drag on forever. Meanwhile more people are being harmed. She thinks you should close the plant, or at least cut back, until the case is settled."

He leaned back in his chair. "That's not likely to happen. Our policy is to play it out in court. It's not just the cost of closing the plant, it's the cost of damages if a link between the plant and the injuries is established."

She couldn't believe it. "Are you saying that, even if the plant is harming people, you're going to defend your right to run it?"

"I'm saying that if we win in court, Sonny might be persuaded to quietly fold the plant, but he'll never admit liability."

"That's monstrous! Is that how you feel?"

Billy twisted unhappily. "If it was up to me, I'd cut back operations in a minute. But it's not up to me. Two of us would have to agree."

"And the others won't agree?"

"Mark is Mr. Bottom Line: Fight them in court. Squeeze out every last dime. Sonny is more erratic. He's been known to show human emotions from time to time. But this RICO lawsuit has driven him over the edge. He's not very receptive to people who are suing him right now."

"What about your mother?"

"If she wouldn't intervene for Walter Lamont, she won't on this."

"We have to persuade Sonny. This is evil. How can you talk about saving the environment when Nash International operates a chemical plant that causes cancer and Down's syndrome?"

Billy looked weary. "Dealing with Sonny is like riding the tiger. You have to move carefully. You make trade-offs. He's been very helpful to us on the theater."

"This isn't the theater. This is people's lives."

"I'll talk to Sonny."

"I want to talk to him."

"We can go together."

"No. I want to do this myself. Right now, if possible."

Billy shrugged and picked up the phone. "Sonny, Jessica's here and wants to talk to you."

He listened a moment, then put down the phone.

"What did he say?"

"He said to hustle your sweet little ass right over."

"Wonderful," she said. "Wonderful."

Jessica had not picked the perfect moment to confront Sonny Nash. His fury had been building for months as his planned take-over of Lamont & Company boomeranged into disaster.

Walter Lamont's young lawyer, Sid Timberlake, armed with the RICO law and Yankee audacity, had given Sonny fits. The discovery provisions of the law enabled him to delve into elements of NI's finances that Sonny considered no one's business but his own.

Sonny's depositions had been agonizing for him and everyone else. He hated the idea that any court or judge had power over his life. He arrived an hour late for his first deposition, and did so then only after his lawyers, in near-hysteria, convinced him that he (and possibly they) faced jail for contempt of court.

Sid Timberlake delighted in this process. Men like Sonny thought themselves above the law, and it was sweet to see them slowly accept the law's reality and majesty, to understand that the jailhouse doors could clang for them too. Sid thought Sonny's lawyers would eventually beat back his RICO offensive, but it had bought time for his client and also treated Fort Worth to the spectacle of seeing Sonny Nash squirm.

Sonny was bitter and unrepentant. He saw a vast conspiracy against him, made up of old farts like Walter Lamont and Judge Grady Pickford who'd always hated him. The court system seemed to him venal, cliquish, and corrupt, and he yearned to smash it as he had smashed everyone and everything that had ever dared challenge him.

Hungry for revenge, he had his staff check into Sid Timberlake's past, and Judge Pickford's, and some other people's too. He didn't know what he'd find or what use he'd make of it, but Sonny knew his day would come, in court or elsewhere.

The strain of the legal battle drove Sonny into a near-permanent state of rage. He'd been drinking hard, pub-crawling with his biker friends and brawling in sleazy North Side bars. He'd been troubled by blinding headaches. Even his sex life had suffered. How could he be himself when these bastards were making a fool of him, calling him a gangster, telling lies about him in the newspapers? He'd fired three sets of lawyers for failing to rout the RICO suit and complete the Lamont deal. Sometimes Sonny thought he would explode from pent-up frustration. He was surrounded by idiots, and increasingly he believed he would have to deal with his enemies himself.

He leaped up when Jessica entered, took her hand, fixed her with his biggest smile. Charm, a politician once told him, was the most lethal weapon known to man.

"Little sister, seein' you has made my day!" he declared. "How about a drink?"

Jessica had never seen him like this: unshaven, his eyes bloodshot and wild, like a caged animal's. His T-shirt featured the mushroom cloud of an atomic bomb. Above the cloud were the words: "Made In America." Below it: "Tested In Japan."

"Thanks, Sonny, but . . . "

"Come on, have a little rum."

"Okay, a little."

While he mixed two drinks, she looked around his office. One wall was covered with pictures of Sonny with Presidents and lesser politicians who had sought his friendship and money—"the whore's gallery," he called it.

"To what do I owe this honor?" He eased her onto a cowhide sofa. "If you're leaving Billy and want me to run off with you—by God, I'll do it!"

Jessica laughed. "I'll stick with him a little longer, Sonny. But I want to talk to you about . . . "

He was looking at her legs, nice long smooth legs, and wondering whether his nitwit brother was giving her what she needed.

"Say what now?" he interrupted, for he had not been listening. Women said precious little that interested him.

"The Carvex plant in Pearl, Sonny. A woman came to see me. Her son has Down's syndrome."

She told him about Tammy Barber's visit, the children with Down's syndrome, what the Baylor doctors said, the whole sad story.

To Sonny, it was the standard bleeding-heart bullshit. If she'd been anyone else he'd have thrown her out. Instead, he thought about her tits. Not big like Puss's, but apple-sized and firm; he imagined her hard little nipples, imagined biting them.

" . . . close the plant," she was saying, "or at least cut back the parts that pollute the worst."

Sonny shook his head. "Folks don't want that. Close the plant and you close the town."

"Sonny, two hundred people in the town are suing. They want to stop other people from being harmed."

"That's not what they want."

"What do you mean?"

"They want money. They've got 'em some radical lawyer and they're talkin' a hunnerd million, two hunnerd million damages. It's nothing but a shakedown. I've got to stand up to 'em. I can't have everybody in West Texas thinkin' if they get sick they can sue Sonny Nash."

"Sonny, there's no doubt in my mind that the Carvex plant caused those cases of Down's syndrome."

"There's a heap of doubt in mine, honey. I've got me a passel of scientists who say there's no link-up been proved."

She wanted to scream in frustration. "Maybe your scientists tell you what you want to hear," she said evenly. "There are objective scientists, at Baylor, at the state health department, who are convinced the plant's pollution is causing Down's, cancer, and lots more. It's monstrous."

Sonny's face flushed. "I'm no monster, Jessie. You show me proof that that plant hurt one man, woman, or child, and I'll close it down so fast it'll make your head spin."

"Do you mean that, Sonny?"

"I said it, didn't I?"

"The Baylor doctor wrote a long report, with case histories. Have you read it?"

He shook his head.

"Will you read it, if I get you a copy?"

"Absolutely."

"I'll have one to you tomorrow. Thank you so much."

She rose up, genuinely excited. Maybe he did have an open mind, maybe he'd be moved by the report, maybe this whole terrible episode could be ended.

At the door, he squeezed her arm. "You come see me any time, little sister."

She hugged him and hurried away.

He watched her go, feeling the warmth of her breasts against his chest, admiring the way she moved. Sonny didn't give a damn about his sister-in-law's high-minded social concerns, but he loved her sweet little ass.

16.

WINGO LIVED FOR ESCAPE.

He had accepted prison as his greatest challenge, the ultimate test of will between him and the government.

His quest for freedom was working on several levels. He was paying some of America's most celebrated lawyers hundreds of thousands of dollars to pursue every possible appeal. He had other, less celebrated lawyers gingerly examining the possibility that certain federal judges, for large amounts of cash, might look favorably on his appeals.

He had still other lawyers, celebrated only in jailhouse legend, taking steps to make his life inside the federal maximum-security prison in Atlanta as bearable as possible. There had been, for Wingo, no hope of bargaining for a "country club" prison. This was hell in a very small place. There were many ways the authorities could encourage the rape, mutilation, or murder of an inmate, like Wingo, whom they despised. Wingo feared no man in hand-to-hand combat, but he did not relish the prospect of defending himself

239

against four or five assassins in some isolated cell or shower room.

But money was a shield, in prison as elsewhere. On his second day in prison, a slender, muscular black man wearing a red bandana and a diamond earring blocked his path in the exercise yard.

Wingo flexed for combat, but the man flashed a cold smile. "My name is Phoenix," he announced. "I'm going to keep you alive."

Phoenix led him around the prison yard. He saw the eyes of the other inmates upon them, knew that Phoenix was giving him his blessing, knew that his least celebrated lawyers had done their job well.

He learned that Phoenix was a member of a black supremacist faction who had shot two policemen after robbing a bank, and was the leader of the black brotherhood that ran the prison. Wingo never knew what his lawyers had paid Phoenix; he didn't want to know. All that mattered was that the black man's protection of him was, insofar as anything could be in that violent world, absolute.

With his personal security assured, Wingo settled into the prison routine. He worked in the prison library. He played chess and read in his spare time. Yet his every word and deed had but one end: freedom.

He did not indulge in the sex and drugs that were readily available, because they dulled the senses. If he made a "friend," it was because that person might have information or resources that could aid his cause. Even his chess games with the stockbroker in the next cell were a means of keeping his mind alert, just as he kept his body fit with daily workouts.

He met others who shared his obsession. They endlessly analyzed legendary escapes of the past. There were tales of tunnels hundreds of feet long and of helicopters landing in prison yards. They marveled at the mob boss who persuaded his lawyer to trade places with him—the inmate strolled to safety, while the lawyer stayed behind to face felony charges. They cheered the shotgun-wielding Americans who raided a Mexican jail and freed friends held on drug charges.

Wingo enjoyed the bull sessions, but he knew that yesterday's escapes were by definition the ones the authorities were prepared for. The challenge was to find the new weakness in the prison defenses, the escape hatch no one had seen before.

In time he was forced to admit there was no obvious way to escape from the prison itself. Inmates sometimes left under escort, for funerals, courtroom appearances, and the like, but Wingo was an unlikely candidate for release. Moreover, because the prison had its own hospital facilities, a medical furlough did not seem a possibility. Wingo nonetheless faked a series of migraine headaches, to take a closer look at the hospital wing.

It seemed as escape-proof as the rest of the facility, but he spent a day there making small talk with the doctors and orderlies, fishing about to see what he could learn.

By the time he left, Wingo had the beginnings of a plan.

He summoned his father to the prison for a talk. When he was on trial, Wingo could easily have incriminated his father; instead, he went to great lengths to protect him. Not out of affection, but because he needed his father free, fearful, and anxious to do his bidding.

He told his father precisely what he wanted. His father was not happy, but he promised to obey.

As he waited, Wingo spent a good deal of his free time reading. The prison library was poorly stocked in most areas, but well supplied with tattered paperback editions of crime novels, notably the works of John D. MacDonald, Elmore Leonard, and Lawrence Sanders.

Wingo read their novels partly to pass the time, and partly for insight into the criminal mind. He raced through MacDonald's Travis McGee novels in a week, savoring the portrait of Florida's sea, sand, and sex, but concluding that MacDonald was a romantic, more interested in his knight-in-shining-armor fantasies than in the realities of crime.

Elmore Leonard was more interesting. He clearly identified with the small-time criminals in his novels—he properly found little to choose between crooks and cops—and he knew the nuts and bolts of crime. But ultimately Wingo found Leonard's petty criminals boring: crime, he thought, should aspire to grandeur, and Leonard was of the kitchen-sink school of crime novelists.

Lawrence Sanders was Wingo's most welcome discovery, particularly his "Deadly Sin" series. Here was a writer who appreciated the marriage of genius and madness that produced great criminals. His killers killed not because they needed a few dollars but because they were angels of darkness, men and women with a grudge against the universe.

In one astonishing novel, *The Case of Lucy Bending*, Sanders succeeded in portraying a Florida that was almost as violent, decadent, and corrupt as the real thing. Wingo did not mind that Sanders's anti-heroes almost always paid in the end—that was a requirement of the genre—for here at last was a writer who understood, as Wingo did, that the first responsibility of the criminal, as of the artist, is to think big.

Wingo waited, thinking big.

One afternoon Phoenix came to see Wingo in the library. A few mournful jailhouse lawyers were hunched over their briefs.

"Merry Christmas," Phoenix said.

"Where's my present?"

Phoenix extended his fist. Wingo put out his hand and received a small pink pill.

"Is that all?"

"They sent two. Said to keep one."

Phoenix asked no questions, although his eyes shone with curiosity. Wingo wondered if Phoenix too had fantasies of escape. Or did he enjoy being king of this particular jungle?

Wingo faced an interesting decision. His father had sent him a pill, but he had only his father's assurance that the pill would do what he wanted, as opposed to killing him, which many people wanted, probably including his father.

But he did not hesitate. The next morning he reported to the library with the pill in his pocket. He felt a certain apprehension, like the first time he'd dropped acid, not knowing what magic or menace the chemicals might bring.

He walked to the water fountain and swallowed the pill.

Nothing happened.

He returned to his desk. A young arsonist asked if he had a copy of *Fear of Flying*, which ranked with *The Godfather* among the library's most popular novels. Wingo was recommending *The Second Deadly Sin* when World War Three broke out inside his head.

"Excuse me," he said, and dropped into his chair.

Throbbing. Lights flashing. Someone had jammed a knife into his brain. Wingo clasped his hands over his ears, trying to ward off the pain. He screamed, sure he was going to die, sure his father had betrayed him. The jailhouse lawyers gathered round in curiosity, and Wingo screamed and crashed senseless to the floor.

He awoke in the hospital wing of the prison. His brain, eyes, and jaws ached, and the rest of him felt as if he'd been hit by a truck. He tried to move and found one of his ankles shackled to the foot of the bed. Not that he could have walked far.

In time an orderly loomed beside the bed, pockmarked and feline. "Well, Sleeping Beauty awakes."

Wingo could not speak. The orderly helped him sip a glass of water, stroking his hands lovingly. Wingo lacked the strength to protest.

"How long have I been here?"

"They brought you yesterday morning, sweets. Looking like something the dog fucked."

After a while Dr. Mudd appeared, a fleshy, owl-eyed man who checked Wingo's pulse, took his temperature, then pulled out a notebook.

"Young man, have you ever had a seizure of this nature before?"

"No."

"Any head injuries? Auto accidents? Recent drug use?"

"I never use drugs," Wingo said. "I'm in perfect health."

By the end of the week Wingo felt fine; it was the doctors who were in discomfort, from their inability to diagnose his problem.

Finally, after all his tests had failed, Dr. Mudd sent for him.

"We find serious abnormalities in the chemistry of your brain.

We're sending you to the Medical Center in Baltimore, which has the technology for more sophisticated tests."

"I feel fine."

"That's irrelevant," the doctor said.

They drove to Baltimore in a black Pontiac station wagon. Wingo was in handcuffs, with shackles on his feet. The four marshalls referred to him as "it," blew cigar smoke in his face, and made clear that they would relish an excuse to blow his head off.

It was not a pleasant trip, but Wingo was encouraged. He was out of prison. He was moving.

The Medical Center was one of the new generation of federal institutions. It did not sprawl amid rural isolation. It was, rather, a modern, twelve-story building on the fringes of downtown Baltimore. It served as a detention and processing center, and also housed, on its upper floors, the most modern medical facilities available to federal prisoners in the northeastern United States.

It was also a fortress. Even as its pastel walls soothed the incoming inmate, its state-of-the-art defenses ensured that he would not depart prematurely. Steel doors, electronic locks, closed-circuit TV, and heavily armed guards welcomed its visitors. Wingo remained handcuffed and shackled as they rode the elevator to the seventh floor. He and the marshalls passed through two more sets of steel doors before they entered the hospital proper and his handcuffs and shackles were removed. He was subjected to an extremely unpleasant strip search.

Wingo was given a room. His door was locked from the outside and his window was barred and high above the ground. Still, he loved the view of Baltimore. A new world of possibilities spread out before him. Wingo slept well.

The doctors arrived in force the next morning. He was poked and probed and subjected to video thermography. The prison guards and marshalls, well aware of his crimes, treated Wingo like dirt, but to the doctors he was simply a puzzle, of no more personal interest than a lab rat. They didn't care about his crimes, only his brain waves.

Only one doctor showed the slightest personal interest in him, an intense young man named Dalton.

"Wingo?" the doctor said, with a hint of amusement. "The infamous Washington coke czar?"

"So they said."

"Do you think cocaine use caused these seizures?"

"You're the doctor." Wingo studied the young man's face and saw something familiar there.

As the tests continued, Wingo learned his way around. He and the other patients had the use of a large day room that contained a TV, a pool table, a Ping-Pong table, and assorted chairs and magazines.

Wingo played chess with a frail man who was dying of cancer and had robbed a bank for money to buy medicine for his dying lover. As he played he studied the day room carefully, because the prisoners were largely unguarded there. Its windows overlooked a major commuter route. But the windows were barred, and even if you somehow cut through the bars it was still a sixty-foot drop to the ground.

The floor was solid concrete. The air-conditioning vents were small and barred. The TV set was bolted down. The pool cues and Ping-Pong paddles had potential as weapons. There was a firehose, coiled in a box with a glass door, which perhaps could somehow be used to sow confusion. It would not be difficult to take hostages. The problem was that the state had long ago made clear its willingness to sacrifice a few guards, or even doctors, rather than let prisoners escape. You could kill your hostages, but you would be killed in turn, and Wingo wanted no part of that bargain.

The unprecedented performance of Wingo's brain waves fascinated the Baltimore medical staff.

"If you have another seizure, we want you back fast," a doctor named McCaffery said in parting. "I'm putting you on ergotamine, an experimental drug that relaxes the arteries of the brain. You understand, your brain does not feel pain, but the arteries in the brain have nerves. That's why your head throbs. Every time your heart pumps, it stretches your arteries. The question is what inflames your arteries. We think it has to do with your brain chemistry."

McCaffery questioned Wingo in endless detail about his cocaine use. His fantasy emerged: He would use Wingo's case to document that cocaine did indeed drive men mad; he would write an article for the *Journal of the American Medical Association* that would bring him fame and major research grants.

Wingo led the good doctor on, pleased to have gained his attention. That precisely had been the purpose of the little pink pill.

The pill had come from a young chemist who had developed a number of designer drugs. Wingo had met him in Colombia and heard him joke about the side effects of some of his concoctions. Wingo had told his father to ask the chemist for a pill that would make him seriously, even spectacularly, ill—for prison doctors were accustomed to world-class malingering—but would cause no permanent harm. The chemist had done well. His pill had been an open ticket to the Baltimore Medical Center. That was the first piece of the puzzle.

But it was not until Wingo and the marshalls had driven halfway back to Atlanta—the same slobs, blowing smoke in his face and calling him "it"—that he recognized the missing pieces, put them all together, and saw the way to freedom.

Back in Atlanta, Wingo honed the diverse elements of his plan. He would need to return to the Baltimore Medical Center, but that was no problem, thanks to his remaining pill.

Once there, he would need a hacksaw blade, and that was a problem. It would not be hard to obtain one in the prison, but there remained that strip search in Baltimore.

He sought out Phoenix.

"I need a hacksaw blade," he said.

"How big?"

"Big enough to work, small enough to hide."

Wingo was telling Phoenix more than he wanted to tell him.

There was always the possibility that the black man was reporting to the authorities.

"Is there a way to get a blade through a strip search?" he asked.

"They check your mouth and your hair and your ass. You can't swallow it and shit it out. You better rethink your plan."

Wingo would have to think more about the hacksaw blade. Those few inches of steel were the key to his freedom.

At length he wrote his father, using a code, and gave him new instructions, and with that, Wingo's plan was in place.

He had nothing to do but wait, and as he waited he thought often of the two mistakes that, as he saw it, had led him to prison.

The first had been letting Lita know his name. It had seemed reasonable at the time. She was his friend in the White House. But by giving her coke, he created a fatal link between his public life and his secret life.

His second and, he thought, greater mistake had been trusting Mickey McGee—as, in court, he had learned her name to be. His hatred of McGee grew with each passing day. Lita had simply been a fool, an addict who did what addicts did.

But McGee was different. McGee had gleefully lured him, duped him, made a fool of him. Wingo might have blamed himself—for the drug use that had warped his judgment, for his political fantasies, for his obsession with the perfect woman, for underestimating his adversary—but here his dispassion failed him. He blamed McGee for doing her job, and he lived for the day when he would make her suffer as he had.

In time his father's letter arrived, with a one-word, encoded message: Proceed.

Before he could proceed, however, Wingo had to calculate yet another element of his plan, one that demanded the cooperation of the very heavens themselves.

He redoubled his study of the weather reports and almanacs available to him. For Wingo needed a storm. Not just rain, but a storm of Shakespearean dimensions. He waited two weeks, until the weather patterns looked favorable, then he acted.

He sent for the second of the pills from Phoenix.

The next morning, in his cell, he swallowed the pill. Within minutes the symptoms began. The explosions in his brain, the all but unbearable pain, the flashing lights, the shortness of breath, the nausea followed by darkness and collapse.

The stockbroker in the next cell called for help.

The authorities moved quickly. Wingo awoke hundreds of miles away, back in his seventh-floor hospital room in Baltimore.

Once again, the tests were endless, and the questions, too. McCaffery, the would-be *JAMA* scholar, begged Wingo to confess that illicit prison drug use had triggered the seizure—the "flashback," he persisted in calling it.

"I promise you total immunity," he insisted.

"I hate drugs," Wingo said. "Maybe it was the coffee."

He was there three days before Dr. Dalton appeared, the tense young doctor who had been amused by his cocaine connection.

He took Wingo's temperature and pulse. Finally, still without speaking, he took a small envelope from his pocket and slipped it under Wingo's pillow.

"Bastard," he said, and hurried from the room.

Wingo could guess what had happened. Two men had knocked on Dalton's door. One had done the talking; the other had been very large. They handed Dalton two packages. One contained several ounces of cocaine. The other: $50,000.

Earlier, the smaller of the two men would have confirmed that Dalton was a heavy user, as many young doctors were. He would also have learned that Dalton was deeply in debt for his medical education, and that his cocaine habit had only put him in deeper. Wingo had guessed all this the first time he saw the doctor's wary eyes, his bitter face. He could read that face like a map of Colombia.

"What do you want?" Dr. Dalton would have asked, although by then he probably had guessed. And the smaller man, the lawyer, had told him about the modest favor, the delivery that now had been accomplished.

Wingo hid the hacksaw blade in his mattress and settled back, dreaming of revenge, waiting for rain.

17.

From the shadowy second-floor bedroom, if you pulled back the damask drapes and looked, you saw lovers strolling beside Turtle Creek, ancient oaks, and the grandest mansions between Palm Beach and Palm Springs. She had borrowed this one from a friend who had married an English lord and didn't plan to return to Dallas until he died.

Every room was ablaze with flowers. She kept music playing, Mozart and Tchaikovsky, low and soothing. She kept champagne at hand, and bonbons and finger foods. The bedroom was dim and cool, magical, an island of calm amid the relentless heat and conflict of the world outside.

He had not felt so relaxed in years. Too many people wanted too many things from him.

"I need a vacation from my life," he said.

"Is your life so terrible?"

"Not terrible. But confused. Tiring."

"This is your vacation."

She lay beside him in the brass bed, her head on his shoulder. They made love at different times, in different ways, and she amazed him, for he thought sex held no more surprises. Her body was white and thin and hard, an ivory dagger. Her body was as unlike Jessica's as her mind. They were both educated, monied American women of the late twentieth century, but they might have sprung from different centuries, different planets.

"May I ask a question?"

"Of course."

"How is your marriage?"

He laughed. "That's the sixty-four-million-dollar question."

"What does that mean?"

"It means I don't know. I love her."

"But."

"Yes. But."

"You want your freedom?"

"Sometimes. That's part of it."

"And pleasure," she said. "It is strange, how few women know how to please a man. They think that because they are attractive and have sex with him and give him children, he should overflow with gratitude."

"Shouldn't he?"

"Those are the basics, like scrambled eggs and toast. There is a difference between a short-order cook and a great chef."

She rubbed the worry lines between his eyes with her index finger; he sighed contentedly.

"You're so sophisticated. I'm not sophisticated at all."

"Shop girls are sophisticated these days. But your kind of wealth is rare."

"I'm really quite normal. That's my secret. I was a patrol boy."

"What is that?"

"It means that in the sixth grade, before school, I helped smaller kids across the street."

"I wish I had been there. I would have been a siren, luring you from your post."

250

"I played Little League. I went on double dates. I had a paper route. I have a middle-class mentality."

"We must change that."

"It's not easy. I was a teenager when Mother inherited the money. When I went to Princeton I was just another tacky Texan, as far as the preppies were concerned. Mother paid my tuition and sent me a hundred dollars a month and if I needed more I had to earn it. I dropped out to work for Gene McCarthy in the New Hampshire primary in 1968. When Bobby Kennedy was killed, I dropped out of school and grew my hair and smoked a lot of dope. I was a very normal kid."

"You must have been adorable."

"Meanwhile, Sonny was starting to amass this incredible fortune. Finally I decided I'd better come back and confront reality, if that's what this is. I still fancy myself a very normal guy. But in an abnormal position."

"You're an extraordinary person. You have to accept that."

"In a sense, we're all pretty normal. Sonny bought a yacht once, for twenty million from a down-on-his-luck Greek. An incredible thing. It was like a floating luxury hotel. He flew us all down for a cruise."

"And how was this voyage?"

"A disaster. Let's face it, we Nashes spend half our energies avoiding each other, and suddenly we're trapped on this goddamn boat. Mark was sick the whole time. Sonny and I had a fight. Puss was tripping. Somewhere off the coast of Mexico, Mother threw a fit and had the helicopter fly her out. The rest of us quickly followed. Sonny never set sail again. He sold the damn thing for twice what he paid for it."

"I hope to meet Sonny sometime."

"Don't be in any hurry. He's in the middle of a lawsuit that has him foaming at the mouth."

"Do you like your brother?"

"I respect him. Sonny has clear goals and total certitude. He wants to be the richest, most powerful, most feared son of a bitch in America. My problem is that I can't decide what I want."

"You must decide. It would be a sin, with your intelligence and money, not to define your goals and achieve them."

"Sometimes I think that what I want is to be a serious man, in this trivial world I move in. It's hard. The more money you have, the more temptations to dedicate your life to trivia."

"You are a serious man. You need support. A woman who understands you."

"I don't want to hurt anyone."

"Money can ease many hurts."

"I love Jessica. She represents a kind of ideal to me."

"Yes, of innocence, and innocence is very appealing at a certain point in one's life, but in time it can become deadly dull."

"I'm not sure she and I want the same things. She has this idea that she wants to go back to teaching. My wife, teaching? Grading papers? The latest thing is, she's after Sonny to close down a chemical plant."

"That's unfortunate."

"She's right, of course. It should be closed."

"It's not her decision. These things are complex. She should leave them to you and your brothers. It isn't her role."

"What is her role?"

"To please you."

"Ha. Tell her that. She's a modern woman."

"Too modern for her own good. Turn over, let me rub your back. I feel such tension in you."

"Do you give good back?"

"I give good everything, love. Turn over."

"Boy, it hit me like a freight train to see you that day at the store," Emmy said.

She was fat and sullen. Anton, whom she called her fiancé, sported a purple shirt and a world-class Adam's apple. They were in Jessica's living room, acting out the charade they had concocted.

"What I always wanted to do, far back as I can remember, is be a writer," Emmy announced.

252

"It's the truth," Anton confirmed. "She's all the time got her nose stuck in some book."

"They say write what you know, and I don't know much except puttin' up with Anton and clerkin' in a drugstore. I don't reckon even Jackie Collins could make a story out of that."

"You could make me a real sexy international playboy," Anton suggested.

"I figure the most exciting thing I know about is that one time I lived at the Gertrude Little Home and there were these twins in the next bunk and one of 'em grew up to be the famous Jessica Nash. And all that stuff with Luther and the boys . . . "

"She told me 'bout that and I like to threw up," Anton confided.

" . . . and the way they split you twins up," Emmy continued. "And how you both kind of vanished, and then you turn up famous, with your picture in magazines, livin' in Westover Hills. I figure I could make a story out of that. I Knew Her When."

Jessica fought to keep her temper.

"I figure the *National Enquirer* would buy it. Or the *Star*. Sometimes they get to biddin' over things."

"Maybe the *Reader's Digest*," Anton ventured. "My Most Unforgettable Character."

"I wrote up a rough draft," Emmy said.

She opened her purse and handed over a handwritten manuscript. Jessica read a few paragraphs.

"You know, of course, that it would be painful to me to have that published," Jessica said.

"That story, it's all true," Anton declared.

"The truth can be painful."

"See, this is journalism," Anton explained. "Like 'Sixty Minutes' or something. People don't always like being wrote about, but we've got freedom of the press in this country."

Jessica thought of the Duke of Wellington's mighty "Publish and be damned!" Did she have the courage to say that to these creeps?

"I hear the *Enquirer* will pay ten or twenty thousand dollars for a big story," Emmy continued.

"I'm sure you could do a lot with that money."

"That's right," Anton agreed. "Pay off all our bills. Maybe even pay down on a house."

"But we don't want to cause you no misery," Emmy added.

"Of course not."

"It's hard for me, seeing a chance to do something for myself, but not wantin' to cause you no misery either."

"What we thought was, Miz Nash, was that maybe there was a way to satisfy us both," Anton said.

"How is that?" Jessica asked.

"Suppose, instead of the *Enquirer*, we was to sell it direct to you? Then you could just, you know, tear it up."

"And how much would you sell it to me for?" Jessica asked. "Ten or twenty thousand, did you say?"

Anton looked grieved. "Well, see, ma'am, that's just what we figure the *Enquirer* would pay. The thing is, this could be a TV movie, too. Maybe a mini-series. This here's a true-life Cinderella story, that's what I told Emmy. She could make a million dollars out of this."

"Then she'd be the Cinderella," Jessica said, but her irony was lost on her visitors.

"I hope you don't think I'm going to give you a million dollars," she added.

"No, ma'am. But we was thinking maybe a hunnerd thousand."

"You want me to give you a hundred thousand dollars for this garbage?" Jessica said angrily.

"Yes, ma'am, that seems about right to us."

"It's blackmail, you understand," she told him.

"Don't you get high-and-mighty on us," Emmy said. "You always did think you were better 'n anybody else. I wish those boys had . . . "

"Hush *up*, Emmy! We figure it's a business deal, Miz Nash. A up-and-up deal, just like your husband and Mr. Sonny Nash, they do every day."

"And then you'd come back wanting more money."

Anton looked hurt. "Why, no, ma'am."

"How would I know that?"

"We'd give you our word of honor."

"I'll have to talk to my husband," Jessica said.

Anton's eyes widened. "Don't reckon you need to do that, ma'am. Be simpler if it was just you and us."

"Do you think I walk around with a hundred thousand dollars in my purse?"

"Look, Miz Nash, make it fifty thousand and we'll close the deal right here and now."

"I'd still have to talk to my husband."

"We'd take a check, ma'am," Anton told her. "Make it twenty thousand."

This had happened too fast; Jessica wanted time to think.

"No, I'll have to talk to him." She could not resist adding, "You understand, he may want to bring charges against you."

"Emmy, I told you," Anton moaned.

Jessica stood up. "Emmy, you ought to be ashamed of yourself. I never did you any harm."

"You bitch, whatta you know about harm?" Emmy demanded. "Whatta you know about workin' on your feet all day for slave wages and never havin' anything? I knew you when you was nothin', and now you're Mrs. Gotrocks in Westover Hills puttin' on airs."

Olivia came to the doorway and looked with dismay at the couple. "Is everything all right, Mrs. Nash?"

Jessica nodded. "Yes, Olivia, my guests are just leaving."

Mr. Eliot was mistaken, Jessica thought. Or he had never been to Texas, where clearly August was the cruelest month. The heat was brutal, one hundred-plus, day after day; it sapped your strength and dulled your mind. Hot blistering winds blew off the plains, and there was no shade, no rain, no mercy. The sun was a tyrant, an angry god on high, defying you to venture out. The rich fled, the middle class grumbled in air-conditioned sanctuaries, the poor suffered and died. According to the *Star-Telegram*, crimes of violence doubled during the harsh days and sultry nights of August. Jessica didn't know why Billy didn't take them away, to Aspen or

Maine, any place cool. He said he was still too busy with the SMU grant.

The temperature was near a hundred degrees when Kay and Myra dropped by for coffee at nine one mid-August morning. Kay, in shorts and a halter, said she and her son were on the way to Shady Oaks for a swim.

"Did you hear about the excitement at Sonny's last night," Kay asked.

"No, what happened?" Jessica said.

"A friendly poker game turned into a brawl. Sonny almost killed a man."

"I'm glad I wasn't there."

"He's at the edge," Myra said. "He'd given another deposition yesterday in that RICO case. I worry about him."

"I worry about the rest of us," Kay said. "I mean, do we have Captain Queeg at the helm? Have you seen him since he started growing a beard? He looks positively Mephistophelian."

"He always has," Jessica said.

"Has he talked to you again about Carvex?"

"He says he's studying it," Jessica said. "I think he's playing games. I'm supposed to meet tomorrow with the people from Pearl. I'll have to tell them not to expect miracles."

"Hi, Mama. Hi, Aunt Kay and Aunt Myra."

Melissa was in the doorway, in her bathing suit, a pail in her hand.

"Precious darling," Myra said, and scooped the child into her arms. "Oh, how you've grown!"

Jessica was always amazed by the impact her daughter had on Myra: the lines were erased from her face; she glowed and seemed decades younger.

"My baby starts in school next month."

"School?" Myra exclaimed.

"Montessori. She's been tested and everything."

"You going swimming, Aunt Kay?"

"Yes, sugar. You want to go with us?"

"Is it okay, Mama?"

256

"Maybe I'll come too," Jessica said. "Billy's in Dallas again."

Myra and Kay exchanged a look.

"Honey, if you have a minute," Myra said.

"I can take the kids to Shady and you catch up there," Kay suggested.

Jessica studied her friends uneasily. A few minutes later, she faced Myra across her kitchen table.

She was glad to have the time alone with Myra. She respected the older woman's judgment and she had thought about asking her advice about Emmy's blackmail. She hadn't yet talked to Billy about it. How much would it matter if the world suddenly learned that she had once been Jessie Ketchum of the Gertrude Little Home?

But Myra spoke first.

"There's something come up, and Kay and I decided to stick our noses in your business."

Jessica forced a smile. "And you're the spokesman?"

"We flipped and I lost. Do you mind if I just bust right out with it?"

"Bust away. I guess."

"I gather you met China Siddons in New York?"

"Alas, yes."

"And I gather she was friendly with Billy?"

"You could say that."

"She's in Dallas. Been there about a week."

"Oh my God!"

"A friend of hers, and mine too, went to London, and China is camping out in her house on Turtle Creek. Mind you, I'm not saying that she and Billy are seeing each other."

"Why else would anyone come to Texas in August," Jessica said bitterly, "except to steal someone's husband?"

"I'd have to agree with that," Myra said.

"You know her?"

"She made a play for an oilman I know in Houston a few years back. To her, Billy Nash is too big a payday not to take a shot at. What has she got to lose? Not her virtue. Not her reputation. Not a husband. Not a goddamn thing."

Jessica fought back tears. "How can he have such poor taste?"

"Men will surprise you that way."

Jessica went to the refrigerator and took out a Carta Blanca. "Want one?"

"I thought you'd never ask."

The cold beer tasted good, straight from the bottle. "It's a shock," Jessica said. "Should I be angry and throwing things? I just feel hurt. I think I've been a good wife."

"Of course you have. It's an old, old story."

"I was suspicious in New York, but since we've been back I put her out of my mind. Never imagining that the Wicked Witch would mount her broomstick and fly to Texas."

"One thing you have to consider is whether you want to document their being together," Myra said.

"How? Go hide in the bushes along Turtle Creek?"

"Your lawyer would know. A private detective, probably."

"That's so degrading."

"I've seen how bitter these things become. A few photographs can be worth millions of dollars. Or did you sign a pre-nupt?"

"No, although Mark wanted one."

"In that case, if you ever divorced Billy, particularly if he was in the wrong, you'd be a very rich woman."

"I can't believe we're discussing this. When you start talking millions of dollars, it's unreal to me. What I care about is what's right for us and our daughter. If he doesn't love me anymore, if he doesn't want me . . ."

"Oh, balls! Of course he loves you, but this Park Avenue *puta* comes along dropping names and her pants soon thereafter and he forgets. Men have poor memories. You have to jog them now and then. Like they say about hitting the mule with the two-by-four, to get his attention."

Jessica laughed. "What's my two-by-four?"

"That boy needs to consider that he could lose the finest wife and child in the world, and wind up with some piece of baggage who, once he comes to his senses, he wouldn't touch with a ten-foot pole."

"I give her credit. She's impressive."

"She's expensive trash. The trouble is, men really are different from us. They're like dogs in heat. You have to be tolerant sometimes."

Jessica shook her head sadly. "I feel so lonely, just thinking about it."

"It's the human condition, honey. In the end we're all alone, no matter how much money we have. You talk to that boy. He's not bad, just a little confused."

Jessica took the older woman's hand. "Myra, I do appreciate your support. You've known Billy all his life. I'm the outsider. Your friendship means so much to me."

Myra's smile was sad and loving. "You and that baby of yours mean more to me than anything in the world," she said. Jessica believed her, and trembled to be loved so much.

Jessica stewed all afternoon and decided to confront Billy that very evening. When she thought about him and China together, she felt such rage that she could imagine killing them both, gunning them down *in flagrante delicto*. It was an alternative that had the virtues of simplicity, brevity, and finality. But of course violence was not her way. Then what was? In the late afternoon she thought seriously about just taking Melissa and leaving, driving to Little Rock or Baltimore or some other place very far away.

Men, she thought, what bastards they are—cold, calculating, conscienceless bastards. You never really knew them. You thought you did, when they courted you, pranced and preened like peacocks, but that was a game, a deception. You saw only what they wanted you to see, or maybe what you yourself wanted to see.

You married them, and the preening stopped, and they began to tune out, except that they needed food and sex and flattery. Then came the moments of truth and you learned that you'd never known them at all. You'd known kind Dr. Jekyll but not the monster Hyde, who wanted to rut with some warthog along the muddy banks of Turtle Creek.

She allowed herself one good cry, then she made her plan. She would not shoot him. She would not flee. No, they were reasonable people—at least she was—so they would Talk Things Over.

To what end? She didn't know. She wasn't sure what she wanted, and she had not the slimmest notion what he wanted. Was Billy bored with domestic life in his hometown? Did he dream of a more sophisticated life with a more sophisticated consort, *la dolce vita* on Park Avenue?

Then let him go! There was always plan B, the one Myra and Kay kept advancing: Get a lawyer, go to court, make him pay!

Myra had spoken of $50 million. She truly could not imagine that much money. When she thought about it, all she could see was Donald Duck's rich uncle, bouncing atop a mountain of greenbacks. It was ridiculous. What would you do with it? She guessed she and Melissa could get by on $50,000 or $60,000 a year—the interest from $1 million would do just fine, thank you.

Then she wondered: What would be the income from $50 million? $3 million a year? What if she had that much money, and used it to help the people in Pearl? Or others like them? She imagined herself as the head of her own foundation. It was a pleasing fantasy.

Of course, what she really wanted was for her and Billy to be in love again, but that seemed the wildest fantasy of all.

"Oh, boy, what a day!"

He kissed her and headed for the bar, shedding his coat along the way. They settled on the deck. It was dusk, and there was enough breeze to make the outdoors bearable. She saw the occasional twinkle of lightning bugs, massed in shadowy treetops, and remembered, despite herself, those boys at the Home who would mash their bodies into phosphorescent balls; their sad glow still lingered in her memory.

"Was the traffic bad?" she asked innocently.

"The traffic? It's those damned academic bureaucrats. 'Just give us the money, Mr. Nash. We know how to spend it, Mr. Nash. You're only an ignorant layman, Mr. Nash.' How did you survive in that world?"

"On poetry and TV dinners."

"They're so damned slick. So arrogant. A bunch of smooth-talking eunuchs!"

She let him ramble. Had he combined real work with his rendezvous that day? God, China Siddons would be work enough!

She watched the shadows engulf their deck, this place where they spent so many happy evenings. Billy had friends from high school he liked to have over, relatively sane young men who were dentists and lawyers and businessmen now, and had nice wives, and did not defer to him. He would grill steaks out here, and everyone would drink too much and flirt a little, and Billy could imagine himself just an average Joe in his backyard.

Other times, it was just the two of them. Sipping Mt. Gay and tonic, after Melissa was in bed. Billy would report on Sonny's latest outrages, or tell long, crazy stories about his hippie days, the people he'd met, the guru who said God had told him to eat only popcorn the rest of his life, the girl who could sing the entire Beatles songbook in seven hours, the time he'd hitchhiked through Nepal, fragments of his wayward youth.

Now those happy evenings seemed centuries past.

"Billy, there are things we need to talk about."

He looked mildly curious. "What's that?"

Class would now begin. L'affaire Turtle Creek wasn't the only item on her agenda.

"Someone's trying to blackmail me," she said.

That got his attention. Might her plight win his sympathy, rekindle his love?

"Who? What for?"

"There's something I never told you about," she began. "Maybe I should have, but it was hard."

She took a deep breath and told him about the mystery of her birth. The foster homes. Jessie and Mickey Ketchum. Her year at the Gertrude Little Home. Her adoption by the Alberts.

And Emmy and Anton and their demands.

"My God," he said when she finished.

But she hardly noticed him. Something quite unexpected had

happened as she spoke. She had been freed from the prison of her fears. She felt not uncertain or ashamed, but liberated. Just telling him her story had done that for her. It was, in literary terms, a catharsis, but Jessica knew this was no literary game; this was one of the great moments in her life.

"My God, I should *thank* Emmy," she told Billy, the words pouring out excitedly. "I've run from the past long enough. I have nothing to be ashamed of. The *National Enquirer* isn't the place to break the news, but maybe in an interview. We could ask your PR people what would be best. My example might help other kids realize you can overcome all kinds of obstacles. I want to visit the Home, to speak there. There's so much I want to do."

She was so caught up in her enthusiasm that she did not notice that Billy remained grimly silent.

"I warned these people that you might turn them in for blackmail," she added.

"Turn them in? Dammit, I may have to pay them."

She couldn't believe it. "Pay them? What for? I told you, I have nothing to hide."

"Jesus, Jessica, it's a hell of a thing."

"What is?"

"For my wife to suddenly announce that she grew up in the Gertrude Little Home. God, what a media circus that would inspire. Just when we're trying to get the theater launched."

"I'm not afraid of publicity. I'm proud of what I've done."

"And this sister of yours, what do we know about her?"

"Nothing. I've tried to find her. She disappeared after high school."

"Well, you'd better believe she'll turn up if this story breaks. You'll have thousands of friends and relations turning up. With their hands out."

"I doubt that."

"Jesus, Jessica."

She thought that if he said that once more she would throw her drink at him.

"It's just so damned sordid."

She let fly: her glass whizzed past his ear and crashed against the side of the house.

He leaped back in amazement. "What the hell's wrong with you?"

"*Me?* What's the matter with *you*, you creep? What do you mean, calling my life sordid? I worked for what I've got! Nobody struck oil and left me a billion dollars! And I'm not aware that any of my immediate family ever pushed any old ladies down a flight of stairs to speed up their inheritance!"

"Who told you that?"

"It doesn't matter. Are you ashamed of my sordid past, is that what you're saying? I never told you I was Miss Magnolia Blossom of 1980. Is that what you want? A pedigree? Is China Siddons aristocratic enough for you?"

She was furious, and enjoying it mightily.

"What about China Siddons?" he asked grimly.

"Do you think I'm an idiot? Do you think you and China can shack up on Turtle Creek and keep it a secret?"

"I don't know what you're talking about."

"Don't lie to me, Billy."

"I haven't seen her since New York."

"She's in Dallas."

"Maybe so. But I haven't seen her."

The denial, his sheer audacity, threw her off stride. She cursed her lack of proof. Myra had been right about photographs.

"That's Sonny's joke, isn't it?" she said bitterly. "What do you do if your wife catches you in bed with another woman? Deny it."

"You haven't caught me in bed with anyone," he insisted.

She believed he was lying, but his stubborn denials took the wind out of her sails; she felt weary, infinitely sad. She looked at him and she thought she knew what the trouble was. She thought it was his money, making him hard and cynical, eating at him the way cancer or alcoholism consumed other men. She knew that at his best Billy was youthful and kind and idealistic, but she had seen him change, in just a few years, as the fact of his wealth tempted and twisted and molded him in ways he could not understand or control.

"Billy, what's happened to us? Don't Melissa and I and our marriage mean anything to you?"

He was unmoved. "I don't appreciate these accusations. Maybe someone's been feeding you a line, but you don't have to believe it."

"Are you telling me you haven't seen that woman in Dallas?"

He glared at her, then rose up.

"I'm not going to be cross-examined," he said. "I don't like being called a creep. I don't appreciate you repeating old gossip about my family. I'll come back when you're more rational."

He marched out of the house. She heard his car engine roar, heard him drive off into the humid August night. She stayed on the deck, staring into the darkness, wondering where the magic had gone.

"I have to be honest," Jessica told the women. "I think Nash International will fight you in court as long as they can."

"How can they do that?" someone cried. "How can they be so cruel?"

"That's easy," Tammy Barber said. "Money."

The dozen women, and their lawyer, were packed into Tammy's living room in Pearl. Jessica had driven over that morning. When she awoke, Billy wasn't there and she hadn't left him a note.

"I guess we had our hopes up," Tammy said. "Thinking you'd be our miracleworker." She held Josh on her lap. Another of the Down's children was there with her mother. The small living room was decorated with china unicorns and rifle-club trophies.

Outside, a hot wind blasted a flat sandy landscape that seemed to roll on forever. Driving into Pearl Jessica had passed the Carvex plant, seen the acrid yellow gases rising from its smokestacks, breathed its bitter air.

"I had my hopes up too," she admitted. "My husband is sympathetic. But it takes two of the brothers to make policy."

"It's Sonny, isn't it?" asked Bo Conway. He was a raw-boned, broad-shouldered, sleepy-eyed man who wore jeans and boots and looked more like a cowboy than a lawyer. He was nationally known for winning several class-action suits that pitted have-not Davids against corporate Goliaths.

Jessica nodded. "That's true. Mark would do whatever Sonny said. Part of the problem is that Sonny is involved in another lawsuit that's made him furious."

"The RICO suit," Bo Conway said. "The countersuit in the Lamont takeover."

"That's right."

"That's interesting," Bo said. "It suggests that Sonny has feelings."

"I'm not sure Sonny has feelings," Jessica said. "But he has ego. He hates the idea that reporters can criticize him or the courts have power over him."

"Our problem is time," Bo said. "I'm sure as I'm sitting here that we can close Carvex, but it could take years. Meanwhile, our people are suffering, and they're making millions off that plant."

Jessica was restless. Now that she was here, she wasn't sure how she could help these people, beyond the check she'd already written for their legal fund. To some of these women she was a Nash, and therefore the enemy, no matter what she did.

"I'm thinking you ought to step up the pressure," Bo continued. "If Sonny Nash doesn't like bad publicity, give him some."

"How?" Tammy asked.

"Last year you asked about a demonstration and I said the timing wasn't right. Maybe it's right now."

"What kind of demonstration?" someone asked.

"Whatever kind you want," the lawyer said.

"What do you think they'll do, if we picket?" Tammy asked.

"If they're smart, they'll ignore you. That way it's a couple of paragraphs. If they arrest you, that's a bigger story. The more publicity you get, the more pressure on them to negotiate."

Jessica was seized by an idea, one that frightened her and yet was irresistible.

"Would it help if I demonstrated?" she asked.

The lawyer laughed. "I expect it would," he drawled.

"We're not asking you to do that," Tammy declared. "It's our fight."

"I want to do it. What they're doing is unconscionable. The only thing is, I have to get back to my daughter. Bo, would tomorrow be possible?"

"It's up to the group," the lawyer said. "But as far as the publicity is concerned, I can get the reporters there tomorrow."

"Then what are we waiting for?" Tammy cried.

They debated far into the night. The safest plan was to picket on the sidewalk across from the plant. The more dangerous plan was to block the entrance to the plant, in which case they would probably be arrested, jailed at least briefly, and brought to trial.

That would probably guarantee TV coverage, the lawyer told them. "But it's no fun being arrested," he cautioned. "I can't advise you to break the law. I can only tell you the consequences."

The women searched their souls. "How will it affect my family?" was a constant refrain. These were good Texas women who'd won gold stars for perfect attendance in church and made straight A's for Good Citizenship in school; it was agonizing for them to contemplate breaking the law, no matter how indifferent the law had been to their misery.

Yet the more they talked, the more militant they became. The Carvex plant was poisoning them and their children. The courts rewarded their suffering with endless delays. How could they, in good conscience, do other than try to shut it down? They talked bravely of Gandhi and Dr. King, men whose teachings had not previously seemed relevant to life in Pearl.

A compromise was reached. They would gather across from the plant at eleven the next morning to picket and make speeches.

At noon, those who wished would cross the road and block the entrance to the plant.

They agreed that this protest would be limited to women (not that they knew of any men who were anxious to join them) and they could bring children if they wished.

When the meeting broke up, Bo cautioned them not to tell their husbands of the plan, lest a leak forewarn the authorities. "Surprise is the best weapon we have," he said.

Jessica phoned Kay, who reported that Billy had called repeatedly, anxious about her whereabouts. Jessica said to tell him nothing. She spoke to Melissa, and then retired to Tammy's guest bed.

Sleep came slowly, in an unfamiliar bed in a God-forsaken corner of the universe. She wondered if she was making a terrible mistake. Probably Billy had come home to apologize, to promise a new start, but this new, public embarrassment might drive him away forever. And what of Sonny? He would never forgive the affront. Even Lily might not approve such radical behavior. Jessica wondered if she had the courage to go ahead. She considered fleeing into the night. But part of her clung stubbornly to a belief that she was right, that helping Tammy and Josh and the others might be the best thing she would ever do.

Sonny and Puss were splashing in the Jacuzzi when a call came from NI's chief of security, an ex-Texas Ranger called Pie Adams. There was, he reported, a problem in Pearl, and the local police chief was on the line to explain. The chief, he added, was nearing retirement and coveted a job at Carvex.

Sonny took the call. "Chief, what the hell's going on out there?" he boomed.

"Bad trouble," the chief warned. "You know that lawyer Conway, the one who's suing Carvex?"

"Yeah?"

"He's got some women all whipped up to demonstrate outside the plant this morning. Eleven o'clock. Gonna have reporters there. One of their husbands told me."

"Well, fuck 'em," Sonny said. "Let 'em march. Probably all pass out from the goddamn heat anyway."

"The thing is, Mr. Nash, after they make their speeches and all, they're gonna sit down at the front gate. I mean, that's bullshit, because you could send your trucks out the back, but . . . "

"Dammit, that's illegal. I have a right to use that gate," Sonny declared.

"Yes, sir, you do," the chief said. "And we'll clear 'em out of there if you say the word."

"Let me think about it," Sonny grumbled, his territorial instincts only barely held in check by the fact of those damned reporters; as Sonny saw it, they were the ones who ought to be arrested.

"There's this other thing, Mr. Nash," the chief continued.

"What's that?"

"Mrs. Jessica Nash? Mr. Billy Nash's wife?"

"Yeah, what about her?"

"She was at their meeting. She gave 'em money and said she'd march with 'em."

"That dumb bitch!" Sonny knew his goal at once: to teach his fancy sister-in-law a lesson.

"It's plumb pitiful," the chief agreed.

"Chief, here's what I want you to do. If these gals want to march on the sidewalk, that's fine. But if they break the law, you move in like gangbusters."

"Arrest 'em?"

"Sometimes you gotta be firm, chief. It's like with kids, you gotta paddle their little bottoms. Nip this thing in the bud, before the radicals take over your town. Then you come see me the next time you're in Fort Worth."

"I'd sure like that, Mr. Nash," the chief admitted.

Sonny called Billy's home number. His brother answered on the first ring.

"How ya doing, kiddo?" Sonny asked.

"I've had better days," Billy confessed. "What's up?"

"It was your better half I was hoping to speak at."

Billy hesitated. It was maddening not to know where Jessica was, and it would be even more humiliating to admit it to Sonny. It had been fun to enjoy two women, but now one had walked out on him and the other was talking matter-of-factly of divorce and marriage. This was not at all what Billy had in mind. In the cold light of day, China terrified him.

"She went shopping in Houston," Billy lied.

"That gal does get around," Sonny said, and hung up.

"What's going on?" Puss demanded.

"You won't believe it," Sonny roared. "You fucking won't believe it."

The Carvex plant, with its sun-bright domes and towers, looked like a huge, sinister space station amid the West Texas wasteland. Tanker trucks came and went, and now and then a human form, tiny as a fly, scaled a distant silver globe. Greenish-yellow smoke rose relentlessly into the air while other wastes seeped down unseen to poison ancient springs far beneath the earth.

By the time the women gathered at eleven, the temperature was 106°; the globes and towers shimmered in the heat.

The otherworldliness of the scene was compounded by a line of police standing ready to protect the plant from marauding mothers. These West Texas warriors were girded in state-of-the-art battle gear, their visors and helmets giving them the look of goggle-eyed aliens.

Jessica, holding her "NIX CARVEX" sign aloft, did not think she and the others could survive an hour of this brutal heat, this rancid air. Her mind was dazed; she marched in a circle that had no end, chanting slogans that had lost all meaning. Six or eight reporters and cameramen watched from the shade of the only tree in sight.

Tammy and other mothers made speeches, their words impassioned but disjointed, scrambled by the heat. The most eloquent message was unspoken: the sight of Josh and the other Down's children marching with their mothers.

They all were strands in the same surreal tableau: the heat-dazed mothers; the bored reporters; the sullen police; the plant that went on churning out its poisons, indifferent as a mountain range. It seemed quite futile to think they could change this plant, that anything could. It seemed, literally, a hell on earth, beyond mortal intervention.

A few reporters sought Jessica out, but she and Tammy had agreed that she should make no statement; her presence would speak for her.

She had decided not to cross the street and face arrest. She told

269

them that she, an outsider, should not detract from the local people whose struggle this was. But there was another reason. Since that long-ago night at the Home, she had hated and feared the very thought of men holding her body, having her in their power.

At high noon, with the heat at its worst, the women formed a circle. The reporters and photographers inched closer. Across the street, the chief spoke through his bullhorn.

"Do not cross the street. Do not trespass on plant property."

"This is it," Tammy told them. "Those who are going, join arms, block the gate, go limp, make them carry you out. But don't resist. Stay non-violent."

Fifteen women locked arms and marched across the street to the gate. The others stayed on the sidewalk with the children. Jessica clutched Josh's hand. She felt disembodied, and infinitely sad. It was like watching from the pier as a troopship left, carrying your friends to battle.

"You are subject to arrest if you do not disperse immediately."

The women reached the gates, stretching from one side to the other, and sat themselves down.

"This is your last chance to disperse."

The women sang "We Shall Overcome," or as much of it as they knew, and snatches of "The Eyes of Texas," as the police advanced. The cameramen were busy now.

The chief had given his orders and his men welcomed them. They hated having to brave the midday sun, having to face the despised reporters, having to confront these crazed women. They knew these women and their husbands, had gone to school and church with them, and now hated them for embracing radical ideas that could only bring trouble.

The chief, in his zeal to impress Sonny Nash, had a surprise up his sleeve, a secret weapon from America's ever-expanding anti-crime arsenal. His men were for the first time using their new MAWR (multi-adjustment wrist restraint) handcuffs, which were expertly calibrated to cut into the wrists like a knife.

Protesters typically "went limp" and demanded to be carried

away, lest they seem to compromise their purity by cooperating with their captors. Police, for their part, hated to carry people, which was both undignified and dangerous. Armed with the MAWR cuffs, they could usually persuade even the most dedicated idealist to stand up and walk.

"Come on, move out, move out!"

The women huddled on the hot pavement, dazed by the heat, squinting into the sun.

The police began to jerk them to their feet and slap the MAWR cuffs on their wrists. "Walk, you can walk!" Arms were twisted, women cried out and struggled against the metal that cut like razors into flesh and bone. Some screamed, begging for mercy, and were shoved toward waiting vans.

Jessica and the others watched in horror.

A reporter was trying to question her.

"Look what they're doing to them!" she cried, but the reporter seemed unconcerned.

Tammy, her hands cuffed behind her back, kicked the policeman who was shoving her toward the paddywagon. Cursing, he clubbed her to the ground.

Her son Josh broke free from Jessica, and ran clumsily across the street toward his mother. The policeman was jerking Tammy to her feet. The child threw his arms around his mother's waist and the policeman pushed him away.

Jessica felt drugged by the heat, by fatigue, by the horror. She was disgusted by the scene before her and more disgusted with herself. She thought this was what she'd been doing all her life, watching from the sidelines. This was life, the good and evil she'd read about in so many books, and she could not stand by passively any longer.

The policeman was dragging Tammy. Josh stumbled after her; it was a scene from Bosch, outside the gates of Hell.

Suddenly Jessica was moving like the wind, into the street, into a new dimension, and throwing herself against Tammy's tormentor. "You bastard!" she cried, as they tumbled to the ground. She hardly knew what she was doing, only that she had never felt so free before. She never saw the other officer who raced up, swinging his billy club.

"Who invited you here, bitch?" the cop asked triumphantly, and she crumpled to the street. He did not immediately understand why he was surrounded by photographers.

Kay was driving up Clover Lane when the news came over her car radio. Her thoughts, until that moment, had been on the upcoming Van Cliburn Piano Competition. She had been asked to head the social committee, but she was reluctant, because when all those attractive young pianists had to be housed and amused, many delicate situations arose. She laughed, remembering Ivan, the apple-cheeked Russian who'd stayed at her house during the last competition. Mark kept trying to engage him in somber talks about God and communism, which drove Ivan half-mad, since his non-musical passions were women, vodka, and fast cars, in that order.

Kay's smile abruptly faded as WBAP aired a bulletin. Jessica had been arrested—injured—during a demonstration outside a chemical plant in West Texas.

She slammed on her brakes, ejected an elderly gentleman from a phone booth, and traced Billy to the Petroleum Club.

"How bad is she hurt?" he demanded.

"They just said 'knocked unconscious.' "

"Oh God!" he cried. Then, pulling himself together, he told her, "I'll leave immediately."

Sonny howled when the news reached him. Three things you could count on: death, taxes, and bonehead cops screwing up the deal.

Within minutes a Jet Ranger was flying Billy to Pearl. A company plane followed with a small army of doctors, lawyers, and security men. Billy was prepared to take Pearl by force if necessary.

Jessica had been taken to a small clinic. An unhappy deputy stood outside, lest Pearl's most celebrated prisoner attempt an escape.

When Billy charged into her room, he found her asleep, her head bandaged. She looked unspeakably fragile. He took her hand and after a moment her eyes opened.

"Are you all right?"

"My head hurts. What about Tammy and the others?"

"They're outside, waiting to see you."

"Billy, close that awful plant."

"Jessica, forgive me," he said. "I've been a fool. I've been the biggest idiot in the world."

"You certainly have," she said.

Then she slept.

Just a week later, Jessica and Billy and their friends the O'Briens were spending a quiet evening on the deck of the Nash chalet outside Aspen. Jack O'Brien was a criminal lawyer in Houston and his wife Mimi sang with the Houston Opera. They owned a condo in Aspen, and Jessica and Billy enjoyed having them over for evenings of bridge and talk.

The Nash chalet was atop the fourth-highest mountain in Colorado. Sonny had bought the mountain for future development, but for now theirs was the only building in sight.

Billy had flown Jessica there as soon as she was able to travel, to get her away from the furor that accompanied her arrest. He had done a lot of thinking that week, and he could only conclude that he was an idiot to endanger his marriage for China Siddons or anyone else.

"I can't have it both ways," he told her. "I finally figured that out. And this is the way I want it, with you."

Jessica was happy to believe him. She had not felt so close to him since the weekend they met. She believed they were truly starting over.

Billy called her "my little fugitive" because she still faced charges in Pearl, although his lawyers promised they would soon be dropped. In truth, Billy was more angry about what had happened there than she was. Her concern was the future of the Carvex plant, but Billy was determined to find out why the women had been so brutally treated. He had vowed, too, to have a showdown with Sonny over the Carvex plant. For Jessica, that made a few stitches in her scalp seem a blessing.

They talked a lot about the future that week. About Jessica working with him on the Nash Foundation. About the upcoming, long-awaited opening of the Billy Ringer Theater. About having another baby. After the turmoil of the past weeks, the placid days and nights in Aspen seemed the happiest time of their lives.

On this lazy Colorado evening they and the O'Briens were having drinks and watching the sunset's distant drama.

"I do believe that sunsets are the most beautiful thing on earth," Billy said. "My wife and daughter excepted. People pay millions for a painting, but you can walk out your door and see something more stunning than any painting for free."

"Weighty thoughts," said Mimi O'Brien, who was thumbing through an old newsmagazine.

"That's because nothing free has snob appeal," Jack O'Brien said. "Imagine if you owned the sunset and could charge admission. The rich would pay tens of thousands of dollars for front-row seats."

"They'd say the poor didn't appreciate it," Jessica added.

"Entire schools of criticism would evolve around sunsets," Mimi said. "Minimalism. Deconstructionists. All that stuff."

"Wars would be fought over control of the sunsets," Billy predicted. "They'd replace oil as a source of human greed and violence."

They laughed, and the men went for more drinks. Jessica smiled contentedly. They'd played tennis that afternoon and she and Billy had beaten the O'Briens for the first time. She daydreamed about their lovemaking that night: it was time to get on with making a baby.

Mimi looked up from her newsmagazine. "Jessie," she said idly, "you don't have a twin sister, do you?"

"*What?*"

"Or did you ever secretly work for the DEA?"

"What do you mean?"

"There's a story here about a drug dealer they caught. And a picture of a DEA agent who I'll swear could be you."

"My God," Jessica said. She snatched the magazine from Mimi's hands.

Then she was staring into a face she knew as well as her own, into a mirror, into the past.

"Isn't it an amazing resemblance?" Mimi asked, and strolled forward to enjoy the sunset's last indigo glow.

Jessica's heart pounded. It was all she could do not to let loose screams of joy that would echo from the mountaintops.

"Yes," she said calmly. "Amazing."

18.

THE DAY MICKEY HAD DREAMED OF FOR SO LONG BEGAN MUCH like any other.

Rafe was out of town and Mickey was spending a gloomy Sunday painting the dining room of their new house. A cooling wind had brought relief from the late August heat and the promise of afternoon rain.

It wasn't *their* house, of course. Rafe had an old Marine buddy who'd been sent to Japan, and he owned this house on a cul-de-sac off Reno Road in northwest Washington, D.C. A brick house, built in the 1920s, two stories, four bedrooms, backing on a park. It was more room than they needed, but it was great when Rafe's boys came. The guy was renting it to them for just enough to cover his mortgage, and they'd promised to do some fixing up. Mickey didn't mind the work. She had a six-pack and some Motown tapes and painting was as good a way as any to kill the time.

When the car slowed out front in the early afternoon it registered more or less unconsciously. Cars were always driving down the street and turning around and driving out. Mickey paid no attention as long as they kept going, but if they stopped she stopped, because in her business that was how you stayed alive.

Not that she expected trouble. Only the DEA knew they were living here; the phone was unlisted, their cars were registered in other names, and their neighbors thought they worked at the Pentagon. Yet Mickey could not banish Dee Wingo from her thoughts, even though he was in a maximum-security prison many miles away. His parting threat lingered in her mind, ugly and unsettling.

So when the car stopped, she put down her paintbrush, wiped her fingers on her cut-offs, and went to the window. A limousine was poised at the curb. Mickey figured it was lost; the only people she knew who drove limousines were dealers, and she didn't think they'd be coming to call.

She was turning away when a chauffeur in a pearl gray uniform hopped out and opened the rear door.

A slender woman with golden hair slid out and stood gazing at Mickey's house.

The woman looked as if she'd just stepped out of a fashion magazine. She wore a white linen suit with a narrow waist and boxy shoulders, and a strand of pearls. You didn't have to be Einstein to figure out that the pearls were real, that everything about this lady was the genuine article.

Mickey laughed nervously to herself. The mysterious lady looked a lot like she had in her Michelle costume.

The woman started toward the house, as the driver gazed up and down the street. Mickey recognized the bulge under his coat.

Mickey felt weak, disjointed. Her brain turned flip-flops. She wasn't sure she was breathing.

"Oh my God," she whispered. She tried not to think because life had taught her that thinking led to hoping, which led inexorably to heartbreak.

Yet there she was in old sneakers and filthy cut-offs and this fine lady was ringing her bell.

She ran to the door and threw it open. The woman's face stunned her; she was looking into a magical mirror and seeing herself made perfect.

"You're Mickey, aren't you?" the woman said. "I'm Jessie."

Mickey reached out. "Jessie, baby," she cried, and the two women embraced.

She felt so stupid, all covered with paint, but she didn't care, she just didn't give a damn. She hugged her sister and they were laughing and crying at the same time.

"Oh shit, I've got paint on you."

"It doesn't matter, it really doesn't matter."

Finally Mickey stepped back. "Jesus, come in," she said. "I don't even know what to call you. Are you still Jessie?"

Her sister followed her inside. "I'm Jessica Nash now," she said. "But I'm still Jessie."

"Boy. Am I shook up or what? You want a beer?"

Jessica grinned and it was like the sun coming out, pure Disney. Mickey wanted to turn flips.

"I could stand a beer," she said.

Mickey popped a pair and they settled in the living room. Mickey remembered the limo out front.

"You want to send that guy on?"

"It's all right. He's supposed to wait for me." She looked around. "Such a nice house."

"It's not ours. I mean, we're just renting. But it is nice. Jessie Ketchum. Jessica Nash. I have to stop and think. It's been so damn long."

Her sister looked wistful. "I never believed much in names. I always thought they were disguises. Books were always more real to me than people. I lived my life in books for a long time, until I married and had a real life thrust upon me. Too real, sometimes."

Mickey didn't understand but it didn't matter. "You'll never know how long I looked for you. I went back to the Home, back to Motley County, I talked to hundreds of people. I joined the fucking DEA just so . . . I'm sorry, but that's how we talk, if you're in it you mostly say the fucking DEA, like that was the official title. Anyway,

278

I joined, so they'd teach me how to find you. I've been using computers. All I had to go on was those people's names, Gilbert. I must have checked . . . "

"It was Albert. Dr. and Mrs. Fenton Albert of Little Rock."

"*Albert*? He called himself *Gilbert*!"

"Maybe you misunderstood. Or they gave it wrong on purpose."

"My God, I terrorized every Gilbert in ten states. Oh well. So how was Little Rock?"

"After the Home, it was heaven. I went to Central High—it's the one President Eisenhower sent soldiers to integrate, back in the fifties. Then I went to Kenyon."

"Kenyon? Where's that?"

"In Ohio."

Mickey groaned. "I went through a million college annuals, looking for your picture. But never in *Ohio*."

"I looked too," Jessica said. "Nobody at the Home would tell me anything. Neither would that lawyer in Dallas, George Peoples, is that his name?"

"Yeah, the old bastard. I went to him, too. He was like a brick wall. The law was all against us. That's one thing I learned, if you're an orphan you've got no rights."

"But then a miracle happened," Jessica continued. "My husband and I were in Aspen and a friend was reading a magazine article about the Wingo case. She said, 'Jessica, do you have a twin?' I looked at the picture and it was you."

"Yeah, in my rich-girl disguise."

"That was last week and all I had to do was . . . "

"How *did* you get this address?" Mickey asked. "We're not that easy to find."

"I called a man my husband knows at the White House. I guess he called the DEA."

"Who is he, your husband?"

"My marriage is so ironic. I went to Kenyon, did my graduate work in Boston, and settled down to teach in Baltimore. I never *dreamed* of going back to Texas. You were the strong one . . . "

"No . . . "

"Yes, you were. For years the very thought of Fort Worth made me physically ill. And then, on a trip to Washington, D.C., Billy and I fell in love. And it turned out he was from Fort Worth. So now I'm *back* there, but so far nobody knows I was there before. Jessie Ketchum and Jessica Nash are two different people."

"Who is this wonderful guy?" Mickey asked. "Your husband, I mean."

"His name is Billy Nash. Do you remember our English teacher, Mrs. Nash?"

"Sure, that's where we read *Huckleberry Finn*."

"Well, she's Billy's mother."

"What does he do?"

"He and his brothers are in oil and real estate and investments. But Billy is interested in a lot of things. We've been helping start a new theater in Fort Worth. And we have a daughter. You've got to meet her."

Mickey grinned. "I'm an aunt."

"Tell me about you," Jessica said.

"Me? Oh boy. Well, I went to wonderful AHHS, after you left. I was Cowtown's first hippie. Tie-dyed shirts, beads, the whole bit—I was Janis Joplin, except I couldn't sing.

"Anyway, after I graduated, I went to North Texas State for a couple of years. It was okay but, you know, I was never a scholar. I knocked around for a while. Painted houses. Went to Alaska. I hooked up with this guitar player, and we went to Nashville, and I learned photography, and I got hired by the paper there. It was a blast. Then I met these DEA people and they told me I ought to join up, and I thought it'd help me find you."

"And you're married?"

"Yeah. A great guy. Rafe Klayman. He's an agent, too. We went through training together. He's kind of a diamond in the rough— I mean, before the DEA he was a Marine, right?—but he's a real sweetheart. He's on a trip—due home tonight."

"No children?"

"Our jobs are so crazy. Maybe in a couple of years. But we're having fun right now. I'll swear, he's the only man I could live with."

"He sounds wonderful."

Mickey made a face. "Billy Nash," she said. "Is he one of those Nash brothers I read about?"

Jessica nodded uneasily.

"Holy shit, they're billionaires!" Mickey exclaimed. *"Those* Nashes?"

Mickey could not immediately digest the idea that her sister had married a billionaire; it was as if she had married a Zulu prince, a fine thing, perhaps, but alien to her experience.

"Not to be crude or anything, but what's it like, having all that money?"

"After a while, you take it for granted. I mean, you still have your troubles, your good days and bad days. It's just that your troubles relate to people, instead of things."

Jessica thought a moment. "It's a world where everything is perfect except the people. Billy and I have had our problems. But I think they're behind us now. It's a different world I've lived in for the past few years. I've grown and changed. I'm tougher than I was. Billy runs the Nash Foundation and I want to help with it. You mentioned orphans' rights, or non-rights. There's a movement to gain more rights for women who give up their children, and for the children when they grow up and want to find their natural parents. That's something I want our foundation to support."

"There's something we ought to think about," Mickey said. "We still don't know who our parents are. I want to know if our mother gave us away or if they took us away from her. She may be out there somewhere trying to find us."

Jessica saw dark clouds coming in, filling the sky. "You're right. When I get back, I'll talk to my lawyers. I should have done something years ago. But for so long I couldn't even go back to Fort Worth. I had nightmares about that night."

"Me too," Mickey admitted.

"We were so helpless. And you were so brave. Remember the

Everclear gin? To this day the smell of gin makes me sick. Even now, married to Billy, I don't feel safe. That one night made me believe in evil."

Jessica tried to smile. "Listen to me. We should be talking about the good old days. Our happy memories."

Mickey grinned. "My only happy memory is cutting Luther Pringle's dick off."

Jessica laughed until she cried. The first raindrops splattered against the windows.

"Want to see some pictures?"

"Sure!"

Jessica took a thick stack of snapshots from her purse. "These were taken last Christmas. That's Billy holding Melissa."

"They're adorable. Who's *that* guy?"

"That's Sonny, my brother-in-law."

"A tough-looking character."

"He's strange."

She went through the pictures, showing Lily and Kay and Olivia, telling how she met Billy and about Sonny's séances and the Billy Ringer Theater, her whole extraordinary life in Texas.

Mickey was captivated, by the story and simply by Jessica. She studied her hands, her voice, her smile, everything about her. She'd pretended to be her sister, to fool Wingo, and now she saw where she'd been right and where she'd been wrong. She thought: I was close, I *could* be you.

Finally Jessica looked at her watch. "I have to go. I'm late to meet Billy at the airport. Talk to Rafe about coming to Texas. We'll send a plane for you, and we'll go to our ranch for a few days."

"Sounds great. I mean, if we can get the time off."

Jessica stood up. "I hate to leave. This has been the happiest day of my life."

They walked to the door hand in hand. The chauffeur came running with an umbrella. Mickey tried to imagine never having to worry about a raindrop again.

"I don't want you to leave," Mickey said. "I'm afraid of losing you again."

"You won't lose me," Jessica promised, and then she was gone, into the rain, into the limousine, toward the Nash International jet that would waft her back to Texas.

The rain, the rain, the blessed rain.

Wingo saw the dark clouds roll in, heard the distant clap of thunder, watched the first raindrops splatter gloriously against the barred windows.

Sweet, conspiring rain come to burn away the bars that held him.

His plan was many-sided and of all its elements the last and least manageable had been the storm that now raged over Baltimore, cold violent windswept rain to keep honest men off the streets and blind the eyes of those few who braved its fury.

A predator's smile played across his face. Tonight the heavens would rage and tomorrow he would be free.

Free to flee, to start anew, to get revenge.

Dee Wingo watched the rain and waited.

They ate dinner in the day room. The wind howled outside and rain pelted the windows relentlessly.

His companions were the cancer patient and a dying Mafia don, who never spoke.

"Can you imagine dying for love?" the cancer patient asked.

"No," Wingo told him.

"I'd do it again," the man said sadly.

After dinner Wingo went to his room and blinked the lights.

At nine he returned to the day room, where the bank robber and the don were settling down to a mini-series about a timber heiress and her lost love.

Czabo, the guard on duty, glanced in at them; he would return at ten.

As soon as he left, Wingo acted. The other men were side by side on a sofa. He slammed their heads together like coconuts.

The men slumped forward. Wingo did not want to kill them but he did not want them bothering him, either.

Satisfied, he took the hacksaw blade from his pocket, moved quickly to the window, and started to work on one of the bars.

The storm raged outside.

Wingo had tested another blade in Atlanta, on bars identical to these. It had taken twelve minutes to sever the first bar and, because of the increasing dullness of the blade, fifteen for the second.

The bars were six inches apart. Removing one created a twelve-inch opening: not quite enough. But removing two provided eighteen inches, and Wingo, slimmed down to one hunded seventy pounds, could pass through that easily.

At nine-thirty, as Richard Chamberlain went off to war, Wingo removed the second bar.

He checked the unconscious men again. He put the don's head on the bank robber's shoulder, hoping that at ten Czabo would think them dozing and it would be eleven before he sounded the alarm.

Wingo broke the window with a pool cue. Then, finally, he opened the box that held the fire hose.

The fire hose had been his breakthrough, the keystone of his plan. By itself it was nothing. But he had realized its potential, and added the pills, the hacksaw blade, Dr. Dalton, even the storm—all the elements that made an impossible escape possible.

The hose unwound easily as he lowered it out the window.

He squeezed through the bars and started down. The rough cotton hose was easily grasped, even in the storm. The rain was sweet on his face and the thunder was a rhapsody. He laughed aloud as he dropped the final dozen feet into a muddy flowerbed.

Wingo was free.

It was not yet ten o'clock as he walked confidently around the corner, where a two-year-old Chevrolet awaited him. Its key was taped under the fender, and the car came equipped with a Baretta 9-mm. pistol, clothes, a driver's license and credit cards, cash, rope, tape, a towel, and an ounce of cocaine.

He dried his face and hands with the towel, put on a dry shirt, and started the car.

He might have driven north to Canada, south to Florida, or west to a cabin he owned in the Rockies.

Instead, he headed for the highway to Washington, D.C.

Rafe hitched a ride back from Colombia on a military plane, only to circle Andrews Air Force Base for hours because of the storm. Rafe hardly noticed the delay, so caught up was he in the offer he'd received in Bogotá. He was dying to tell Mickey. Even more, as he contemplated this new milestone, he wished his mother had lived to see the dreams they shared come true.

Rafe's full name, which neither of his wives nor any of his friends had ever known, was Raphael Rembrandt Klayman. His mother, an educated woman, had married an uneducated man, hoping to raise him to her level of society. Instead, he pulled her down to his, where there was precious little she could do for her children except give them illustrious names and try to supplement the meager education they received in the hardscrabble schools of West Virginia.

She had been raised in the fox-hunting country outside Middleburg, Virginia, and when she eloped into West Virginia it had been like entering a Third World nation. In time she focused all her frustration and passion on her children, and it was with Rafe, the youngest, that she was most successful.

By the time Rafe started school she had him reading better than most adults in the little mining community called Hawk Hollow. He was one of the few of his contemporaries to complete high school, but there was no money for college. She was pleased when Rafe enlisted in the Marine Corps. Her great-grandfather had, as she often reminded the boy, ridden with Stonewall Jackson.

When Rafe looked back, he felt great gratitude for his mother's sacrifices. Yet he felt, too, that both his parents had contributed to whatever success he'd achieved. His mother's gift was the more obvious: she taught him to use his mind, because the life of the imagination was what she knew.

But his coal-miner father made his contribution, too. His father taught him that a man keeps his word, respects decent women, and brooks no insult from any man. The boys in Hawk Hollow fought constantly, and Rafe was taught to fight until either he won or was disabled. He bore scars from his early years, but by the time he was fifteen no boy or man in the county would cross him.

He thought that if he had known only his mother's influence, he would have become some kind of do-gooder, perhaps a school-teacher if he'd had the education. And if he'd heeded only his father's lessons, he might have wound up in prison.

But the combination of the two had made him something more complex: a soldier, a warrior, but one with a certain depth, a certain idealism that set him apart from his fellows.

Rafe's mother had made him a lover of underdogs, of heroism, of lost causes. He thrilled to "Give me liberty or give me death" and "I only regret I have but one life to give for my country." He was inspired by Lancelot and Horatio Alger and the Dutch boy with his finger in the dike. His heroes included General Lee and the doomed Confederate legions at Gettysburg, Tennessee's Sergeant Alvin York and West Virginia's own Chuck Yeager—the latter two, his mother often reminded him, sprung from origins as humble as his own.

Rafe would always remember the first time his mother read to him about Lindbergh's flight. The image of the Lone Eagle, in that frail craft, low on fuel, sailing only a few feet above the waves, to be greeted by a million cheering Frenchmen—that long-ago image left a boy of ten in Hawk Hollow, West Virginia, weeping for the glory that might never be his.

In the Marines, Rafe was a tough, taciturn soldier who burned to embrace a cause greater than himself. He arrived in Vietnam ablaze with anti-communism, thinking he had found his crusade, but he soon decided that the war was less crusade than tragedy.

He left Vietnam with a Purple Heart, a Silver Star, and a top sergeant's stripes. His Silver Star citation said: "In the aftermath of the ambush, Sgt. Klayman, at extreme risk to his own safety, rallied his men, led a counterattack, and rescued four severely wounded men under his command." To Rafe, it was simple: you didn't leave your wounded behind, any more than you ran away from a fight in a schoolyard. He would have been nominated for the Medal of Honor had he not, in the heat of battle, called his commanding officer a chickenshit son of a bitch.

Post-Vietnam, the Marines offered only ass-kissing, ticket-punching, bad marriages, and cheap whiskey. At thirty he felt fifty, felt his life slipping away.

Then, as he had fled West Virginia for the Marines, he fled the Marines for the DEA.

There, at least, a real war was being fought. Rafe had seen in West Virginia what rot-gut booze did to men and in Vietnam what hashish and heroin could do. He knew all the arguments for recreational drug use and he thought them beneath contempt. The weekend smoker or snorter or chipper would damn well have to go back to booze because his pleasure wasn't worth the misery of a million addicts and the crime they created.

Rafe loved his new crusade, the daily skirmishes, the instant gratification: every pusher he busted made his day. It would be a long war, but in time the "recreational" users would see it wasn't worth it and the dealers would figure out that prison was the end of the line. He'd almost burst with pride when Mickey had busted that bastard Wingo—he couldn't have been more proud if he'd done it himself.

Mickey was such a jewel. So tough on the outside, so gentle underneath. So fierce making love and such a kitten afterward. So brave. It was crazy but wonderful how she'd joined the agency to find her sister. He intended to move fast on finding the sister.

But the immediate payoff, for them both, was the job he'd been offered in Bogotá, as the ambassador's liaison with the Colombia military. As far as the drug war was concerned, it meant going to the front lines, to the lion's den, to challenge the cartels on their home turf. To be chosen was a stunning honor, and marked him as a man destined for leadership at the DEA.

The deputy chief of mission had promised him that a job could be found for Mickey in the embassy. But what Rafe wanted, if he could talk her into it, was for Mick to take leave and have a baby. The DCM had driven him around and shown him the kind of house they could rent, a mansion with high white walls and a red-tiled roof, with servants and a pool, in the hills near the embassy.

Rafe could only laugh: they'd be living like millionaires.

He didn't kid himself. It would be dangerous work. But it would be a new life for them, too. The rain pounded reassuringly on the roof as he departed Andrews Air Force Base and sped along the Suitland Parkway, hurrying home to break the news to Mickey.

After Jessica drove away, Mickey was too excited to keep painting. What she wanted most was to tell Rafe of this miracle. She called the office, but on a Sunday evening there was only a part-time employee on duty, a nitwit named Hazel who did little more than answer the phones. Hazel checked around and said Rafe had left Colombia and he'd be back that night, except flights were being held up by the storm.

Mickey put away the paintbrushes and opened a beer. She nibbled at some leftover Popeye's fried chicken but she wasn't hungry. Mainly she thought about Jessie. The last time she'd seen her sister, she was thirteen and running down Camp Bowie Boulevard after a Buick. Now Jessie had reappeared, as magically as if she'd floated down on a cloud, and she'd been all Mickey had dreamed she would be. Beautiful, delicate, a perfect lady. She laughed. And with a rich husband, too. Mickey was game to fly to Texas and visit their ranch and be real cowboys for a change—Rafe would love that.

Soon Mickey was sleepy. She guessed the beer on top of the day's excitement had been too much for her. Rafe would come stumbling home in the middle of the night and she'd tell him her news and they'd make love with the rain beating on the roof. Mickey kicked off her jeans, took a hot shower, and rubbed herself dry until her body burned. She slipped into bed, thinking of Rafe. She always slept naked. In the long run it saved a lot of time.

Just inside the Washington Beltway, Wingo stopped at a phone outside a 7-Eleven. The worst of the storm had passed. The woman who took his call quickly told him what he wanted to know. "Many thanks, Hazel," Wingo said.

He followed the Southwest Freeway to the Rock Creek Parkway, then Massachusetts Avenue to 34th Street, which became Reno Road in northwest Washington. The wet streets glistened under his headlights. In time he turned off Reno Road and stopped beside a school. He moved quietly across a muddy soccer field and through the woods toward the dark, silent house where Mickey McGee lay sleeping.

Billy and Jessica listened to the news as they drove home from the airport. Tornadoes had raged across North Texas that day, leaving hundreds dead and homeless. In the Panhandle, children had been swept up like dolls.

"That's awful," Jessica said. "What would you *do* if one was coming at you?"

Billy shook his head. "Did I ever tell you about the time I was in a motel fire?"

"No."

"It was in New Mexico. About two, the sound of people yelling woke me. I went to my door and found the corridor filled with smoke. My room was filling up. It was all so unreal, yet it was the realest thing that ever happened to me. I figured out that I had to break the window and jump—I was on the second floor. The men on either side of me died in their rooms from the smoke."

"How awful," Jessica said.

"My point is that, fire or tornado or whatever, when something like that happens to you, it just happens, and if you're lucky you survive."

For the first groggy moment she thought it was a dream.

Then she saw him, huge in the darkness, felt the blade at her throat, and knew it was her worst nightmare made real.

"I told you, McGee," he whispered, almost lovingly. "I told you that one night you'd wake up and I'd be there."

289

She struck out, but his fist crashed against her head and Mickey spun into darkness.

She awoke wet and choking. He had thrown water in her face. She struggled and found herself spreadeagled, her wrists and ankles tied securely to the bedposts.

The tip of his cigarette glowed in the darkness.

"You'd better get out of here," she said. "This is the first place they'll look for you."

"How good of you to warn me."

"They'll be here any minute."

"I don't think so, McGee. I don't think anybody will be here for a long time."

Mickey searched for some advantage, some plan, some hope. They must be looking for him. The prison people would alert the DEA. But how, when? A call to that idiot Hazel in the middle of the night? Or would they screw around until office hours on Monday morning? Rafe was her best hope. He might be here at any moment. She had to hold out until then.

Wingo, as if reading her mind, said, "And where is your dear husband?"

"He's out of town."

"You know what I think? I think that if he was out of town, you'd say he was on his way home. And if he's on his way home, you'd say he's out of town. You need to be more clever than that."

"You'd better get out of here, Wingo."

"Brave talk, McGee. Brave talk from someone who's naked and helpless, at the mercy of a psychopathic killer. Brave talk, indeed."

"They'll come."

"You sent me to prison, didn't you, McGee? You were so clever. So proud of yourself. Did they give you a raise? Are you writing a book? But there was one problem. They couldn't keep me in prison. I've come for you, just as I said I would."

"What do you want?" Keep him talking, that was her only hope. In training they'd devoted only part of one class to what you'd do if you were taken prisoner. They didn't like to admit it could happen. You worked in a team and took precautions and it wasn't

290

supposed to happen. But if it did you did the obvious things. Agree with them. Keep them talking. Say anything. But save your life.

His hand stroked her belly. His fingers played lazily in her pubic hair. Her innards roiled with rage and fear. Don't panic, don't scream.

He licked his finger, touched her. She gasped, felt weak and liquid all over.

"I dreamed of you in prison, McGee," he said. "No lover ever dreamed of you with more passion. Does that excite you?"

"I was doing my job." Did her voice break? Did she sound desperate? "It was nothing personal. You were breaking the . . . "

He held the red tip of his cigarette a half-inch from her nipple. She twisted away from the heat, the pain, but he followed.

"Don't lecture me, McGee. Speak when you're spoken to. And say 'Sir' to me. Do you understand?"

She hesitated, until the fire brushed her nipple. "Yes, sir," she said meekly.

"That's better, McGee. And don't think about screaming. Because you know what I'll do if you scream?"

"No, sir."

"I'll stuff a sock in your mouth and then I'll have fun with this cigarette. Maybe that's your sentence. Instead of thirty years, one cigarette. Do you think you could stand it? Would you like to find out?"

"No, sir."

"Are you brave, McGee? Let me tell you something. Pain always wins. Over youth, over courage, over virtue, over justice—pain always wins. We're born in pain and we die in pain and we spend our lives trying to escape it. I sold a drug that helped people escape their pain, and you sent me to prison. But now you're the prisoner."

He brushed one nipple, then the other. It was like a blowtorch sending fire into every nerve ending, a thousand hot needles of pain.

"Did you like that, McGee?"

His words did not immediately penetrate the inferno that consumed her.

"I asked you a question. Did you like that?"

"No, sir." Numbly.

"That was just a lover's kiss. I can make you purr like a kitten, McGee, or cry like a baby, or pray to the great god Wingo. Do you doubt me?"

"No, sir."

"Would you like to fuck me, McGee?"

"No, sir. Yes, sir. I don't care."

Rafe, where was Rafe?

"I was a businessman, McGee. I never bothered you. All you had to do was leave me alone. Don't you wish you'd left me alone?"

"Yes, sir."

"In prison, McGee, I saw a boy raped by six men. The more he screamed, the more they enjoyed it. Prison isn't a pretty place, McGee, is it?"

"No, sir."

"Have you ever been fucked in the ass, McGee?"

Despite herself, she started to cry.

Wingo put out the cigarette and lit another.

"So the little girl's not so tough after all?"

"Please, go away."

"No, McGee. You had your day. Now I have my night. Are you afraid I'll kill you? There are worse things than dying."

What could she do, to mislead Wingo, to warn Rafe? For an instant she felt herself surrender to her fear, to the void, wishing herself dead, then she fought back. Wingo was smiling at her. She tasted the blood in her mouth and dreamed it was his.

He held the glowing cigarette an inch from her navel.

"Would you like more pain, McGee?"

"No, sir."

"Would you rather have pleasure?"

"Yes, sir."

He licked his middle finger and touched her clitoris.

"Does that feel good, McGee?"

"Yes, sir." She hated herself for saying it, but all she could think was that he might not burn her again.

"Maybe you'll have an orgasm, McGee. Wouldn't that be nice?"

292

"Yes, sir."

"Pleasure and pain, McGee," Wingo whispered. "They go together. And the end of the road is death."

Rafe reached Reno Road at one in the morning, a time of solitude and clarity, a time for decisions. He would take the job in Bogotá. Mickey would take leave and have a baby. He laughed, thinking what a pistol his and Mick's kid would be.

Tired as he was, Rafe hummed with excitement. To tell Mick his news, to spin out his plans, to make sweet, crazy love.

He parked in the driveway and crossed the soggy yard. He frowned to see the porch light off, the house dark. They should pay more attention to security, but it hadn't seemed urgent, because no one outside the DEA knew they were here.

He unlocked the door and let himself in, smelling the paint, glad Mickey had started on the dining room. He put down his suitcase and reached for the light. The house was still and silent. Rafe tensed, felt the hairs rising on the back of his neck; some primordial sense alerted him to danger, an alien presence. He was dropping into a crouch when something crashed into the back of his head and he sank to the floor like a stone.

Rafe, too, awoke to water, gagging, dazed, confused, disbelieving. He struggled against his bonds and strained to see.

What he glimpsed, distorted by shadows and rage, was too terrible to believe.

Mickey tied to the bed.

Wingo, leaning against the bed, holding a cigarette, grinning foxlike. The shades were drawn and a candle burned on the dresser, the one Mickey liked to make love by.

Rafe was on the floor, tape over his mouth, both wrists tied to the radiator by nylon cord. He struggled, raged, but his shouts came out muffled and meaningless.

"Welcome to the party, Special Agent Klayman."

Rafe raged anew. To be mute was the final insult.

"You'd like to talk, wouldn't you, Klayman? To threaten? To warn me that your colleagues will arrive any moment?"

"I'm sorry, Rafe, I'm sorry. He . . . "

"Quiet, bitch," Wingo said, and backhanded her. Rafe saw her head snap back onto the pillow. He struggled against the cord but it gave not at all.

"Actually I know just what your colleagues are doing," Wingo boasted. "Do you wonder how? Your agency is growing so fast it has had to hire part-time help. Not all of the newcomers are as loyal and dedicated as you. Some of them, like poor Hazel, even need money."

Rafe struggled anew. If Wingo was telling them his source in the agency, it meant he planned to kill them.

"Very good, Klayman. Pull the radiator loose from the floor. Is that your plan?"

Rafe saved his strength. His feet at least were free. If the bastard came close enough . . .

"I've been in prison, Klayman. Haven't had a woman in ages. And here's McGee."

"Rafe," Mickey cried, "whatever happens, I talked to my sister today. I've got that."

Wingo was amused. "Talked to your sister? Where is she? Does she want to join the party?"

He puffed at the cigarette. "Do you know what the number-one sport is in prison, Klayman? I'll give you a hint, it's not volleyball. And here's Agent McGee, an anal virgin."

Rafe struggled to no avail.

"Oh, cheer up, man. It's a party. I'll fuck her. Then you can fuck her. Then I'll fuck you, to round things out."

That was Rafe's first glimmer of hope. If the bastard would come close enough.

"Are you ready, McGee? Is your rosebud aquiver?"

"Fuck you, you bastard," Mickey said defiantly.

Wingo sucked on his Marlboro, then jabbed Mickey's breast with it. Her scream filled the room, until Wingo clamped his hand over her mouth. When he took his hand away, her face was barely recognizable.

Wingo laughed and pulled a vial from his pocket. "Too much hostility here," he said. "Maybe a little powder will help. My first in a long time."

He snorted, twice in each nostril, then laughed. "Look at you, McGee, stiff as a board. How about a snort? It'll change your whole attitude. You've got to look at this as a broadening experience, McGee, no pun intended. What do you say? A little toot?"

She would gladly have used any drug that promised to ease the shame to come.

"Yes, please," she said.

"Very good."

He dabbed cocaine onto his finger and held it under her nose. She sniffed some and he laughed and gave her more.

"Goodness, aren't we the little cokehead? Feel better?"

In fact, she was amazed at how fast the drug took hold. She felt herself relaxing, distancing herself, drifting away.

"Are you ready, dear?" he repeated.

"Yes, sir." A whisper, a voice not her own.

"Very good, McGee. You'd be popular in prison."

He fondled Mickey. She lay still and looked away. She imagined the little boy she and Rafe might have had. She saw him, looking like Rafe, riding a bike, tossing a baseball with his dad, learning to read.

Wingo looked her body up and down. "We need you on your tummy, McGee, that's the preferred posture. I'll have to untie your legs."

He loosened the ropes from her ankles. "Now, turn over, dear. Let's put on a good show for hubby."

She slowly did as he said. Then she said, "Please, could I have some more coke?"

Wingo took out the vial, had a hit himself, put more powder on his finger, and held it under her nose.

"You're a fun date, McGee."

"Yeah, right," she said, and sank her teeth into his hand.

He howled and tumbled backward off the bed.

Patrick Anderson

"You little bitch," he raged, and grabbed at her ankle.

Mickey kicked at him savagely. With her wrists still bound, she was like an animal in a trap, struggling for life.

He retreated to the dresser, where he'd left his gun and knife.

"You want pain, bitch, I'll show you pain."

He slashed her leg. Mickey felt the pain, the blood, but she kept kicking because it was all she knew to do, because it was that or surrender.

Wingo grabbed at her flailing legs. His plan had changed. He would kill them and be on his way. Their colleagues would get the message.

Both of them, locked in combat, forgot Rafe Klayman.

No one could ever fully explain what happened next. DEA experts, after an extensive study, concluded that what Rafe did was a physical impossibility.

As Mickey struggled with Wingo, Rafe summoned up all the strength he had ever possessed or imagined, from his Confederate ancestors, from his boyhood heroes, from the schoolyards of Hawk Hollow and the battlefields of Vietnam, from his love of Mickey and his hate for Wingo. He summoned that strength and he braced his feet against the floor and pushed until something had to yield: rope or flesh and bone. One moment he was bound and the next the cords snapped and he flew at Wingo.

They tumbled to the floor, grunting, groaning, cursing, bleeding. Rafe knocked the knife from Wingo's hand, and Wingo leapt for his Baretta. Rafe tackled him and they tumbled about, the gun between them.

Mickey, her wrists still bound, screamed at the top of her lungs, imagining that someone in the world of sanity would hear.

The gun exploded, once, twice. Mickey's heart stopped.

"You son of a bitch!" Wingo moaned. She saw him slowly rise, holding one hand to his gut, a startled look on his face. He clutched the gun at his side and stumbled out of the room.

"Rafe!" Mickey screamed, and then he was leaning over her, his face twisted in pain, blood everywhere, cutting her wrists loose.

"You're shot," she cried. "We've got to get you to the hospital."

296

"He's hit too," he whispered.

She screamed when she saw the wound in his chest.

"You've got to lie down."

"No, help me to the car."

"Oh God, Rafe," she said, but she helped him down the stairs.

"Wait," he said. He knelt and opened his briefcase, seizing his .45. Blood pumped from the wound in his chest.

"Rafe, please, to hell with him." She threw on a raincoat. She was bleeding from wounds she had forgotten. For God's sake, what was the nearest hospital? Sibley? Georgetown? They stumbled out to the yard. The wet grass comforted her bare feet.

"Look," Rafe muttered. His face was pale, demonic.

Near the end of the street, Wingo was leaning against a light pole.

Rafe sank to one knee and raised his weapon. His hands were unsteady. She couldn't bear to look at his chest.

"Rafe, for God's sake, come on."

He fired. The explosion was like a cannon on the silent street. Wingo staggered away and Mickey pulled Rafe toward the car.

"Did I hit him?"

"I don't know, I don't know. Come on, the hospital!"

"I'll drive," he said. She wanted to protest but she wasn't sure she could drive now. She thought he must be going on pure adrenaline, pure hate. Lights were popping on, up and down the street.

Rafe gunned the engine, backed out of the driveway, then to her horror started the wrong way, toward the turnaround where Wingo was hobbling toward the trees.

"No, the hospital, please!" she screamed.

"I'll get the bastard," Rafe vowed.

The night shimmered with blood, soft rain, unreality. Rafe clutching the wheel, Wingo on one knee, firing the Baretta. Bullets shattering their windshield. The car leaped the curb, skidded in the wet grass, then crashed into their enemy.

She saw Wingo broken and still on the grass. "You got him," she cried, "You got him!" But when she turned back to Rafe, he was slumped over the wheel; the car was out of control, they were hurtling toward a tree. Mickey threw up her hands and screamed.

19.

THE TEXAS PAPERS CARRIED WIRE-SERVICE STORIES ON THE violent clash between the escaped drug lord and the two DEA agents, but Jessica did not see those stories. Once she returned to Fort Worth she was caught up in round-the-clock preparations for the opening of the Billy Ringer Theater.

Everything else went to the back burner. Even the visit of Mickey and her husband, she realized, would have to wait until after opening night. She tried to call Mickey, but the phone had been disconnected; puzzled, she waited for Mickey to call her.

The problem of Emmy and Anton had been abruptly resolved. Billy had his lawyer call Anton and threaten to call the district attorney. Soon thereafter the couple departed for parts unknown. Jessica still planned to reveal her background at the Home in an interview, and combine the announcement with a major donation, but that, too, would have to wait until after the opening of *Romeo and Juliet* and the visitation of Ronald Reagan.

Even the future of the Carvex plant was left unresolved, although Sonny did agree to install new anti-pollution technology, at a cost of several million dollars. Billy said other action would have to wait, particularly while Sonny was being so helpful on plans for the theater.

It was Sonny whose determination brought the Reagans to the opening; that was undeniable. The problem had been that, since his reelection, the President was spending more and more time at his California ranch, and at the outset had showed not the slightest interest in a visit to Texas. But Sonny was not easily rebuffed.

He enlisted the aid of Vice President Bush, who, as an adopted Texan and a potential President, wanted to show his clout as well. While the Vice President pressed their case to the White House powerbrokers, Sonny opened delicate negotiations on another front. Although Nancy Reagan was deeply rooted in the culture of southern California, she was not unaware that there were people of wealth and taste in Texas, and she had often been treated royally there.

Kay was recruited to seek out Texas friends of the First Lady, people whose calls and letters might persuade her that she and her husband would be greeted in Texas by an outpouring of love, luxury, and *haute couture* that would satisfy even her exacting standards.

Soon Kay was receiving daily bulletins on the First Lady's state of mind. Word came that she had told an aide that Texas might be "amusing," might even be "great fun." Kay boldly sent the First Lady a pair of ostrich-skin cowgirl boots, complete with silver spurs. A report followed that Mrs. Reagan was actively championing the trip.

There remained opposition within the White House staff. One problem was memories of John Kennedy's ill-starred visit to Texas more than twenty years earlier. And there was a more tangible problem: If the White House power merchants sent their man to Texas, what would Texas send back in return?

One blunt White House political operative told Sonny, "Mr. Nash, money talks and bullshit walks!"

That was reasoning Sonny understood, and he agreed to organize a $10,000-a-plate "appreciation dinner" which would raise some $10 million for Republican campaign coffers.

The combination of cash and culture carried the day: a deal was made. The President would fly to Dallas on Friday for the fund-raising dinner, and would proceed to Fort Worth on Saturday for a reception at the Kimbell and the premiere itself.

Jessica watched with dismay as the presidential visit began to turn the theater opening into a three-ring circus. She could not deny that the theater had reaped priceless publicity from the visit. The entire run of *Romeo and Juliet* was sold out, and the sale of season tickets had been phenomenal.

Yet it bothered her that the excitement focused on the wrong man: Ronald Reagan, not William Shakespeare. It was Reagan who drove so many wealthy Texans into frenzied admiration, for he had, like some mighty warrior of legend, championed the cause of the rich, even as he put the presidential imprimatur on their lust for a regal lifestyle.

Jessica was consoled that in the long run of things it was her man whose glory would endure.

One agonizing problem was deciding who would be invited to the reception at the Kimbell. She and Kay were in nominal charge of the list, but the White House kept full control. Gradually guidelines emerged. Not more than sixty guests would be allowed, because Mrs. Reagan did not wish to confront a "mob." There were detailed rules about media coverage, food and drink, proper dress, political approval, and who might or might not approach the First Couple.

Despite these restrictions, there were hundreds of people clamoring for invitations. The First Couple was a Royal Couple, and their loyal subjects longed to pay homage. Some rejectees vowed never to attend the Ringer Theater or to speak to Kay and Jessica again.

Feelings were running high when the Reagans finally arrived. "I feel like I've been fucked flat," Kay complained, as the fateful weekend began. "Those White House people are the biggest bastards in the world. They make Sonny look like a choirboy."

The "appreciation dinner" was being held in Dallas, for the good and simple reason that it contained more money than Fort Worth. The Reagans checked into a home on Turtle Creek, rested for several hours, had drinks with friends, and at nine o'clock were driven to the downtown hotel where a thousand Texans were paying $10,000 each to break bread with their President.

It was then that Sonny Nash's disillusion began.

Sonny had assigned himself the role of welcoming the guests and introducing the Republican leader who would introduce the President. He was wrong. The White House chief of staff bluntly told him that he was not to speak. In fact, he was not even to sit at the head table, or be photographed with the Reagans.

"You back-stabbing, shit-faced son of a bitch," Sonny raged at the White House nabob, but the gentleman had already turned on his heel and left.

An ill-timed newsmagazine story on the President's visit, dredging up the details of the RICO suit and the Carvex plant, had abruptly made Sonny persona non grata with the White House. The Ringer Theater was fine, the rest of the Nash family was fine, but Sonny would be kept at arm's length, lest the Reagans risk contamination. In other circumstances, Sonny might have argued, or bullied his way to the head table, but one does not argue where the President is concerned because the President is surrounded by armed men who do not argue. Even Sonny understood that.

He went, instead, to the bar and downed several shots of whiskey, muttering and cursing to himself, then stumbled out of the ballroom just as the President was rising to speak. A Secret Service agent followed him out and watched him drive away.

At nine the next morning, Jessica arrived at the Gertrude Little Home, accompanied by her Romeo and Juliet.

April Flynn and her young English co-star, Ian Ridley-Campbell, had proved to be delights. April, just turned seventeen, still projected a rare innocence. She bubbled with enthusiasm, yet retained a serenity, an inner stillness. On stage, with her oval face, milky skin, and midnight black hair, she was irresistible.

301

Ian held his own with her. At nineteen, he had more acting experience, and a loose-limbed grace that made him a dashing Romeo. There had been speculation about a romance between the two young stars, but as far as anyone knew their dealings were entirely professional. April's ever present mother, Doris Flynn, did not encourage hanky-panky.

It was Jessica's first trip back to the Home, after twenty years, and she was amazed at how much it had changed. The original Victorian mansion still stood, but a new dormitory, gym, and auditorium had gone up. It all seemed bright and cheerful, nothing at all like her dark memories.

The Home's director escorted them into the auditorium, where every seat was filled. He introduced Jessica as "one of Fort Worth's leading citizens, a courageous lady who stood up against pollution in West Texas," and asked her to speak.

She gazed out at row upon row of faces. Everything had changed except those faces: still confused, vulnerable, fearful. There was a great deal she wanted to say to those children, but she was not the star today. She waved and sat back down. The children applauded her, nonetheless, and she was proud.

April and Ian were introduced, to much greater applause, because the kids knew April from her movies and Ian from a mini-series role as a doomed RAF pilot.

They spoke about acting, took questions from the audience— "How much money do you make?" "What's it like to kiss her?"— and then performed the balcony scene. The audience—ill-starred Texas waifs, bastard Edmunds and rejected Cordelias—listened in a hush.

Jessica was caught up in the music of the poetry, but she heard the sadness beneath its youthful wonder.

The girl's wistful:

> I have no joy of this contract tonight.
> It is too rash, too unadvis'd, too sudden;
> Too like the lightning, which doth cease to be
> Ere one can say it lightens.

And the boy's:

> O blessed, blessed night! I am afeard,
> Being in night, all this is but a dream,
> Too flattering-sweet to be substantial.

April finished the scene flushed, luminous, virginal, trembling at the power of the words she had spoken, an American teenager who had by some magic made herself Juliet. In that moment, as the children cheered, Jessica wept, not just for the beauty of the poetry, but for all the youth and innocence that fled so suddenly, like lightning, "which doth cease to be/Ere one can say it lightens." This was what she'd worked for, not to bring Shakespeare to the rich, or the President to Texas, but to bring art to children who might love it as she had.

As she and the two teenagers left the Home, she found Sonny's red Cadillac parked behind her car. Sonny leaned against it, grinning at them.

Over coffee that morning Billy had said something about Sonny being snubbed by President Reagan the night before. Now, seeing Sonny, bearded and haggard, she sensed the anger behind his charm.

"How'd it go?" he asked the teenagers.

"It was fun," Ian said.

"The kids were so sweet," April added. "You can tell when it's the first time for them, and they begin to feel what's happening."

"Yeah, that first time's a killer," Sonny said, laughing to himself. "Hey, tonight's the big night. You nervous?"

"I always am," April said.

"Whatta you gonna do all day?" Sonny asked. "Study your lines?"

April laughed. "I know my lines. Mostly I'll just relax. Read a little. Take a nap."

"How about you, son?"

"I watch TV," Ian confessed.

"That's a sorry way to spend such a fine day," Sonny declared. "Tell you what—I'll take you both waterskiing!"

April's face registered uncertainty. "That's awfully nice, Mr. Nash . . ."

"How many times do I have to tell you to call me by my name?" Sonny demanded playfully. Jessica felt pangs of alarm. She wished April's mother was here.

"Honey, a little exercise would do you good," Sonny told April. "Maybe we could talk about that contract of yours."

"Well . . ." April hesitated. Her proposed three-picture deal with Excelsior was still unsigned.

"I'll feed you and get you back by two," Sonny promised.

"Sonny, I don't know," Jessica said. "Tonight's the opening, and if anything went wrong . . ."

His glance was chilling. His beard made him look even more evil than before. "Miss Jessie, they ain't gonna break a leg, if that's what you're worried about. Come on, kids."

He eased them into his Cadillac. Jessica held back, frozen. For all her newfound courage, she still feared Sonny.

The two young actors climbed into Sonny's convertible and roared away.

"Tell my mom," April called, laughing and waving.

They were no sooner gone than Jessica began to fear she'd made a terrible mistake.

The *crème de la crème* reception for the Reagans began at the Kimbell at six. Later, a caravan of limousines would take the guests out to the Billy Ringer Theater for a fireworks display and, finally, the premiere of *Romeo and Juliet*. That at least was the plan.

Jessica watched the handpicked guests cross the long sweep of grass, past cheering crowds and sullen, roped-off reporters, a band of rich and joyous pilgrims, framed by the distant Amon Carter Museum and the setting sun, arriving at the Louis Kahn museum that was hailed worldwide as a masterpiece. It was for Fort Worth a social event whose equal could hardly be remembered: the ill-fated Kennedy visit of the sixties and the rip-roaring Casa Mañana opening in the thirties came to mind. But to students of Texas social history this superlative blending of money, politics, and culture was more, a milestone, a cowtown's long-awaited coming of age.

Texas, Jessica had come to believe, was a land of the most amazing and maddening extremes. It was home to some of the kindest, most generous, most cultivated people she ever hoped to meet, and also to some of the most ignorant, mean-spirited sons of bitches on earth. The people here worked harder, drank harder, prayed more fervently, drove faster, loved more, hated more, gave money more generously, wasted money more absurdly, and in general explored the possibilities of human goodness and depravity more relentlessly than people elsewhere on the planet.

It was not so much excessive wealth that fueled their passions, she thought, for money was not as abundant as in decades past, as it was a kind of stubborn pride, a feeling that, for better or worse, they had a tradition to uphold.

The men tonight were mostly tanned and trim, impressive in their tuxes; these were men who had more likely attended Yale than Texas A&M, who were more comfortable in Paris, France, than Paris, Texas. With few exceptions they had survived the oil bust intact. Theirs was old money; it clung to them like barnacles. They were proud to be associated with the new theater, proud to greet their President, but they knew full well that this evening belonged to their wives.

For, if the men were quietly elegant, their wives had, for this most special evening, conjured up an explosion of high fashion that was spectacular even for Texas.

As the couples entered the museum, a kind of informal fashion show evolved. The world's great designers were represented, in shimmering miracles of color and fabric, ego and sensuality, gowns that were near-Shakespearean in their invention and complexity. The women entered with chins high, aglow, savoring this perfect moment in their lives, then abruptly the spotlight passed and they were watching the next arrival do her turn.

Jessica, who had come early, was struck by how few surprises there were. If many of the women had looked at hundreds of gowns, almost all of them had eventually picked the one that was preordained to be hers. Puss, to no one's surprise, arrived in a shimmering Scaasi gold lamé mini-gown that was backless and all but frontless. She was stunning—she was Puss—and no one had expected her to arrive in a Mother Hubbard.

Kay, while more discreet, chose to reveal a good deal more of herself than the city was accustomed to beholding. Her jade green Oscar de la Renta swept the floor, but her shoulders, back, and milky breasts were abundantly displayed. "What the hell, we don't live forever," she told Jessica earlier that day.

Jessica was amused by the arrival of one celebrated hostess whose weakness for little-girl ruffles and feathers and frills was a joke in their circle. "Poor Anne always looks like a little bird who can't get off the ground," was Kay's oft-repeated remark, and that was how she looked tonight, in a fluttery baby blue gown that embodied one very rich woman's rather poignant wish to be twelve again.

Jessica herself had opted for a simple, strapless white silk gown by Saint Laurent, with pale satin flowers at the waist, one that she hoped would balance Billy's desire for her to be gorgeous with her own determination not to be overshadowed, as she felt many women were that night, by their gowns and spectacular jewels.

The fashion show was a treat, but Jessica was alarmed to see Puss arrive on the arm of Philip Kingslea.

"Where's Sonny?" Jessica asked. She had handed April over to Sonny that morning and been uneasy ever since.

"Aw, he said screw it, you seen one President you've seen 'em all," Puss replied. "So Philip gets to be my walker tonight."

"I ask only to serve you," the novelist said humbly.

Philip was impressed by how artfully Puss dissembled. Actually she had called him barely an hour earlier in hysterics and said Sonny was out of control, refusing to attend the reception, and that she needed an escort.

Walter Lamont and his wife arrived, to scattered applause. His success in keeping Sonny on the defensive in court had made him a hero to many who despised Sonny.

Jessica turned to Billy. "Did Sonny stay away because of the Lamonts?"

Billy shook his head. "The Reagan people came down on him hard. It's better that he didn't come."

Lily Nash, regal in royal blue, arrived on the arm of Alex Molina, her young Spanish lover. It was his first trip to Fort Worth: Lily calculated that the scandal would be minimized on such a busy weekend.

"Where's the Gipper?" Puss demanded, just as the President and First Lady made their entrance, to thunderous applause.

Jessica clapped without enthusiasm. She thought Mr. Reagan was a sweet man, and she loved the way his cheeks turned pink when she laughed, but she could never quite believe he was President of the United States. In that, of course, she was distinctly in the minority amid this adoring throng. Mrs. Reagan, wide-eyed and tiny beside her husband, was resplendent in a red sequined gown that more than held its own with the finest in the room.

The guests began to move through a receiving line. Puss, never shy, led the way. In high heels she was as tall as the President, and she looked as if she might devour him on the spot.

"You're cute!" Puss roared, and the leader of the free world blushed delightedly.

Lily Nash followed, and the line stopped moving as she was given a presidential hug and told about the time he made a movie in Fort Worth forty years before.

Jessica held back, in no hurry to bask in the presidential sun. She thought she should keep an eye on things, then bring up the rear.

She saw a museum employee take Kay aside, and her sister-in-law quickly left the line—for a phone call, it appeared.

Jessica chatted with Philip Kingslea. "So how do you like our little party?" she asked.

"The mind boggles," the novelist admitted. "When I was growing up here, culture had not yet been discovered. Just football and the Golden Gloves and the rodeo and wrestling matches at the North Side Coliseum. Bar-hopping was the art form of my youth."

"How about fireworks displays, did you have those?"

Jessica was still annoyed that Sonny had insisted on having a sensational fireworks show outside the Billy Ringer Theater that evening.

"You don't like fireworks?" Philip asked.

"Mr. Shakespeare will supply enough fireworks for me."

"Ah, but you're an elitist," Philip said. "Sonny's right. People who'll never set foot in the theater will still think it's wonderful because of those fireworks. Sonny's a hero in this city, because of gestures like that."

They were near the head of the line when Kay rushed back, pale and shaken, and gripped Jessica's arm.

"You have to come with me, *now*," she whispered.

Jessica stared at her sister-in-law in confusion. What tragedy could have wrought this change in her? "What is it? What about the opening?"

"Dammit, there may not be an opening. Come on."

They slipped out a side door and soon were in Kay's limousine, speeding downtown.

"Kay, for God's sake, what is it?"

"What happened today? Ian and April, where did they go?"

Jessica told her about Sonny coming to the Home and taking the two actors waterskiing.

"And you *let* them?"

"Yes," she confessed.

"And then what happened?"

"I don't know. Sonny said he'd have them back by two."

"Oh God!" Kay cried. "Doris Flynn called me at four in hysterics, asking where her daughter was. She called again just now. Something terrible has happened and the opening is off."

"Off? It can't be off," Jessica moaned. "All those people. The President. What do you think . . . ?"

"I'm afraid to think," Kay said. "I don't want to think. Please God, don't let me think." She squeezed Jessica's hand, and the limousine slid to a halt at the Hyatt Regency.

. . .

The two distraught, begowned women hurried through the big, plush lobby of what was once the legendary Hotel Texas, where the Murchisons and Hunts and Wildcat Billys had swapped lies and oil leases a half century before. Now it was filled with software salesmen, Japanese tourists, and TCU students on their way to a dance.

Doris Flynn threw open the door to her penthouse suite. The cool backstage mother had been reborn as Medusa. Her dark eyes burned with the fury of a mother wronged.

"Come in," she said. "Damn you, come in and see what you've done."

Ian was immobile on the sofa, still in a bathing suit, his head in his hands.

"You! I entrusted my daughter to you and you sent her off with that monster."

"Where is she?" Jessica whispered.

"The doctor is with her."

"What happened?" Kay demanded.

"What happened? What do you think happened? That monster attacked my daughter. He . . . "

She could neither finish nor bring herself to speak Sonny's name.

The bedroom door opened and the doctor beckoned. Doris Flynn vanished behind the door.

"Oh, God, what about the opening?" Kay cried.

"What about April?" Jessica asked. "Ian, please, tell us what happened."

"We went waterskiing. At first it was fine. But then he sent me up to the house for beer. When I came back, he'd taken April out without me. They were gone for an hour. When they came back, April was crying. He said she was seasick. He took her inside and more or less got her calmed down and then he had someone drive us here."

"Damn him!" Jessica raged. It seemed the end of decency, of life as they had known it. She could not imagine what could come next.

"Ian, can you perform?" Kay asked. "With April's understudy?"

He looked at her in horror. "I only want to leave this place. April's mother asked me to stay and talk to the police."

"Oh my God!" Kay groaned.

The door opened and the doctor and Doris Flynn emerged.

"You two know Dr. Holloway?"

"Of course," the doctor said. "Jessica, Kay, I'm sorry to meet under such circumstances."

"Tell them," the mother said impatiently.

"Well, based on what the girl says, and the physical evidence, there's not much doubt what happened," the doctor said.

"Can she perform?" Kay asked the doctor.

"Perform?" Doris Flynn cried. "Are you insane?"

"She needs rest," the doctor said.

Kay looked at her watch. "I have to call the theater. All those people. Ian, can you . . . ?"

The door opened and April appeared, drawn and listless in a faded blue robe. She looked at Jessica and seemed not to know her.

Jessica yearned to embrace the girl, to comfort her. She thought of her own near-rape, so many years before. She wanted to tell April that this would pass, that she would be strong again someday, but she dared not risk the mother's fury. It was Ian who moved to April's side.

"I feel dirty," the actress murmured. "Sticky and terrible, inside and out."

"No, no," Jessica said.

"I wanted to throw myself into the lake and drown."

"Go back to bed, darling," her mother urged.

"No, I'm going to the theater."

"You'll do no such thing!"

April turned to Jessica. *"He* won't be there, will he?"

"No, I promise you."

"Then we should go," April said. "It's late."

Doris Flynn was livid. "You Nashes," she said. "I want you back here, after the performance, all of you. We're going to settle this."

April put on a coat and Kay herded them down to her car. Kay and the doctor sat up front, Jessica took the jump seat, and April and Ian huddled in the back, holding hands. Soon they were speeding out the Jacksboro Highway. Sonny's fireworks display filled the sky ahead.

The fan-shaped jewel of a theater, all burgundy and gold, hummed with excitement as Kay and Jessica hurried to their box. Lily Nash shot them an anxious glance, then turned back to the First Lady. Moments later, the audience broke into spontaneous applause as the curtain rose for the first time on the Billy Ringer Theater.

> Two households, both alike in dignity
> In fair Verona, where we lay our scene . . .

Jessica clutched Billy's hand. There had been no time to tell him the news. For most of the show she kept her eyes closed, unable to trust her emotions. She heard the murmurs of the audience, and the beauty of the play, and most of all she heard April's heartbreaking voice speaking Juliet's words. The critics, the next day, would praise the "grace" and "maturity" of April's performance. Only the *New York Times* critic would note that she had been, as he put it, "strangely muted."

As the curtain fell, a Texas-style ovation greeted the company. The President himself was leading it, pink-cheeked and beaming. Melissa Nash emerged from the wings, bearing roses for April. As the cheering reached a crescendo, April bowed low, smiling her wistful smile. How incredibly tough she is, Jessica thought. What a great star she will be.

People filed into the moonlight, buoyed by the brilliance of the evening. The presidential motorcade slid away, followed by cheers.

Kay told Lily and the men that there was a terrible problem, and they all must go, immediately, to meet April's mother. On the way, Jessica whispered the facts to Lily, who reeled in disbelief.

It was past midnight when they gathered in Doris Flynn's suite. She was accompanied by a grim little man whom she introduced as "Mr. Giddings, my lawyer."

Lily offered an apology on behalf of the family, but Flynn cut her off. Her anger had become more focused, more terrible.

"Let's understand one another. Your son, Mrs. Nash"—she still could not speak Sonny's name—"abducted and raped my daughter. She was seventeen and a virgin. These are facts to which Dr. Holloway can testify. Ian witnessed the abduction. And April herself can attest to"—her voice broke—"to the horrors he inflicted upon her."

She glared at them. No one dared speak.

"My daughter, out of inexplicable goodness, saved your opening. But in the morning she's leaving this God-forsaken city.

"What remains now is this crime, this outrage. I can call the police and that brute will be arrested and if there's a God in heaven he'll spend the rest of his life behind bars. Nothing could please me more."

"Hold on," Mark injected. "Sonny may have a different story."

"Shut up, you fool!" Kay cried.

"I would dearly love to see that man rot in jail—to see him rot in hell!" Doris Flynn continued. "I'd glory in seeing the Nash family disgraced, all of you shamed and ruined by this, as you so richly deserve."

"It's true. We do deserve it," Lily Nash whispered.

"But I must think of my daughter's well-being. It would cause her great pain to relive this outrage in court. So I must consider an alternative to legal action."

"You've suffered damages, no question," Mark said.

"And you have a great deal of money. But I'm not here to blackmail you."

"Mrs. Flynn, anything within reason . . . " Billy began.

She turned on him furiously. "Don't talk to me about reason! Here are my terms. Excelsior Films will sign a contract with my daughter for three films, one in each of the next three years. For the first she will be paid three million dollars. For the second, five million. For the third, seven million. And ten percent of the gross, in each case. We will have approval of scripts and directors. If we find no acceptable script, she will be paid nonetheless. That man

312

will never speak to or in any way communicate with my daughter again. Take it or leave it."

"Fifteen million dollars?" Mark protested. "For a girl of seventeen? It's . . . "

"It's entirely reasonable," Billy said, and his mother nodded her agreement.

"My lawyer will draw up the contract," Doris Flynn said. "Now get the hell out of here."

The Nashes returned to Lily's house. Everyone converged on the bar, then slumped in a semicircle on Lily's overstuffed sofas and easy chairs.

"Fifteen million," Mark muttered. "It's an outrage."

"*I'd* have demanded double that," Kay said.

"She had too much pride," Lily said. "I admire the woman."

"You know what's the worst of it?" Billy asked. "We bailed Sonny out. What's fifteen million to him? He's laughing."

"We mustn't let this leak," Kay warned.

Billy ignored her. "Sonny started planning this from the moment he laid eyes on that girl. Her innocence was an affront to him. That's why he invited her here. To show his contempt—for her, for our family, for our values, for the theater, for everything decent people stand for."

"That's a bit extreme," Mark protested.

"I blame myself," Lily said. "I kept quiet too long, year after year, outrage after outrage, because of the money he was making me."

"Making all of us," Billy reminded her.

"Yes, but I was his mother. I made my pact with the devil."

"We'll have to talk with him," Mark declared.

"It's past talk," Lily said. "We have to be rid of him."

"How?" A cold smile lit Kay's face.

"It's a legal matter now," Lily said. "Billy and Mark and I each own twenty-five percent of the company. It's simple. We vote him out."

"Hold on," Mark said. "If Sonny did what this girl claims, it's a bad thing, I'll grant you that. But let's don't lose our heads. Sonny is the goose who lays the golden eggs."

"Are you saying you'd stick with him?" Kay demanded.

"We've done well together," Mark said stubbornly.

"I'd divorce you," Kay said. "Which would offset your profits for several years."

"You'd be cut off from the rest of us," Billy said. "You have to choose, Mark. Us or Sonny."

"You're all so moralistic," Mark grumbled. "Money is money. He's never been convicted of doing anything to that girl. Maybe she made it up."

"He could be convicted easily enough," Lily said.

"Don't be so sure," Mark warned. "I don't know that a Texas jury would accept the word of an actress over one of the state's leading citizens."

"Here's something nobody made up," Kay said, flushed with anger. "The night of our first anniversary party, you'd passed out, and Sonny raped me in our bed. Rather crudely. Because he knew I wouldn't dare tell you. It hasn't been a pleasant memory to live with, and I was no teenage virgin."

Mark's face crumpled; he looked like a hurt child. "Did you have to make a public announcement?"

How like a man, Jessica thought, to see himself the victim.

"She's among people who love her," Billy said. "The question is where you stand."

Lily Nash stood up. "If you're choosing Sonny, then leave now and we'll see you in court."

Mark grimaced in frustration. "No, I'm with you," he said finally. "But don't think it will be easy. Sonny won't take this without a fight."

"He'll walk away with twenty-five percent of Nash International," Billy reminded him. "He can set up on his own and not be bothered by us."

"Twenty-five percent!" Mark said incredulously. "Don't you understand anything? He thinks it's *all* his."

"Then show him!" Kay declared. "Call the lawyers, take him to court, get this mess behind us."

Mark's thick body was limp as Jell-O. "It won't be that easy," he warned again.

Billy and Mark met with NI's chief counsel on Monday morning. The lawyer was shocked and wary. Billy thought he feared both Sonny and the breakup of a company that had enriched him.

Yet, when pressed, he admitted that the legal situation was simpler than they had imagined.

"You all signed the Uniform Partnership Act," the lawyer explained. "There is specific provision for the expulsion of one partner by a majority of the other partners. You don't even have to show cause or go to court. The ousted partner can go to court, of course, and you owe him an accounting—but the burden of proof is on him. On the face of it you simply give him notice and he's out."

"How much notice?" Billy asked. He was nervous and Mark was a basket case. Sonny had not come to the office that morning, but they felt his presence, his menace.

"The agreement calls for twenty-four-hours notice."

"Then what?"

The lawyer shrugged. "Then you can change the locks. If he comes on your property, he's trespassing."

Billy said, "It's incredible to me that Sonny would sign an agreement that allowed him to be ousted without cause on twenty-four-hours notice."

Mark managed a dour laugh. "You miss the point. We signed the agreement when you came into the company. He wanted an easy way to be rid of you if you made trouble. No one dreamed it would be applied to Sonny."

The lawyer left and Billy and Mark faced one another uneasily.

"How will we tell him?" Mark asked.

"I'll do it," Billy said. "We have to get it over with."

"I want protection when it happens," Mark said.

"What do you mean?"

"Security men. Police. Witnesses."

"Dammit, Mark, this is sick. Are we going to spend the rest of our lives being afraid of our own brother?"

"Our brother is a dangerous man," Mark replied grimly.

Just then the door opened and he was there, bearded and sardonic, in jeans and a red Izod shirt.

"Gentlemen," Sonny greeted them, in a rich, ironic voice. He had surrendered none of his flair for the dramatic. His smile chilled them. He might have been the Devil confronting Faust.

"Come in," Billy said.

"A little bird said you were looking for me."

Sonny sprawled across Billy's sofa. He pulled out a pocket knife and began to trim his nails.

"We have business to discuss," Billy said.

"Always glad to talk business."

"Sonny, let's be honest. What you did to that girl was unforgivable. That ripped it. We bailed you out, to protect the family name—to protect ourselves—but we can't stay in business with you."

Sonny put the knife away. "You understand, baby brother, I don't know what the fuck you're talking about."

Billy shrugged. "Have it your way. The bottom line is, we've voted you out. You have twenty-four hours to vacate. We'll give you a full accounting, and your full share of the assets. Money isn't the issue."

There was a moment of silence. Billy saw the contempt in Sonny's eyes, contempt and the shadow of something worse.

Then Sonny smiled.

"Money is always the issue," he said. "Some folks make it, some folks piss it away."

His smile was like a rattlesnake's: you had be extremely naive to expect anything good to follow.

"You two assholes will be broke in a year," Sonny added. "You know that, don't you?"

Billy had to laugh. "It's possible."

"I never figured you'd turn on me," Sonny said to Mark. "The

316

kid here, he was always a fruitcake, but I thought you had some sense."

Mark was staring out the window. Far across the prairie, an ominous purple-black wall of clouds was moving in.

"You abused my wife," he said woodenly.

"Oh come on, you ugly pig-fucker," Sonny said. "You weren't doing the job."

"You're a cruel man," Mark said. There were tears in his eyes. "You always have been."

"Yeah, so cruel I made your dumb ass rich."

"Let's leave it to the lawyers," Billy said. "I'd like to issue a statement that puts the best possible face on this. This isn't the end of the world. You'll probably be a lot happier without us to hold you back."

Sonny stood up and stretched. "You can bet on that one, kiddo," he drawled.

Then he was gone.

Billy turned back to Mark, and saw a blade of lightning flash to earth, far to the northwest.

"That wasn't so bad," he said. "For Sonny, that was a picnic."

Mark looked at him in anguish. "That wasn't Sonny," he said. "That was only a mask."

Billy felt a surge of sympathy, even of affection, for his brother. He thought that for years, caught up in his own drama, he had ignored Mark's. Perhaps now, as partners, they might at last come to know one another.

"Mark, he's gone," he said gently.

His brother would not be consoled. "No," he moaned. "Can't you see? He'll never be gone!"

Billy called the lawyers and PR people, then his mother, and headed home as the first rain began to splatter against the cars on Camp Bowie Boulevard. He passed the old Bowie Theater, where he had spent so many Saturday afternoons; it was a bank now, but they had saved its Art Deco facade. When he reached home and told Jessica how well the encounter with Sonny had gone, they agreed to leave for the ranch the next morning, and perhaps escape to France after that.

Kay dropped her son Christopher by to spend the night; there'd been a mix-up with the babysitter, she said. Christopher was a moody boy of eight, athletic and handsome, nothing at all like Mark. Jessica suspected, although Kay had never confirmed it, that he was Sonny's son, the offspring of the rape she had revealed.

The four of them watched "Mork and Mindy," Melissa's favorite TV show, and then Olivia served tacos and guacamole at the kitchen table.

After dinner Christopher returned to TV, and Billy read Melissa two chapters from *Charlotte's Web*. The storm had arrived; thunder and lightning crashed outside, but they were playing Beatles tapes and hardly heard the storm. They loved the isolation it gave them, the sense of being alone in their own universe. At last Melissa began to nod.

"I'll take her up now, Mr. Billy," Olivia said.

"No, let me."

He lifted his daughter and carried her up. The beanbag of her body against his shoulder was warm and thrilling. He sat on the edge of the tub while she went to the bathroom, then carried her to her cluttered bedroom. He eased her into bed, holding her hand.

"We're going to the ranch tomorrow, 'Liss," he told her.

"Can I ride Pancho?"

"Sure. And we'll fish in the creek."

"I want to catch a big fish and have it for dinner."

"You catch it and I'll teach you to clean it."

"To cut all the guts out?"

"That's right."

"Yuck."

"If you want to catch fish, you have to clean them. That's part of the deal."

He felt strongly that it was part of the deal, for her to learn to clean a fish, to paint a fence, to change a tire, all the workaday chores that might keep her in touch with reality.

The child yawned.

"Goodnight, Princess."

"Night, Daddy."

"Love you."

"Love you."

In the hallway, he passed Olivia, going up to her room. Christopher had taken a book and retired to the guest room.

Downstairs, Jessica was sitting on the floor. He knelt and kissed her.

"Let's have champagne," he said.

"Great. Why?"

"I feel like celebrating."

"About Sonny?"

"He took it well."

He popped the cork and poured.

"I've been thinking about the people in Pearl," she said.

"So have I. With Sonny out of the way, I'll put in new equipment, cut production, whatever it takes."

"That would be so wonderful," she said. "In the long run it will help NI, by gaining respect for you."

Billy smiled. "Sonny would consider that a wimpy point of view."

"Billy, I'd like to work with the foundation."

"What about teaching?"

"When you come right down to it, there are a lot more people who want to teach literature than want to help people in need."

"I wish you'd run the foundation," he told her. "I'll have to spend more time on NI business now."

Jessica laughed.

"What is it?"

"I want it all. The foundation and France and a new baby too."

"I don't know why two clever people can't manage that. My God, it's just sinking in. I won't have to deal with Sonny anymore. He was making me crazy. I feel sane now."

She squeezed his hand. "You've always been sane."

"Just a little crazy?"

"Maybe," she agreed. "But brilliantly sane now."

319

She felt expansive, maternal; she was glad to forget the China Siddons episode. She, like Sonny, was the past now.

"What about Mickey, your sister?" he asked.

"I called again. Phone disconnected. I'll try through the DEA tomorrow."

"I want to meet her. Let's get them to the ranch."

"I'd love that. I'm so happy. I feel like we've just begun to live."

"Me too."

She smiled. "The champagne made me sleepy. I'm going up."

"I'll be along."

She kissed him. "Don't keep me waiting."

He watched her move up the stairs, slender and serene. He loved the cornucopia of her body, loved the thought of her bearing another child.

"Abbey Road" was playing, the second side. The aching sadness of Paul's farewell to John. He could remember the first time he heard the album, in college; he and his friends had spent a weekend adrift in the music. His roommate believed that the Beatles had come from another planet, and "Abbey Road" had been their parting gift before sailing back to a more perfect corner of the cosmos.

Tonight was a parting, too, his and Sonny's, sad in its way. He wished it had been different, but he had never understood Sonny, nobody had; it was as if he, too, had arrived from elsewhere in the universe.

Billy moved with the music, restlessly. He knew Jessica was performing her nightly ritual: washing her face, brushing her hair, looking in on the children. He went to his desk and found a joint that had been there for months. At Jessica's urging, he had stopped smoking, but he wanted this special night to be heightened, magical.

He deactivated the security system, stepped onto the deck, under the canopy, and lit the joint. Soon he was utterly at peace. He savored the rain on the roof, the caress of the cool air. He finished the joint and flicked it into the night. He stood in the darkness, thinking of Jessica, imagining the love she would give him, the son she would give him, and he blazed with the totality of his happiness.

Only when he turned to go in did he realize he was not alone.

320

20.

MICKEY SLEPT ON. TIME PASSED UNCLOCKED IN A WORLD AS dark and silent as the depths of the sea. Sometimes she drifted up into fields of light, where memories rippled and fled, then she would pass back into darkness.

It was those at the bedside who suffered. Her DEA colleagues were there in shifts, around the clock. The nurses bathed her and fed her through tubes, and when she was able her friends would feed her liquids with a spoon. "Got to keep meat on them bones, sugar," Ruby would say.

Her friends marked the milestones in her struggle. The times her eyes fluttered. The time she cried, "Rafe, watch out, watch out!" They understood that, but they did not understand the times when she whispered, "Jessie, baby."

She was there and not there, alive and not alive, and the doctors could not say if her sleep would last another day or another decade. Two thousand miles away, in a kingdom called Texas, there was tragedy and turmoil, but Mickey knew nothing of it. She slept, deep in her shadowy sea.

21.

ON THE MORNING AFTER BILLY AND JESSICA NASH WERE murdered, Jay Taggart's phone rang as never before in his three years as Tarrant County District Attorney.

Sonny Nash was by then a free man, thanks to a JP who had granted bond of $1 million, which Sonny paid by certified check twenty minutes after the banks opened. He had spent most of the night in the JP's office, joking with a pair of deputies, because the jurist did not think a man of Sonny's renown should be subjected to the indignities of the county jail.

The people who were calling Jay Taggart mostly had never called him before. They certainly hadn't called when he announced for reelection, because he was considered a one-term fluke. He had blundered into the office, in the wake of a local scandal, on his credentials as a yellow-dog Democrat, honest to a fault, who gamely stuck with the national ticket every four years while the country club crowd, self-styled "Texas Democrats," made their peace with whomever the Republicans put up.

But now the good citizens were calling and what they were saying was, "You're the District Attorney, and why is that killer walking the streets of our fair city?" The callers blamed Jay, not the JP, for Sonny's freedom, and many were none too subtle in suggesting that Jay's tenure in office would be brief unless justice was quickly done.

Not that Jay Taggart minded the calls. They were a quick, if unscientific, survey of local opinion. The callers were mostly people who had known Sonny Nash for years, and who without exception considered him a rotten, violent, amoral son of a bitch.

"Sonny was always crazy and when they took away his toys he just flat freaked out," said one lawyer, echoing a popular view.

"It's a dual tragedy," said a more reflective caller. "Not only the murders themselves, but that they should come so soon after the other Nashes built that theater. It's like one day the city was groping toward the twenty-first century, and the next day we were dragged back to the Wild West days of the nineteenth."

No caller expressed the slightest doubt that Sonny was guilty. And Jay Taggart, for his part, had rarely been more rock-solid certain of guilt. He had known the Nash family all his life. He was Billy's classmate, and thought him a bright, funny, decent guy, and he remembered Lily Nash fondly. But Sonny? He thought him the scum of the earth. He remembered Sonny best from high school: a cold, arrogant loner, consumed by some inner rage.

He had watched Sonny grow rich and powerful without otherwise improving. Sonny was smart, and possessed a certain roguish charm, but he remained a predator, a disaster waiting to happen.

Now the disaster had come, far worse than anyone had imagined.

Once the good people of Fort Worth accepted that Sonny would be free until convicted—that in fact he would go to his office each day, eat lunch at the Petroleum Club, and loudly proclaim his innocence—they began to demand a speedy trial. They assumed, of course, that a speedy trial would lead to his speedy conviction and removal from the local scene.

Jay Taggart devoutly hoped that was true, although he was aware of certain weaknesses in the state's case.

Jay knew that Sonny would not be tried, strictly speaking, by a "jury of his peers." Did a man as rich as Sonny truly have any peers? Nor would the jury consist of those well-informed citizens in whose minds Sonny was already convicted. No, the jury would by definition be made up of the city's least-informed citizens, people who lacked opinions, people who did not read newspapers, people to whom Sonny would be a distant, enigmatic, perhaps glamorous figure.

The district attorney's concerns multiplied when Sonny imported Stump Wildeman from Dallas to be his lead lawyer. Jay had thought Sonny might plead insanity, or at the very least submit to plea bargaining. But Stump Wildeman had not made his fortune by pleading his clients guilty. He had made his fortune, rather, by winning acquittals for very rich men and women who were charged with murders (usually of a spouse) that everyone believed them guilty of except the jury.

Jay Taggart had a method of sampling public opinion that rarely failed him. He patronized certain dingy taverns two or three evenings a week, where he would sip a Lone Star and commune with various barflies. Whenever possible, he would guide the talk toward local politics and its near relation, local crime. He had found no better way to keep in touch with the prejudices of potential jurors, and he was therefore troubled, after Sonny Nash's arrest, when he began to encounter a certain recurring sentiment.

"Hell, ain't no way a man that rich is gonna kill somebody," people would say. "That's dumber'n dogshit. Man that rich, he'd hire somebody to do it for him!"

The words were always spoken with a canny grin, an air of received truth, as if the speaker possessed amazing insights into the hearts and minds of the very rich. The fourth time he heard that opinion, Jay Taggart began to worry.

The trial of Sonny Nash began less than three months after the rainy night when Billy Nash was beaten to death in his home on Westover Drive.

Sonny had insisted from the first that he, no less than the prosecution, wanted a speedy trial, and he had refused to seek a change of venue because of the relentless publicity in Fort Worth. "This is my town," Sonny told reporters, "and I'll sink or swim right here."

The case was assigned to the most recently appointed of the District Court judges, Roland T. Balthus, who was largely a mystery to Jay Taggart. That he was a black man who called himself a Republican was not in doubt. That he was a large, formidable man who had been a respected trial lawyer was not disputed either. But how this T&P Railroad porter's son might feel in his heart about such a creature as Sonny Nash remained a mystery.

To the scores of reporters who had descended on Fort Worth, and to local citizens who hungered for scandal and/or justice, the initial week of the jury selection process was a bore. But to the lawyers on both sides, picking the jury was the crucial first round of the trial, one that might well determine its outcome.

Jay Taggart started at a disadvantage. Sonny's lawyer, Stump Wildeman, so-called because his right arm ended at the elbow in a round, pink nub, which he wielded in the courtroom for maximum dramatic impact, was blessed with unlimited funds and had hired a small army of investigators. No sooner had the first panel of prospective jurors been called than the defense's gumshoes were out, seeking every detail about their debts, politics, jobs, marriages, and the like. This data was fed to a team of psychiatrists who sought to determine what sort of juror would look most kindly on a murder suspect who was also a billionaire.

In most murder trials, it is the state that seeks solid, law-abiding jurors, and the defense that looks for the rebel, the outsider, the dope smoker, the rock-'n'-roller, anyone who might feel sympathy for a poor wretch on trial for his life. But Sonny was not your typical poor wretch and this was no ordinary trial. Here, both sides were looking for solid citizens.

Stump Wildeman wanted older jurors, jurors who would respect, not resent, his client's money, jurors with the imagination to accept the concept of "reasonable doubt." Wildeman was well aware that most leading citizens of Fort Worth thought his client was guilty, but that did not bother him. For a jury is a newborn creature, and he intended for this jury to see a newborn Sonny Nash, one he would create before their eyes.

After two weeks of jousting, they had a jury that was discernibly older and better educated than most. There were seven women and five men, three black people, four college graduates, a retired Marine sergeant, and one elderly woman who said she was unaware of the murder because all she watched on TV were the soap operas. The jury's most conspicuous lack was that of women under thirty. Stump Wildeman's experts and his instincts told him the same thing: most young women, particularly secretaries, would loathe his client; it was their mothers who might love him.

The jury filed in warily and took their seats for the first morning of the trial, the opening statements.

"Each side will give you evidence, not argument," explained Judge Balthus, massive in his robes, and did not warn the jury what a fine and oft-disputed line runs between the two. "Mr. Taggart."

Jay Taggart, sandy-haired, youthful, stepped up in a new pin-striped suit and red tie. He was the State, the People, the defender of justice, and he gloried in the role.

"May it please the court. We have here a wealthy and prominent citizen brought to trial for murder. Your duty, ladies and gentlemen, is to see that justice is done, in the case of this powerful man— no more and no less than any humble or penniless person accused of a crime."

Jay paused, caught the eye of a juror, then another, seeking the personal contact without which his words would mean little.

"The evidence will show—beyond a reasonable doubt—that on the afternoon of September 17, the defendant Howard Nash, Jr., better known as Sonny, a partner in a great company that you all know about, was voted out of that company—expelled from it—by his mother and two brothers. The evidence will further show that about ten o'clock that night, Sonny Nash gained entry to the home of his brother, Billy Nash, and in a fit of rage and revenge beat his brother to death. Eyewitnesses will testify that he carried away Billy Nash's wife, Jessica Nash, whose body has never been found."

Jay looked at the jurors: their faces were inscrutable, but rapt; he—or the grisly crimes—clearly had their attention.

"The state will demonstrate a motive for the murder: the violent rage of a powerful man who could not bear to have his power taken from him. We will show that other members of the Nash family feared for their lives when word of his rampage spread. We will show you that this defendant would have killed everyone in that house—would have left behind no witnesses—but was foiled by one brave woman.

"We ask only, ladies and gentlemen of the jury, that you be just as brave in doing your duty, and in proving that Texas justice applies to the powerful as much as to the most humble citizen."

Jay Taggart sat down. He tried to look brisk and self-confident. But he had a terrible feeling that he was waltzing on quicksand.

Stump Wildeman marched to the jury box with the pride and confidence of an old gladiator, scarred but never defeated. In this very courtroom, twenty years before, he had won one of his first famous cases, that of the oilman Wade Kingslea, accused of murdering a now forgotten beauty named Jenny Rhodes.

"Reasonable doubt," he began. His sharp East Texas twang invaded the ear, lulled the mind. "The state must prove guilt beyond a reasonable doubt."

He pointed to Sonny Nash, clean-shaven now, perfectly groomed, a paragon.

"The prosecutor tells you that my client is rich. Well, praise the Lord, that's not yet a crime in Texas. What the prosecutor does not tell you is that my client is innocent. In the eyes of the law, he is innocent until proven guilty beyond a reasonable doubt. And we will show that doubt, a thousand times over.

"The evidence will show that Billy Nash was very likely the victim of his own lifestyle. We will show that he was a rich man who led a double life, who liked to run with the underbelly of society. We will show that the state's supposed eyewitnesses are in fact a great deal less than that."

Stump Wildeman paced relentlessly before the jury box. He was an ugly little man, with short legs, a barrel chest, greasy hair, and mean eyes set close together. Yet he had star quality; few jurors could take their eyes off of him. Jay Taggart, watching him, felt a pang of despair.

"We agree with the prosecution on one thing, ladies and gentlemen. You face a challenge. But we say the challenge is to prove that a man of wealth, a prominent citizen, cannot be railroaded by . . . "

"Objection," Jay Taggart boomed.

"Mr. Wildeman," the judge said, "let's stick to the facts—the closing argument comes later."

The lawyer nodded. "I stand reproved, your honor." Then, to the jury, he repeated passionately: "Reasonable doubt, ladies and gentlemen, reasonable doubt."

Jay Taggart began the state's case by calling one of the police officers who first arrived at the Nash house on the night of the murders, followed by the county coroner, and the detective who'd led the investigation. He hoped to brand the jury, at the outset, with a searing memory of the crimes committed.

The officer, Randy Bray, pockmarked and solemn, said he and his partner had responded to a radio call and arrived at the Nash home at 10:47 p.m. They found the front door locked, but went around back and gained entry through the French doors. They found lamps and furniture overturned, then, in the hallway, they discovered Billy's body at the foot of the stairs.

Over Stump Wildeman's objections, the police officer said that Billy appeared to have been beaten with a tire tool and that he appeared to have died trying to protect his family.

He said he and his partner, guns drawn, went upstairs, where they found Olivia and the two children. After hearing Olivia's story, they radioed headquarters and issued an all-points alarm for Sonny Nash, warning that he might be armed and dangerous.

Stump Wildeman, on cross-examination, established that the officer had not seen Sonny Nash at the scene, or any sign of Jessica

Nash, or any weapon, or any sign of forced entry. Officer Bray answered Stump's questions with wary respect; all policemen in Texas knew how many of their fraternity Stump had left looking like fools, and they treated him as gingerly as they would a drunk with a shotgun.

The coroner, testifying next, said that Billy's wounds suggested he had tried to fend off his attacker but had been beaten down and killed by "three or four" severe blows to the head. He gave the opinion that the attacker was a large, powerful man.

Wildeman's cross-examination revealed that traces of both marijuana and alcohol were found in Billy's blood. Pressed hard, the coroner said the fatal blows "might possibly" have been struck by a woman.

In the afternoon, Detective Orin Vestal took the stand. Vestal said he reached the murder scene at 11:22, and took charge of the various detectives and technicians who were arriving.

Jay Taggart used the detective to introduce the photographs of Billy's body. He himself, after three months, could not look at those pictures without shock and horror, and he knew what impact they would have on the jury. He watched their faces as the photos were handed around the jury box, some of the men impassive, most of the women shaken; he noted with pleasure how many of the jurors, after studying the pictures, looked immediately at Sonny Nash.

After the jury finished with the photographs, Jay resumed questioning the detective. "Did you form an opinion as to how Billy Nash met his death?"

"It appeared that he opened the French doors to admit someone, or just to go outside. Someone was there, and they went into the house and fought. Mr. Nash was beaten down and his skull crushed with a blunt instrument."

"Did you find evidence that Jessica Nash took part in the struggle?"

"We did not."

Jay handed the detective one of the crime scene photographs. "Mr. Vestal, in this photo of the living room, I ask you to identify this object."

"It's a tennis racket."

"You found, in the shambles of the living room, a woman's Prince tennis racket, is that correct?"

"Yes, sir."

Jay left the mystery of the tennis racket unresolved. "That's all for now."

Stump Wildeman strutted forward like an angry pit bull.

"Mr. Vestal, did you or your men find any drugs at the scene of the crime?"

"We found a small amount of marijuana in a plastic bag in Mr. Nash's desk."

"How small?"

"Less than an eighth of an ounce."

"Enough for four or five marijuana cigarettes?"

"Something like that."

"And did you find other evidence of drugs?"

"The next morning, we found the butt of a marijuana cigarette in the flowerbed, beneath the deck."

"In the flowerbed, where it would have been tossed by someone who smoked it on the deck, is that correct?"

"It could have been thrown there from the deck."

"Did you find any other drugs, Mr. Vestal?"

"Prescription drugs, not illegal drugs."

"No cocaine?"

"Only the marijuana, Mr. Wildeman."

"Based on your professional experience, was this crime scene consistent with a drug deal?"

"This was a murder scene."

"We know that. But here we have a man who's had a little to drink. He . . . "

"Your honor, he's asking for gross speculation," Jay Taggart objected.

"The District Attorney didn't object to speculation when he had the witness," Stump shot back.

"You may continue, Mr. Wildeman."

"He smokes a joint and realizes he's about out of marijuana. So he calls his supplier. 'Bring me some over right now,' he says. 'Come to the back door.' The supplier comes. Or sends someone else. Maybe they quarrel over money. Or maybe the dealer decides there's more money to be had by murder than by selling an ounce of dope. Is that a probable scenario, based on your experience, detective?"

"I renew my objection, your honor," Jay Taggart repeated.

"Counsel will approach the bench."

The two lawyers huddled with the judge, out of earshot of the jury and spectators.

"Mr. Wildeman, you're roaming far afield," the judge warned.

"I disagree, your honor. We've placed marijuana at the crime scene. We've shown that the deceased had been smoking it. He opened his back door to the killer. We intend to show that this crime could have been the direct result of a drug deal."

"Mr. Taggart?"

"One marijuana cigarette doesn't make a drug deal. We have witnesses who saw the defendant at the scene, not a drug dealer. Mr. Wildeman is dealing in ghosts and scare tactics."

The judge looked troubled. "I'm going to let the witness answer."

Jay sat down angry and discouraged. He thought that both Stump's "theory" and the judge's ruling reflected the prevailing political winds. Jay and his classmates had smoked their share of dope in law school; he ranked marijuana with beer on the scale of dangerous drugs. But that wasn't what a lot of mothers thought, and that wasn't what the politicians were saying. What black Republican judge wanted to look soft on drugs? Jay would have to trust the jury to have more common sense than Stump Wildeman thought they had—and Stump was no fool in reading Texas juries.

"My question, Mr. Vestal, is whether this crime scene is compatible with a drug deal that escalated into a murder."

The detective stared at the lawyer with unvarnished scorn. "The scene could be compatible with a one-ounce marijuana sale, but in my experience they don't turn into murders."

"Never, or not often?"

"Never, in my experience."

"Are you saying that the people who sell marijuana are harmless hippies?"

"I'm saying what I said."

Stump retreated to the defense table and thumbed through some papers.

"Did your men find the defendant's fingerprints at the scene, Mr. Vestal?"

"No, sir."

"His hair, his blood, any evidence that he'd been there that evening?"

"No, sir."

"That'll be all," the defense lawyer said.

Jay Taggart stood up. "One more question, Mr. Vestal. Did you find any sign of a robbery?"

The detective shook his head. "Billy Nash had his billfold in his pocket, with credit cards and about a hundred dollars cash. There were valuable paintings and jewels in the house. Nothing was taken."

"That's all, your honor."

The judge looked pleased. "Gentlemen, we've moved along nicely. We'll adjourn until tomorrow morning."

Olivia Winston, the state's witness the next morning, approached the witness stand slowly, with determined dignity. She wore a navy blue suit, white blouse, and a black hat over her steel gray hair. She took the oath, lifting her head high, and awaited Jay's questions.

"Mrs. Winston, tell us where you were employed last September 17."

"I worked for Mr. and Mrs. Billy Nash."

"And how long had you worked for the Nash family?"

"Fifteen years. First for Miss Lily, then, after the baby was born, for Miss Jessica and Mr. Billy."

"May I call you Olivia?"

"Yes, sir, you surely may."

"Olivia, tell us what happened at the Nash home, on the night of September 17."

"Mr. Billy came home about seven-thirty. He was all excited, because they'd put Mr. Sonny out of the company. He and Miss Jessica, they hugged and talked about taking a vacation. Then they played with Melissa . . . "

"Their little girl?"

"Yes, sir. They read to her and played games. Chris was there, too, Miss Kay's son."

"You mean Melissa's cousin, Christopher, son of Mark and Kay Nash?"

"Yes, sir. I fixed dinner and we all ate and they played some more and then Chris went up to the guest room and Mr. Billy carried Melissa up to her bedroom."

"And you did what?"

"I cleaned up the kitchen, then I went up to my room and looked at TV."

"At what time?"

"He took her up about nine-thirty."

"Your room, and the two children's rooms, were all on the same floor?"

"Yes, sir."

"Was the evening in any way boisterous?"

Olivia frowned. "How do you mean?"

"Was there excessive drinking? Were the Nashes loud or acting unusual? Was it a wild party?"

"No, sir. He drank a bottle of beer and she had a glass of wine, but it was just a quiet evening."

"All right, Olivia. You and the children went up to your rooms. What happened then?"

"I heard Miss Jessica go to their bedroom."

"On the third floor?"

"That's right."

"Do you know what time it was?"

"I was watching the ten o'clock news."

"What about Mr. Nash?"

"The music was playing downstairs, so I guessed he was still down there."

"So, Billy was downstairs alone. What happened next?"

"I heard yelling and glass breaking. I ran to the stairs and looked down and saw Mr. Billy fighting with a man."

"Did you recognize the man?"

"He had a bandana over his face. I thought I did but I wasn't a hundred percent sure."

"What happened next?"

"I just froze up for a minute. Then Miss Jessica came down. She saw what I saw and she said, 'Olivia, lock the children in your room and call the police.' "

"Then what did she do?"

"She ran to the hall closet and took out a tennis racket and she ran down the stairs."

"How was she dressed?"

"In her nightgown."

"She armed herself with a tennis racket and raced downstairs to help her husband, who was struggling with the intruder. Is that correct?"

"Yes, sir."

"And what did you do?"

"I woke up the children and took them to my room and locked the door. I tried to call the police but the line was dead."

"There were no back stairs? No way for you and the children to escape without passing through the room where the struggle was in progress?"

"No, sir."

"Could you hear what was happening downstairs?"

"I heard more crashing. I heard Miss Jessica scream."

"How many times?"

"Too many, God rest her soul. Then it got real still."

"What were you doing?"

"I was holding the children, trying to quiet them. I heard somebody coming up the stairs, and he started kicking on my door."

"You had a gun, didn't you, Olivia?"

"Yes, sir."

"How long had you owned it?"

"Maybe ten or twelve years."

"Had you ever fired it?"

"No, sir."

"Did the Nashes know you had it?"

"No, sir. Mr. Billy, he didn't believe in guns. He wouldn't have let me keep one in the house."

"But you did anyway?"

"Mr. Billy never lived where I've lived and saw what I've seen."

"All right, Olivia. You heard someone in the hallway. Did you get the gun?"

"Yes, sir."

"Where was it?"

"Under some sheets, on the shelf in the closet."

"Loaded?"

"Yes, sir."

"Someone was kicking on the door. Then what?"

"I yelled for him to go away."

"Did you warn him that you had a gun?"

"No, sir. I thought if he had a gun, it was better if he didn't know I had one."

Jay looked at the jury and saw several nods of approval.

"Then what happened?"

"I put the children in the closet and stood in front of it. The door flew open and the man was standing there."

"Did he still have the bandana over his face?"

"It was down, around his neck."

"How was the man dressed?"

"In blue jeans and a T-shirt and a windbreaker."

"Was he wearing gloves?"

"Yes, sir, rubber gloves."

"Did he have anything in his hand?"

"A tire tool, with blood on it."

"Objection!"

335

"Overruled."

"Olivia, you say the man was no longer wearing the bandana over his face. Did you recognize the man?"

"Yes, sir."

"Is he in this courtroom now?"

"Yes, sir."

"Would you point him out?"

Olivia, unbidden, rose to her full height and pointed one thick finger like a weapon: "It was Mr. Sonny Nash."

Sonny stared back at her with a kind of bemusement, while the courtroom hummed with excitement. Olivia sank back to her chair.

"How long have you known Mr. Nash?"

"Ever since I went to work for Miss Lily, fifteen years ago."

"You have no doubt it was he that you saw?"

"As God is my witness."

"What happened next, Olivia?"

"I saw his tire tool and he saw my gun. I knew he intended to kill me and those children like he'd . . . "

"Objection!" Stump Wildeman ruled.

"Sustained."

"You feared for your life, Olivia, and those of the children?"

"Yes, sir. So I shot at him."

"How many times?"

"I think twice."

"Did you hit him?"

"He didn't show any sign of it."

"What did he do?"

"He yelled and ran down the stairs."

"What did you do?"

"I kept the gun pointed at the door. I wanted to protect the children but I thought maybe I could help Mr. Billy and Miss Jessica. Finally I put the children in the guest room and told them to lock the door until I got back. I went downstairs. I walked right past Mr. Billy's body. The front door was open. I went out, holding the gun in front of me. I saw Mr. Sonny over at the driveway. He had Miss Jessica over his shoulder, putting her in his car."

"Was she struggling?"

"No, sir."

"You recognized the car?"

"It was his Cadillac, with the longhorn on the front."

"He was putting her in the front seat or the back?"

"The back."

"And what did you do?"

"I yelled, 'Let her go, you devil.' I couldn't shoot, for fear I'd hit her. He drove off in the rain. I went next door and called the police. Then I went home and waited with those two poor babies."

Her composure cracked. The judge called to a bailiff for water, and the courtroom was hushed while she drank.

"One final question. When you shot at Sonny Nash, did you intend to hit him or just to scare him off?"

The woman hesitated, as if struggling with an unwelcome truth.

"Mr. Taggart, I wanted to kill the devil and send him back to hell."

Someone in the back of the courtroom cheered.

"Let's have quiet," the judge commanded.

"No further questions," Jay said. It was the best he had felt since the trial began. To send the devil back to hell: that seemed to him a commendable goal.

They broke for lunch and Jay invited Olivia to his office. "You did good," he told her.

"I only told the truth."

"You told it well. But it won't be so easy this afternoon. He'll try to confuse you, any way he can. The best chance he has of winning this case is to discredit you."

"I know what I saw."

"I know you do. Just stick to it. Take your time. Don't be angry, don't be rushed, don't be confused. Whatever he says or does, tell the truth."

At the Mexican Inn, a few blocks away, Stump Wildeman was having an enchilada platter with one of his young associates. Stump

337

was capable of hard, solitary work, but he was happiest when surrounded by disciples.

"How far can you push the drug deal theory, Mr. Wildeman?"

"From here to Chicago. Dammit, boy, we know that a respectable citizen like Sonny Nash didn't kill his brother, so who did? It's clear as glass: a drug deal gone bad."

"But all you've got is one roach," the young lawyer protested.

"You've heard that great oaks from little acorns grow, haven't you?"

"Yes, sir."

"Well, from that one little pissant of a roach a mighty defense is gonna sprout!" Stump laughed heartily.

"That black lady, she looked pretty good this morning."

Stump's close-set eyes narrowed, giving him a slightly demented look: "She may not look so hot this afternoon."

At two minutes past two, Olivia was back in the witness box, gazing serenely at the defense lawyer. Then, he jolted her with his first question.

"Mrs. Winston, would you tell us where you resided from January of 1945 until July of 1946?"

A slap in the face would not have changed Olivia more abruptly. Her mouth quivered, her body sagged, as if she had been dealt a mortal blow. She struggled in vain to frame an answer.

"Shall I repeat the dates, Mrs. Winston?"

"I was in prison," she finally whispered.

"And why were you in prison?"

"A man tried to attack me and . . . "

"No, Mrs. Winston, you were not in prison because a man tried to attack you. You were in prison, were you not, because you killed a man with a butcher knife?"

Her eyes downcast, Olivia said, "Yes."

Jay Taggart watched in horror. He could not object, because felony convictions can be used to impeach a witness. He was heartsick—Olivia had assured him she had no skeletons in the closet of her long life.

Stump Wildeman quickly established that Olivia had told the grand jury she had no criminal record. She protested that she had driven the long-ago incident from her mind: "I locked the door on that and threw away the key."

"Let's look at the night in question," Stump pressed. "When you were downstairs with the Nash family, did you observe Mr. and Mrs. Nash smoking marijuana?"

"No, sir!" Olivia said emphatically.

"Had you ever seen them smoking marijuana?"

A slight pause. "No, sir."

"Did you ever smell marijuana in their house?"

"I don't know what it smells like."

"You don't know what it *smells* like?" The lawyer looked astonished. "Isn't it a fact that your son Omega has been convicted of selling . . . "

Jay Taggart shouted his objection. The judge waved the two lawyers to the bench.

"This has gone far enough," Jay protested. "Her son has nothing to do with this case."

"On the contrary," Stump rejoined. "This woman's truth and veracity are in doubt. She's a convicted felon who misled the grand jury. Now she says she doesn't know what marijuana smells like. I can show that her son's a dealer."

The judge scowled. "Gentlemen, if I'm going to err, I'll err on the side of giving the jury information, not keeping it from them. I'll permit the question."

Under more questioning, Olivia admitted that her son Omega had twice been convicted of selling marijuana.

"Did your son come to the Nash home on the night Billy Nash died?"

"No."

"Had he not visited the house in the past?"

"He'd been to see me."

"You said you once worked for Sonny Nash?"

"Once, about ten years ago, but not for long."

"Isn't it a fact that he fired you for stealing?"

Olivia swelled up in anger. "As God is my witness, that's a lie! I left because he was rude and ugly."

Stump smiled. "You don't like Sonny Nash, do you?"

"No."

"You say you shot at him, wanted to send him to hell."

"That's right."

"Isn't it a fact that you never saw Sonny Nash that night, and you've made up this story . . . "

"Objection!"

"Sustained."

"What about the two children you say you protected? Did you tell them it was Sonny Nash who killed Billy Nash?"

"They saw what they saw."

"Didn't you tell them, 'It's Sonny, he's gone crazy'?"

"No!"

"No further questions," Stump Wildeman said.

Jay Taggart reexamined the witness, trying to repair the damage. According to Olivia, a white soldier had followed her home and tried to rape her, and she'd fought him off with a butcher knife, wounding him fatally, only to be convicted of manslaughter by an all-white, all-male jury. It was a convincing story, yet the harm had been done. His hardworking, churchgoing eyewitness had been knocked off her pedestal. Any juror who wanted to disbelieve her had an excuse now.

Jay took one shot in the dark.

"Olivia, you said you worked for Sonny and left because he was rude and ugly. Could you explain what you meant by that?"

Stump howled his objection, but the judge permitted the question; he owes us one favor, Jay thought bitterly.

"He drank and hit his wife and little boy and called me names."

The judge cut off the questioning and adjourned. Olivia seemed dazed as she left the courtroom. Jay Taggart retreated to his office for a stiff drink. He'd had some bad days in court, but this was the first time his star witness had ever been unmasked as a murderer.

.   .   .

Kay Nash called Jay at home the next morning and said it was urgent that she see him at once. Jay feared the problem was either Melissa or Christopher Nash, who were to be his witnesses that day.

Jay needed their testimony, but he knew how delicate it was, legally and emotionally. Juries were historically reluctant to convict adults on the testimony of children, most often for fear that a child could be coached by one parent to speak falsehoods against the other. Yet in recent years, as child abuse had become a national issue, courts had been more willing to hear young witnesses.

Jay talked to both children the day after the murders. Both had supported Olivia's story. Convinced they were telling the truth, and would make persuasive witnesses, Jay told the judge of his intention to call both to testify. The judge, in turn, had interviewed the children, concluded that they knew right from wrong, and given his approval.

All parties involved knew how sensitive this process was, particularly with regard to Melissa. No one wanted to see the child exposed to further pain; it was only in their desire for justice that they would consider putting her on the stand and subjecting her to the wiles of Stump Wildeman.

When Lily wavered, it had been Kay who argued that Melissa herself, when she was old enough to understand what had happened to her parents, would never forgive them if they had denied her the chance to testify.

An unsmiling Kay arrived at his office at eight, petite and sexy in jeans, an open-necked blouse, and a white jacket. She and Mark had separated: the violence that killed Jessica and Billy had shattered their fragile marriage too.

"Coffee?" he asked. "I've got instant."

Kay cut him off impatiently. "I had three cups before I left the house."

She curled on the leather sofa across from his desk. He came around to take a chair near her. Kay was a billion-dollar-baby; you went to her.

"Chris has changed his story," she announced. "Now he says he never saw the man's face."

"Oh, God!" Jay groaned. "What happened?"

"What do you think happened? Mark got to him."

"What is it with Mark?"

Kay recrossed her quite perfect legs. Jay regarded her with a certain awe.

"Mark's interests lie with Sonny," Kay said. "Billy's dead. Lily doesn't care about the company anymore. Mark on his own is a rich man who is terrified of making decisions. With Sonny, he doesn't have to worry."

"Except that maybe the son of a bitch will kill him."

"He probably thinks that if he can keep Sonny out of prison, Sonny will finally appreciate him. In any event, he's convinced Chris that he didn't see what he saw."

"Did you try to change Chris's mind?"

"How far can I push him? He's an eight-year-old child. I'm just warning you where things stand."

"If what you say is true, I can't call him as a witness. If the defense does, I'll have to point out that he previously told a different story."

Kay's pain showed. For all her money, he thought, for all her toughness, she was still a mother. "Jay, if it comes to that, go easy on him. This isn't his fault."

"I know," Jay Taggart said wearily. "I know."

The courtroom was hushed as Melissa settled into the witness chair. Her feet dangled. When she gazed up at the judge, her eyes were a bright Chagall blue, her shoulder-length hair a sunlit blond. She wore a pink dress, white stockings, black Mary Janes, and ribbons in her hair.

Melissa took the oath and assured the judge that she understood what it meant.

Jay greeted the child with a cautious smile.

"Melissa, how old are you?"

"Four."

"Do you go to school?"

"Yes, sir, to Montessori school."

"Do you understand why we're here in this courtroom?"

The child hesitated. "You're trying to find out what happened to my momma and daddy."

"That's right. Do you remember the last night you saw them?"

"Yes, sir."

"Do you remember what you did before you went up to bed?"

"We watched TV—my cousin Chris was there—and Daddy read me *Charlotte's Web* and Olivia fixed dinner."

"Do you remember going up to bed?"

"My daddy carried me up. We talked for a while."

"What about?"

"We were going to our ranch the next day. He said I could ride Pancho and we'd go fishing and if I caught a fish, he'd teach me how to clean it."

"And then you said good night?"

"He kissed me and I went to sleep."

"You went to sleep. What is the next thing you remember?"

"Olivia took me to her room. She got Chris, too. She locked the door but we could hear a fight downstairs."

"Then what happened?"

"Somebody started banging on the door. Olivia told him to go away but he broke the door open and he was standing there."

"Where were you then?"

"Olivia had put us in the closet, but we had the door open a crack."

"Did you know the man standing there?"

"It was my uncle Sonny."

"You're sure?"

"Yes, sir."

"Do you see him here today?"

"That's him right there."

She looked at Sonny, who abruptly gave her a smile and a wink. He was wearing a handsome smoke gray suit and a tie the color of her eyes.

343

"How was Sonny dressed?"

"In jeans and boots and a jacket. And a red scarf around his neck."

"Was he holding anything?"

"He had a thing in his hand, like I've seen my daddy change tires with at the ranch."

"What happened then?"

"Olivia shot at him and he ran away."

"When the police came that night, did you tell them about Uncle Sonny?"

"Yes, sir."

"Did anyone tell you what to say here?"

"My grandmother told me to tell the truth, just the way I saw it."

"And you've told us the truth, just the way you saw it?"

"Yes, sir."

"Thank you, Melissa. God bless you. No further questions."

"Mr. Wildeman?"

Stump approached the girl warily.

"Melissa, I'm your Uncle Sonny's lawyer and I'd like to ask you a few questions. Is that all right?"

"Yes," the child said without enthusiasm.

"Do you love your Uncle Sonny?"

"No."

Jay was pleased to see a few jurors smile. Who the hell did love Sonny?

"When the man came to the door that night, you were in the closet?"

"Yes, sir."

"And how wide open was the closet door?"

"Just a crack."

"But you could see the man all right?"

"Yes, sir."

"He had a beard?"

"Yes, sir."

"Could it have been a man with a beard who looked a lot like Sonny?"

"Nobody else looks like Uncle Sonny."

"After the man left, what did you do?"

"Olivia went downstairs, then she came back."

"You love Olivia, don't you?"

"Yes, sir."

"Did she tell you that the man in the doorway was Sonny?"

Melissa looked at him as she might at a dull playmate. "She didn't *have* to tell us who he was. It was *Sonny*."

Stump Wildeman retreated. "Thank you, dear," he said. "No further questions."

Jay studied the jury. One of the women was blinking back tears, and all looked sobered; for once, the Nash money seemed not to matter, alongside the tragedy of a child who had lost her parents. And he couldn't ask for a more rock-solid identification than Melissa had given—*if* the jury didn't discount her story because of her age, *if* Stump didn't convince them that the killer nanny had brainwashed the child.

Sonny's trial was a circus from the start.

There were only about thirty courtroom seats allotted for the public, and to win one you had to line up at dawn. But there was excitement outside the courtroom as well. The courthouse steps and lobby had become a stage and a bazaar, teeming with reporters, hustlers, publicity seekers, and curious citizens who coveted even walk-on roles in the drama.

One desperate-looking character hawked T-shirts, soon marked down from $20 to $8, that proclaimed: "IF YOU'VE GOT THE MONEY, SONNY, I'VE GOT THE CRIME."

Women, in particular, seemed drawn to the drama. Some compared it to a Greek tragedy, some to a soap opera, but almost all found it irresistible. Women of all ages occupied the courthouse steps and gawked at the players, particularly the Nash women. Puss, as a potential witness, could not attend her husband's trial, but when she came to meet Sonny she was greeted by squeals and Instamatics like some homegrown Marilyn Monroe. Kay, unsmiling in wraparound dark glasses, projected the aura of a moody Italian movie goddess.

Sonny himself was the main attraction. He drove alone to the courthouse in his notorious red Cadillac convertible, weather permitting with the top down. At the outset, the women greeted him with a muted, ambiguous reception as he bounded up the steps.

They neither cheered nor jeered. They were struck mute by the contradiction of a man who was so rich, so glamorous, yet charged with so heinous a crime. Fantasy and reality collided, and they stared at him nervously, torn by conflicting emotions, uncertain of the socially approved response. Sonny, unconcerned, waved and winked, leaving them speechless in his wake.

On the morning that Lily Nash arrived to testify, scores of curiosity seekers applauded the ill-starred matriarch who was mother to both the victim and the accused in Texas's best murder in years.

Lily took her seat in the courtroom, only to find that her testimony would be delayed. The day's first battle was in progress in Judge Balthus's chambers, where Jay Taggart was seeking permission to question Lily about Sonny's rape of April Flynn.

"I don't believe this," Stump Wildeman raged. "You've got no victim, you've got no charges, you've just got this *tale*. If the District Attorney wants to charge my client with rape, he'd better produce a victim."

"Nobody's charging him with rape," Jay shot back. "We simply want Lily Nash to tell exactly why she voted to expel her own son from the family business."

The judge was not moved. "I can't permit it, Mr. Taggart. The fact that he was expelled is relevant. The reason for it, in this case, is not."

Stump Wildeman laughed scornfully. "The fact that she subsequently signed a fifteen-million-dollar deal with my client's film company suggests that the alleged rape must not have entirely disagreed with her."

The judge scowled. "Let's get to work," he said, and led them into the courtroom.

Lily looked profoundly sad as she took the oath. She had let her hair return to its natural gray, and in other, less tangible ways a spark had gone out of her.

"Mrs. Nash, did you and members of your family meet at your house on the night of September 15?"

"Yes, we did." .

"Can you tell us who was present?"

"My sons Mark and Billy, and their wives, Kay and Jessica."

"And what was the purpose of the meeting?"

"My sons and I agreed to expel my other son, Sonny, from our company, Nash International."

"Can you explain how this was done?"

"Each of the four of us owned twenty-five percent of the company. Any three could vote to expel the fourth. We did so, with regard to Sonny."

"How was he notified of this action?"

"Billy and Mark were to tell him on Monday."

"And Billy was murdered on Monday night?"

"Yes."

"As you discussed this decision, were you concerned about Sonny's reaction?"

Stump leaped up. "He's asking for a conclusion."

"The witness may testify as to her own state of mind," Judge Balthus ruled.

"I was concerned. We all were."

"Mrs. Nash," Jay continued, "can you tell us, in round numbers, what Nash International is worth?"

"It's very complicated. Something in excess of four billion dollars."

A few whistles sounded in the courtroom.

"Sonny was the chief executive officer?"

"Yes."

"As a result of your decision, he was to leave the company and to be given one quarter of its assets, is that correct?"

347

"He would take his share and go off on his own, yes. That's what we expected."

"Do you credit Sonny with being the genius behind the phenomenal success of Nash International?"

Lily shut her eyes, as if the question pained her. "There's no question about it," she said.

Sonny smiled at her reply, but his mother did not look his way. She had not, since she took the stand.

"So your decision was to throw him out of the company he had built?"

"Yes, it was."

Jay paused to let that sink in. This was crucial: Sonny's motivation. His anger, his insane rage, at being cut off from the company he had built. The danger was that to most people, being "thrown out" with a billion dollars might not sound like a reason to kill.

Jay desperately wished he'd been able to demand psychological testing of Sonny in the days after the murder. He thought Sonny was an extremely clever psychopath, but might not have entirely beguiled the experts. However, Stump Wildeman had seen to it that no psychiatrists advanced within a country mile of his client. Jay had to rely upon the good judgment of the jury, and perhaps on Sonny's own erratic ego, if he was so bold as to take the stand.

"Mrs. Nash, do you now have custody of your granddaughter, Melissa?"

"I do."

"Is Olivia Winston back in your employ?"

"Yes."

"Were you aware that she had been to prison many years ago?"

"Vaguely. I consider Olivia one of the finest women I've ever known."

"You are willing to entrust Melissa to her care?"

"I do, every day."

Jay hesitated for a moment. "Mrs. Nash, do you consider your eldest son, Sonny Nash, to be a hot-tempered, or violent, person?"

Stump Wildeman was on his feet. "He's asking for an opinion."

"Which this lady is uniquely qualified to give," Jay shot back.

"Sustained," the judge said.

"I'll rephrase the question. Mrs. Nash, can you remember specific examples of violent behavior on Sonny's part?"

"Same objection!"

"I'll let her answer."

Lily, ignored in the legal spat, had quietly begun to weep.

"My question, Mrs. Nash, is can you recall specific violent acts by your son Sonny?"

"I can," Lily whispered. "But I'd rather not."

Jay knew when to stop.

Stump Wildeman approached the witness as he might a minefield. Gone was the pit-bull aggression he inflicted on lesser witnesses. He knew that a wrong word with this matriarch would explode in his face, yet he had a point to make.

"Mrs. Nash, you're saying that Sonny was leaving the company with a billion dollars in his pocket?"

"At least."

"So it wasn't like he was being thrown out to starve in the street?"

"No one who knows Sonny would expect him to starve in the street," Lily said bitterly, and Stump left it at that.

Philip Kingslea had an assignment to write about the trial for *Playboy*, and he arrived at the courthouse early most mornings to savor the carnival outside. It was there, on Monday morning, that he first sensed a new mood in the air.

The crowds had been cool to Sonny at first, but this morning, as he bounded up the steps, a gaggle of middle-aged women cheered, and proclaimed their faith in his innocence to anyone with a notepad.

Philip suspected that two photographs in the *Star-Telegram* had sparked the new pro-Sonny climate. The first, on the previous Saturday, had shown a fiftyish woman giving Sonny a homemade chocolate cake. "I just love him," she proclaimed. "Everybody does. He's so sexy."

The second picture, that very morning, was of Sonny and Puss

349

outside the First Baptist Church, exchanging pious smiles with its celebrated minister after his Sunday-morning sermon. When Philip saw the picture at breakfast, he'd laughed and wondered if Sonny had dropped a thousand or two in the collection plate. Good PR didn't come cheap.

But there on the windy courthouse steps, as the women giggled and squealed, Philip wondered if that one-two punch of chocolate cake and God hadn't somehow made it acceptable to cheer this man who so many Texas women, with so little glamour in their lives, wanted so much to cheer.

In the days ahead, the ranks of Sonny's admirers grew. They were mostly middle-aged women who were given to pastel pantsuits, harlequin glasses, and elaborate hairdos. They had never dined at the Rivercrest Country Club, nor graced the mansions of Westover Hills, nor were likely to. But they entered his life vicariously now, cheering him outside the courtroom and, when they won seats inside, waving at him with girlish abandon and pressing upon him cakes, cookies, and other evidence of their affection. They became known around the courthouse as Sonny's Honeys.

When Philip saw Jay Taggart later that week, he commented, "You're making Sonny a star."

The prosecutor was not amused. "Those women ought to be horsewhipped. He's a cold-blooded killer."

Philip shrugged. "You'd better convict the son of a bitch or he'll run for governor."

In the days ahead, Sonny's fan club grew ever more numerous and vocal. Fan mail began to arrive, addressed to "Mr. Sonny Nash, The Courthouse, Fort Worth." Somehow Sonny's wealth, his charisma, even his notoriety, had won him a place in the Sam Houston/Clint Murchison/Lyndon Johnson/Hud Bannon pantheon of Texas mythology. He was revered as a rugged individualist, a man's man, an anointed lord of this rugged frontier kingdom.

The trial, for the next two days, was far less interesting than the rise of Sonnymania, as Philip called it. The state's next witness was a police technician who testified on the blood found in the house. That a great deal of Billy's blood was found downstairs was not in dispute. But there had also been a small amount of blood found which the technician said "could" have been Jessica's.

This evidence was important to Jay Taggart. He had been troubled that Jessica's death had seemed so little a part of the trial: Sonny had been charged with two murders, but only one was much discussed. Billy's fate was clear enough—there were photographs—but hers remained cloaked in mystery. Stump Wildeman had at various times hinted to the media that Jessica might not be dead at all, but might have fled to parts unknown. The implication was that she had killed or helped kill her husband, although Stump was too clever to come out and say that.

For all these reasons, it was important to Jay to produce even a trace of Jessica's blood, to make her death real, to remind the jury that this was her tragedy too.

When Jay finished questioning the evidence technician, Stump began a cross-examination that lasted two days and put several jurors to sleep. He went over the highly technical blood-type data in mind-numbing detail; if there were five ways to ask the same question, he found them all.

Jay understood Stump's tactic. He was stalling, giving the jury a chance to forget Olivia and Melissa and Lily and the pictures of Billy. He saw Sonny's popularity growing and hoped it would infect the jury.

Jay Taggart thought the wave of support for Sonny was sick and disgusting, but he did not discount the pull of mythology, or its potential damage to his case. The jury was sequestered, but in the courtroom they could hardly ignore Sonny's Honeys as they swooned over their hero.

Nor could Jay deny that in the hothouse of the courtroom, where anger and confusion were the prevailing emotions, there was only one man who was always cheerful and self-confident, who always seemed certain of the outcome, and that man was the defendant. However black his heart or sordid his past, Sonny sat at the defense table looking like the most innocent man in Texas.

The night the blood expert finally left the stand, Jay's chief investigator, Al Gillette, came to see him.

"A surprise for you, chief," Al began. He was a blade-thin, sardonic man whose job was to search the Texas demimonde for witnesses against Sonny Nash.

"It better be good," Jay said.

"Good is not the word," Al said. "His name is Curtis Dubois and he is an exceptional piece of work."

Curtis Dubois was a small, nervous man of twenty-five. His face was pointed and pimply, his stringy hair a dingy brown, his eyes watery and elusive, his garments dirty and ill-fitting. He sat in the witness chair blinking as if he had just emerged from under a rock.

"Tell us your name, please," Jay began. He had interviewed the young man the night before and called him as a surprise witness this morning.

"Curtis Dubois."

"Where do you now reside?"

"In the Tarrant County Jail."

"You were arrested two weeks ago on burglary charges?"

"That's right."

"And you've served two prison terms for burglary?"

"That's right."

"Would it be fair to call you a professional burglar?"

The young man reflected. "I've held day jobs, you understand. But that'd be fair enough."

"Tell us what you were doing on the night of September 17."

"I was driving around Arlington Heights. Out Crestline Road, out that way."

"Do you live out there?"

The young man chuckled. "That's kinda rich for my blood. I was just driving around."

"In fact, weren't you looking for a house to burglarize?"

"I was thinking about it, that's a fact."

"Do you remember the weather that night?"

"It was raining."

"Good conditions for a burglary?"

"Real favorable. People stay inside and they can't hear so good."

"Did you, in the course of driving around, turn into Westover Hills?"

"Yes, sir."

"Why?"

"There's a lot to steal there, sir."

Laughter broke the courtroom tension.

"Did you know which was Billy Nash's house?"

"It was my business to know things like that."

"Did you stop to observe the Nash house?"

"I did for a fact. I cut my lights and took a good look up the driveway. I seen lights in the house and the Cadillac in the drive."

"Did you recognize the Cadillac?"

"Yes, sir, it was the red '57, with the longhorn on the hood, that Sonny Nash drives."

The courtroom exploded with excited talk. Judge Balthus beat his gavel for silence.

"You'd seen the car before?" Jay continued.

"Shoot, everybody knows that car."

"And you could see the longhorn hood ornament, despite the rain?"

"It glittered real bright 'n clear."

"What time was this?"

"About ten-thirty."

"Did you see anyone at the house?"

"No, sir, I just seen the Cadillac, thought things over, and hauled ass. Beggin' your pardon."

"Tell us how you happen to be testifying here today?"

"Yesterday, we was watching TV in the jail, and we saw the news on the trial, and I got to thinking about the Cadillac and Westover Drive and all, and figured I ought to own up to what I knew."

"Have I or anyone else offered you any special treatment, of any kind, in exchange for your testimony?"

"No, sir."

"You're here simply to tell the truth?"

The seedy little man swelled up with pride. "Mr. Taggart, I may be a burglar, but I got no use at all for a man what'd kill."

Jay stepped back. "No further questions."

Stump Wildeman was at him like a dog on a bone. "You're a professional criminal?"

"You could say that."

"A two-time loser?"

"Twenty times is more like it."

"You know that a third burglary conviction will send you to Huntsville for the rest of your life?"

"It could, that's true."

"So you heard about the Sonny Nash trial and figured you could lie your way out."

"I seen the Cadillac."

"You figured all you had to do was say, 'I saw the Cadillac,' and you'd talk your way out of life in prison, which you so richly deserve."

"Objection!" Jay said.

"No further questions," Stump Wildeman said.

Jay was lost for a moment, distracted, trying to call up a detail, one of a thousand details in the mosaic of this case. It came abruptly.

"One more question, your honor." He turned to Curtis Dubois. "When you saw the Cadillac, was it parked head-in, facing the garage?"

"No, sir. It was backed in. That's how come I could see the longhorn, because it was facing out to the street."

"That's all," Jay said, and was pleased to see Stump's puzzled expression.

After the lunch break, Jay recalled Olivia Winston.

The black woman, hurriedly summoned, took the stand a second time. Jay faced her with some papers in his hand.

"Mrs. Winston, I'm going to read to you from your grand jury testimony. Mr. Taggart: 'Was the Cadillac parked head-in?' Mrs. Winston: 'No, sir, it was backed in.' "

He lowered the grand jury transcript and looked directly at the witness. "Olivia, is that what you told the grand jury?"

"Yes, sir."

"But did I ask you on the stand this week about which way the car was parked?"

Olivia was as puzzled as everyone else. "I don't believe you did, sir."

"If I didn't, it couldn't have been on TV, could it?"

"Objection!" Stump roared. "There's a lot of ways things get on TV, as Mr. Taggart well knows, and a lot of ways information gets into the jailhouse!"

"That'll be enough," the judge declared. "Mr. Taggart?"

"Your honor, the prosecution rests," Jay said.

That afternoon, at the Naval Hospital in Bethesda, Maryland, Mickey awoke as abruptly and completely as, an eternity before, she'd collided with the tree near her house on Reno Road.

"Miss McGee!" a nurse cried. "God be praised!"

Mickey blinked uncertainly. "Where's Rafe?" she demanded.

The nurse summoned doctors, who gave her drugs and called the DEA.

When Lon Tate told her about Rafe, she asked bitterly why they hadn't let her die too.

On Monday, after Stump's futile plea for a directed verdict, he called the first defense witness, Mark Nash.

"You are the brother of the deceased William Nash and of the defendant Sonny Nash?"

Stump Wildeman had thought long and hard before leading off his case with a witness who possessed all the warmth of a frog. But Mark was the man in the middle, the brother of both men, and the jury had to be impressed that he was testifying for the defense.

"I am," Mark said gravely.

"Were you at the meeting on the night of September 15 when it was agreed to oust Sonny from Nash International?"

"I was."

"And you supported that decision?"

"Reluctantly."

Several jurors looked puzzled. They still didn't know why Sonny had been ousted, and the defense had no intention of enlightening them.

"Can you tell us how that news was conveyed to Mr. Sonny Nash?"

"The following Monday afternoon, Billy and I were in his office, discussing how to break the news, when Sonny walked in. Billy told him, right there and then."

"What were the particulars?"

"There weren't many. That he would be given an accounting and his share of the assets. That he had twenty-four hours to vacate the premises. That we wanted the parting to be as friendly and positive as possible."

"And what did Sonny say?"

"He was entirely reasonable. He joked that without him we'd be broke in a year."

"What did Billy say to that?"

"He laughed and said we probably would."

"You saw nothing to suggest that Sonny might seek revenge against either of you?"

"Absolutely not. We were both elated at how well he'd taken the news. Billy said he was going home to celebrate."

Stump Wildeman gave the jury a small, cold smile. "No further questions."

Jay approached the witness.

"Mr. Nash, this exchange you've been describing, when Billy told Sonny he'd been expelled from the conglomerate he'd built—this was some six hours before Billy was brutally beaten to death in his home, is that correct?"

"You know it is, Mr. Taggart."

"And you're telling us that you see no connection between the sudden ouster of as proud and hot-tempered a man as Sonny and . . . "

"Objection!"

"Sustained."

"I'll rephrase the question. You're saying you see no connection between Sonny's ouster and Billy's murder?"

"None has been proven to me."

"Has it occurred to you that except for Olivia Winston, your own son might have been murdered that night?"

"I don't believe it's at all clear what happened at Billy's house that night."

"You don't? Tell us how you got the news of the murders."

"The police called me."

"Called you before Sonny was taken into custody?"

"That's correct."

"And did you not say to the officer who called, words to this effect: 'Oh my God, it's Sonny, he's gone crazy, he'll come for me next!' Did you not request immediate police protection, out of fear of your brother Sonny?"

"Objection!" Stump roared.

"Overruled. The witness may answer."

Mark's face was pale and sweaty. "I couldn't have said that, because I have no reason to fear Sonny. I was in a state of shock. I must not have made myself clear."

"You made yourself extremely clear, Mr. Nash," Jay said coldly. "No further questions."

The second defense witness was Mark and Kay's son Christopher. Kay, grim in sunglasses and a tan Binatti suit, watched from the front row. Her friend Myra Fontaine was beside her. Myra hated courts, and had rarely been in one since her own hearing after she shot her father, many years before, but she came because Kay said she couldn't face this alone.

Myra had thought her heart would break when she learned of Jessica's death. She'd been spending much of her time since the murders helping Lily and Kay care for Melissa. Except for the child, she might have left Texas; she'd seen too much violence there for one lifetime.

Stump Wildeman led the boy through the events of the evening:

"Mork and Mindy," dinner, bed. As had his cousin Melissa, he told of being awakened by Olivia and taken to her room, of hearing voices and violence downstairs, of someone forcing Olivia's door open.

"You saw this man?" Stump asked the boy.

"Yes," Chris said grimly.

"Was it anyone you knew?"

"No."

"You're positive it wasn't your uncle Sonny?"

"Yes." The boy's voice was both frightened and defiant.

"Can you describe the man?"

"I couldn't see him very well. He was white. He had long hair, kind of light brown. He saw Olivia's gun and jumped back, just before she shot. We heard him yelling and somebody downstairs yelling back."

"You heard two voices?"

"Yes."

Stump Wildeman gave the jury a knowing glance. "Chris, the night it happened, you told the police you'd seen your uncle Sonny in the doorway, didn't you?"

"Yes."

"Why did you tell the police that?"

"Olivia said she'd seen him. She said I had to say it was Sonny, because he'd gone crazy and killed Jessica and Billy. I was afraid, so I did what she said."

"Why did you decide to tell the truth?"

"I felt bad. I talked to my father, and he told me to tell the truth."

"And that's what you've done here today?"

"Yes, sir."

"Thank you, son," Stump said.

"Mr. Taggart?"

Jay approached the boy with profound despair. It was not just that the boy was lying. It was his sense that corruption filled the courtroom, tainting them all. Sonny had corrupted Mark, Mark had corrupted his son, and where would it end? Could one man with enough money corrupt the entire system?

"Chris, you told the police and the grand jury that you saw Sonny, is that correct?"

"Yes. But . . ."

"Wait. When you talked to the judge, did you tell him that Olivia had told you to lie?"

"I was afraid."

"It was not until later, after you talked to your father, that you changed your story, is that correct?"

"He told me to tell the truth."

"And now you and your father are both telling the truth for the defense," Jay said bitterly.

"Objection!" Stump cried. "He's bullying the boy."

"I'm not bullying him," Jay said. "I feel profoundly sorry for him."

"That's enough!" Judge Balthus roared. "The jury will disregard Mr. Taggart's remarks."

"No more questions," Jay said, and sat down.

Omega Winston, a sullen, wary man of thirty, lowered himself reluctantly into the witness chair. He hated being here, but he was intimidated by the court, the subpoena, the power that white men had to put black men in jail for breaking their rules.

Under Stump's questioning, he told the jury he was Olivia's son, that he worked as a janitor, that he'd twice been arrested on marijuana charges, and that Billy Nash had once hired him as a driver for Nash International.

"And how long did you keep that job?"

"About two months."

"Why did you leave it?"

"I got tired of it."

"But you continued to be friendly with Billy Nash?"

"You could call it that."

"You visited his home occasionally?"

"I'd go see my mother and maybe I'd see him."

"Did you ever give drugs to Billy Nash?"

Jay howled his objections, and once again the lawyers huddled with the judge. "This is a murder trial," Jay protested. "This entire line of questioning is a red herring for Mr. Wildeman."

"Your honor, we intend to show that Mr. Nash's death resulted from his illegal, drug-oriented lifestyle, and this witness is essential to our case."

It was, Jay thought, a turning point. Who was running this trial, the judge or Stump Wildeman? Lawyers liked to pretend that the law was majestic, immutable, but in truth it gave wide latitude to trial judges, who were variously liberal and conservative, brave and craven, foolish and wise. It was a crap shoot, and here he faced a newly appointed black judge whom he believed to be intimidated by Stump Wildeman, fearful of being overturned on appeal, and unwilling in any way to seem permissive toward drugs.

The judge ruled for the defense.

"I gave him some marijuana," Omega admitted.

"How much?"

"An ounce."

"How many times?"

"Two or three."

"How did this come about?"

"He said he liked to smoke and I said I had some good weed."

"Did the two of you ever smoke together?"

"Once or twice."

"Did any of your friends ever accompany you to the Nash home, and do drugs with you and Billy?"

"The man wasn't running a social club."

"That remains to be seen," Stump shot back. "No further questions."

"Mr. Taggart?"

Jay thought the judge was wrong, that the defense's whole "reefer madness" premise was wrong; he thought that juries had more sense than that. He didn't want to practice law the rest of his life if they didn't.

"Mr. Winston," Jay began, "did Billy Nash pay you for the marijuana you gave him?"

"No, sir."

"Why not? He had plenty of money."

"It was a gift."

"He'd been a friend to your mother, he'd given you a job, and it was a favor you did for him, is that right?"

"That's right."

"What kind of man was Billy Nash?"

Omega hesitated. He had never been called upon to evaluate a white man's character. "He was a good man," he said. "He treated people with respect."

Stump was on his feet. "Your honor, I object to this love-in."

The judge smiled. "He's your witness, Mr. Wildeman. This is cross-examination."

"Did you know Mrs. Nash too?"

"A little. She was a nice, polite, gentle lady."

"Omega," Jay said, "can you imagine what kind of person would kill Jessica and Billy Nash?"

"Anybody'd hurt them is the worst kind of trash in the world."

Omega glared at Sonny Nash as he spoke, his voice filled with scorn, and hoped the jury understood.

News reports of Mark and Chris's support of Sonny, and the defense revelations of Billy's consorting with a drug dealer—his "secret life," Stump called it—inspired ever-widening sympathy for the accused billionaire. When he arrived at the courthouse the next morning, a growing army of Sonny's Honeys pushed and shoved for a glimpse of their hero. One lovesick matron broke through the police lines to plant a sloppy kiss on Sonny's cheek; another handed him a rose.

Moments later, the frenzied Honeys were struck dumb by the spectacle of the next defense witness lumbering into view.

Brother Amos Moon was a large, florid man in his forties whose flowing white robe did not conceal his ample girth. His reddish hair was thinning, his thick red beard was turning gray, and his bright green eyes sparkled like a pickpocket's at a hanging. He wore sandals, and a wreath of wildflowers around his neck, and he clutched a Bible in the vicinity of his heart.

Brother Moon's arrival excited the media, but it amused neither the judge nor the prosecutor. The judge heard Brother Moon's testimony with the jury out, then the prosecutor and the defense clashed once again on whether a witness's lurid tales were relevant. Stump Wildeman, red-faced, jabbing with his nub, won the argument: the jury was recalled.

"You are Brother Amos Moon?" Stump began.

"I am."

"Where do you live, sir?"

"At Tranquility Ranch, outside Taos, New Mexico."

"And what do you do there?"

"I am the director of WISH."

"WISH?"

"The World Institute for Spiritual Healing."

"Just what does your institute do?"

"We open our arms to the weary and afflicted."

"Has the Nash Foundation supported your efforts?"

"Generously."

"So you knew Billy Nash as a benefactor?"

"And loved him like a brother."

"Is it true that several people were arrested at your ranch a few years ago for using mescaline?"

"Unfortunately, yes."

"How did this come about?"

"It is our belief that mescaline and certain other substances, while not ends in themselves, are guides on the path to enlightenment."

"Did you and Billy ever use mescaline together?"

Jay was on his feet. "I renew my objection, your honor. The dead man is not on trial for drug use in New Mexico."

"The witness may answer."

"We did, on several occasions, when he was visiting the ranch."

"And what happened?"

362

The guru bobbed his bushy eyebrows. "Enlightenment and peace."

A few snickers greeted the pronouncement. Stump was walking a fine line. He wanted Brother Amos to be seen as a freak, but a freak who was telling the truth.

"Did you ever use drugs with Mr. Nash in Fort Worth?"

"When visiting here, I would sometimes bring him gifts of mescaline and ganga."

"That's marijuana?"

"Yes."

"Sir," Stump said—he could not yet bring himself to address his witness either as Brother Amos or Mr. Moon, which seemed the only alternatives—"were you in Fort Worth on the night Billy Nash was murdered?"

"I was."

"Did you talk to him that day?"

"Yes, I called his office."

"Did he mention drugs?"

"He asked if I'd brought him a gift."

"Had you?"

"In point of fact, no, I had not. The harvest was not yet in."

"What did you do later that night?"

"I met friends for dinner at the Sidewinder Restaurant on Camp Bowie Boulevard."

"And what happened?"

"Many people came and went. We had fifteen or more around our table."

"You didn't know them all?"

"I knew very few of them. But I open my heart to strangers."

"Did the subject of drugs come up?"

"It did. Two men joined us and hinted that they had drugs to sell."

"What happened?"

"The conversation went back and forth. I commented—and I shall regret this through all eternity—that if anyone had any drugs

363

I had a rich friend who would be glad to take them off their hands."

"Did you identify who you meant?"

"One of the men pressed me. Finally I said I meant Billy Nash, who lived not far away."

The courtroom buzzed with excitement, until the judge demanded silence.

"What happened to these men?"

"They left the restaurant around ten o'clock."

"Can you tell us how far it is from the Sidewinder Restaurant to Westover Hills?"

"Less than a mile."

"You never knew their names?"

"No."

"Can you describe them?"

"They were white men, rather seedy-looking, in jeans and boots and plaid shirts, with dark, longish hair."

"Did you tell them Billy's address?"

Brother Amos lowered his head into his hands. "I believe I did," he sobbed.

Water was brought to the bereaved witness. Jay thought he might throw up.

"Why didn't you tell the police about this incident?" Stump asked gently.

"Billy's death left me in a state of profound negativity. I was slow to do my duty."

"No further questions," Stump Wildeman said.

Jay Taggart stalked the burly, berobed witness.

"What is your name?" he began.

"Brother Amos Moon."

"The name you were born with."

"That was many years ago."

"Do you know your name or not?"

"Ira Schwartz."

"Born where?"

"Jersey City."

"And you are a professional guru?"

"Through God's grace, a healer."

"Have you ever been in prison?"

"Once, many years ago, a misunderstanding . . . "

"Two years for mail fraud, California, 1969, right?"

"Those are facts but not the truth."

"Just for the record, it's the Sidewinder Saloon, not the Sidewinder Restaurant, is it not?"

"Perhaps."

"You said this ranch of yours was raided for drugs. Wasn't there a little matter, just last year, of statutory rape? You and a girl of fourteen?"

"I was deceived and betrayed," Brother Amos said.

"Isn't it a fact that you were taking Billy Nash for a ride, as you have scores of people for twenty years?"

"He admired my work."

Jay sighed. "Yes, I suppose he did. For your kind, there's a sucker born every minute, isn't there?"

"I advocate freedom, Mr. Taggart, not imprisonment. I teach love, not hate."

"How much money has the Nash Foundation given you?"

"The foundation's annual donation has increased from seventy-five to a hundred and fifty thousand over the past four years."

"With Billy dead, who decides if that funding will continue?"

"Whoever takes over the management of the foundation."

"And you don't know who that is? You haven't been in touch with them about your status?"

"Mr. Mark Nash is the interim director."

"So it's up to Mark Nash—perhaps to Sonny, if they stay in business together—to decide if your money continues?"

"Apparently so."

"But a spiritual healer like you wouldn't tell a few lies for a hundred and fifty thousand dollars, would you?"

Stump Wildeman leaped to his feet, but Jay had nothing more to say to Brother Amos.

. . .

There were many in Fort Worth who thought that Puss's testimony was her finest hour. Not that they believed a word she said, but almost everyone agreed it was a brilliant performance.

To the surprise of some, Puss did not arrive in court wearing one of the plunging necklines for which she was famous, nor did she trail an ermine wrap behind her to the witness stand. She did not precisely arrive carrying a prayer book, but Puss had done what she could to clean up her act. She wore a prim, high-necked blouse, and a loose-fitting gray jacket above a long, full tweed skirt that permitted nothing more enticing than a glimpse of her trim ankles. Her hair was several shades darker than usual, drawn back in a most un-Pusslike bun; she wore glasses and no jewelry except her wedding ring.

"You are Mrs. Emily Nash, wife of Sonny?" Stump began.

"Yes, sir," Puss purred.

"Might I ask, Mrs. Nash, is he a difficult man?"

Puss smiled brightly. "Sonny's bark is worse than his bite. He's a sweetheart, if you want the truth."

"Do you have children?"

"No, sir, Sonny and I don't, but we see a lot of his little boy from his first marriage, and Sonny's got the Little League team he sponsors."

"And how do you occupy yourself, Mrs. Nash?"

Jay Taggart recalled a novel in which a famous writer's wife, asked if she inspired her husband's great works, replied, "Lady, I just fuck."

"Well, I have my charities, hospitals and the Girl Scouts, things like that. But I guess you'd say I'm just a housewife."

Various people in the courtroom rolled their eyes at that howler—Puss, just a housewife?—but Jay had to grudgingly admit she was good, feminine and appealing, sucking the jury in, or at least the men.

"Mrs. Nash, I have to ask you about the tragic events of last September."

"Yes, sir, I know you do."

"What did you do that evening?"

"I was home all afternoon, fixed dinner, and then watched TV, until Sonny came home."

"And what time was that?"

"About eight-thirty."

"What happened then?"

"We ate dinner and he told me about his brothers voting him out of the company."

"Was he upset?"

Puss grinned merrily. "He was *happy*. His brothers needed him; he sure didn't need *them*."

"What happened next?"

"Well, about ten I went up to bed, and he stayed downstairs and watched the news. About eleven he came up to bed."

"You were at your home on Eagle Mountain Lake?"

"Yes, sir."

"All right, Sonny came up about eleven. What happened then?"

Puss lowered her eyes. "This is kind of personal."

"That's all right, just tell us the truth."

"Well, Sonny and I, we started playing around."

"Sexually, you mean?"

"Yes, sir. Sexually. And one thing led to another and I had to go to the bathroom for a minute."

"Yes?"

It had to be said that Puss had captured the courtroom's attention, her and Sonny's sex life having been a subject of unbridled speculation for years.

"And we have this telephone in the bathroom?"

"Yes?"

"And the darn thing rang!"

Stump nodded sagely. "The phone rang, while you were in the bathroom, preparing to make love."

"That's right. It's a private line, but it rings all the time, day and night. And I was just so frustrated. I answered it and somebody asked for Sonny and I said he wasn't there and hung up."

"Wasn't it the police calling, Mrs. Nash?"

367

"I realized that later. At the time, I just wanted to get rid of whoever it was."

"But before you hung up, did you tell the caller that your husband wasn't home and maybe they should try his apartment at the Nash Tower, downtown?"

"I guess I did. I mean, they didn't say there'd been a murder or anything."

"To recapitulate, your husband arrived home at eight-thirty, you had dinner and talked, you went up at ten, he watched the news and came up at eleven, and you were together until the police arrived sometime after midnight. Is that correct?"

"Yes, sir."

"And if you've given other accounts, it was because of confusion or modesty on your part?"

"Yes, sir, that's precisely correct."

Stump Wildeman made a courtly little bow and surrendered the witness.

Jay Taggart had known Puss casually over the years and rather liked her, or at least been amused by her. But he was not amused now.

"Mrs. Nash, this story you're telling us now, is this not the second story you've told?"

Puss looked sheepish. "I guess it might be, Mr. Taggart."

"And is this the final version, or will there be another next week?"

"This is the truth."

"Let's take them one at a time. The police called about eleven and asked for your husband?"

"Yes, sir."

"And you told them he wasn't there and they should try his apartment downtown, correct?"

"I guess I did."

"And now you're telling us that the reason you said that was that you were about to make love and you didn't want to be bothered."

"Yes, sir."

"Isn't it a fact that you told the police the truth the first time?"

"No!"

"That you were at home alone, you had no idea where your husband was, and maybe they should try downtown—that was the truth, but it turned out to be inconvenient. Then he came home and the two of you had to cook up a new story?"

"No! I just wanted privacy." Puss composed herself. "I guess you could say I was aroused, Mr. Taggart. Most people would understand."

"So you're telling us that you made love, and it was nearly an hour later that you mentioned the call to your husband and he called the police?"

"That's right."

"You made love for an hour, Mrs. Nash?"

Puss cocked an eyebrow. "Haste makes waste, Mr. Taggart."

The courtroom exploded in laughter; Puss's words were soon immortalized on a T-shirt that was hawked outside the courthouse.

"All right, Mrs. Nash, those are versions one and two. That you didn't know where he was and that he was right there in your bed."

"It's the truth," Puss said stubbornly.

"It doesn't make sense," Jay shot back.

Puss smiled serenely. "Mr. Taggart, in my experience, the truth is often extremely confusing."

Jay's temper flashed. "It's not confusing. He was out disposing of Jessica Nash's body and you're lying for him!"

"You're the liar, you bastard!" cried the unvarnished Puss of old, as Stump Wildeman shouted his objections and the judge angrily banged his gavel. When the hubbub settled down, they adjourned until after lunch, when Sonny Nash would tell his story.

A small but determined Foreign Legion of the media had encamped in Fort Worth, and by and large its grizzled mercenaries approved both the trial and its locale. Fort Worth, with its agreeable mix of loud bars and tacky blondes, of cheap marijuana and bizarre millionaires, was never boring, and the trial had hinted at enough upper-crust scandal to justify their expense accounts.

One particularly odious London tabloid had dubbed this "The

Case of the Billionaire Basher"; other, more sedate journals were calling it "The Trial of the Century," confident that their readers had forgotten Leopold and Loeb, Scopes, the Lindbergh kidnapping, the Boston Strangler, Jack Ruby, and other Trials of the Century of yesteryear.

Most reporters were hoping for an acquittal, on the theory that Sonny would toss a memorable victory party, at which they could eat and drink to glorious excess, explore the inside of his fabled lakeside castle, and (this fantasy clouded many men's minds) come to know Puss more intimately. About the only reporters hoping to see Sonny convicted were those with book contracts, for whom an acquittal would present legal problems if they portrayed him as the colorful but cold-blooded psychopath he was widely believed to be.

Given the bizarre, conflicting, sometimes sensational testimony that preceded it, Sonny Nash's long-awaited day on the witness stand struck reporters, and everyone else, as anticlimactic.

That was Stump Wildeman's strategy. The freaks, druggies, felons, and perjurers had all had their say; now it was time for his very rich and respectable client to clear the air.

Stump had given Sonny Nash the same advice he gave all new clients—"Let me do the talking"—and Sonny had reluctantly complied.

Sonny's silence only inspired endless speculation and gossip. Bets were made on whether he would testify in his own behalf, with one camp saying he would make a brilliant witness, since he was a natural-born liar, while others predicted he would come unhinged under cross-examination and explode with a violence that would seal his fate.

There were stories that he was using powerful drugs, to keep calm during the trial, and that he was being coached on how to appear modest, kind, truthful, and otherwise unlike himself. There were reports that he had paid Mark and Puss many millions of dollars for their testimony. Tales were told at the Sidewinder, the Hop, the Rhinestone Cowboy, and the White Elephant of Sonny's escape plan, which involved gunmen, a waiting jet, and a banana-republic fortress where Texas justice could never penetrate.

Local bookies were giving 6 to 5 for acquittal, and there were those who would further wager, if given decent odds, that if acquitted Sonny would be murdered within a year. One popular version of this scenario was that Lily Nash had put out a million-dollar contract on him, an assertion that did nothing to lessen the lady's popularity. And while Sonny still drove himself to the trial in his red '57 Cadillac convertible, it was rumored that he now wore a bulletproof vest, and it was a fact that two well-armed men followed in a black Oldsmobile and were never far from his side.

Everyone agreed that Sonny had comported himself admirably during the trial, dressing well, staying alert, smiling at friendly witnesses, establishing eye contact with jurors, and showing no sign of anger, impatience, or arrogance. To those of the jury who had known little of him until this trial, he might appear the most sedate and respectable of citizens.

The jury had surely noticed that, during breaks in the trial, Sonny conferred not only with his lawyers but with earnest young aides from Nash International who came bearing memos and reports for him to act upon; he was a dynamic executive even when on trial for his life. And the more alert jurors would have noticed some of the city's leading businessmen stopping by to shake Sonny's hand and offer words of encouragement. These businessmen had to consider that, if Sonny went to prison, the great concentration of capital that he had brought to their city might fly to God-only-knows where, and many jobs, loans, and executive salaries would vanish with it. Some of the jurors might even have wondered if their well-being, or that of their family and friends, might suffer if Nash International collapsed.

As the trial progressed, Sonny's smooth exterior was a source of endless frustration to Jay Taggart. The rules of evidence, he thought, were cruelly stacked against the prosecution. Almost everything important and relevant about a person on trial, from ill repute to actual crimes, was barred from admission. With the jury kept in the dark about key facts, the prosecutor had to count on its sophistication, its ability to make leaps, to take one hint, one fact, one outburst, and from that to imagine the other, unseen truths.

But most juries lacked that boldness, and it was their caution, their refusal to trust their own common sense, that let killers walk the streets.

Or so it seemed to the prosecutor.

"You were born right here in Fort Worth, weren't you, Mr. Nash?"

Stump Wildeman, aided by the lenient judge, led his client on a leisurely tour of his life: local boy, Arlington Heights High graduate, successful businessman, family man, Little League patron, civic leader, philanthropist. Sonny was composed and self-confident; his manner was less that of a man on trial for his life than that of a corporate statesman granting an interview to *Fortune* or *The Wall Street Journal*.

His story, as to the charges against him, was simple; its essentials had already been suggested by other witnesses. He had not been at all unhappy to end his partnership with his brothers. He had worked in his office, sorting out his papers, until nearly eight on the night of the murders. Then he had driven home in a rainstorm, eaten dinner with his wife, watched the news until eleven, and gone up to bed. He and his wife had besported themselves until well past midnight, when she mentioned an earlier call from the police. He had immediately called to see what was the matter, only to learn that his brother and sister-in-law had been killed and that the police wanted to talk to him.

"Did you kill your brother and his wife, Mr. Nash?"

"No, sir, I did not. I loved them both."

"Do you have any idea who did kill them?"

Sonny shook his head sadly. "No, sir, I don't."

"Your witness, Mr. Taggart."

Jay had been awaiting this moment, imagining it, preparing for it, for months, and yet he stepped forward with a terrible dread. He had his motive, his eyewitnesses, but he faced a witness as unyielding as the Rock of Gibraltar. He hammered at Sonny with angry "Isn't-it-true?" and "How-do-you-explain?" questions, but

Sonny remained unshakable. He had been at home all evening. He loved his brother and could not imagine who had killed him.

"How do you explain Olivia Winston's sworn testimony that she saw you in her doorway?"

"Maybe she made a mistake," Sonny said calmly. "Or maybe she's got a grudge against me."

"What about little Melissa, do you think she has a grudge against you?"

"Maybe Olivia put it in her head—that's what Christopher said."

When Sonny brushed aside the contradictions in Puss's story, saying she'd been "overcome by modesty," he had some jurors laughing along with him.

The cross-examination lasted two hours, and when it ended, it was the prosecutor who was angry and shaken.

After court adjourned, Sonny Nash shook hands with his lawyer and stepped out onto the courthouse steps, where a sea of adoring Texas womanhood cheered him.

As the courtroom battle progressed, another war was being fought in the city's meaner streets and less fashionable bars. Both sides had men out searching tirelessly for witnesses to bolster their cases. Curtis Dubois, the burglar who claimed to have seen Sonny's car at Billy's house, had been the first of these, and both the prosecution and defense hoped for more, preferably of higher repute than Dubois.

The prosecution had three urgent goals: to find witnesses who had seen Sonny abroad on the night of the murders; to find Jessica Nash's body; and to find the murder weapon, believed to be a jack handle. The DA's men strongly assumed that both Jessica's remains and the jack handle now rested somewhere on the bottom of Eagle Mountain Lake. They had dragged the lake and followed up many tips that led them to shallow graves throughout the county, but with no success. They had searched all Sonny's cars, too, without finding blood, hair, a missing jack, or a murder weapon.

The prosecutors estimated that Sonny had almost two hours,

373

between the time he left the murder scene and his arrest, to cover his tracks. The police had been slow to pursue Sonny, until a SWAT team was assembled, because of fears that he was primed for a shootout. Confused by Puss's report that he was not at home, they'd taken close to an hour to reach the Nash Tower, gain entry, and inch their way to his penthouse, which proved to be empty as a tomb. They were still regrouping when Sonny called to ask what the trouble was. The foul-up, the prosecutors believed, had given him time to dispose of Jessica's body, then return home and concoct his alibi with Puss. That was what they believed, but they needed proof, and time was running out.

Sonny was to have been the last witness, but then the surprises began.

The prosecution's first surprise was a nervous young man named Wendell Gaines, a senior at Paschal High, who swore that on the night of the murders he and his girlfriend had been out in his father's boat and had seen Sonny's cabin cruiser, the *Royal Flush*.

"How far were you from Mr. Nash's boat?" Jay asked.

"I passed about thirty feet from it," the boy said. "It like to scared me to death."

"Were his lights on?"

"No, sir."

"How could you be sure, in the dark, that it was his boat?"

"Well, from my lights. And it was clearing—the moon was out. I've seen that boat a hundred times."

"His boat was not moving?"

"No, sir."

"Did you think he might be in trouble? That you should offer help?"

"I figured Mr. Nash didn't want to be bothered and I'd better get out of there."

"And what time was this?"

"Eleven-thirty. I know, because my girlfriend was due home at midnight."

"Why didn't you report this earlier?"

The boy grimaced in discomfort. "I didn't want to get involved. Mr. Nash is a pretty important man."

"Yes, I know," Jay said. "No further questions."

Stump Wildeman glared at the young man.

"Son, how much had you had to drink that night?"

"A couple of beers."

"You'd had a couple of beers and your girlfriend was late getting home and you saw a boat in the dark and knew it was Sonny Nash's, right?"

"There was some light."

"Do you know what kind of boat Mr. Nash owns?"

"A forty-foot Sun Runner."

"And do you know how many others like it there are on that lake?"

"No, sir."

"Suppose I told you there were at least six others, would you doubt that?"

"I don't guess I would."

"That's all," Stump said scornfully.

The next morning the press gallery perked up as the prosecution put a second surprise witness on the stand, a dark, slender, graceful woman who looked as if she did not belong on the same planet with this increasingly bitter, dirty trial.

"State your name, please," Jay began.

"Felice Mendelson."

"You were previously married to the defendant, Sonny Nash?" Jay asked.

"Yes."

Felice did not look at Sonny; her luminous eyes were fixed on the prosecutor. She was simply dressed and wore no makeup and no jewelry except a wedding band. Reporters rolled their eyes: who but Sonny could progress from this serene beauty to the glorious excesses of Puss?

"How long were you married to him?"

"Five years."

"During that period, did he ever strike you or . . . ?"

"Objection," Stump roared.

"Approach the bench." The two lawyers looked ready for fisticuffs. Everyone's nerves were on edge now, after weeks of bitter combat.

"This is an outrage," Stump protested. "He can't bring the man's ex-wife in to say he's a wife-beater."

"Your honor, they opened the door for this. They had his present wife say he was a 'sweetheart.' They had his brother say he was a perfect gentleman. This man is on trial for two violent murders and this woman is uniquely qualified to testify to his violent nature."

"I'll permit the testimony," Judge Balthus said.

"Note our exception," Stump said angrily, warning that this might be grounds for appeal. Jay hated that almost as much as the judge did. But he thought he needed Felice's testimony. She had told him, months before, that she would not testify, but that very morning Kay Nash had called and said that she had persuaded Felice that she must speak out, lest Sonny go free.

"Mrs. Mendelson, did the defendant ever strike you during your marriage?"

"Yes."

"How often?"

"On five or six occasions."

"With his open hand or with his fists?"

"Both."

"For what reasons?"

The witness lowered her eyes, then raised them again, meeting his gaze. "When I challenged his authority. When I protested his mistreatment of his son. When he didn't like something I cooked. Once . . . for sexual reasons."

Tears glistened in her eyes. "No further questions," Jay said.

Stump shot forward. "Did you complain to the police about these alleged attacks?"

"No."

"You stayed married to the man for five years?"

"Yes."

"Is your father, Walter Lamont, not engaged in a protracted and bitter legal battle with Mr. Nash?"

"He is, yes."

"Did you ever tell Mr. Nash that you'd have your revenge if it took the rest of your life?"

Felice Mendelson looked genuinely shocked. "I certainly did not. He's the one who deals in revenge."

"No further questions," Stump growled.

At that, finally, both sides rested.

Jay Taggart, giddy with exhaustion and dread, escorted Felice past shouting reporters to his office, where Kay Nash embraced her.

"Thanks for gracing our little cesspool," he said, by way of parting.

Outside, on the courthouse steps, Sonny Nash was again hailed like a conquering hero.

Jay Taggart faced the twelve unsmiling strangers who soon would settle the matter of *Texas* vs. *Nash*.

"The state's case starts with a motive," he began. "A rich, proud, powerful man is suddenly expelled from the company he built and considers his own, thrown out by his two younger brothers. He curbs his temper in public, but that night, in a rage, he goes to his brother's home. He gains admission. He attacks his brother, beats him to death, kills him as surely as Cain killed Abel. You've seen the pictures: Billy Nash dies trying to defend himself and his family. His wife Jessica hears the struggle, and rushes to help her husband, only to be herself knocked unconscious and carried away.

"How do we know? Because there were two eyewitnesses, two people who knew Sonny Nash well. One is a woman who had worked for his family for fifteen years—Olivia Winston, whom the defendant's own mother calls 'One of the finest women I've ever known.' The other witness was the dead couple's child, the defendant's niece, who told us without doubt or hesitation that she saw her uncle in that doorway. Nor is there any doubt that, had Olivia not produced a gun, she and Melissa would have met the

377

same bloody fate. Sonny might have committed the perfect crime—but he was driven away.

"A third eyewitness, Curtis Dubois, saw Sonny's red Cadillac in the driveway. Yes, Dubois is a burglar. But the fact remains that he knew something—that the car was backed in—that he could not have known unless he had been there. Because that fact had not appeared in the media.

"Olivia saw Jessica being carried unconscious to Sonny's car. Wendell Gaines saw Sonny's boat out on Eagle Mountain Lake an hour later, with no lights on. The terrible implication is that Jessica's body now rests at the bottom of the lake, that vibrant young mother who had committed no sin except to try to defend her family from the wrath of her brother-in-law.

"Mr. Wildeman is going to talk to you a lot about 'reasonable doubt.' What doubt is there here? A boy who told the police, the grand jury, and the judge that he saw Sonny Nash, then changed his story at the prompting of his father, who also testified for the defense?

"What did Sonny's wife say, when the police called her, a half hour after the murders? She told the truth: 'My husband is not here.' Oh, she changed her story later, but she was right the first time: a half hour after the murders he was out disposing of Jessica Nash's body.

"Ladies and gentlemen, murderers do not often confess and ask to be punished. They lie, and they find others to lie for them. I submit to you that Sonny Nash is lying, his wife is lying, and even his nephew has been persuaded to change his story and lie as well.

"The defense, on the basis of the butt of one marijuana cigarette, has conjured up the fantasy of a drug deal murder. Brother Amos Moon has conjured up two phantom killers. But are you going to believe this Amos Moon, as dedicated a con man and liar as you are ever likely to encounter?

"Do not be deceived by lies and fantasies. We have a young father beaten to death. We have a young mother abducted and killed. We have a child orphaned—but surviving to bear witness. These are crimes that cry out for justice. This defendant may look respectable here in court. But we have the testimony of his first wife as to his capacity for violence. And we have overwhelming evidence that on this one crucial night in his life, he was a killer.

"Forget the wealth of the Nash family. This is a simple case of murder. On the one hand we have a motive and eyewitnesses. On the other hand we have lies and fantasies. On behalf of the state of Texas, on behalf of law and decency and reason, on behalf of Jessica and Billy Nash, I ask you to do your duty and make this defendant pay for his crimes, even as you or I would."

Jay sat down and clasped his trembling hands together. Within seconds, Stump Wildeman was pacing before the jury box, gathering steam, trying with all his energy and passion to erase every word the prosecutor had spoken.

The older jurors recognized the hellfire-and-damnation fire in Stump's eyes, for he was heir to the tent preachers who had pounded pulpits and brought young sinners to Christ in decades past.

Stump's sermon began with a hymn of praise for the Golden Rule of reasonable doubt. That point made, he began to pick at the state's case, scornfully, expertly, finding it as riddled with doubt as Satan's heart is rotted with sin.

Who are the state's witnesses, he demanded. A convicted murderess who calls the defendant a devil. An impressionable child. A burglar. A teenager out for a joyride with a six-pack and his girlfriend. The accused man's ex-wife. Gossip, speculation, hearsay, and out-and-out revenge.

"What really happened here? Billy Nash posed as a model citizen, but he was secretly a drug user, leading a dangerous double life. Getting high with the likes of Omega Winston and Amos Moon. Endangering himself and his family by his disregard of society's rules.

"Is Amos Moon a freak, a crazy, a drug user? Perhaps he is. But he was Billy Nash's friend. Billy gave him hundreds of thousands of dollars. And what did he ask in return for all that money? Only 'gifts' of drugs.

"Amos Moon called Billy on the seventeenth. Billy asked if he'd brought him a 'gift.' Moon had not, but that night he met two men who were selling drugs. He told them he had a rich friend who was looking for drugs. He even gave them his address. And the men left.

"It wasn't far from the world of drifters and drug dealers to the billionaire's world in Westover Hills. Just a mile. Just a few whispered words. Just a lust for drugs—that was enough to pass from a world of dreams to a world of danger."

Stump had hit his stride. His eyes gleamed, sweat glistened on his brow. Every soul in the courtroom was caught up in the tale he told, even those who believed it the most loathsome of lies. For the moment, his passionately imagined reality gripped them all.

"Perhaps we'll never know who those two men were. Perhaps they've vanished back into the world of darkness from whence they came. But we know that some cruel fate led them to Billy's mansion. They told him they were Amos Moon's friends and he let them in. He had already said he wanted to 'celebrate' the expulsion of Sonny from their company.

"But the strangers weren't there with a 'gift' of drugs, they were there for robbery, and robbery became the terrible gift of death. Christopher Nash testified to seeing one of the men and hearing the voice of the other.

"The prosecutor talks about fantasies. Where is *his* evidence? Where is the murder weapon? Where is evidence tying this defendant to the scene? His blood? His hair? Where were the bruises on this man who supposedly had just fought a battle to the death? The police examined Mr. Nash's car—where was any sign of a body in it? The state doesn't give you physical evidence. It gives you so-called eyewitnesses whose testimony is riddled with uncertainty and doubt.

"The prosecutor says justice is threatened by Mr. Nash's wealth. I say that, except for his wealth, he would never have been brought to trial. With all the publicity, with all the pressures and the politics, the District Attorney's Office decided they had to put Sonny Nash on trial. And they've done their best. But their best is a case based upon an old woman, a child, and a burglar, a case as filled with holes as a pound of Swiss cheese. The state should be ashamed to have wasted its time and our money on this big nothing of a case."

He returned to "reasonable doubt," pounding his fist, shouting, flailing his arms. Jay Taggart, watching, was captivated by Stump's passion. He feared in his heart that Stump Wildeman, who almost surely believed that his client was guilty, had summoned more passion for his lies than he, the prosecutor, had invoked for the cause of truth.

Was that inevitable? Were lies, by their nature, bejeweled and painted strumpets, while the truth was like a plain girl, virtuous but dull?

Stump ended his sermon, leaving himself and everyone else exhausted. Local lawyers who had packed the courtroom agreed that Sonny had gotten his million dollars' worth.

The next morning, the state had the final word: Jay's brief lecture on facts versus fantasies, his final plea for common sense. The judge delivered his charge, and then, at last, the fate of Sonny Nash passed into the hands of twelve people he could have bought and sold.

"I've always believed in the law," Jay told Philip Kingslea. He had known Philip a long time and did not try to hide his despair. "I've believed that the law is essentially logical and fair, and that nine times out of ten it produces the right result."

"This could be the one out of ten," Philip warned.

They were alone in Jay's office with a bottle of Wild Turkey between them. The jury had completed its second day of deliberations without a verdict. The possibility of a hung jury grew ever more real.

"No, it can't be," Jay protested. "Sonny is too blatantly guilty. If he walks, the system is a farce and I want out of it."

"Sonny is lucky," Philip said. "I don't figure he planned it. Probably he was drunk. He's driving around. He stops there, spur of the moment. With any luck, Billy won't let him in. Or Olivia shoots him. Or a neighbor sees him. Or he gets scratched and leaves some blood behind. A hundred things could have cooked him. But, as it is, you don't have physical evidence and your eyewitnesses are shaky. Maybe you'll get lucky with the jury. But if Sonny walks, it's not that the system is fucked, it's just that one rotten son of a bitch had a lucky night. And the best defense lawyer in Texas."

"That bastard," Jay muttered.

"No use blaming Stump," Philip said. "Oh, sure, he'd gladly defend Hitler. But if it wasn't Stump, there'd be a hundred other lawyers lined up to take Sonny's money."

"We deserve justice," Jay said. "The city needs it. Decency demands it."

"I'm not so sure the city wants Sonny in prison," Philip said. "He wouldn't be any fun there. I think most people want him right here, making money, making jobs, driving his red Cadillac, putting Puss on display, doling out his bread and circuses."

"It's sick," Jay protested.

"What do you expect? The state is going broke, and here's this charming rogue who reminds everybody of the glory days. Sonny is to his era what Hunt and Murchison were to theirs—every raggedy-ass son of a bitch in Texas thinks that with a break or two he could have been just as rich."

"But he killed those people," Jay said dully.

"That's the trouble," Philip said. "Nobody cares about the dead. Oh, you do, and their family and a few friends. But to the world at large, dead people are depressing. Live people you can get drunk with and get mad at and even forgive, but the dead only remind us of our own mortality."

Jay was not listening. "What are we gonna do if the bastard walks?" he demanded. "I don't want to live in the same city as Sonny Nash. He's an affront to everything decent in the world."

Philip laughed darkly. "Cheer up," he said. "Maybe somebody will kill him."

A few blocks away, in his office overlooking Sundance Square, Stump Wildeman was having a drink with a gambler named Leland Webb. Leland Webb was an elegant man, gray at the temples and exquisitely groomed, who many people might have thought looked more like a lawyer than Stump. In fact, Leland's father was the senior partner of a celebrated Houston law firm, and his uncles, brothers, and male cousins were all prominent members of the Texas Bar. But somewhere along the line Leland had "gone wrong," although as he saw it he had gone right. He thought gambling was a lot like practicing law, except that the hours were more erratic and you paid no taxes.

"What are my odds on a hung jury, Mr. Gambler?" Stump demanded.

"I never bet on human beings," Leland said. "They're unpredictable at best and dishonest at worst. Dice, cards, wheels, sometimes horses, but never people."

"Then I'm the gambler," Stump boasted, "because I bet on people all the time. I bet that I can sell 'em my story better than some prosecutor can sell 'em his. The difference is, he has to convince twelve people, but I only have to convince one. That's why defense lawyers can afford yachts and ex-wives."

"And you think you have your one?"

"Maybe two or three," Stump said. "Maybe that gal in the front row with the funny glasses, who kept making eyes at Sonny. Or that Marine—he looks like a hardass on drugs. Or that old gal with the cracker accent who said all she watches on TV is soap operas; *she* won't believe what a black woman says."

"You observe the jury closely," Leland said.

"That's my job, like you watch the cards. The thing is, you take any twelve people, there's gonna be at least one contrary son of a bitch among 'em. You know the type. You say up, he says down. You say black, he says white. Me and that guy are in cahoots, right from the start."

Stump sipped his drink. "He's locked up for a month, he thinks the other jurors are idiots, he hates the DA and the judge, and he wants to say a big fat fuck-you to them all. How? By letting my man walk.

"My job is to give him a theory that lets him do what he wants to do. In the present instance, that my client is a distinguished citizen, and his brother was a misguided young man who managed to get himself killed by drug dealers. Which, as you and I know, is almost certainly God's own truth."

"And you think the jury will buy that scenario?" Leland asked. His voice was silken.

"Sure, one of them will," Stump said contentedly. "The only question is which one."

First they elected a foreman, Ray Boyle, an engineer at General Dynamics, who'd been angling for the job all along. Boyle knew what outcome he wanted and he guessed some persuasion would be required.

He suggested an initial vote, to see where things stood. It came to eight for conviction, four for an acquittal. Worse than he'd expected. They went around the table, giving everyone a chance to speak. The three blacks were solid for conviction—they'd believed Olivia one hundred percent. Emotions ran high. Some of those who wanted to convict were incensed that anyone could doubt Sonny's guilt. Boyle urged calm. The worst mistake would be to paint anyone into a corner. "Let's reason together," he kept saying. "We have a big job to do."

After the first go-round, they changed one vote, Miss Teague, the nurse, whose reasoning was vague but who was more comfortable with the majority.

The other three weren't so easy.

Mrs. Apple, who ran a beauty salon on West Berry, peered at them through blue harlequin glasses and told them they just didn't understand Fort Worth. "I've lived here all my life. Ladies from the finest families come to me. These are *not* the sort of people who settle disputes with tire tools. The Nashes are cultivated people— look at that theater they built."

"But Billy *was* beaten to death," Boyle said patiently. "Two eyewitnesses said they saw Sonny. And two defense witnesses changed their stories."

"Men of Mr. Nash's standing don't commit crimes of that nature," Mrs. Apple said with finality.

Next was Hirsh, the Marine, a husky, red-faced man with a crew cut. "You reap what you sow," he told them. "You had a rich boy doing drugs, breaking the law, and it caught up with him."

"How can you ignore the facts?" another juror demanded. "Sonny Nash is clearly a psychopath!"

"What do you know?" Hirsh demanded. "Drugs ensnare people. They ruined my son's life!"

"Which has absolutely nothing to do with this case!" the other juror shot back.

"Let's keep calm," Boyle urged. He had not given up on Hirsh, far from it. Hirsh was a military man, a man who respected authority; if Boyle could swing the vote to eleven to one, he thought Hirsh would fall into line.

There remained Ila Medill, a plump little woman in her sixties whose passion was soap operas, and to whom this trial had become the greatest soap opera ever written.

"That Mr. Taggart," she volunteered, in the mushy accents of her native Georgia. "He was mean to poor little Christopher Nash."

"Mean?" Boyle repeated.

"Callin' him a liar an' all."

"Well, the boy did change his story," Boyle said. "His father may have persuaded him to lie."

Mrs. Medill's face was set. "Maybe he did," she conceded. "But that's no excuse for meanness to a child."

Ila Medill resented their questions, because she believed a lady should almost never say what she thought. A lady should say what was proper, that was what defined her as a lady.

She had come to Texas as a bride, with her husband, Owen Medill, who took a position with a Dallas bank. She left four sisters behind in Georgia, all of whom married brilliantly. Ila, to her shame, had not done so well. Mr. Medill, a man of great promise, had succumbed to a heart condition. Mrs. Medill opened a dress shop and worked hard and achieved modest success, all out of love for her daughter, so Isabel could marry well and have the perfect life her mother had been denied. The second tragedy of Mrs. Medill's life came when Isabel was a senior at TCU and was proposed to by the son of a millionaire oilman. She impulsively turned down the boy—he drank too much, Isabel said—and eloped with the editor of the school paper, who was now a columnist for the Dallas

Morning News. Mrs. Medill had never recovered. Her daughter might have risen to the pinnacle of Texas society, but instead she drove her children around in a four-year-old car and went to country music concerts on weekends, while her mother watched soap operas in a cramped apartment.

"But what about the eyewitnesses, Mrs. Medill? What about Olivia Winston's testimony?"

Ila glared back at her inquisitors. "Mr. Medill and I had a maid like her once and she stole from us," she declared. "Would you send a distinguished gentleman like Mr. Nash to prison on her say-so? The very idea!"

"But what about Jessica Nash, a young mother murdered?" Ray Boyle demanded.

"She should have married him," Mrs. Medill said. "She could have stopped his drinking. Think what a life she would have led."

Ray Boyle felt a great sense of despair enter his heart. He was a logical man, and this woman's reasoning defied all logic. "Let's run through it again," he suggested.

Judge Roland Balthus figured Sonny had killed those people—not that the state had proved it—but that wasn't the point. Poor black men went to prison for murder, not rich white men. Sending a man as rich as Sonny to Huntsville was about as likely as electing a man as black as Roland Balthus to be governor. The judge figured they were looking at a hung jury.

He'd tried the case with a sure sense of where his own interests lay. Acquittal or conviction—that didn't matter, that was the jury. A hung jury would be unfortunate but bearable. A reversal on appeal was a kick in the ass, but it was a risk you ran. The one thing that he would not do—had not done—was let them say he'd been soft on drugs. They had a rich white victim who smoked a little dope, and Stump hellbent to use that, and the prosecutor desperate to keep it out, and in the middle a judge who continued to be a political animal despite his black robes.

He could have kept the drugs out, perhaps he should have—it was a narrow line—but if he had there would have been talk about the black judge who tried to hush up drug use among the Nash family. Some would have said he was in cahoots with drug dealers, and others would have said the Nash family had bought him off. Neither theory would have done an ambitious man any good at all. So Roland Balthus had let Stump concoct his drug deal fantasy for the jury, and he would live with his decision. The only thing he wouldn't do was listen to Sonny Nash's lies and Stump Wildeman's theatrics again. Life was too short to spend on garbage like that.

After four days of debate and passion, tears and rage, came a numbing, humiliating acceptance of failure. One stubborn man and two stubborn women, one possibly senile, had frustrated the majority. Ray Boyle sent word to the judge that the jury was hopelessly deadlocked.

Stump Wildeman immediately moved for a mistrial, which the judge refused. Instead, he ordered the jury to keep trying, but at the end of the fifth day he surrendered to the inevitable.

Philip Kingslea saw the jury's rage as they returned, the judge's relief, Jay Taggart's grief, and the euphoric grins of Stump and Sonny as they embraced. Philip slipped out to a phone.

"Kay, it's a hung jury."

She was silent for a time.

"It's so damned awful."

"I know."

"What're we going to do?"

"Life goes on," he told her. "He's what he is and we're what we are."

Philip went out to the courthouse steps. It was a bright day with the temperature in the mid-sixties; the Christmas decorations were up on Main Street.

Sonny emerged to yet another roar of approval from a huge crowd. He stopped to hug one of the jurors, an old woman who looked like a frog. "Ah just think you're the greatest," she giggled.

Microphones had been set up at the top of the steps. Stump spoke first, declaiming about justice, but it was his client this multitude wanted to hear.

Sonny faced his people after months of enforced silence. "I tell you, I'm mad as hell. They never had a case. It was all politics and that two-bit radical in the DA's Office. It doesn't matter how much money you have, it's no fun having your good name dragged in the mud."

Sonny descended the courthouse steps triumphantly, stopping to shake men's hands and embrace women. When he reached his car, he turned and waved and the cheering reached a crescendo. Then, Puss at his side, he drove away in his Cadillac, his chariot of fire.

Into the sunset, Philip thought. Like Shane, or a John Wayne cowboy.

The crowd started to break up. Reporters headed toward Stump Wildeman's office on Sundance Square, in search of an open bar and meaty quotes.

Philip reentered the courthouse, the very courthouse atop which, in his youth, the world's largest neon flag had proudly flickered. Then he hurried to Jay Taggart's office. A cold wind was blowing, and he didn't want his friend drinking alone.

22.

M ICKEY AWOKE TO THE MOST BITTER OF IRONIES. THE DOCTORS said only her indomitable will to live had brought her through the coma. Now she lost that will. The world of light was infinitely more dark and terrible than the netherworld she had escaped. Rafe was gone, his life traded for Wingo's, the cruellest of exchanges. She raged, lusted to kill, but there was no one left to kill, except possibly herself.

She had exchanged one limbo for another. She lived with Lon and Ruby, but she ate little, spoke seldom, and rarely left her room. She thought endlessly, maddeningly, of Rafe, and blamed herself for his death. When the shrink came, she wouldn't even look at him.

Then she felt a spark one April day. She let herself remember Jessie, and the joy of their reunion. She found the number Jessie had left her; her hands trembled as she dialed it. "Nash residence," a black woman answered (Olivia, she remembered from the pictures), and Mickey asked for Jessica. She didn't say who was calling because this was her surprise. But the real surprise came when Olivia cried, "Don't you know? Miss Jessica . . . she's dead!"

Mickey had a DEA agent in Texas send her a transcript of the trial. As she read it, her disbelief became all-consuming rage. She stirred from her room at last. As spring bedazzled Washington, she began to run and work out, and slowly her strength returned. Ruby and Lon thanked God that she had regained the will to live. Ruby even noticed that Mick was letting her hair grow and thought that strange but no doubt a good sign.

In June, when Mickey returned to the office for the first time, everyone met her at the door and cheered. Some of the women giggled about how they loved her hair. Mickey was oddly unmoved. Her old colleagues were like ghosts; they hugged and kissed her but never connected.

The agent in charge took her to his office. He urged her to return to work and said she could have any assignment she wanted. She asked if she had any money coming. In fact, she had a lot coming, her salary and Rafe's benefits. She said she wanted a check as soon as possible.

The check arrived by messenger, the most money she'd ever had. She took Ruby to lunch at Hamburger Hamlet and then said she was going to the bank. She never came back. She'd withdrawn $10,000 in cash and taken a cab to National Airport, where no one remembered the slender woman in jeans and dark glasses who paid in cash and knew everything there was to know about leaving no trail. Her co-workers told themselves she'd slipped off for a vacation, that she needed time alone. The trouble with that theory was she'd left her credit cards behind and taken her gun.

As the new year began, Sonny and Mark formed a new company, Nash Brothers International. Lily took her money elsewhere. The remaining quarter of the Nash fortune belonged to Melissa. A judge made Lily the child's guardian, with Kay to succeed upon her death or incapacity. In the division of assets, Lily took control of the Nash Foundation. Kay, separated from Mark and still seeing Philip Kingslea, became the new administrator of the foundation.

390

In the aftermath of the hung jury, there was little outcry for the ordeal of a new trial. Jay Taggart had announced he would not seek reelection, and he made a suitable scapegoat. Sonny walked the streets, unregenerate. In the eyes of many, he had become the city's cross to bear: Dallas had the Kennedy assassination, and Fort Worth had Sonny Nash.

Sonny finally beat back Walter Lamont's RICO suit and completed the takeover of Lamont & Company. He continued to resist the lawsuit brought by victims of the Carvex plant, although the new anti-pollution devices stayed in place. Tammy Barber gave birth to a second, normal child.

Sonny started his own foundation with a flurry of good works. His image was on all the news shows and front pages when he established a ten-million-dollar William and Jessica Nash Scholarship Fund. Sonny's enemies spoke bitterly of his "rehabilitation," and in truth polls showed him to be one of the most admired men in Texas. His lakeside mansion became a popular stop on the tourist-bus circuit, and T-shirts and beer mugs bearing his likeness sold in souvenir shops alongside DON'T MESS WITH TEXAS stickers.

Mickey landed at D-FW and took a cab, not west to Fort Worth but east to Dallas. She checked into a big, anonymous hotel and spent a few days watching TV, studying people's voices, and reading everything the public library had on the Nashes.

One day she walked to the Highland Park Shopping Center. It had been built in the thirties, its style a lazy blend of Spanish and Art Deco, and it remained in fashion. She went to an expensive hair salon and told the woman precisely the style and shade she wanted, and the woman gushed, "Oh, it will be so perfect, so natural, so chic." Her hair did, in fact, look lovely when it was done, almost identical to Jessica's on the afternoon of their reunion, so many months before.

Back at her hotel she turned on the news and found Sonny Nash's face on the screen, awarding the money for a new Little League stadium in Fort Worth. Mickey smiled as she watched him deliver a pious little speech. She pointed her index finger at him and cocked her thumb and made a click with her tongue. It felt good, to hate someone so much who didn't even know you existed.

After the news she studied the snapshots Jessica had given her. They were all there: Billy and Melissa, Sonny and Puss, Kay and Mark and Christopher, Lily and Olivia. Her phantom family, the family she'd never met. It was funny. For thirty years she'd dreamed of being her beautiful, perfect sister. Now she was.

Kay's divorce suit had turned ugly. Mark's lawyers were gathering data on her affair with Philip Kingslea. Kay suspected that Sonny was calling the shots, out of sheer meanness.

Philip was in town and she wanted to see him, but the lawyers were urging discretion. She hated the lawyers, the restraints, the uncertainty.

Kay had never imagined how difficult single life could be. Half the men she met were afraid of her and the rest were in love with her money. Philip had his faults, but at least he treated her like a flesh-and-blood woman.

Since her separation from Mark, Kay had been living in Jessica and Billy's house in Westover Hills. People asked how she could stay there, after what had happened, but she liked the house and she wanted to keep it, in case Melissa ever wanted it. On this sultry June afternoon she was locked in a dispute with Olivia, all because Kay wanted to do her a favor.

"I do need a driver," Kay was saying. "Why not Omega? I could pay him more than he's making."

"I thank you, Miss Kay," Olivia said. "But it won't work."

Kay had tried for years to persuade Olivia to drop the Miss, but she deemed it proper and that was that.

"Why couldn't it work?" Kay demanded.

"I know that boy," Olivia said. "He'll be late or he won't come to work or he'll be drinking or something."

"Frankly, I expect that with any driver. We can work it out."

"But he wouldn't be any driver, he'd be my son," Olivia said. "Omega's doin' fine where he is. If you need a driver, I know a good man at my church. A retired minister."

Just what I need, Kay thought, a man of God.

The doorbell rang.

Olivia went to answer it. Kay wanted a drink but it wasn't even three yet. She moved restlessly around the room and saw a cab leave.

Then she heard Olivia scream.

The first thing she thought was that it was Sonny, he's come back. They lived with that nightmare. Kay raced to the foyer.

She found Olivia huddled in a chair, sobbing like a baby.

A woman hovered in the doorway. Kay blinked into the light that silhouetted the slender figure, the graceful sweep of golden hair.

Kay shuddered from deep within, choked back a cry. She reached out with trembling hands.

"Jessica. Is it *you*?"

"It's me, Kay. I'm back."

Kay was giddy with shock and disbelief. Jessica waited, smiling the way she did, self-effacing, patient, until Kay embraced her. Then Jessica took Olivia's hand. "Don't be afraid of me," she said. "Could I have some tea, please?"

The black woman struggled to her feet. "Child, child," she sobbed. They, too, embraced, then Olivia went off to the kitchen.

"Come in the library," Kay said. "I need a drink."

She poured herself straight gin and in a moment Olivia brought tea for their guest.

Mickey smiled at the two women who were gazing at her in such confusion. She did not fear their scrutiny. She and Jessica had been identical twins; the differences in their bone structure had been too subtle for anyone else to detect. Their bodies, too, were too nearly identical to be told apart, unless perhaps by a doctor or a lover. She knew she had the hair right, and she thought she had the voice, the clothes, and enough facts to bluff her way; unless she did something stupid there was no one alive who could prove she was not her sister.

"Is Melissa here?" she asked.

"Her class went to the Children's Museum," Kay explained. "They'll bring her home soon."

"What about Lily?"

"She's in London."

Mickey sipped her tea. "I owe you an explanation."

"You don't owe us anything," Kay said. "Make it easy on yourself. My God, I'm shaking all over."

The phone rang. It was Philip, calling from the Sidewinder, and Kay told him to come at once. She hoped he would know what to do; she sure as hell didn't.

When Philip arrived, Kay met him at the door and tried to prepare him for the shock, with only partial success.

He stepped into the library, gazed open-mouthed, and demanded, "Who the hell are you?"

Mickey smiled wanly. "I read your article in *Playboy*. What was it Mark Twain said? 'The reports of my death are greatly exaggerated?' "

Philip knelt by her chair. "What's Melissa's birthday?"

She laughed and told him.

"What's yours?"

She told him that, too.

"Where did you grow up?"

"In Little Rock," she said. "Before that in an orphanage. I never told anyone except Billy."

Philip nodded slowly. "That's true. I found that much out, researching my article. Okay, but you're going to have to answer a lot more questions. It isn't going to be like you came home late from the movies."

"I know it's strange," she said. "I'll do whatever I have to."

"Why don't you tell us the whole story?" Philip said.

"I was in Arizona," Mickey began. "I don't know how I got there. An older couple took me to their ranch and cared for me. I didn't know who I was or where I'd come from. There's still a lot I can't remember."

"Amnesia?" Philip asked.

"I suppose so. I helped the people on their ranch. They had no TV or newspapers. We didn't know about the trial."

"Who were these people?" Philip asked.

"I can't tell their names. The last thing they would want is publicity."

"Let her tell it her way," Kay snapped.

"One day I drove to town for groceries. The store had a magazine stand. I saw the *Playboy*, with the caption on the cover: THE NASH MURDER TRIAL. Something exploded and sent all these names and faces and places flying around my brain. I read the article and knew who I was, and that my husband was dead and I had a daughter in Texas."

"But do you remember what happened the night Billy was killed?" Philip demanded.

She recoiled from the question. "I knew you'd ask," she began. "But if you knew how painful it is to . . . "

The front door banged open and Melissa rushed in. "Aunt Kay, we went to the . . . "

The child saw the woman in the Queen Anne chair and her small, perfect face froze in wonder. Mickey swept across the room and took the child in her arms. She felt the love her sister had lost, the happiness that had been torn from her, and her tears were real.

"Baby, I'm come back to you," she whispered.

The child stared at her solemnly. "Are you really my mother?"

"I really am, darling. I've come back now. Nobody will ever hurt us again."

"Then come see what we've done to my room," Melissa said with perfect logic.

Kay and Philip watched them go.

"Jesus H. God," Kay said, and refilled her glass.

Philip groaned. "I believe it and I don't believe it."

"What are we going to do?"

"I'm thinking," he said. "She has to see Jay Taggart—she's the missing witness to her husband's murder. As well as the heir to a billion dollars."

They asked no more questions that night. After dinner, Mickey played with Melissa until the child went to bed. Kay said her clothes were still in her closets, and she tried a few things on.

"I've lost a pound or two," she said.

"You look good," Kay said. "Ranch life must have agreed with you."

"I'm stronger now. I loved it."

"We don't mean to rush you, but Philip thinks you ought to talk to Jay Taggart in the morning."

"All right," Mickey said. "If you think so."

The next morning, Kay called Jay and asked him to come for breakfast. "Be prepared for a shock," she warned.

When Jay arrived he was shocked into near-immobility. He had for so long carried in his mind an image of Jessica beaten, brutalized, and sunk to the bottom of the lake, that his mind rebelled at the idea of her alive and well. He stared at her in bewilderment, like a drunkard confronting a puzzle he cannot possibly solve.

Finally he turned to Kay. "Are you sure?"

"Look at her," Kay said. "Listen to her."

"I know it's strange," Mickey said.

Mickey told her story a second time, adding a few details about her life in Arizona.

"Look, I'm sorry," Jay interrupted, "but you haven't told us about the night Billy was killed."

Mickey turned away. "I'm sorry," she said. "I can't talk about it."

"You'll have to, eventually."

"I know. But not yet."

"Who will she have to tell?" Kay asked.

"Me," Jay Taggart said. "The grand jury."

"I'll tell the grand jury," she said. "But don't make me tell it now. Philip, when I read your article, it was like the earth swallowed me up. I broke down, people thought I'd lost my mind. Give me time."

"We understand," Jay assured her. "Just get your strength back. Then we'll go to court."

"I'm not interested in courts," Mickey said. "All I want is my daughter."

"There's a lot of money involved, Jessica," Philip said.

"I don't care about money." Mickey hesitated. "But there is one thing I want."

"What?" Kay asked.

"I want to see Sonny."

It made sense to Mickey. Sonny would learn of her return soon enough. She wanted the pleasure of seeing his face and also a chance to size him up. This was her raid on the enemy camp. The opening salvo in her psychological war.

Jay Taggart had no business with Sonny, and left for the courthouse, but Kay and Philip were intrigued.

"Can we get in to see him?" Philip asked.

"*I* can," Kay said. "He's been issuing lewd invitations to me ever since I left Mark."

They drove downtown in Kay's Mercedes. Mickey sat in the back and watched the city unfold. She'd forgotten how ugly it was. A new museum or two didn't change anything, not in her book. She saw the Nash Tower ahead, tin-can bright in the morning sun. The killer was up there, thinking himself invulnerable.

Kay parked in the underground garage. She had a key to the private elevator to the executive suites. Mickey put on dark glasses, lest Jessica's abrupt return alarm the secretaries. She need not have worried; it was Kay (rich, sexy, newly single, newly discovered by Liz Smith and *Women's Wear Daily*) the girls stared at as she blazed a trail to Sonny's suite.

Kay entered first. Sonny was sitting at his desk, reading a newsmagazine with Michael Jackson on the cover. Seeing Kay, he grinned and stood up. "Couldn't stay away, huh?"

"I wouldn't say that," Kay replied.

Sonny waved the magazine. "It's a crime how much money this boy is making," he said.

Mickey slipped through the door. For an instant, she saw Sonny before he saw her. Photographs had not prepared her for the reality of him, his arrogance, his cruelty. She slipped off her dark glasses and mocked him with her sweetest smile.

Sonny's eyes flicked from Kay to Mickey, and she was rewarded by the horror that gripped his face. He dropped the magazine and staggered away from her.

"You bitch!" he cried. "You're dead."

She drank him in, this monster she had come so far to see. She might have killed him then and there, but that would have been too easy.

"How do you know I'm dead, Sonny?"

"You're a ghost," he said.

She stepped toward him. "No, Sonny. I'm alive. Touch me."

He gripped her hand. "You *are* alive," he whispered.

"Don't you know that if someone is mean enough, their spirit lives on? I am meaner than you thought, Sonny. I came back."

She jerked her hand free, loathing his touch.

"Back from where?" he demanded.

"From a dark world far away, where I dreamed about you."

Sonny fought free of her gaze and turned to Kay and Philip. "Hell, this just proves what I said all along. She skipped town and now she's come back for the money."

Mickey's laugh shocked them all. "No, Sonny. You killed Billy and you tried to kill me. I've come for justice."

His body swelled with rage; he stepped toward her menacingly. "Fuck you, sister! Jessica is dead and a jury set me free. I don't care who you are. A ghost or an actress or some nut off the street. Get out of here and don't come back."

A cloud drifted across the sun. The office floated in a pale half-light. Mickey's eyes were cold as death. "I'll be back, Sonny," she promised. "I'll be with you as long as you live."

She marched out of the office. Kay and Philip, too shaken to speak, followed after her. Philip, looking back, saw Sonny reach for the phone.

"Well, you certainly *look* like Jessica," Lily said cheerfully. "If you're not her, you're her twin."

Mickey smiled. "I can understand why you're uncertain."

It was early evening, and they sat facing one another in Lily's den. Lily had started the day in London, taken the Concorde to

398

New York, then at Kay's urgent request flown directly to Fort
Worth.

"My dear, if you are Jessica, I apologize for prolonging your
ordeal. But, you see, my daughter-in-law disappeared months ago
and has been presumed dead. If she returns, she will be a very rich
woman. And it isn't unthinkable that some enterprising young
woman who looked like her might try to pass herself off as Jessica,
is it?"

"Of course not."

"I guess we all feel a certain uneasiness. We prayed for a miracle
and now it seems to have happened and we think it's too good to
be true. Human nature is like that. Anyway, I thought we might
talk. There are things that only Jessica would know."

"Of course," Mickey said. "What would you like to know?"

"Tell me how you met Billy."

Mickey felt in perfect control. Her sister had told her an abun-
dance of personal detail, that day in Washington.

"We met on the Mall in Washington. At the Vietnam Memorial.
We walked to the National Gallery and he showed me his favorite
picture, Gainsborough's portrait of Mrs. Sheridan."

Lily nodded. "That's all quite true. But I suppose some of it has
been in the newspapers."

"Did he tell you about our honeymoon, at Wintergreen, in Virginia? Or about the pearls he gave me for our anniversary? Or the
new house we were planning?"

"Yes, he told me all that."

"There are things I can't remember. Names that are still coming
back."

"I talked to my lawyer before you came. He said that if I had
the slightest doubt, there were objective tests to prove your identity."

"What sort of tests?" Mickey asked. She knew, but Jessica would
not have.

"Oh, fingerprints, that sort of thing. But I don't think that's
called for. As far as I'm concerned, my daughter has returned!"

It was potentially a moment of high drama. The two women

might have embraced. Instead, they stayed in their chairs, studying one another. Mickey was thinking this was the shrewdest of the Nashes, the only one who worried her.

"Lily, let me be honest, too. If all this hesitation is about money, it isn't necessary, because I don't want money. All I want is my daughter."

Lily poured them both more tea. "I'm afraid it's not that simple, my dear. As Billy's widow, you will inherit a great amount of money. I suppose you could give away your share, but you can't give away Melissa's share. If you tried, I'd take you to court and the jury would clearly think you unfit, if not insane. If you want to raise Melissa, you'll have to raise her as a Nash, which means you'll both live in considerable comfort."

"I don't mind comfort, but I don't intend to stay in Fort Worth," Mickey said.

Lily's temper flared. "Listen to me carefully, dear. I lost my son—I lost all my sons—and that child is my reason for living. If you try to take her out of this city, I'll fight you with everything I have. You would be unwise to underestimate my legal, financial, political, and emotional resources."

"I don't want to fight you."

"Then take off your shoes and stay a while. Live in your house, spend time with your daughter, and let Olivia care for you both. Enjoy yourself. I know you've always felt alien to Texas, but maybe you'll wake up one morning and realize you've become one of us."

Mickey had to laugh. "Maybe I will," she said. "But I doubt it."

Kay and Lily and Lily's lawyer, Ben Pegram, talked by conference call the next morning. The lawyer was unhappy: that he had not yet seen Jessica, that she had confronted Sonny, and that Lily did not demand blood tests and fingerprints immediately.

"It would seem that just about everything we've done is wrong," Lily commented.

"I don't have to tell you how much money is at stake here," the lawyer said grimly.

"She says she doesn't want money."

"And you believe that?" he demanded.

"I don't know what I believe anymore," Lily admitted.

"Then why not make a few simple tests?"

"Why not?" Lily said heatedly. "Because I believe this *is* Jessica, and she's been through an ordeal we can't even imagine."

"Need I remind you, Lily, that if you can prove she isn't your daughter-in-law, Melissa remains in your custody?"

"Do you think I haven't thought of that? But I'm accepting her, at least pending some new revelation."

"What do you say, Kay?" Pegram asked. "Is this Jessica?"

"I lay awake last night thinking about it," Kay said. "The problem is that it's so bizarre. Someone virtually coming back from the dead. But when I just look at the woman before me, I can't believe that an impostor could be that much like another person. The cheekbones, the mouth, the eyes—it simply is *her*."

The lawyer sighed. "All right. Since she's made her ill-advised visit to Sonny, we have to assume that her return will soon leak out. It will be very big news, and we must try to keep control of the story."

"We'll issue a statement," Lily said. "I'll say she's back, she's resting, and the family is overjoyed."

"You can't get away with that. If you say she's back, you have to say back from where. You have to let them see and hear her, or God knows what rumors will start."

Scores of reporters and photographers flocked to Lily's house the next morning. They didn't know what was to be announced, but for Lily Nash to summon the media was news in itself. The camera crews set up in the front yard, as golfers putt-putted by in white carts on the Rivercrest course across the street. Lily came out at eleven and read a brief statement. It said that Jessica Nash had returned home, that she had been in another state suffering from amnesia, that the family was grateful for her return, that she was recovering her strength, and that she would in due course tell her story to the proper authorities.

When Lily finished her statement, a dozen reporters began shouting at once. She shushed them like the impatient schoolmarm she once had been, then abruptly her front door opened.

Mickey emerged, in a white skirt and blue blouse, and dark glasses. The startled reporters called out questions.

Ben Pegram raised his hands. "Ladies and gentlemen, please."

Mickey could barely be heard. "I'm very happy to be home. I want to rest and be with my daughter. That's all I have to say now."

The reporters whipped themselves into a frenzy, but their quarry retreated into Lily's house. The news conference was over.

The return of Jessica Nash set off a tornado of news, speculation, and debate. Calls poured in from Barbara Walters, Mike Wallace, and Phil Donahue. Several Hollywood producers called proposing a mini-series. Ben Pegram returned those calls himself, vowing legal action against any such project.

The media staked out Jessica's house, eager to photograph even Melissa's departure for school, but with the help of a sympathetic judge they were kept a hundred yards away.

Mickey ignored the furor. She devoted her energies to Melissa; she loved the child and she thought Melissa loved her and accepted her as her mother. That was important, because as far as Mickey was concerned, they were together for the long haul. Someday she would tell Melissa the truth. She knew as well as anyone how important that was. But for now she wasn't looking that far ahead.

She was focusing on the short term, and her plan was on track. Jessica was back, the Nash family accepted her, the grand jury wanted to see her, and she figured Sonny Nash was starting to sweat.

Mickey had been expecting Jay Taggart's call.

"Jessica, I'm taking a lot of heat. People are asking me when you'll go before the grand jury."

"I dread the ordeal," she said, for Jessica would indeed have dreaded it.

"I understand, but it has to be done. The grand jury adjourns in two weeks. I need you to testify before then."

And he could, of course, back that up with a subpoena.

"All right. Two weeks from now."

"Good," Jay said. "Off the record, I had a call from Stump Wildeman. He talks in circles but the gist of it is this. He assumes you'll testify that Sonny killed Billy. He questions your identity. He'll want dental records, a lie detector, whatever. His theory is you're someone Kay hired to frame Sonny. He'll do anything he can to keep you away from that grand jury."

"It's funny," Mickey said.

"What is?"

"In the trial, he said so dramatically, 'Jessica Nash might walk in that door tomorrow!' Well, I did, and you'd think he'd be glad to see me."

Stump Wildeman's threats were what Mickey had expected. Even if she were willing to take the stand and perjure herself by claiming to be Jessica and having seen Sonny kill Billy Nash, Sonny's lawyers would expose her before she got to a jury. She might finesse the lie detector, and she had learned that Jessica had never been fingerprinted, but dental records were a killer. She had to settle with Sonny out of court. But Sonny didn't know that. He didn't know what to think. He was a half-mad psychopath who had killed a woman who had come back to haunt him. Sonny had to figure that, whoever she was, she was hellbent to put his ass in Old Sparky and he couldn't count on dental records to save him. So Jay Taggart's grand jury was a deadline for them both: she to dispense her justice, he to silence her.

Mickey's plan was becoming clear to her. She had to kill Sonny, she started with that. He had killed the person she loved most in the world, the courts had failed to punish him, and she must be her sister's avenger.

Sometimes she thought of Wingo, how he had hated her, and she felt a terrible kinship with him, because she hated Sonny Nash with that same white-hot intensity. She had to kill Sonny, and he had to know why he was dying. That ruled out the simplest form of assassination, a rifle shot from afar. This had to be a personal encounter, Mr. Sonny Nash's first and last meeting with Ms. Mickey McGee.

And there was this complication, too: she had to survive. That had not been part of her original plan. She'd figured that if it came to it, she'd trade her life for his, that with both Rafe and Jessie dead it was a fair bargain. But that was before she met Melissa. Now she had to surrender a certain recklessness in her planning.

She didn't underestimate the challenge. Sonny hardly ever went out of his mansion now, which raised the possibility that she might have to go to him, and he was surrounded by electrified fences, armed guards, and attack dogs. She would go after him if she had to, but life would be simpler if she could lure Sonny to her.

One afternoon Mickey started crying and couldn't stop for an hour; she thought she was truly insane, as crazy as the man she intended to kill. Later, purged of her tears, she thought she was the most sane, serene person in Texas. In the end it didn't matter. She had a job to do.

Lily invited her to dinner one night that week, along with Kay and Philip and a woman she had not met before, Myra Fontaine.

They had drinks on Lily's side porch, where the air was scented by magnolias, then gathered around the Chippendale table in Lily's dining room.

Myra, fiftyish and bittersweet, apologized for not seeing her before. "I was on a pilgrimage in India when I heard you were home. It was as if I had to go to India for there to be a miracle in Texas."

"Did you enjoy India?" Mickey asked. She had become expert at asking questions. People would talk endlessly about themselves if given any encouragement at all.

"I love India, despite the pain and poverty. There's a grandeur to it, an acceptance of all that is human. But an awful thing happened on this trip. My party included an Englishwoman. One day we took an elephant ride. The two of us, side by side on these quite tame elephants. Hers went under a tree and she collided with a hornets' nest and suddenly hundreds of hornets were swarming around her. I'll never forget her screams."

Myra paused for wine. "She leaped from the elephant's back and broke her ankle and tried to hobble away. You could barely see her for the hornets. She died in the hospital. She was a kind, cultivated woman. I prayed that night, for the first time in decades. It was the next day that Lily's message reached me. I lost one person I loved and gained another one back."

"What a terrible story," Lily said.

"A very Indian story," Myra said. "Death and rebirth. Just as we've had here, with Jessica's return."

Myra's eyes kept returning to Mickey throughout dinner, making her uneasy. She liked the woman, but she was troubled because Myra seemed to be trying to peer into her soul, and Mickey welcomed no one there.

As dinner progressed, they spoke of many things, but never of Sonny, although he seemed to Mickey to hover beside their table like Banquo's ghost. It was as if they were pretending that he didn't exist, when in fact his murderous presence dominated all their lives.

They had all drunk heavily of Lily's exquisite La Fleur. When the third bottle was empty, Philip went to the kitchen and opened another.

"Philip, do you know what that wine costs?" Kay protested.

"As much as several barrels of oil," the writer told her. "But methinks I heard the ghost of Billy Ringer telling me to drink one for him."

Lily laughed. "Perhaps you did," she said. "Let's all have some more."

Philip filled everyone's glass. The candles had burned down and the Texas night was still as eternity.

"I think of Billy Ringer often," Lily said. "I'll tell you something I've never told anyone, about the time he first reappeared in the early sixties. He had a terrible row with my husband, Howard, but finally Billy told us he was leaving me all the money from his field in Louisiana. Perhaps a hundred million dollars, he said. We were astounded. I was trying to thank him—perhaps I was crying too —and he looked at me and said, 'It's only money, Lily. It ain't like I was doing you a favor.' "

Lily sighed. "Billy was wiser than I. He had to give me the money, and I had to take it, but he understood that it was more likely a curse than a blessing."

She raised her glass in a gesture of wistful acceptance.

There was a moment of silence, and it was then that Philip chose to mention the unmentionable. He turned to Myra. "No offense, but why are you so chummy with Sonny?"

"Philip, shut up," Kay snapped.

"It's a fair question," Myra said. "Perhaps chummy isn't the word, but we talk. I spoke to him yesterday, in fact."

"You do believe he killed Billy, don't you?" Philip pressed.

"You know I do."

"Then how can you deal with the bastard?"

Myra returned his stare without flinching.

"I'm not a judgmental person—perhaps writers are more given to that. I enjoy your books, but they present a world more black and white than I see it."

"We're not talking about books, we're talking about murder," Philip said angrily.

"Perhaps I feel a kinship with Sonny—after all, I killed someone once."

"It was hardly the same," Kay interjected.

Myra shrugged impatiently. "At a certain level, to kill is to kill is to kill."

"You're talking in circles," Philip protested.

"Perhaps I am," Myra admitted. "Let me put it this way. If Lily or Jessica asked me, I'd never speak to Sonny again. But I've known him a long time. I think of him as being, in a certain way, a cripple, born without the basic human decencies. Perhaps I think he needs me."

"Oh for Christ's sake!" Philip groaned.

"No, Myra is right," Lily said quietly. "If there's anyone on earth who needs compassion, it's Sonny. I can't bring myself to bestow it. I call myself a Christian, and I've tried, but I hate what he did too much. Perhaps God will grant him compassion someday. Until then, I'm glad Myra can."

. . .

Sonny and Leland Webb were having a drink on Sonny's balcony, high above the lake. Sonny watched moodily as a girl water-skied far across the water, while Leland idly dealt hands of solitaire. After a while Sonny turned back to the gambler. He enjoyed watching his hands, the tricks he could play with a deck of cards.

"You could have been a safecracker."

"A lonely business. I prefer poker."

Sonny turned away. His thoughts kept returning to the lake, to that stormy night that was now months in the past.

He had seen the bitch go under, that was the hell of it. Broken, weighed down with chains. Harry Houdini couldn't have escaped. Sure, he'd been in a hurry, but he knew what he'd done. Jessica Nash was at the bottom of Eagle Mountain Lake.

Then who was this bitch who said she was Jessica, who looked so much like her she almost gave him a heart attack?

An actress? If so, she deserved an Oscar.

Or *could* she be a spirit? Sonny took the spirits very seriously, but he didn't believe his dumb-ass sister-in-law could be one because she wasn't strong enough. Only the very strong came back.

She had to be an impostor, hired by Kay or even by his mother to mess up his head, to trick him into court again. She'd tell the grand jury he'd gone crazy and killed Billy and carried her off and thrown her into the lake. And how she slipped out of the chains and swam to shore.

Except she wasn't going to tell that tale. He wasn't going to let her. His lawyer had his fruitcake plan about lie detectors and fingerprints, but this girl was smart, she'd have a way around that, and he wasn't going to wait to be railroaded. Sonny would have to solve this problem himself.

He stood up and stretched.

Leland watched him carefully. Sonny had been restless all afternoon. Leland sensed something coming and he would have bet a thousand dollars that he knew what it was.

"Refill?" Sonny asked.

"No thanks."

Sonny poured himself more Black Label.

"Did you know that lake froze over, back in the twenties? They drove cars over it."

Leland tried to look impressed. Sonny sat down.

"I need a man I can trust. A professional, from out of state. He comes in, does a job, and leaves. When he's here, I'm somewhere else. You follow?"

Leland shuffled the cards. They arched and whispered into a neat pile. "I think so."

"Maybe you know a guy. In Vegas, maybe."

"They exist."

"I need him soon. How about you check it out?"

Leland's friendship with Sonny had been a profitable one. He organized a game for Sonny every few months, and won serious money from rich men who fancied themselves poker players. But this was dangerous business. The question was, which was more dangerous, to help Sonny or refuse him?

"I could fly out tomorrow," he said.

"Good," Sonny said.

Leland stroked the cards unhappily. Sonny's drinking bothered him. Was he thinking clearly? How much did he imagine he could get away with? Even for Sonny, there were limits.

"In that chest by the door, there's money," Sonny added. "Take what you need. For the guy and yourself, too."

Leland nodded. He had seen that drawer once, filled with thousand-dollar bills.

"But remember, a professional. And I'm a long-gone daddy when he does the job."

"I understand," the gambler said, and cut the cards for luck.

Myra Fontaine took her to lunch at the Old Swiss House.

"I'm bored beyond words with the country clubs," she explained. "It's like purgatory. The same dull people eating the same bland food forever. The food is interesting here and you may even glimpse an unfamiliar face."

"I love it here," Mickey said cautiously.

Myra waved for another martini; Mickey sipped iced tea.

"I loved Jessica from the first moment I laid eyes on her," Myra said. "She was beautiful and loving, everything . . . everything you could hope for."

Mickey was alerted by Myra's choice of words, but guessed the martinis had muddled her thinking.

"Billy and Jessica and Melissa had a beautiful life ahead," Myra added.

Mickey was annoyed. "Myra, I *still* have a good life ahead."

"Well, of course you do. But you're not Jessica."

Mickey widened her eyes. "That's a heck of a way to start lunch. Why do you say it?"

"Call it instinct. You're remarkably like her, but you're not Jessica."

"Then who am I?"

"How should I know? Oh, I have a theory, but I'll keep it to myself. Understand me, child, I don't dislike you. If you're not Jessica, you're the next best thing. I care about you, more than you know."

They had reached an impasse. Mickey tried to laugh off Myra's skepticism, and the older woman, for her part, remained cheerful and friendly. Mickey knew the story about Myra shooting her father and wondered if she might be a little mad. No matter—she was a threat.

"Well, you'll go before the grand jury soon?" Myra said, when their coffee came.

"I'm scheduled for Friday."

"But there's a legal battle, isn't there?"

"Sonny's lawyer is demanding a blood test, lie detectors, all sorts of things."

"Well, that could be inconvenient, couldn't it?" Myra said.

Mickey ignored the barb. "Lily's lawyer, Mr. Pegram, is arguing that tests are insulting and unnecessary. We expect a ruling this week."

Myra arched an eyebrow. "Well, happy lie detectors."

"How well do you know Sonny?" Mickey shot back.

Myra laughed, and her sad face was abruptly lovely. "Well enough."

"Someone said you play poker with him."

"I have, but I prefer bridge with the ladies. The table talk is more interesting."

"But he still has his games?" Mickey was thinking that one of Sonny's poker nights might be her best hope of penetrating his mansion.

"He was supposed to have one next week. Leland Webb was organizing it. But instead Leland flew off somewhere and Sonny's leaving town."

Warning bells sounded, a three-alarm fire. "Leaving town? Where for?"

"London, then the Middle East. Very hush-hush, of course, but Puss was complaining that she wasn't invited."

"When did you say he was leaving?"

Myra smiled. "I didn't. But I will. Today is Monday and he's leaving Wednesday. Congratulations. You've run Sonny Nash out of town, something no one else was able to do."

Mickey went home and locked the door and thought hard. If Sonny was going away, that meant she had only forty-eight hours to kill him. But her every instinct told her there was more to this. He wasn't fleeing because he was afraid of her, not Sonny. It didn't make sense. She was about to go before the grand jury and he would want to be there, in control, telling Stump Wildeman what to do.

Or wasn't he worried about the grand jury anymore? Why not? Because a fix was in? No, she trusted Jay Taggart. Or did he know she'd never testify? *She* knew that—but how could he?

The answer burst across her mind like the Fourth of July, so obvious she felt like an idiot. Sonny was a killer but not a fool. Last September he'd gone berserk, acted impulsively, and escaped by the skin of his teeth. He wouldn't make that mistake twice.

This time he'd send an expert to do the job.

It made perfect sense. He wasn't worried about the grand jury because he knew she'd never make it to the grand jury, and he'd be halfway around the world when the deed was done.

That meant once Sonny left town, it was open season on her. She'd walk out the door, or be driving down the street, and—pow!—Sonny's man would pop her.

If she was right, she was safe for another forty-eight hours.

But Sonny wasn't safe. He'd let his plan slip out. Now she had two days to kill Sonny before he killed her.

Fair enough, she thought. Fair enough.

Mickey was drawn to the lake that night. She left her car among trees and slipped through the woods, black-clad and invisible, until she reached a bluff overlooking Sonny's fortress. The fence that surrounded it on three sides was electrified, and an armed guard was stationed in the gatehouse. As she watched, he left his post to walk the perimeter, an automatic weapon under his arm and four Rottweilers racing like hellhounds beside him. Sonny's cabin cruiser rocked gently at the dock. Mickey saw no flaw in his defenses. If she came by water, the dogs would greet her at the water's edge. She could overpower the guard, shoot the dogs, and charge the mansion, but with Sonny alerted inside that would be a kamikaze mission. No, tonight she would watch, remember, and temper her resolve.

She was not surprised when Sonny stepped onto his balcony and peered out over the lake. He was drawn to her, she thought, just as she was drawn to him. They were partners in a dance that only one could survive.

Watching Sonny, she thought of Luther Pringle, two decades before. What was the difference between them? Sonny had more brains, sure, but they were brothers at heart. Wingo was another. Thugs, throwbacks to the jungle, predators who took their pleasure in the pain of others.

So what did you do about them, the bullies, the thugs, the rapists and killers? Mickey had been wrestling with that question all her life. Up to a point, you avoided them. But sometimes you had to take a stand. All by yourself. She'd learned that at thirteen, when she took a razor to Luther. The world was full of bastards who wanted to grind a woman down, and the instinct to fight back had defined her life.

Mickey felt herself in the grip of a power greater than herself—call it love or hate or justice or madness, it came out the same. She had to settle with Sonny. He had killed Jessie and she had to kill him. She had no choice. She wanted to do it a certain way, up close, so he understood, so she could taste his fear, but if she had to she'd gun the bastard down in the street.

On the distant balcony, the shadowy figure tossed a glowing cigar into the darkness, and retreated into the sanctuary his money had built.

Mickey watched, ablaze with passion, a child of the night, as pitiless as the stars.

Time was running out and she saw only two choices. One was to hit Sonny on the way to his plane, knowing that his bodyguards might get her first. The other was to lure him into the open, to trick him into coming to her. But how? Who would help her? Who could she trust?

Myra Fontaine had the best lines to Sonny, but Mickey couldn't be sure what game Myra was playing. How could she trust someone who called Sonny a friend, who spoke of compassion for him?

She trusted Kay, and Kay's hatred of Sonny approached her own, but he was smart enough to be wary of Kay. Still, she needed ideas, so she went to see Kay.

Kay had her settlement, a million a year, and she had a decision to make. Philip Kingslea had taken a house in Malibu and invited her for the summer. She was tempted, for she liked the film world. It was a world, like Texas, where money ruled supreme, but the people were more interesting than Texans. Instead of making deals they made movies, and Kay found them creative and cynical and reckless in ways she enjoyed.

But did she want to live with Philip? Kay had married too young, to the wrong man, and she had some catching up to do. She needed to live alone for a time.

Her dream was to rent a house in Paris, but two new realities kept her in Fort Worth. One was the Nash Foundation. She'd been running it since the spring and she had discovered how addictive work could be.

Chris was the other, and he was an even more urgent concern. He had always been fragile, and lying for Sonny at the trial had tipped his inner balance. He ignored school, hated Mark, and had withdrawn into a shell she could rarely penetrate. He was seeing a psychiatrist three afternoons a week, and Kay was not sure she could drag him off to California or France, no matter how renowned the doctors there or how regal their lifestyle.

Kay had reached the only decision she could: to stay in Fort Worth and run the foundation, and coax her son back to health. So much money, she thought, and so little comfort.

Jessica and Melissa's visit cheered her. The child played out back with Kay's poodle while the women settled by the window with coffee.

"You said once you wanted the foundation to do something to help adopted people find their parents."

Mickey blinked. "Yes. That would be wonderful."

"Some people have submitted a proposal. Want to see it?"

"You know I would. What's their approach?"

"Legal, mainly. Court tests of the old laws. Ideally a Supreme Court ruling on adoptee's rights."

"Good for them," Mickey said.

"So how's your legal battle?"

"A mess," Mickey told her. She watched Melissa tossing an old tennis ball to Kay's poodle. The child was so self-contained. She wondered what she thought, how much she knew.

"I've been thinking I'd like to talk to Sonny again," she added.

"What in God's name for?" Kay demanded.

Mickey shrugged. "Maybe to ease tensions."

"Honey, I think you'd better keep your distance from Sonny. Seriously."

"I understand. But suppose I wanted to talk to him. Who could help? Myra?"

Kay shook her head. "It would have to be family. His mother."

"Are they speaking?"

"No, but she's the only one of us he'd talk to. Oh, he'd talk to me, but only because he wants you know what. No, Lily is the one. But run it by your lawyer first."

Mickey nodded. Kay had given her ideas. "Probably it'd be crazy."

"Anyway, Lily is leaving town tonight."

"Oh? For where?"

"New York."

Mickey looked out the window at Melissa and the poodle. "Look at them. We ought to have a picture."

Fluff kept bringing the ball back but she was tired of throwing it. She sat down in the soft wet grass and held the dog in her lap and laughed as it wiggled and licked her hand. Silly old Fluff, silly old poodle. She could see her mother and Kay beside the window and she wondered what they were talking about. Everyone had changed. They tried to pretend they hadn't but they had. Ever since her father went away. Her father and mother had both gone away and she'd gone to live with Lily and then her mother had come back except she wasn't as happy as before. Nobody was as happy as before. She was glad she never saw Sonny anymore. Sometimes when she said her prayers, she prayed that he would die just like she prayed for her father to come back. They said he wouldn't, but if her mother had come back, why couldn't her father? She was glad Chris wasn't home. Chris was mad all the time now and when they were alone he said ugly things to her. Everything had changed. When she grew up she was going to live on a ranch and have a hundred dogs and horses and never get married and maybe then her mother would be happy again and her daddy would come home if she prayed enough. She saw her mother get up and she stood up too and tossed the ball and Fluff ran after it. She loved Fluff. She loved everybody except Sonny, but she didn't know why they all kept changing and making her so sad.

. . .

Mickey drove pell-mell to Lily's house, Melissa seat-belted at her side.

Olivia let them in, and whisked Melissa away for milk and cookies. In a moment Lily came down, silver-haired and unsmiling. How strong she was, Mickey thought, and how afflicted.

"You're going away."

"Only for a few days."

"Hi, Grandmother!" Melissa burst into the room, a milky mustache on her upper lip.

Lily brightened, lifting the child into her arms. "Did Olivia give you cookies?"

"They were still warm."

"A little bird told us you'd be by. How is your school?"

"I made a horse out of clay."

Olivia swept in. "Come along, child, and we'll make another batch—you like to ate the first one up."

Lily turned back to Mickey. "Is something on your mind, dear?"

"Yes. Yes, something that may sound strange."

"Not much sounds strange anymore."

"I want to talk to Sonny."

Lily gasped. "What on earth for?"

"To spare everyone a lot of misery. The grand jury for me. Maybe another trial for him."

"No trial? Don't you want him punished?"

"It's complicated, Lily. I can't explain everything now. But maybe it'd be better if he'd just leave Texas."

Lily looked skeptical. "Sonny leave Texas? That doesn't sound likely."

"He might if the alternative was prison."

"Jessica, I don't have to tell you what a dangerous man he is. I don't think you should talk to him, much less threaten him."

"Think what agony another trial would be, and he might go free again. Wouldn't it be better if he just went away?"

"How strange that you should propose it," Lily said pensively. "Twenty years ago, I ordered his father to leave Texas."

"History might repeat itself," Mickey said.

"Sonny is more formidable than his father," Lily said. "What is it you want of me?"

"I want you to call him. He might not talk to me, but he'll talk to you."

"I don't like it," Lily said stubbornly.

"Please, trust me," Mickey said, and Sonny's mother finally did as she was asked.

"Sonny, it's your mother."

"Lord have mercy, I believe it is."

"It's time we talked."

"What about? Money?"

"Perhaps. I'm not happy with my present situation."

"That clown you hired don't know his ass from a teacup."

"It's not just money. We need peace in this family."

"I never made war."

Lily gritted her teeth. "I'm leaving for New York in the morning. Could you come to my house tonight?"

Sonny hesitated. "Just the two of us?"

"Yes. Just the two of us. Will you come at ten? I'll be at church until then."

Sonny laughed. "I never refuse a lady. Ten o'clock."

Lily put down the phone.

Mickey nodded. "Good," she said. "Now, go to New York. Everything will be fine here."

"I don't like it," Lily said again, but she finished her packing and left for the airport.

Mickey drove home, taking Melissa and Olivia with her. Lily's house was empty now and she had the key. She thought it the one place he would venture without fear or suspicion.

She sat with Melissa while she ate dinner. Olivia and the child kept up a running dialogue. Mickey felt herself slipping away, there and not there. Part of her was planning her showdown with Sonny. She was operating on pure instinct now, a hunter at the dawn of time.

The phone rang and Olivia spoke briefly.

"Who was it?" Mickey asked.

"Miss Lily, calling from the airport, wanting to know if every-thing was all right."

Mickey smiled.

After dinner she watched TV with Melissa until it was time for the child to go up. Then Mickey dressed quickly in jeans, sneakers, and a cotton shirt. She took her gun out of the closet and stuck it in her belt, under her shirt. It was a silenced 16-shot Sig-Sauer 9-mm. semi-automatic, a powerful weapon.

Then she slipped into the night.

She arrived at Lily's at nine, up the alley, entering by the back door. She turned the porch light on, closed the curtains, and settled in the study. An odd tranquility engulfed her. She thought Sonny needed most urgently to die. Mickey didn't precisely believe in God, but she did believe in goodness. Right now Melissa was all the goodness in the world to her. She was the future, as soon as Mickey had settled accounts with the past.

At two minutes past ten, Lily's doorbell rang.

Mickey smiled and stood up.

"This one's for you, Jessie," she whispered.

Mickey opened the door and stepped back.

Sonny filled the shadowy foyer.

"What're you doing here?"

"Waiting for you."

"Where's my mother?"

"On her way to New York."

"What's your game, sister?"

"I want to talk. You're not afraid of me, are you?"

She kept her distance, coiled to act. If he made a move she'd blow his guts out.

He followed her into the study and took the chair by the lamp.

"You thought you'd killed me, didn't you?"

"You talk crazy, girlie."

"Does it bother you, to have killed your brother?"

"That's not what the jury said."

"You and I know better."

"Who the hell are you?"

"Why don't you believe I'm Jessica? Because you know you killed her?"

Sonny laughed. "You think I'm gonna confess, sister? You gonna tape it and haul my ass back into court?"

"There's no tape here. You want to look around?"

He shrugged.

"Once I testify, they'll indict you, with or without a confession."

"That's assuming you testify, sweetheart. You're not there yet. My lawyer doesn't think you're who you say you are."

"Everyone else does."

Sonny was unimpressed. "You look like her. But you're different. Jessie was a high-toned lady."

It was Mickey's turn to laugh. "And what am I?"

"I don't know, honey, but that looks like a gun under your shirt, and Miss Jessie wasn't any pistol-packin' mama."

"Maybe I've changed. Maybe I'd like to blow your ugly head off."

"And mess up my mama's pretty parlor?"

"She'd forgive me."

Sonny laughed. "She probably would. But you'd be in a heap of trouble."

"Would I? I don't think anyone would spend five minutes worrying about who killed you, Sonny. You have a bad reputation."

"A nasty disposition, too. I might take that gun away from you."

Mickey's smile glowed. "Make my day."

Sonny's eyes shone with sudden understanding. "You're a cop, aren't you? A nasty little bitch of a cop made up to look like Jessie."

Mickey stood up and jerked the gun from her belt. "You guessed it, cowboy, and now the bullshit is over. Start talking. I want to hear what you did that night."

A faint smile lit his face. "No, sugar, it's tonight we need to talk about."

Her finger caressed the trigger. "I'm gonna gut-shoot you, Sonny. It'll be slow. But I'll let you talk first."

"How come you hate me so bad, girlie?"

"I might tell you later. Talk, damn you!"

"You dumb bitch, do you really think I came here alone?"

"Yeah, I do," she said, but with the first tremor of doubt. The door was to her right, out of her line of vision.

"You think I trust my dear old mama that much? Gimme a break!"

He winked at her. "Fact is, my friend Vince has got you covered right this minute."

She wouldn't take her eyes off him. That was what he wanted, a moment's lapse. But she hesitated.

"Take her out, Vince."

His eyes cut to the doorway and, despite herself, hers did the same, and were lost among the shadows there, and in that instant Sonny flung himself at her. He crashed into her, fell atop her. His fist crashed against her jaw. Suddenly, Sonny towered over her, her gun in his hand.

"Some tough cop," he said contemptuously.

"Fuck you, Sonny," she could not help but say.

The weapon exploded, and suddenly she burned with more pain than she had ever known existed.

He had shot her in the right kneecap. She screamed, writhed, and finally lay still, whimpering because she could not help it.

"Fuck me, huh?" Sonny said. "You're gonna gut-shoot me, huh? How's it feel, you dumb cunt?"

She could not speak.

"Okay, now you'll do the talking. Who are you?"

The terrible pain in her knee was slowly giving way to another, inner pain. She had failed. She should have killed him, but she'd played games and let herself be outsmarted. Now he would kill her and she didn't care except that she'd failed, failed Jessie, failed in the most important moment of her life.

"Shoot me, you bastard," she muttered.

"What's the hurry?" Sonny said. "Who are you?"

Mickey was sobbing. "Damn you, you'll never know."

He pressed the barrel of the gun against her head. "You bitch, I killed you once and I'll kill you again. Who are you?"

She wanted to live. Despite everything.

"Her sister," she told him.

Sonny lowered the gun and shook his head in amazement. "Her fucking sister. Ain't that a kick in the ass?"

He went to the bar and poured two glasses of brandy. "How 'bout a drink, little lady? Might ease your mind."

He held the glass to her lips. She wanted to spit in his face but she wanted relief from the pain even worse. She thought she must be in shock, for the pain had lessened. The brandy burned, helped.

Sonny squatted beside her, the gun loose in his hand. She felt the strange, terrible intimacy between them, a union of hate.

"This house is where I started my life of crime," he told her.

"How was that?"

"Poor old Aunt Ida wouldn't die. It was about to drive my daddy crazy, he wanted Billy Ringer's money so bad. So I pushed her down the stairs."

Mickey pulled herself up. "Your mother knew."

"She blamed Daddy. It was a good thing she ran him off. He'd have pissed away the money before I got my hands on it."

His face blazed with malice. "Her sister, come for revenge, and blew it—right? A fucking cop?"

"Yeah, and pretty soon you're gonna see a million more cops."

He smiled smugly. "I don't think so. I think you're a dumb bunny who went off half-cocked. I think I can put you under and nobody'll ever know."

"You like killing people, Sonny?" It was all she knew to do. Feed his ego, hope for a miracle. Someone might come. Or she might go for his eyes, if she had the strength.

He shrugged. "Sometimes it's part of business."

"Is that why you killed Billy? Business?"

"He tried to steal my company. You could say I overreacted."

"And killing Jessica? Was that business, too?"

He leered at her. "No, honey, that was pleasure. That bitch had been bugging me for a long time. I'll say this for her, she put up a fight. She was tougher than she looked."

"You bastard." Her leg throbbed mercilessly. She felt herself slipping away. But she would have suffered an eternity of pain for one shot at him.

"They'll get you, Sonny. You'll burn."

He stood up. "You're starting to bore me, sister. We're gonna take a ride out to the lake. A one-way ride, for you."

"No, Sonny."

The woman's voice leapt out of the night, one they both recognized.

Sonny turned slowly, until he saw his mother in the shadows by the doorway.

"What the hell do *you* want?" he demanded.

"I have the truth now," Lily Nash said. "All I want is peace."

Sonny slowly pointed his weapon toward his mother. Mickey screamed and seized his ankle. He kicked at her, and at that moment Lily Nash fired her small revolver. Sonny cried out in disbelief, then crumpled to the floor.

The two women watched in silence as he groaned and then lay still.

"It had to be done," Lily Nash said finally. "It should have been done long ago."

Mickey gripped the other woman's hand.

"I was so worried," Lily said. "I drove to the airport and turned around and came back. I couldn't leave you alone with him."

Lily began to weep. "It's okay, Lily," Mickey told her. "Everything will be better now."

Mickey drifted in and out of consciousness. When her eyes were open, the doctors gave her powerful drugs and asked her questions she didn't answer. A toe-to-thigh cast encased her leg, and the drugs only numbed the pain. Sleep was better, but she awoke one day and found Lon Tate beside her bed.

She spoke his name and he hugged her gently.

"How are you, Mick?"

"Lousy. What day is it?"

"Saturday. You were out like a light."

She groaned. "Sonny's dead, right?"

"Right."

"Lily, is she in trouble?"

"The guy was in her house with a gun in his hand and you half-dead at his feet. They'll give her a medal. Everything's fine, Mick, except your knee. You may not be kicking down doors for a while."

"They gonna terminate me?" She felt sudden panic. The DEA was a million miles away, yet it had been her home, the best home she'd ever had.

"Don't worry about it. But . . . "

"Yeah?"

"Some of us are ticked off that you pulled this Lone Ranger crap."

"It was crazy," she admitted. "But he killed my sister and I had to."

"It's a miracle you're alive. Didn't we teach you anything?"

"Next time I take an army. Except there won't be a next time."

"What's your plan?"

"To be a junkie until my leg stops hurting. Then, oh God, there's Melissa, my sister's little girl, and I don't know what will happen."

"There's a few thousand reporters outside, wanting to see you."

"I don't want to see them."

"And Lily Nash, she's out there, too."

"Oh God," Mickey said. "Oh God."

Lon squeezed her hand. "What's the matter, baby?"

"I'm scared. I was Jessie, but now I'm just me again."

Her friend smiled wistfully. "There's nothing wrong with being you, Mick. Most folks, they'd be doing real good to be you."

"May I come in?"

Lily Nash was in the doorway, wearing a tweed skirt and pale blue sweater. After Lon left, the nurse had given Mickey more Percodan and brushed her hair.

"Sure. Please." She tried to smile.

Lily took her hand. "Is the pain awful?"

"Not so bad," Mickey lied.

"Are you sure? Would you rather I came back?"

"No, I want to see you. To thank you for saving my life."

Lily's face darkened. "Let's not talk about that. It was a terrible act. I had no choice."

"I agree."

"Can I sit on the edge of the bed, or will it jostle your cast?"

"It's okay. I mean, don't bounce or anything."

"I won't bounce, dear. I think my bouncing days are over. May I call you Mickey?"

"Yes, ma'am, if you want to."

"Don't be afraid of me, child."

"I . . . it's just that I guess you think I'm crazy."

"No, I think you're unspeakably brave and reckless. And you're gripped by a passion for justice. Do you remember what Bacon called revenge? A kind of wild justice."

Mickey grinned. "That's a good way of putting it."

"We have a lot to talk about. You are Jessica's sister, and . . . "

"How did you find that out?"

"Let's come back to that. The point is, as Jessica's sister, you will inherit a great deal of money."

"I don't care about money. That's not why I came here."

"No, you came for your wild justice. But now you want Melissa, as do I. That child is my heart. I have at least ten good years left and I hope to devote them to her."

"I love her too."

"Perhaps not as obsessively as I."

"I want to raise her. I'm her aunt."

"Fine. Move into Jessica and Billy's house. We can both raise her. If you try to take that child away, Mickey, I'll fight you with every breath I have."

Mickey gazed with awe, and affection, at her adversary.

"Lily, look at my leg," she said. "I'm not going anywhere for a while."

The older woman smiled. "No, that knee needs time and therapy. We'll employ the best doctors. If they're not here, we'll bring them here. When you can leave the hospital, go back to Jessica and Billy's house. It's yours now. Olivia will care for you. Or take Melissa and spend some time at the ranch."

"Which ranch?"

"Billy's. Didn't you ever go there?"

"No, but Jessie told me how much she loved it."

"Consider it yours. We can fly the doctors out, and me too, when I want to visit. There are horses and a pool and a river and a comfortable house. Autumn is quite wonderful there."

Mickey was dazed. She longed more than anything to be at that ranch with Melissa, in that solitary house by that slow-moving West Texas river, with a million stars at night. In her imagination it was heaven on earth, the home she'd always dreamed of.

"All I'm saying," Lily continued, "is don't make any decisions until you know us better."

"I won't," Mickey said. "I promise."

"Good. Now, if you're up to it, there are other matters."

"I'm up to it," Mickey said.

"Do you remember a boy named Herbert Lavender, from the Gertrude Little Home?"

"You know about us and the Home?"

"Yes. I even remember teaching you two girls. The Ketchum twins. Don't look so alarmed, I'll explain all of this. What I want to say is that little Herbie Lavender, one of your classmates, is a policeman now. Ever since Billy married Jessica, her face tormented him. He knew he'd seen her before, but he couldn't make the connection between the girl at the Home twenty years ago and Jessica Nash."

"It was a big leap," Mickey said.

"As luck would have it, he was one of the officers who came to my house after the shooting. He saw you when they carried you out to the ambulance and it all came together in his mind. He told me that night, at the hospital, that he was convinced you were one of the Ketchum girls. I called my lawyers and the next morning they went to the Home and demanded some answers."

"Tell me," Mickey pleaded.

"You two girls were taken there when you were twelve, from a foster home in West Texas. State law required at least some minimal record keeping; you couldn't have children passed around like sausages. But a powerful man was pulling the strings in your case. Money was exchanged, and a vow that your case histories would never be revealed."

"That old lawyer in Dallas."

"He was the agent. Your mother's father had taken you girls from her at birth and he didn't want ever to hear from you again. When he died, it seemed that you two were forever cut off from your past."

"The bastard," Mickey said. "I tried. We both did."

"I know you did. But my lawyers could do more. My lawyers can be extremely unpleasant men."

Mickey's pain was forgotten. The door to the past was poised to open, and if that cost a kneecap, so be it.

"Tell me what you learned, Lily. Please. I know you must think I'm terrible, but . . . "

"Jessica was my daughter and you're my daughter now, if you choose to be," Lily said. "That's what I think. But it's not my place to answer your questions."

Mickey choked back a sob. "Then whose is it? I've waited so long to know who I am."

Lily embraced her. "You've been through so much. Can you stand just a little more?"

"Yes, yes."

"You remember my friend Myra?"

"Of course. We had dinner at your house. And lunch, later on."

"She's a wonderful person who's had a hard life. She'd like to talk to you, if you're strong enough."

"I'm strong enough."

"I'll get her. Later, I'll come back with Melissa."

"Thank you. And Lily?"

"Yes?"

"I'm your daughter, too."

As Lily left, a nurse looked in, smiled at Mickey, and went out again. The afternoon sun burned like eternity. Somewhere down the corridor Mozart played and a woman wept.

"Hello, Mickey."

Myra Fontaine stopped at the foot of the bed.

"You're a brave woman," she said.

"Not really," Mickey told her. "There are different kinds of brave. Jessie was brave, too."

"I know she was. But I was right about you. When I said you weren't Jessica."

"You were the only one who knew. Come closer."

Myra took her hand. "I hate it about your leg."

"It doesn't matter," Mickey said. "Really." The pain was still with her, would always be, the pain of lost love, but new emotions were stirring, too.

"I have a long story to tell you," Myra said.

"Good," Mickey said.

"It begins a long time ago, when I was young and foolish, and went on a trip to New Orleans."

Myra turned away, fighting back tears.

Mickey waited serenely. "I've never been to New Orleans," she said. "But I always heard it was wonderful."